T0123697

IN THE COURSE OF HUMAN EVENTS

IN THE COURSE OF HUMAN EVENTS

a novel by
Mike Harvkey

soft skull press

Copyright © 2014 Mike Harvkey

All rights reserved under International and Pan-American Copyright
Conventions. No part of this book may be used or reproduced in any manner
whatsoever without written permission from the publisher, except in the case
of brief quotations embodied in critical articles and reviews.

This book is a work of fiction. Names, characters, places, and incidents
either are products of the author's imagination or are used fictitiously.
Any resemblance to actual events or locales or persons, living or dead,
is entirely coincidental.

Library of Congress Cataloging-in-Publication Data

Harvkey, Mike.
  In The Course Of Human Events : A Novel / Mike Harvkey.
      pages cm
  1. Young men—Missouri—Fiction. 2. Temptation—Fiction. 3. Good vs
evil—Fiction. I. Title.
  PS3608.A78933I5 2014
  813'.6—dc23
  2013044834

ISBN 978-1-59376-608-5

Cover design by Debbie Berne
Interior design by Domini Dragoone

Soft Skull Press
New York, NY

www.softskull.com

For P.D., and
for Jake

*The tree of liberty must be refreshed from time to time
with the blood of patriots and tyrants.*

—*Thomas Jefferson*

THE SACKING OF LICK SKILLET

Winter, 2012

That morning in Lick Skillet Jan took Clyde to the cemetery at the top of the hill to show him where she found her daughter's name. With difficulty they walked in the open road, the snow thick and nearly unmarked, and along the High Street to a red gate draped with ice and frozen to the ground where it hung open. They took the narrow path that wound at sharp angles through the overgrown graves, low-leaning trees making it too narrow for Clyde and Jan to walk side by side. She went ahead, stopping at an old tomb half buried under snow. Some of the stones of the tomb were missing, leaving deep holes, and the roof, over years, had collapsed, making the Celtic cross at the top point not to God but Lick Skillet. The carving on the face was shallow; Jan dug a handful of grass from the snow and rubbed it against the stone, revealing words: *Tina Louise, beloved daughter, born 18 Jn 1831.* There was no date of death.

Jan took off her gloves with her teeth and got the cigarettes out of her pocket. She passed one to Clyde and burned four matches lighting them. "Tina

Louise Birch. Her husband . . . " Jan rubbed another stone. "The Reverend Wilhelm Birch. Killed in the Civil War. December 1862. The Sacking of Lick Skillet. Their two sons too. William and Gerhardt. Thirteen and fifteen. Tina had three other kids by the time she was twenty." Jan ran her fingers over their names, delicately, as if they were her own kin. "None of 'em made it long. If we lose a goldfish now we cry like babies. In 1831 there weren't nobody who hadn't lost at least *one* kid to *somethin*. Wilhelm and Tina were the head of this community. People say Tina treated their slaves better than the reverend did."

Jan pulled Clyde off the path to reach a higher vantage, her boots making deep impressions in the snow. She pointed to the last tree line before the distant gray horizon. "Napoleon Hudsputh had a farm over there in 1862," Jan said, "a sorta meeting place for most of the Confederate guerrillas around. But one day late fall that year a bunch of Kansas Redlegs rode up to Hudsputh farm looking for a fight." The standoff that followed became known as the Sacking of Lick Skillet 'cause, when all was said and done, that's exactly what it was.

REDLEGS AND JAYHAWKERS HAD BEEN SHOOTING UP HUDSPUTH FARM LEFT and right for years trying to disrupt the Confederates in Missouri. But on this day, Hudsputh, along with Bloody Bill Anderson and William Quantrill, were minding their own business when the Redlegs rode in. The Redlegs weren't alone either. They had Jayhawkers and half the First Kansas Colored Infantry with 'em and they'd met up with some of the Missouri militia. It was a powerful army and they ambushed the farm, pushed everybody into these woods.

Jan poked the glowing tip of her cigarette at the second ridge, marking Cass County line. "They came through there, right into Lick Skillet."

Back then Kansas had an open-door policy for slaves. If you were a slave and you could get yourself across the state line, Kansas would give you a gun and *pay* you to kill whitey. When Hudsputh got pushed into Lick Skillet, Reverend Birch and Tina Louise got everybody ready to fight, including children, including slaves, though they most likely didn't give the slaves guns. Tina Louise wasn't *that* stupid. A lot of those slaves ended up fighting hand to hand with the First Kansas Colored Infantry. Slaves trying to strangle escaped slaves who were fighting to abolish slavery. Imagine it.

After about five weeks, Napoleon Hudsputh fled. But that didn't end a thing. The Redlegs had surrounded Lick Skillet. In the falling snow—the first snow of the year, like this one—the people of Lick Skillet fought them off. Three more weeks passed and things weren't looking good at all. Then Wilhelm was shot, in the middle of the road at the bottom of the hill not thirty feet from the corner cabin. Their boys died in the woods, most of the villagers along with them. But Tina Louise and the men and women she owned, at least the ones who weren't clubbed to death by the Kansas Colored, kept fighting. This was around the end of the year, the earth frozen hard and the air cold and damp, but Tina held her ground. The whole time her husband's body lay in the road, right in the open, a line of blood in the snow behind him marking how far he'd managed to crawl before finally dying. Word was he lasted two days. Back then bullets were less lethal, it could take a long time to die. Nobody had attempted to move his body since one black boy tried and ended up lying next to him. Tina desperately wanted to move him out of the open, so she finally armed her people. It would have been easy for any of them to cross over to the other side, or turn on Tina, kill her. The Kansas Colored were in the woods shouting, "We making seven dollar a month, all the food we can eat!" But not a one of 'em did. For another week Tina and her slaves held them off, with no food and little water, clothes falling off their backs, hard as burlap, rotten.

JAN PAUSED. "AND THEN," SHE SAID, SPREADING HER HANDS IN FRONT OF Clyde in an imitation of magic.

Clyde said, "What?"

"Vanished. Nobody ever saw 'em again. That's why there's no date of death on that headstone. Some say they got away on the river, but it woulda been awful cold for that." Jan shrugged. "Never know. Women were tougher back then. Maybe she sailed down to Jeff City and ran for office."

"I can't believe her slaves didn't run off," Clyde said.

"They was loyal," Jan said. "More loyal to Tina Louise than their own skin. So loyal to the white woman who owned them that they fought against their own interests. Stranger things have happened."

"Stranger things have happened," Clyde repeated, following Jan out of the cemetery and into the road that curved downhill to the old High Street.

To anyone but the Smalls, Lick Skillet was a wild, overgrown place. What minor significance it may have ever held was now lost to all but a few. This was not strictly true, but it was the perception preferred by one fierce family. Aside from a single strand of cables bringing electricity over the mountain that stood against the clear eastern sky, there was nothing that placed Lick Skillet in any decade, any century.

Clyde shouldered his rifle and thought of all the blood that had been spilled on this hard patch of earth in the name of freedom.

AMERICAN DREAMIN'

The year before

Clyde hadn't been awake long. His truck was the only vehicle on the road between Strasburg and Gunn City and he knew the gray smoke rolling up his hood couldn't have come from anyone else. But Clyde was daydreaming, his eyes heavy, muscle memory alone keeping him out of the ditch, and his confused mind had registered the smoke as somebody else's problem. But it wasn't somebody else's problem, it was Clyde's problem. "Son of a bitch!" he shouted, snapping off the engine. He hadn't checked his levels. Radiator had been leaking almost as long as he'd owned the truck, topping it up was routine. Most days he could afford the time it took to pull off and refill from the watered-down antifreeze he kept in back. Most days all he had was time, endless, fat, and dull, nothing at all to fill it. But today was Tuesday, his only work day. He had to be on time.

Outside Ekland Field—named for the doctor, now dead—he brought his truck off the road. He got the kit from the back, popped the hood, and brought the engine back on, raising his middle finger to that field, a flat slab of dirt he'd spent many a summer night on, bored, sweating, bothered by bugs. Just beyond it, the Potty Pond wormed with a crust of flies Clyde could hear from the highway. Downwind, it stank of shit, not piss.

With a rag he twisted off the radiator cap. He'd made the mistake in the past of pulling a cap from a dead engine. Clyde had never really had a dad to teach him how to not hurt himself as he went through life. He slipped the funnel in and poured, the spill burned against the block, engulfing him in smoke. If he had to do this again before Independence he'd be late and that fucker Leon, his boss, wouldn't let him forget it.

Back on 58, Clyde rolled his windows into their felt. Gravel dust and pine erased the scent of Strasburg's human waste. The air rushing in ruffled the old food wrappers on the dash. Clyde moved the six-shooter he kept up there—a silver Colt .45—to pin them down, took a gulp of sweet tea to wake him up. "Rocket fuel" he called it, his own recipe: a gallon of water, twenty bags of Lipton, a cup of sugar. It usually did the trick.

Driving Northwestern Missouri's uncluttered highways for five years had taught Clyde what the bastard deputy sheriffs would let a driver get away with and what they would not. Sixty-two in a fifty-five was about it. Back when he worked for Mr. Longarm he'd kept a working Fuzzbuster, but that purchase had long since crapped out, like most of what he'd acquired between '06 and '08, the only two years of gainful employment in Clyde's short life. The biggest purchase had been this deep blue Ford F-150 he'd got secondhand three years after it rolled off the factory floor in Lee's Summit, MO, home of just about the last UAW plant left in the Midwest; now into its eighth year it too was worse for wear. Even if Clyde had possessed the money to fix its many problems, he just didn't care enough to do so.

He knew he'd be late when he made Independence, the onetime crystal meth capital of the world. Growing up, Clyde had come upon plenty of chances to sample the drug. Half the people he knew had snorted it off the hood of somebody or other's car. But he never had, being either a good boy or a pussy, depending on who you asked. It was 8:38 by the time Clyde rolled through the gates of the auction lot and Leon made a big show of checking his watch. "Sorry, Leon. Had to stop to fill the radiator." The day was thick with atmosphere and blasted white so Clyde covered his eyes with his Oakleys.

"That's funny, I thought you said your radiator overheated again, Twitty." Clyde mumbled.

"Why that's funny," Leon said, "is because I told you a long time ago to get that fixed. Right?"

Clyde kept his mouth tight. He nodded and wanted to snatch the tire iron from his flat kit and swing it into the side of Leon's stupid fucking lumpy head. He saw himself do it: dropping the flame-haired prick right to the pavement. Leon walked to a Firebird and signed it out to Clyde rolling a raw, freckled arm to study the time again. His watch was small like a lady's and cut deeply into Leon's ballooning wrist. "You got an hour to get eighty miles." Leon flipped his red ponytail around his neck so that it came to rest on the other side of his denim vest. "Good luck."

Clyde collapsed into the Firebird's molded bucket seat. He never could get used to a low-riding vehicle. Even though he was of average height and only about twenty pounds over his fighting weight, he didn't fit well in the car. The seat was so rigid he had to take his wallet out of his back pocket. He checked the route and turned the key, feeling the vibration of a glass pack. In Clyde's experience, cars with aftermarket glass-pack mufflers thought themselves much tougher than they were. Once he got out onto the highway he was as rough with the gears as he pleased, grinding second to third, third to fourth, hoping to leave a few pieces on the highway for Leon to think about.

Clyde made the auction with time to spare and parked the car in its designated slot. With a Mr. Pibb from the machine, he stood back watching about fifty people wait to bid on ten vehicles. He was always curious to see who won what he'd driven personally. The bidding on the Firebird started at $250. When it hit $1,000, a bidder bowed out. The two remaining took it to $1,500 before one of them left the girl standing at his side and marched over to the other bidder. "Jay Smalls," the man said, big loud voice, hand out. The other man shook it.

The auctioneer paused and confusion spread through the crowd. The girl Jay Smalls had left yelled, "Dad!" and said, "I don't know him," hiding her face in her hair. People laughed and the auctioneer asked if there was a problem.

"No problem," Jay Smalls said. His arms were long and tobacco brown and roped with veins and muscle. "Just wanted to meet the competition!"

That brought more laughs, then Jay Smalls leaned in and whispered to the other bidder for a solid ten seconds, patted him on the shoulder, said, "All right?" and returned to his daughter. "Fifteen hundred, was it?" Jay Smalls said to the auctioneer.

"Yes sir," the auctioneer said. "Do you mind if I continue?"

Jay Smalls laughed, making his large moustache, black and thick as a shrub, curl up. He whistled. "Lot of money, boy."

The auctioneer started up again, waving his little hammer. Jay Smalls jerked his head and raised a hand for sixteen hundred, staring at the other bidder.

The auctioneer continued. "Do I have a seventeen? Seventeen hunert, folks, come on now, seventeen hunert for a fine automobile." The other bidder tried to hold Jay Smalls's gaze, it looked like he was going to be sick. Jay Smalls never once dropped his big friendly grin, and finally the other bidder shook his head, walked off.

Clyde retreated to the shade with a frosted honey bun from the machine. Jay Smalls signed papers and searched the crowd until his eyes settled on Clyde. He pointed and yelled, "You Clyde Twitty?" Then he seemed to cut the remaining distance between them in a blink. He had his hand out again, straight as an arrow, and his daughter looked embarrassed trailing in his wake.

Clyde took Jay's hand. "Yes sir."

"Jay," he said. He leaned in and patted Clyde's gut, snickering. When he did, one eye squinted shut, the bottom lip flipped out wet and purple, and that moustache curled. Clyde thought there was something naughty about it, like a bulldog who's just pissed in your shoe. "I'm just joshin. Hell, I like the occasional sticky bun myself." He drove a fist into his own stomach to a hard *thud*. "I just work it off is all."

"I used to, uh, play baseball," Clyde said, feeling like an idget, because Jay's daughter, now that she was right in front of him, was pretty in an odd-looking way. She was a big girl, not chubby exactly, her eyes up close were a striking pale green and set wide on her face, too wide, really. Her mouth was enormous, full of tiny little teeth that locked together in two straight rows. She wore a full face of makeup, a clear orange line running along the jaw, making her look more alien or animal than human. Clyde was intrigued.

"Great American pastime, they tell me," Jay said. "You drove the Firebird?"

"Yes sir," Clyde said.

"Anything I need to know? My daughter gonna be driving it and I don't wanna have to worry about the front tire falling off on I-70, know what I mean?"

"Uh, Dad," his daughter said. "You won. Pretty sure that means you bought the car."

Jay dug a hand in his pocket and withdrew a wad of hundreds. He waved them. "Until I hand over sixteen hundred dollars, I ain't bought shit."

Clyde flushed with worry. He hoped he hadn't actually hurt the clutch. "It's, uh, not as fast as it sounds."

The daughter made a noise and Jay said, "Good. Good! That's what I wanna hear."

"I don't want no sissy car," she said. She flicked a hand and made a big show of folding her arms across her chest. "I want a car with some cajones."

"Why ain't she as fast as she sounds?" Jay said. "What's wrong with her?"

"No, nothing," Clyde said. "It's a two-fifty two-barrel. Aftermarket glass pack makes it sound like it's got more horses than it does."

"Ah," Jay said. "I gotcha. All right. She's naturally slow, like my sister. Anything else? This thing gonna be Tina's sixteenth birthday present, Clyde. I find out it's a lemon, I'm coming to your house to git my money back." Jesus. Clyde stepped back. Jay grabbed his arm, laughing, but the hold was firm enough. "Just kidding. I got no idea where you live." He snickered, looked at his daughter, and leaned in. "Course, wouldn't be too hard to find out." He slapped Clyde's arm. Even though Clyde felt like the threat was only about half real, he wouldn't have been at all surprised to find Jay Smalls outside his bedroom window in the moonlight. Now he knew why the other bidder had bowed out.

Jay smacked his daughter on the arm and said, "Say thank you, Tina."

"Thank you, Tina," Tina said, all teeth, and Jay dragged her away.

Back in Independence, Clyde waited in line with the other drivers until Leon slipped three ten-dollar bills and two fives off the stack in his hand, which made it seem like more than the measly $40 it was. Clyde waved the bills and said, "Thanks for nothing."

ndependence, a loud, cluttered sprawl, gave way in time to Boonville, but at twenty-thousand souls even its population was beyond Clyde's comfort zone. When he was a boy he'd made the trip to this town with his dad to buy feed nearly once a month. Even though Boonville in those days had been half the size it was now his dad always griped. "These city folks just as soon run you off the road as look at you," Clyde remembered him saying, though it was possible he'd made it up, he'd been only five or six at the time. Memories of the first half of his life were as unreliable as daydreams. Since the economic collapse, Clyde had heard there'd been carjackings in Boonville, robberies where they intentionally rear-end you to bring you out of your vehicle. Clyde's thinking was, If I get out, it'll be with the Colt in hand.

At the Sinclair station, half the day's pay went right down the fucking tank. Thank you, Obama. Across the road was the Walmart Clyde had to visit next. He hated shopping there but it was the cheapest option. Since high school a few extra pounds had maybe settled in around the middle. Clyde knew this, he wasn't blind. He knew he couldn't drive a hard punch into his gut the way Jay Smalls had done. But he also knew that he hadn't let himself go completely, like most of the Walmart shoppers he saw now. None of them had even paused at the point of no return.

Here it was, a Tuesday afternoon, and the lot was nearly full. Where did these bastards come upon the lucky combination of money and leisure in 2011? In the three years since Mr. Longarm closed, Clyde had almost become a stranger to work. His savings were gone, he'd cashed out of his retirement. To get unemployment he'd had to humiliate himself to some bitch at the government office, only to have it stop when he got the driving job. Apparently $40 was enough to make him ineligible for any government aid, thank you very much. Forget insurance—health, life, truck—he had none of it. All this had beaten Clyde down in ways he didn't even know. As a boy he'd been an early riser. He remembered winters spent hunting, bundled up to immobility by his dad and uncle and trying to step in their deep bootprints before the sun was even up. He hadn't hunted in ages, hardly shot his guns at all anymore. These days he slept late, and that wasn't all. He watched too much TV, avoided his few friends, drank himself to sleep. Work was a hell of an important thing to a man.

Crossing the pavement of Walmart Country, he shook his head at Boonville's fortunate sons and daughters; the suffering of the people of Strasburg, not forty miles east, was evident: houses lost, yards overgrown, vehicles left on roadsides. Half the town's residents, no more fight left in them, had thrown in the towel, walked away. Strasburg was the town the American Dream forgot.

The doors parted and Clyde jerked a basket. He needed Spam, baked beans, eggs, milk, hot dogs, white bread, mayonnaise, margarine, whisky, cigarettes. He checked prices, kept track of the total in his head. Then he looked for Esther Hines in checkout.

This was a girl who turned her hair a new color almost every other week. This was a girl who sang Christian songs with a closed-eye passion while scanning your purchases; she thought of Jesus Christ as savior and boyfriend both. This was a girl who smoked up a storm, partied in the woods, drank herself unconscious, and claimed the next morning with a straight face that her body was a temple into which she took nothing unholy. Clyde had happened upon her checkout once, months back, and had been seeking her out since. When she saw him, Esther moved her *next register please* sign behind his items. "What'd you drive today?" she said, scanning the Spam. Her fingernails, chewed to the quick, held tiny chips of black polish.

"You woulda liked it," he said. "Firebird."

"You're shitting me." She bit her thin pink lip and cast her eyes to the ceiling. "I'm sorry, honey," she said, scanning the beans. The apology, Clyde knew well enough by now, was for Jesus.

"Sits too low for me though."

"I know how you like to be up all high to look down on the rest of us." Esther winked and scanned the whiskey. "Now what do we have here? Baked beans, Spam, and whiskey? Looks like you're about to have yourself one heck of a party." She leaned in. "You are nothing but a heathen. I knew it first time I saw ya." Her voice, now that Clyde heard it up close, trembled. If a baby bird could talk, it'd sound like this.

Clyde pointed at the cigarettes behind Esther and said, "You mind adding a carton."

"GPCs," Esther said, going with her key to the cabinet. "I don't know how your uncle can smoke these."

Clyde said, "When I asked if he wanted something better he said, 'Much as I smoke I can't afford to smoke good cigarettes.' " Clyde watched the blue tips of Esther's white-blonde hair brush her slim shoulders, thinking, again, about trying to see Esther outside of Walmart. So far thinking was as far as he'd got, the right moment never seemed to come and Clyde felt most of the time like he was living under a heavy winter quilt, he had no energy, none at all. She totaled the bill and Clyde groaned. How did this math make sense to anybody? Prices kept going up when the salary went down, it was a conflict of interest he couldn't see ending well for anyone but the extremely fortunate. He reached into his back pocket and his hand slipped right in. "Shit," he said.

"What?"

"Wallet's gone."

Esther bagged the groceries while Clyde stood around, flushed with embarrassment. In the faces of the other shoppers he saw pity. "Think that stuff'll be okay for an hour or so?"

"What?" Esther said. "All this was on special today, Clyde. Prices are *a-fallin'.*" Esther squealed like a bat and punched buttons on the register until it popped out with a ding. She tore off a receipt that showed a grand total of nothing. "See?" she said.

Clyde shook his head. "Whiskey alone's ten. Cigarettes too."

Esther lowered her shaking voice. "It was on . . . *special*. Now, don't make me have to call the manager on your perky little butt."

Clyde remembered what remained of his driving pay and slapped it on the scale. Twenty bucks. "I appreciate it," he said. "But I don't need no handouts. I'll come back with the rest."

Esther threw up her hands. "You're more honest than I am and I been born again!"

Clyde went into the bright outdoors. All those vehicles like hard candy in the sun. He searched his truck but didn't find the wallet. This was the last thing he needed, the last goddamn thing. On the way back he pulled off at Ekland Field and walked in the grass among the empty beer cans and bottles and cigarette packs and dry food wrappers. He picked up a beer bottle and threw it over the fence. It skidded across the baseball diamond. He heaved another at the bleachers. It went high, but the next one smashed into a million pieces. Clyde yelled, "Bull's-eye, motherfuckers!" He broke three more the same way before his shoulder started hurting. Then he drove to his uncle's.

Since his visit last week, Willie had repainted the deck that wrapped the trailer, a deck he'd built himself two summers after he broke his neck. He had only one working arm and walked slow as a turtle leaning on a rubber-tipped cane the pharmacy had sold him for ten times what it was worth. Out on the deck now with a cigarette, Willie raised his good hand, seeing Clyde pull in.

"Uncle Willie," Clyde called. John Wayne, Willie's fourteen-year-old bird dog, lifted his droopy head to eyeball Clyde through a milky cataract film. "How you doing?" Clyde said. Willie made a thumbs-up; he couldn't nod anymore. On the deck, Clyde waved the GPCs. "Got your food," he said, waving the whiskey. "And your water."

"I thank you."

Clyde put them down on the raw pine table next to his uncle. "This is new."

"S'morning," Willie said, running his thumb along the edge with a hand that was dried up, tanned to leather, its thumbnail black from some missed impact. "You all right?" Willie said, turning at the waist to look in Clyde's direction.

"Yeah, why?"

"You're fidgeting."

"Oh." Clyde squinted at the yard. "Lost my wallet." Willie began the difficult chore of reaching into his back pocket. Clyde said, "That ain't what I'm sayin, Uncle Willie, come on."

Willie let the wallet open, dug out a twenty, and slapped it down. "I don't want no back talk neither. More where that came from too, if you need it."

Clyde sighed and picked up the bill. It was fresh from the bank. Willie had already given him grocery money last week and Clyde had already spent it. "Probably just left it at home this morning."

Willie worked to open the cigarette carton and slip out a fresh pack. "Smokin and drinkin are two occupations that are almost gettin to be more trouble than they're worth. I don't know what this country's coming to; half this is tax."

Clyde watched Willie get the pack open, pinch a cigarette in his teeth, and light it all with the one hand. He exhaled a cone of smoke out the one working channel of his nose across a moustache that was yellow down one side and light brown down the other. When the cigarette was finished, Clyde helped him into the house and put some hot dogs in water on the stove. Looking out back he saw the shooting range he'd built out there years before. He made a pot of coffee for the week and decided why the hell not? "Mind if I fire off a few rounds while the wieners are cooking?" he called from the kitchen. It had been almost a year since he'd discharged a weapon.

"Let me alert the neighborhood watch," Willie said, and Clyde heard him punching buttons in the tan tabletop phone.

Clyde huffed. "Your property," he said, loud enough for Willie to hear. Going out to get his Colt from the truck, Clyde burned all over again with anger about the run-in he had the first time he shot a gun in his uncle's yard. Willie's neighbor to the west had come running over like the place was on fire, waving his arms, screaming about how dangerous this was. Dangerous? You ever even *held* a gun? Why was it that the people pitching shit fits about what you were up to were always the ones who knew the least about it? Hell, before firing a single shot Clyde had built a large berm at the back edge of Willie's yard. Beyond it was a field of twenty acres, and this complainer's property bordered that on only one side. He said he had pets, a family, a wife with the jitters. He would sue, goddamn it. When Clyde didn't immediately throw down his weapon and beg forgiveness, the neighbor said, "You're an asshole," which still made Clyde spit whenever he remembered it. And that was four years ago. Clyde was the type to hold a grudge.

The Colt was fully loaded and Clyde fired all six shots in a minute, reloaded watching the distant field, and came back to the house. These days guns were for Clyde like cigarettes and whiskey for Willie: a habit that was getting too damned expensive to maintain. Clyde brought in their supper and set up the trays. On the TV, a pretty blonde in a low-cut red, white, and blue dress was singing her guts out. Clyde poked his uncle and nodded at the screen. "What do you think, Uncle Willie?"

Willie chewed his hot dog, eyes on the screen. "What do I think about what?"

Clyde pointed. "What it'd be like to screw her?"

Willie swallowed his food, it looked like it hurt. "Mm," he said, drinking beer and dimpling the can in his fingers. *Pa-tink.* "Probably about the same as screwin any woman, I reckon."

efore Clyde could even get halfway across the yard his mom saddled him with chores. In the last light of day he unrolled the hose and sprayed the sunbaked bird dirt off the house. Birds liked to roost on the top of the sign that turned his childhood home into a constant advertisement for his mom's shop: *Pretty Lady*, it read in giant letters the color of Pepto-Bismol. Christmas lights that hadn't been lit in months circled the sign. With half of Mrs. Twitty's clientele dead, near death, or moved out of state, it didn't make sense to pad the wallets of the electric company's CEOs. Clyde sometimes wondered what sleeping behind that big pink sign half his life had done to his manhood. He yanked and the roller spun, squeaking. A length of hose bucked on the lawn. Lightning bugs drifting in the gray stillness pulsed.

Clyde was just going in when he heard a horn out on the road. A Plymouth Fury ran past, packed with people. "I tawt! I tawt! I tawt I taw a putty tat!" they yelled in unison.

"Fuck off," Clyde growled, opening the front door, which was always jammed and required both hands and feet to open. Clyde's last name had plagued him all through school. Thanks to these aging burnouts, it still did.

Except for a piece of mail from the IRS that was addressed to him, Clyde dropped the rest on the table inside the door, adding to a growing pile no one wanted to face. During his time with Longarm, and for a good while after, the mortgage had been paid in full and on time. It was only in this last year that they'd struggled, sometimes sending in less than the minimum due. But Clyde's feeling was, We're still trying, we haven't given up like most people, don't count us out.

Clyde took the IRS letter into the tiny salon where his mom sat, in one of her two shop chairs, her head capped by the milky plastic drier. Smoke from the cigarette in her puckered lips swirled about her frosted hair, making it look like a smoldering fire. Clyde tore the letter open and resisted the urge to rip it to shreds when he read what it said. "You've got to be shitting me!" he yelled, making his mom jump.

She slapped the oversized magazine she'd been reading onto her lap. "Clyde! What is it?"

"IRS says I owe them eight hundred sixty-two dollars 'cause of a error *they* made on my tax bill *three years* ago!"

Clyde handed her the letter. She plucked the cigarette from her mouth and read with moving lips. Some of it she read out loud as Clyde paced the tiny, checkered pink and baby blue linoleum floor. It was the ugliest floor Clyde had ever seen. "Well," his mom said, dropping the hand that held the letter. "I don't know. Just ignore it."

Clyde snatched the letter and slapped it down on the counter by the old push-button cash register that didn't work anymore. It hardly needed to. "Can't ignore it. Just makes it worse. You ignoring everything's why we're in the mess we're in."

"Well, ex-*cuse* me."

He sat opposite her in one of her striped folding chairs, shaking his head. Getting this letter felt like a punch to the chest, it really did. "This is all I fucking need. They know how much I make in a week?" His mom watched him in a way that made him sick. He didn't want to see pity in her eyes so he changed his tune. "Ah," he said, waving a hand. "Whatever. You're right. Anyway, I don't even *have* eight hundred dollars. If I had eight hundred dollars, I'd . . . " His thoughts drifted off into the possibilities.

She looked at him a moment longer before lifting the magazine again. "Lose your wallet?" she said behind it.

He jumped. "You find it?"

"No." She shook her head against the drier. "But somebody did."

Next to the register a phone number had been scribbled on an envelope in her shaky hand. "They leave a name or anything?" His mom didn't say but when he looked over she was still shaking her head. He went into his small bedroom and closed the door. His TV was on, muted. Usually he just left it on, day and night, for company. He dialed, looking at the mounted buck above the television, a gift from Willie and, with a six-point rack, still the biggest deer Clyde had ever bagged. When the call connected, he heard TV noise in the background of the other end.

"What you want?" A man's voice.

"Uh." Clyde was confused. They were watching the same show as him but there was a slight delay between the sound in the phone and the picture on his TV.

"This Clyde Twitty, ain't it?" the man said. That made Clyde even more confused. "Born August thirty-first, nineteen eighty-nine?" The man snickered. Okay, Clyde got what was happening. "Brown eyes, five foot eight inches tall, organ donor? Gonna save some alkie's life with your virgin pink liver, are ya? You're a regular Superman, Clyde Twitty. Hang on," the man said, smothering the phone and yelling a name. A brief conversation followed before another phone picked up with a beep and a scrape. No one said anything.

"Hello?" said Clyde.

A girl spoke. "Uh, Dad, you can hang up now, I got it."

"What are you wearing?" the man whispered, breathing heavily.

"Oh. My. God," she said. "Dad!"

"So solly, daughter-san, belly belly solly," the man whined. "Don't be, uh, mad-oo wiz papa-san." He put the receiver sloppily onto its cradle and was gone.

The woman said, "Sorry, buddy. My dad's crazy. This Clyde Eugene Twitty?"

"Uh, yeah, but," Clyde started. The sound of the TV coming through the phone fell away.

"You left your wallet in my Firebird, dipshit." Now he remembered the hard seat, rushing to beat the clock, Jay Smalls, his daughter. "I'm just kiddin," she said.

"Okay," Clyde said. He got a pen off his bed and uncapped it. "Where you live?"

"My dad won't let me say our address over the phone." Clyde laughed, touched the pen to paper. "I'm serious," she said. "Where *you* live?"

"Strasburg."

"I know Strasburg ain't exactly a thriving metropolis or nothin, buddy, but I figure you still got an actual street address?"

"You gonna bring my wallet to my house?" Clyde said. She didn't reply. He gave her his address.

"I'm gonna send you an invitation to an event I'm holding Saturday. Come to that and you can have your wallet back."

"That's four days away."

"Is it?"

"I could kinda use my wallet the next four days."

"I don't know what to tell you, buddy."

Clyde figured his uncle's twenty would last him. It didn't look like he had any other choice. In the salon, the dryer shut off and his mom shuffled around the kitchen, making noise. She called Clyde's name a couple times before giving up. When he finally came in a small chocolate cake and coffee sat on the table. "What's all this?" he said.

"*I*," his mom said with a great emphasis, "was offered a job." She finished setting the table. "The Omega's got a new hairdresser."

"The old folk's home?"

She nodded. "Sunday. One o'clock." In addition to being her son, house cleaner, and accountant, Clyde was also his mom's driver. "Don't forget."

"All right."

"You gonna write it down?"

"When's the last time I forgot to do something you asked me?" His mom looked up at him smiling. She was small, and getting smaller. "How about, uh, never?" he said.

Two days later Clyde got Tina's invitation. It was a card covered by a picture of an old man with a droopy face looking surprised.

> *Dear Clyde Twitty,*
> *You are cordially invited to the Summer 2011 Amway Sales*
> *Event at the Smalls residence in Liberty Ridge in Boonville, Missouri,*
> *this Saturday, May 28, to begin promptly at noon. Please arrive early for*
> *a good seat!*
> *Sincerely,*
> *Tina Smalls*
>
> *P.S. Your wallet will be returned to you at the end of the event.*

Clyde checked inside and out, but there was no house address, just "in Liberty Ridge in Boonville." Tina had put a little asterisk after the word "residence" and written at the bottom, *You'll know it when you see it!*

When Clyde got to Liberty Ridge he saw what Tina meant. Starting at a rock and metal sign by the roadside, which today had a handmade *Amway Sales Event* banner draped over it, the Liberty Ridge development spread out across an enormous slab of flat, barren land. There was a grid of new roads, hundreds of telephone poles and streetlamps, empty foundations as far as the eye could see, but only one house. It was a big house, more than twice the size of Clyde's, split-level, painted yellow and white, and built on a square of springy green sod that ended at road on one side and dirt on the other three; it was the only real grass in the whole place.

A few vehicles were parked in the road. Tina waved from a picnic table in the yard where a small group had gathered. She said something to a woman and the woman walked over to Clyde. "Clyde Twitty?" she said, moving her cigarette to her other hand so they could shake. "I'm Tina's mom. Jan." Jan Smalls, Clyde thought, must have had Tina very young because she didn't look much over thirty. She looked more like an older sister than a mother: the same pretty green eyes and summery skin, but darker hair, bigger teeth, and no makeup. Her fingernails were plain and saw-edged. She was thinner than Tina, with the hips of a boy and a flat ass, but her top half was all breast. A stained white T-shirt pulled so tightly around her front that Clyde had to curse himself not to look. His eyes flicked behind Jan to Jay, coming out of the house, and he thought he saw in the man's crooked grin something like, I see you looking at my wife's big tits, boy, I see you.

Clyde said, "I just . . . came to get my wallet."

Jan nodded and led him through the yard. Jay, wearing a white karate outfit, crossed toward Clyde with an exaggerated stiff-legged wobble, thumbs hooked in a black belt so worn it was gray. He elbowed Tina out of the way and said, "*Hai*," then somersaulted over his arm and came to standing right in front of Clyde with both hands out. Clyde took Jay's right hand and Jay gripped, covering their clasped hands with his other. "Osu-oo, Cryde-san," he said slowly, his eyes crossed. "Belly belly pleased-uh to see-oo you."

"Good to see you again, sir." Clyde laughed. It was impossible not to.

"Bullshit," Jay said, letting go and slapping Clyde on his arm. It hurt. "Call me Jay."

"Nice car you sold us," Jan said. The Firebird was in the driveway. Clyde hoped she wasn't kidding.

"Well, I was just the driver."

Tina hurried over and grabbed Clyde's arm. "I'm glad you came. We're just about to get started." She led him over.

"I could just take my wallet and get out of your hair," he said.

"Silly," Tina said. She stood behind Clyde and pointed at people. "That's my Aunt Missy, Jimmy-Don," she said, pointing to an enormous mass of a man, "and his brother Dale, they're my cousins. And those are some dudes my dad knows, I don't really know them."

Jimmy-Don was the size and the shape of a deep freezer. Dale, half as big, was tanned the color of Skoal spit and draped with a ratty poncho, white sport socks up to his knees. Both of Tina's cousins were covered in tattoos, lightning bolts, Celtic crosses, eagles, handguns, the number 88, almost all of them dull-edged and green. But Jimmy-Don had Frankenstein bolts on both sides of his neck done by a pro. Dale had a widow's peak of deep green ink creeping from his hairline. And both were wearing a weapon. Dale's couldn't be missed: a bolt-action rifle around his shoulder. J.D.'s was a bulge beneath his shirt. Before Clyde knew it, J.D. was standing in front of him, and Tina giggled. "Jimmy-Don," she said, "this is Clyde."

"Clyde," J.D. said, wrapping an arm around Clyde's shoulders and walking him across the yard. Clyde had no choice but to let him. "I feel like I've known you my whole heavy life, my friend." The rest of the family stayed where they were, watching. Clyde didn't even try to alter his course, the man was like a destroyer, not easily or quickly turned. "Remember when we used to ride our bikes out to the lake and skinny-dip with the Sprull twins? You used to say, 'I'd drag my cock through a mile of broken glass just to get a look at one of her fat titties.' Remember that?"

"Jimmy," Jan said.

"Hey, I'm just repeating information here, Aunt Jan. It's all coming back to me now, Clyde. The times we used to have. Some of the best times of my life. Real Kodak moments is what I'm saying. Oh, Clyde. Clyde Clyde Clyde. Or should I call you mister . . . ?"

"Uh, Twitty," Clyde said.

"Uhtwitty," J.D. said. "That's a peculiar name, if you don't mind me saying so."

"Just Twitty."

"Justwitty? That's even worse, Clyde, even worse."

"Twitty," Clyde said. "It's Clyde Twitty."

"Twitty then. I think I got it. Now it's coming back to me. Twitty's an interesting name, you know. A long, distinguished pedigree. Derived from the Latin *twitus*, meaning dim-witted or dull. Slow, if you will, though not, I'm told by my sources in the Academy, to the point of retardation. On the road to retarded? Mayhaps. Halfway up retard hill? I dare say so, dare I do. But not, for instance, not at the high high peak of gork mountain. Not where the flag flies, if you get what I'm saying, and I think you do."

J.D. turned him and they began heading back.

"Good," Jimmy-Don said. "*Bueno*. Am I right? Clyde gets what it is that Jimmy-Don says. He understands. Mucho intiendo, maybe even todo intiendo, who's to say? Me? Doubtful. You? Don't be ridiculous. Clyde gets the intiendo combo platter, eats it up, and orders one more." Jimmy-Don let Clyde free and Clyde's eyes skipped to the bulge under his arm. "I see you took note of my sidearm," Jimmy-Don said.

"Oh," Clyde said, wanting to step back but forcing himself not to. J.D. was practically standing on top of him. "I, uh . . . I was just curious. I've got a Colt .45."

Jimmy-Don reached inside his jacket and pulled it out. It was a Smith & Wesson like Clyde's, but a .357 Magnum, and in J.D.'s hand it looked like grandma's pop gun. He flipped it around and held the barrel. "Care to try it on for size?" Clyde took the gun. It was heavier than two of Clyde's pistols. He'd never fired a bigger handgun than his .45 and wondered about the explosive kick. "Never accept the offer of another man's gun, Clyde Twitty, silly wabbit."

Clyde handed it back.

J.D. slipped it into his holster. "Now you'll be the one riding the lightning for Jimmy-Don's three-state killing spree. I sure do appreciate it." J.D. went to his chair, waving his fingertips.

Dale lit a rolled cigarette and blew tan smoke that Jan waved away with a sour expression. Missy said, "You smoking a goddamn monkey turd, Dale?"

He grinned, smacked his lips, attempted a smoke ring. "Drying my own tobacco now," he said.

Tina hurried around to the other side of the picnic table behind a bunch of bottles, labels all facing out, and said, "Wow, thanks for coming, everybody." Clyde found a chair. "First off, I'd like to tell you about Amway's Artistry line of facial care products." For the next ten minutes, Tina talked about how her Time Defiance line stopped aging where it started. The whole time she barely took her eyes off her Aunt Missy. From what Clyde could see, Missy was no stranger to hard living, so he guessed it made sense, though he could see the woman squirming. Later, Tina would tell Clyde that she'd used techniques during the presentation that she'd been taught at an Amway conference in Joplin: engage the customer, make eye contact, create a connection, build a bond. When Tina finished the first part of her pitch, Missy actually clapped, her cigarette standing at attention.

Jimmy-Don stood up and his chair seemed to explode from his hips, tumbling in the grass. "Forget Marx and Engels and Ché and all those other faggots in their fancy hats," he said. "Ladies and gentlemen, the revolution will be brought to you by the People for the American Way. It's actually brilliant, cousin. I want in on the ground floor." Jan said something to try to get him to stop, but Jimmy-Don was unstoppable. "I'll clean," he said, "sweep, if the Mexicans haven't taken all the available spots. I'll do anything."

"Anything?" Jay said, two chairs down.

"Anything, Uncle Jay."

"How about you shut up then?"

Jimmy-Don ran two fingers across his paper-thin lips and crossed his arms. After a moment of quiet, Tina said, "I'll be happy to answer any questions you might have about my skin-care products."

Missy said, "You're a professional fucker, ain't ya?" and went to Tina, pulling money from her pockets. Clyde could see that this wasn't the way the presentation was supposed to go; he could see Tina trying to hide her frustration. Missy went back to her chair cradling three bottles. "Shit's so expensive I better look like goddamn Madonna!"

"Remember," Jay said, "it was *like* a virgin." Missy flipped him off and Jay jumped up laughing and ran around knocking down chairs.

Jimmy-Don took a shampoo bottle off the table. It rested in his palm like the travel size. "I'm sorry, cousin, I wish you that big big success, know what I mean?" he said. "But I'm afraid I won't be a cog in your capitalist machinery today, not this day, not Jimmy-Don. I make my own shampoo from tree bark and lard." He ran a hand through his long blonde mess and shook his head like a model on TV. "I ever tell you about the time in Russia where they felt the need to shoot all the poets?" As Jimmy-Don talked, Tina started throwing her bottles in a box and Clyde felt bad for her.

A little while later, standing in the yard with a beer somebody handed him, he was thinking about just asking for his wallet back when he felt a tap on the shoulder. He turned into a smack in the face that put him on the ground.

From across the yard Jan said, "Goddamn it, Jay." She hurried over and knelt beside Clyde. "Let me see."

"He ain't hurt," Jay said. He didn't look embarrassed or anything. "You hurt?"

Clyde didn't know whether he was hurt or wasn't hurt. What hit him, he now realized, had been Jay's *foot*. But it had barely touched his cheek. "He looks pretty damn stunned to me," Jan said.

Tina came over. "What'd you do to poor Clyde Twitty, Dad?"

"Stunned he is," Jay said. "You can stun a guy with a well-chosen *word*, mama. But hurt? I don't think so. Get up, boy, come on now."

Clyde allowed Jan and Tina to help him up. Jan growled at Jay, "You have to go around kicking everybody you meet?"

"Careful, mama," he said.

Now that he was standing, and knew what had happened, Clyde calmed down. "He's right. I ain't hurt. Just surprised." He didn't like to have everybody's eyes on him so he said, "Hope I didn't wet myself," and they all laughed.

Jay threw some kicks and punches in the air, his sleeves and pant legs making snapping sounds. "I just wanted to see what he was made of."

"Flesh and blood," Jan said. "Like everybody."

"Not everbody," Jay said, throwing combinations with more speed now. "Wanted to see if he'd *trained* maybe."

"Uh, yeah, I think you got your answer," Tina said.

"Trained," Clyde said.

"Karate." Jay pronounced it *kara-tay*. "I looked at you and I thought to myself, He looks like somebody who knows how to handle his self." Jay stopped and stood in front of Clyde, held his hands out to shake like before. "So solly, Cryde-san." They shook and Jay bowed.

"That's okay," Clyde said. "I, uh, I used to play baseball."

"I know." Jay put a fingertip on Clyde's chest. "Never trained karate, though?"

"Uh, no sir."

"Want to?"

Tina and Jan stood watching. They wore the same expression, an uneasy mix of wonder and dread.

Jay put an arm around Clyde's shoulders and turned him away from the women, like J.D. had, leading him into the flat even grid of Liberty Ridge, the sun shifting overhead. Jay talked about training, hard training, training his way, the Jay Smalls way. "This ain't sport karate," he said. "Ain't a *work*out. Ain't *ex*ercise. Ain't about vanity, looking good, having lots of muscles to impress the ladies. This about life an death." He raised a fist and squeezed, the muscles on his thick forearm rippled. They walked on and Jay asked Clyde if he knew the history of the martial arts. Clyde didn't know much. The Japanese, Jay told him, had invented karate, which, by the way, meant both "open hand" *and* "China hand," out of ne*cess*ity, centuries ago, to fight the invading Chinese bastards. Them Chinese, Jay said, all of 'em knew kung fu. But the problem was, kung fu takes *years* to master. Years. "You can't generate no power whatsoever in the first, oh, four years of training kung fu. It's all," Jay let go of Clyde and jabbed him with his fingertips a few times in various spots. Clyde laughed. "Gotta study anatomy and train ten, twenty years 'fore you can put somebody through a wall with a finger." He wrapped the arm back around Clyde's neck, talking close to his ear, making fists, making eye contact, throwing punches. "So finally the Japs, after getting whooped too many goddamn times, after watchin too many wives and daughters get raped in rice paddies, finally realized they had to learn how to fight, uh, *today*. Not next week. They didn't have no twenty years to perfect their technique. In twenty years the whole country'd be gone, the babies all half-breeds. That's when they came up with karate. The practical application of the martial art. China hand. The hand that will kick China's ass. Forget sticking a finger in a lymph node. We gonna put a fist through your goddamn sternum." Jay drove a slow punch into Clyde's chest, just enough to shove him. Clyde felt Jay's swollen knuckle there. "Gonna dislocate your knee with a kick. Collapse your throat, gouge your eyes, knee your balls, drive my fingers into your guts, snap your neck." In front of Clyde, Jay executed these techniques at half speed with hands and feet, his whole body rotating, the black belt slapping side to side. "They figured out where the power is," Jay said. "It's in the hips. Everything, Clyde, everything everything everything in karate comes from the hips. Just like fuckin." They walked on, Clyde's chest warm, his head buzzing. He could have listened to Jay talk all day.

"Karate is just the ability to do," Jay said. They passed open foundations that stank of standing water and filth, basements poured to be topped with houses that never arrived. Clyde squinted at the bright day and let Jay lead him. He wasn't sure if he really got what Jay meant by "the ability to do." Maybe you had to train to understand something so basic. As if Jay could read Clyde's mind, he said, "Modern man don't git it. The ability to do? All I need 'to do' is the money I got in the bank. A nice-looking wife, no buck teeth or lazy eyes, a couple kids who, uh," Jay slipped into a funny voice, "play by the rules. A good job at a respectable company, fine neighbors, a supportive community." With each phrase Jay's voice grew more ridiculous until he finally made a retching sound and snickered, his moustache curling. "Save *that* bullshit for the suckers. I'm building an army," he snickered, "to fight against the stupidity of the modern age. Karate men, Clyde, we're super-human." Clyde huffed and Jay nodded. "Superhuman don't mean we can dodge bullets, leap tall buildings, although, if I trained hard enough," Jay laughed. "You wanna jump a house, you figure out how, then you train, then you do it." Jay wrapped his arms around Clyde again and led him on. "Just means what it means. Super. *Greater than*. The way we train, it's true. With karate, Clyde, like nothing else on earth, man can perfect his character—if he wants to bad enough. You ever hear how we only use about ten percent of our brains, Clyde?"

"Yeah."

"Most men these days only using about ten percent of their character. It's the same. Modern man is stuck in a rut. We been castrated. By society, by our wives, our mommies, our job. And we don't even know it!" Jay laughed. "Well, *I* know it. But I is in the minority." He snickered and looked around quickly, as if someone was coming. "In more ways than one." Clyde grinned. "Let me tell you something you may not know, Clyde Twitty. There's no better mirror than training. People say mirrors don't lie. The hell they don't! Half the goddamn mirrors out there are *made* to lie. That's their *pur*pose. Make you look thinner, make you look fatter, make you look dumber, depending on what the mirror maker wants from you. But the mirror of hard training does *not* lie. You train hard, you train with conviction and an open heart, you learn things about yourself you never knew. You never *would* know, your whole *life*." Jay shrugged at this simple fact. "Dojo koan says it all: we will train our hearts and bodies, for a firm unshaking spirit. We will pursue the true meaning of the martial way, so that in time our senses may be alert." Jay nodded and they walked on.

After not speaking for so long, Clyde's voice broke when he tried. He cleared his throat and said, "Can you break boards and stuff?"

Jay ran ahead, looking around an abandoned lot until he found a brick. He laid it between two upturned cinderblocks, drew a long breath through his nose, raised his right hand so far over his head his thumb touched his back between shoulder blades, and brought it down with a loud *"Yah!"* The brick snapped in two and fell in the dirt and Jay stood up.

"Damn," Clyde said. His grin was huge. He'd never seen anything that impressive.

"Train with me," Jay said, "you be able to do that." He stepped into the street and Clyde followed. "Hell, Clyde, my *daughter* can break a board. Breaking boards is nothing." Jay held up a finger. Clyde saw that it was bleeding. "Know *why* karatekans break boards?"

"No sir."

"Back when the Chinese were overrunning Japan, their armor was made of wood. Swords slide off. But you put a fist through the wood," Jay threw a punch then straightened his fingers and jabbed, "easier to poke 'em. That's why."

"I didn't know that."

"Nobody does, Clyde-san," Jay said. "Stick with me I teach you all sorts of shit you never knew. And, I give you an outlet for that rage that's aching to get out." Jay tapped the center of Clyde's chest.

Clyde didn't know what Jay was talking about. "I'm fine," he said.

"You're fine."

"I mean . . . " Clyde didn't know what to say.

"You're, uh, *fine.*"

Clyde shrugged. He was fine, nothing to worry about.

"What you're telling me is you are not at all, uh, pissed off?"

Clyde considered the question. He knew there was something in him, but he couldn't place it. "At what?" he said.

Jay spat and closed the distance between them, keeping his eyes on Clyde. Normally Clyde was uncomfortable with this much eyeballing, being this close to another man, but for some reason it felt fine with Jay.

"Everybody thinks anger's a *bad* thing," Jay said. "Some kind of *problem.* This what I'm talking about. Modern man been castrated like a goddamn dog. Fuckin neutered. You don't have to pretend around me, Clyde. Never forget that. You pretend, I see right though it anyway, so don't bother. You got a *right* to be pissed off, Clyde. I were you, I'd be furious."

"Furious," Clyde said. The way Jay said it made it attractive. "At what?"

Jay spread his arms. "Look around, Clyde. Take your fuckin pick!"

Jay grabbed him by the back of the neck and brought their faces close. Jay's breath was smoky and sharp. "Fury, properly directed, is a *good* thing, Clyde, a powerful force. What makes the world go round." Jay let go and walked on. "Sosei—that just means "founder," by the way—Sosei wasn't a Jap, he was Korean, an orphan. Ended up in Japan. Before he was twenty he was a second-degree black belt in Judo. He'd trained Shotokan, tae kwon do, boxing, wrestling. He took the best elements of each style and made something new." Jay rolled his fingers into a tight fist in front of Clyde's face. "With a focus on power. Nothing flashy, it's not *poetry,*" Jay whined. "Sosei decided he needed to go into the mountains alone to perfect his craft. He trained all day, every day, year and a half. Punching and kicking trees to condition his knuckles and shins. Shins is sensitive, boy," Jay said, throwing a soft kick into Clyde's right leg. He was right, it hurt like hell. "That bone's one of your best weapons. But if you scared to use it 'cause it gonna ache like a bitch, you already lost. When Sosei came down off that mountain, he fought by himself, no school or nothing, in the All Japan Tournament. Nobody'd ever heard of him." Jay leaned in and grinned. "Guess who won."

Clyde smiled.

"Month later, Sosei had the most popular karate school in Japan."

Clyde's head was full to bursting with everything Jay had said. They stepped into the yard. "Door's always open," Jay said, and gave Clyde a printout of the class schedule. Then he went in and the screen banged twice behind him.

Clyde got in his truck. By the dashboard clock, he'd been with Jay ninety minutes. Fury, Clyde thought, rage. Anger. After Longarm closed, the truth was the slightest thing *had* set Clyde off. He hadn't realized until his mom had asked what he was so *mad* at, a question that had stumped him. Longarm? They'd done only what they'd had to. The bank? They'd *loaned* the money, it wasn't a gift, there was no ribbon on top. During the period after Longarm Clyde had almost gone around looking for a fight, a fight that he probably wouldn't win, which meant what he'd really been looking for was a beating. He didn't know what that said about him—or his character, as Jay might put it—but it couldn't be good. But that had been years ago. He hadn't felt angry—furious as Jay might say—for a long time, hadn't felt much of anything, really, beyond numb and tired. Sitting outside Jay's house he felt something, an emotion so distant that Clyde had no memory of ever having felt it before. To have power over others, to dominate, to radiate confidence. Jesus, how cool would that be? Clyde wanted to feel powerful. It was the first thing he'd wanted in years.

Jay was a far, far better salesman than his daughter.

Clyde had started his truck and put it in gear before he realized he still hadn't got his damn wallet back. That's why you came in the first place, dipshit. Halfway across the yard she came out waving it. "Time to pull your head out of your butt hole?" she said, laughing. They met by one of the two tiny saplings surrounded by small white wire fences in the middle of the front lawn. Clyde saw that there was still some money in his wallet, and resisted the urge to count it.

Tina handed him a bottle of Amway shampoo. "I might be wrong but it seemed to me like you were interested."

Clyde had shampoo at home, but thanked her all the same.

"It's ten dollars."

"Oh. Ten bucks?"

"Healthy hair requires daily treatment with a quality shampoo that's got more essential vitamins and minerals than any other brand," Tina said, touching a fingertip to the bottle. "You can't get this in stores. It's too good. They're afraid to stock it." She grinned with all her teeth and cocked her head. Her eyes sparkled.

Clyde opened his wallet.

Tina put a hand on his arm. "I already took the money."

Turns out Tina was a pretty good salesman herself.

From Liberty Ridge, Clyde headed to Walmart to give Esther the rest of what he owed her. He walked all the checkouts before someone told him that Esther had been moved to Pets.

Clyde smelled the Pets Department before he saw it, all mossy water and dead fish. The floor where Esther was working was cluttered with aquarium parts, bags of fish food, crates of baby turtles, and loads of junk. Esther was tapping the glass of an aquarium and whispering to a fish when Clyde saw her. "Good thing I'm not with those animal rights people," he said.

Esther flapped her arms at her sides. "Clyde!" she whined. "Mrs. Asbury had a stupid stroke so they stuck me in this shithole." She cast an eye upward. "Sorry, hun, but it is, and not even one of your miracles would change that." She whispered to Clyde, "This is the worst department in the whole store. Everybody knows it."

"Well," Clyde said. "At least you got the fish to keep you company."

"Poor fishies," Esther said. "I was just telling this one that it's gonna be okay on the other side. His water's filled with poop and half his friends are dead and rotting." She leaned toward the glass again and sang, "But everything gonna be all right . . . "

Clyde pushed a box out of the way to reach her. He took out his wallet.

"Hey!" she said. "You found it. I knew you would."

"Yeah." Clyde held out a twenty. "This cover it?"

"Oh my gosh, Clyde, really?"

He shrugged.

"At this point that twenty-dollar bill will cause more trouble than it's worth. Seriously. You think Walmart needs your money?"

"No," he said.

"Then put that away 'fore somebody gets the wrong idea." Esther fluttered her white eyelashes and twisted sideways with a hand on her chest. "I am not that kind of girl, Clyde Twitty. Shame on you," she said with a lot of breath, batting a hand in his direction. "Shame on you, naughty boy. I have half a mind to turn you over my knee." She straightened up and then stared into a tank. Clyde slipped the bill back into his pocket. She's right. Walmart's doing just fine without my money.

Esther flinched like she'd been slapped, grabbing Clyde's arm and making him jump. "Mrs. Asbury!" She bounced up and down. "There's an opening now. You could work here! You're always worrying yourself half to death over the groceries, pinching pennies and, no offense, Clyde, but there is not a single nother man who comes in here with coupons. You must be pretty sure of what you got 'twix your legs to lay a stack of coupons on my belt."

Clyde's cheeks burned with embarrassment. Esther was right, of course, about all of it. He didn't know she'd been paying such close attention.

She shouted, "Work here! Work here!" twirling on one foot. "Every paycheck you'll wanna cry or kill yourself, but the job's easy, we get a thirty percent discount at the Starbucks and a fifteen-minute smoke break every two hours. But best of all, of course, you'd get to work with moi, Esther Hines."

It was hard to argue. She walked him right then to the office in back and knocked at the open door. Behind a plain desk sat a man with thin, tan arms poking out of a short-sleeve button-down. A Walmart tie choked him around the neck, that or high blood pressure making his face look boiled. "Esther," he said.

She dragged Clyde in by the elbow. "Mr. Wilson, meet Clyde Twitty, totally the guy you should hire to replace poor Mrs. Asbury." Esther gave Mr. Wilson an exaggerated sad frown and extended the arm she was holding so that there was nothing Clyde could do but open his hand above Mr. Wilson's desk. A fake wood plaque said *Jerry Wilson, Manager.*

"Mr. Wilson," Clyde said.

The manager stood up, revealing a comically distended belly, a complete surprise given the bony arms. Clyde half expected to hear one of his shirt buttons *zing* into a corner. Wilson shook Clyde's hand. "It's only part time," he said.

"That's fine," Clyde said. "I got other work too."

"Is that right?"

"Yes sir."

"Such as?"

"I drive cars to auction."

"See?" Esther said. "He's reliable, he's nice, he also takes care of his uncle, who's a paraplegic. He didn't say that 'cause he's all modest. It don't get any better than Clyde. He won't let you down, Mr. Wilson."

"Thank you, Esther."

"He used to make extension rods," Esther said. "Before the economy tanked and the place went kaput." She really had been paying attention. She took a small ceramic pig from Wilson's desk and held it a couple inches from her right eye; her left scrunched shut. "Ask him what he got paid."

"Esther," Mr. Wilson said.

She put the pig back on Wilson's desk and said, "Eighteen bucks an hour!"

Wilson's eyes flared, but narrowed quickly. "Well, this position starts at significantly less than that," he said. "Try seven seventy-five."

Clyde grimaced. At the rate he was going, he'd be paying the IRS every month for the rest of his life. "How's anybody supposed to pay the mortgage with seven seventy-five an hour?"

That pushed Mr. Wilson back in his chair. "You own a house?"

Clyde lied. "I do. Bought at the top of the market, too."

Mr. Wilson's eyes narrowed. Clyde could hear him breathing through his nose. "Well, I'm sorry, but Walmart's not responsible for poor timing."

Clyde knew he needed a job. Now more than ever, with this goddamn out-of-the-blue IRS bullshit. But letting one of the world's most profitable companies pay him minimum wage seemed like a particularly hard kick in the balls. I've had enough kicks in the balls to last a lifetime. Clyde shrugged. "I mean, I guess I'll take it."

Mr. Wilson laughed. "Will you, now?"

"Yes sir. Just until something better comes along."

"Well well." Mr. Wilson shook his head, making notes and chuckling like Clyde had just made his day. "Don't do us any favors, uh . . . "

"Clyde," Esther said.

"Clyde," Mr. Wilson said, looking closely at his writing. "It's *very* nice of you to put yourself out for us, Clyde, it really is. I'm sure Sam Walton will appreciate it."

Clyde had known this guy two minutes and he already had him figured out: prick.

Mr. Wilson nodded at Esther. "Help him fill out an application."

At home, Clyde told his mom that she wasn't the only one who'd been offered a job. He wasn't sure that he'd get it now, but for her sake he made it seem certain.

"Boy," she said, "*Wal*mart. It doesn't get any better than that."

"Pays less than half what I used to make. Richest company in the world too."

"Well, I don't know about that, but with the head you got on your shoulders, Clyde, I wouldn't be one bit surprised to find you running the place in five or ten years. I think what we're seeing here is proof of the economic recovery. At last!"

Clyde nodded but he wanted to spit. Even with Walmart and driving and what his mom made setting hair, they'd still be struggling. Here he was, about to start a new job, and he felt like he'd just lost one.

After supper he went around stapling *Pretty Lady* fliers on the telephone poles between Pleasant Hill and Grain Valley. He heard the Plymouth Fury before he saw it and looked around for a place to hide. The ditch was too wet. The car rolled by and the same group shouted, "You did! You did tee a putty tat!"

"Hey, fuck you!" Clyde yelled, jumping into the road behind them and walking down the asphalt with both middle fingers raised. This had been happening for ten years. Literally.

Clyde pounded one of the roadside *Pretty Lady* signs he'd made last week into the mud. The four or five vehicles that would pass by—the Plymouth Fury dicks included—ought to appreciate that. It was pathetic, he knew, but what was the alternative? Give up? Then what? He was standing on the side of 58, still pissed about those townies, when his phone buzzed. He didn't recognize the number and thought it might be Walmart. "Hello?"

"Clyde?" a woman said.

"Yes."

"It's Tina," she said. "Smalls. From earlier."

"Oh," Clyde said, immediately thinking about the ten-dollar bottle of shampoo. What a scam. "How you doing?"

"Good," she said. "Here, my dad wants to talk to you." She smothered the phone.

Jay came on. "Clyde-san?"

"Yeah, hey, Mr. Smalls."

"Special class tomorrow, Clyde. Be a real good introduction for you. Nothing too clazy. Just some basics. Running, stretching, *kihon*, *kata*, light *kumite*, no big deal. You gonna love it. Eight o'clock. Can you make it?"

"Um," Clyde said, looking out at the endless stretch of road, not a car in sight past his own truck in the grass. "Sorry, can you hang on a second, Mr. Smalls?"

"Call me Jay," Jay said, and Clyde lowered the phone. With no voice in his ear there was nothing to hear but wind and a lawn mower so distant it was probably coming from Grain Valley. Clyde wanted to train, but there was no way he could afford to, especially without knowing whether or not he'd got the Walmart job. "Mr. Smalls?" he said.

"Jay. Or sensei."

"Well, I'd really like to make it but . . . I just can't," Clyde said.

"You can't," Jay said.

"I'm sorry."

"Why can't you?"

"Um," Clyde said. "Well. I haven't worked much in the last couple years."

"I don't teach to make money, Clyde. This ain't one of these 'you give me five hundred dollars and I give you a black belt' deals, and believe you me, them deals exist. Half the black belts walkin 'round out there's garbage."

Clyde laughed. He said, "Okay. I, uh, I just can't really afford, uh, anything right now. Especially since I got this letter from the IRS."

"What they want?"

"They say they made a mistake three years ago and now I owe them more money than I got in the bank."

"In my opinion, the IRS is a rogue agency. I don't recognize their power. Personally I ain't paid them a penny in years."

Clyde had never heard such a thing. "You haven't?"

"Do me a favor, Clyde, and bring the letter when you come over tomorrow."

Clyde wanted to, but he didn't want to be anyone's charity case.

Jay said, "Clyde?"

"None of your students pay?"

"Don't you worry about my other students, Clyde. Every case is unique unto itself."

"You sure, sir?"

"I'm sure, Clyde, I am a hundred percent sure. Question is, are *you* sure? You've plumb run out of excuses."

Clyde grinned. Jay could already read him better than some people Clyde called friends. What the hell? he thought. If he didn't like it, he could always quit. "Okay," he said.

"Hot damn! What I like to hear. See you Sunday morning. Be on time, that's all I ask." Then Jay said, "Osu," which sounded like "oh" followed by a long hiss. Clyde didn't know what it meant but Jay hung up before he had time to say anything.

Getting back in his truck, Clyde wondered how Jay had got his cell phone number.

At eight the next morning, breath visible on the air, Clyde stood in the cold grass in his bare feet, shivering. The belt Jay had tied around his waist was the same color as his gi but dirty and limp. Jay grunted some Japanese stuff before Clyde, the only student there. "Let's start with a little run," Jay said, jogging into the street on bare feet. "Five miles." Clyde nearly stopped right then and there; he hadn't run five miles since junior high. The macadam was hard and cold. Less than a mile in, Clyde stumbled to the edge of a pit and threw up, vomit the color of tea dappling the water below. He hadn't eaten any breakfast and had drunk only half his bottle of rocket fuel on the drive over. Puking, he was sure, would excuse him from training. "If you're gonna puke, puke hard," Jay said.

When Clyde finished he said, "Sorry."

"No 'sorry' in training. No shame in upchucking. The body gets rid of what it don't want. The more you train, the better it gets at doing it."

Clyde wondered when Jay would say, "Well, you done good. That's enough for today." Jay executed a series of techniques. Clyde had never seen anybody with so much raw power and it gave him a chill. "Four laps left," Jay said. "Then we train. Don't worry about puking. Don't worry about what happens later. Worry about entering the *mai*." He didn't elaborate on that, pulling Clyde by his gi back into the street. By the time they were in the yard again the sun was up and the balls of Clyde's feet, what Jay called his *chusuku*, were bloody, the bones of his heels bruised. The left side of Clyde's chest ached. When he headed for the house, Jay said, "Get back in line, Clyde-san. We ain't done, we're just getting started."

"I was just gonna see what time it was." Clyde hadn't forgotten that he had to drive his mom to the Omega today.

"When we train, we leave everything else at the door of the dojo. And dojo don't mean a little room with mats an' shit, some cross-eyed Jap pouring tea. Wherever we choose to train becomes our dojo. Right now, it's this patch of grass. We decide to do some *kihon* in a McDonald's lobby, that lobby's our dojo."

"Osu," Clyde said, already understanding that much. He also understood that he probably wouldn't make it home in time to drive his mom to her first day of work. He understood that, without a fight, he wasn't going anywhere until Jay said class was over, and no part of him wanted to fight this man.

All morning they trained against the cold and Clyde pushed his mom from his mind. It felt good learning how to throw a punch, straight and fast and hard. At midday, Jay went into the house and came out with a big kick bag. He held it against his body and Clyde threw front-snap kicks, what Jay called *chusuku mai geri*, into the bag as Jay yelled, "Gotta move me, Clyde. Push me back!" Clyde never did move him, but after a hundred kicks, his toes were stubbed and swollen and he'd overextended both legs.

When Tina and Jan came out of the house and took to the front porch, watching, Clyde again wondered about the time. The sun was high. He thought that he might, if he left right now, still make it to Strasburg in time. Distracted by the women, Jay said, "All right, let's take a break. Clyde-san, you bring that letter?"

"Osu," Clyde said, getting it from his truck. He handed it to Jay and turned his phone on.

Jay stood in the yard, a cigarette in his mouth and the letter held up to his face. He made noises as he read. He laughed. When he finished he tucked it inside his gi.

"How'd he do?" Jan asked.

"I think we got us a damn warrior here," Jay said, snickering, and Clyde couldn't tell if he was joking. "Light lunch, Clyde. Banana. Some crackers. No more than one glass of water. Ten minutes, then we train till five. Dale's on his way." When his phone powered on, Clyde tried to read the time, but sweat ran into his eyes. The muscles that wrapped his ribs burned and his hands shook. It was one thirty. He'd missed five calls, all from his mom. Clyde stood with the phone in his hand, staring at Jay.

"Ought oh," Jan said.

"Think you just broke him, Dad," Tina said, giggling.

"Nah, Clyde's tougher than that."

Clyde crossed the distance in the yard so that only Jay would hear what he had to say. "I'm really sorry, sir."

"Sensei. And say 'osu' when you want to talk to me."

"Osu. Sensei," Clyde said. "My mom needs me to drive her to work."

"Do she?"

"Yes sir. Osu."

"Sunday class don't end till five though."

"Yeah, I didn't know that. Osu."

"When we train, we leave everything at the door, Clyde. That's all I ask."

"Osu. I'm sorry."

"You were doing so well too."

"I guess, sir, Sensei, if I'd known this was all day . . . I woulda had to . . . skip it."

"What's the problem?" Jan asked Jay from the steps.

"Turns out," Jay said, loud enough for everyone to hear him, "Clyde-san's got other obligations."

"Oh, man." Tina fixed her mouth in a grimace. "You screwed up, buddy."

"I'm sorry," Clyde mumbled to Jay. He hit the button on the side of his phone. 1:43 now.

Jay snickered and slapped Clyde's shoulder. "I'm just playing with you, Clyde. Go on, git. Your mommy needs you, don't let us keep you." Jay said all that grinning but he still looked mad, Clyde thought, still looked disappointed. Clyde bowed the way he'd bowed at the beginning and limped to his truck just as Jimmy-Don pulled up in front hollering about the FBI. Dale slammed his door and ran off down the street on bare feet in a filthy gi.

"What's happening?" Jay said, hurrying across the yard. Clyde wiped his eyes and saw a brown sedan parked near the entrance of the Ridge, a K-car or some other shitty make and model. When Dale got close, the engine started and the car lurched from the curb. Dale yelled after it and snatched up rocks to throw. They peppered the trunk. The car jerked into second, getting a scratch, and raced away.

"You're shitting me," Jay said to Jimmy-Don. He spat, looking worried. His lips crimped into a tight line.

Jimmy-Don had his huge pistol in his hand. "Correct me if I'm wrong, Uncle Jay, is it me or is the FBI getting positively brazen in its surveillance of us?" He waved the Magnum.

Jay and J.D. stood watching Dale walk back to the house. "Get the plates?" Jay said.

Dale shook his head.

"Same fuckers as last time, you think?"

Dale said he thought so, yeah.

At the moment Clyde was more worried about his mom than about a car the Smalls thought was FBI. He didn't feel like he could leave before somebody said something, so he stood in the open door of his truck, watching Dale, J.D., and Jay talk in a circle. When Jay noticed Clyde standing there waiting, he said, "Oh, Clyde-san. Monday through Thursday class at six in the basement. It's only two hours. Two-hour class for mama's boys who got other obligations. Hope to see you."

"Osu." Clyde got quickly up into the truck, feeling pain in his fingers, hands, arms, shoulders, ribs, stomach, ass, legs, feet, and toes. He cranked the engine and shifted into drive when he heard his name, or a version of it.

"Clydus Twittus." Jimmy-Don lumbered into the street, put a paw on Clyde's open window, and handed Clyde a book. *The Turner Diaries* was the title. "Ever read this?" he said.

"Huh uh," Clyde said. The paperback was tattered, worn, much used. Its spine broken, the book fell open to a page with several passages underlined and handwritten notes choking the margins. The cover was familiar. He might have seen it at a gun show.

"I hope you don't mind, Clyde. Twitty. The book is *used*. I did not purchase this book *new*. I did not *participate* in our national *pastime*, I did not, I confess, *stimulate* the *economy*, and for that I will undoubtedly hang. From the neck. Until dead. Or maybe just sleepy." Jimmy-Don tapped the cover. "Read it, Clyde Twitty, read it and weep, my tweety-bird friend. Do you tweet? Have I seen you on Twitter? Can I give you a titty twister?"

Clyde grinned. "It's like a . . . novel?"

Jimmy-Don nodded and wagged his head at the same time. "I dare say you might find some of my notes insightful. Profound even."

"Thanks," Clyde said. He resisted the urge to check the time again.

Jay stepped to the curb and called out. "Think of that book as part of your training, Clyde-san. Read it."

"There will be a quiz later," Jimmy-Don said, slapping Clyde's hood so hard Clyde jumped.

lyde called his mom from Highway 50. She picked up on the first ring, her voice wet with worry until Clyde started in on his excuse. Concern flipped to fury and all Clyde could do was listen to her rant and rave about how many times are you gonna disappoint me? Finally she told him to forget the whole thing, just forget it. She hoped he was happy. Clyde told her he'd pick her up in ten minutes and he did, breaking the speed limit from Boonville to Strasburg, punching the wheel, cursing Jay Smalls, praying for luck. He honked pulling up and helped her in the passenger side. She never could lift herself up. He put her hair kit, a big pink tackle box, in back. The four miles to the Omega she didn't say a word, just sat there looking beaten down and worn out, Clyde knew that he was the cause of it. He hated to disappoint people who depended on him.

At the Omega he went in after her with the tackle box. She told them who she was, apologizing all over herself to somebody who didn't know or care. Clyde hung back, just inside the second set of doors that opened only from the inside with the push of the receptionist's button. It was a jail. A tall man entered the lobby and said, Mrs. Twitty, in a way that didn't hide his irritation. Clyde's mom blamed him, her son, he could see very clearly by how often she looked over. Clyde resisted the urge to wave. The man shook his head, wore a sour expression, threw up his hands, shrugged, and crossed his arms over his thin chest while Clyde's mom apologized and apologized and apologized, working herself near to tears. Finally satisfied that she had crucified herself enough for today, the man told her to follow him. It was almost like he'd gone out of his way to humiliate her in public.

There was no way that Clyde was going to stand around inside the Omega, it was depressing as hell. If he'd had his druthers, he would have gone back to Jay's and trained the rest of the day like he was supposed to. He hadn't felt the burn of a hard workout since baseball and he missed it.

In the truck he sat watching the Omega's front doors. Every few minutes a resident appeared, hands on glass, staring with cloudy gray eyes—*Let me out! Let me out!* Clyde couldn't sit there watching that; he went around to the back of his truck, stepping into the first stance he'd learned that morning. It hurt his knees but he did it anyway, going through every technique Jay had shown him, all the punches and strikes, the blocks that made his shoulders ache. He breathed the way he'd been taught—in quickly through the nose, out slowly through the mouth—and sweat ran down his face. Jay had said, "If you're gonna punch, punch hard," and Clyde executed every technique with as much power as he could muster. He kept count, then tried some kicks, but fell off balance too often and got frustrated. Jay could stand on one foot and raise the other to your face, gently tap your cheek, and bring it back to the ground. Clyde kept to knee kicks and threw a hundred. Sweating and tired but feeling strong again, he got back in his truck. He'd chased all the aches away. He opened the book that J.D. had given him.

> *September 16, 1991. Today it finally began! After all these years of talking—and nothing but talking—we have finally taken our first action. We are at war with the System, and it is no longer a war of words.*
>
> *I cannot sleep, so I will try writing down some of the thoughts which are flying through my head. It is not safe to talk here. The walls are quite thin, and the neighbors might wonder at a late-night conference. Besides, George and Katherine are already asleep. Only Henry and I are still awake, and he's just staring at the ceiling.*
>
> *I am really uptight. I am so jittery I can barely sit still. And I'm exhausted. I've been up since 5:30 this morning, when George phoned to warn that the arrests had begun, and it's after midnight now. I've been keyed up and on the move all day.*
>
> *But at the same time I'm exhilarated. We have finally acted! How long we will be able to continue defying the System, no one knows.*

Maybe it will all end tomorrow, but we must not think about that.
Now that we have begun, we must continue with the plan we have been
developing so carefully ever since the Gun Raids two years ago.

Now Clyde remembered. He *had* seen this book at gun shows. Word was, the assault-weapons ban that passed in 1994 had been pretty much predicted by this book. At gun shows he heard the talk about the erosion of rights and the Second Amendment. He just never thought it would come to that.

The Omega's automatic doors parted and his mom came through blinking, almost two hours after they'd arrived. It had been years since she'd worked this way, one customer after another, and it had taken it out of her. At home, she rarely had more than three appointments any given day, and only about a dozen clients total, a third of what she'd had when Mr. Longarm was open. After it closed, almost half of Strasburg's population had left town in search of work, some left the state entirely. Clyde had considered leaving himself, had been given a golden opportunity when his best friend, Troy, moved to Nashville a few months back. In fact Troy and Clyde had talked about Nashville, or something like Nashville, for years. Troy played the drums and had always urged Clyde to take up guitar. Clyde had tried but he had no aptitude for it so Troy had told him he could manage the band instead. To Clyde, it had just been talk, the silly daydreams of a couple small-town boys, he'd never expected it to lead to anything and had always figured Troy hadn't either. Between the announcement of the move and packing the car neither of them had mentioned Clyde riding shotgun. He guessed Troy had by then realized that there were certain responsibilities that would keep him right where he was.

Somebody once said that luck brought more luck. Clyde thought this must be true when a few minutes before six a.m. Monday morning he got the call from Walmart. Jerry Wilson wanted him at the store by seven. He'd slept only about four hours and didn't even have time to make any rocket fuel.

When he got there, he was given paperwork and put in a dark room with the orientation video. It started with a middle-aged white guy grinning into the camera. "I'm Walmart," he said. Then he was joined by a black woman. "I'm Walmart," they said together, and on like that. A young guy that looked Mexican, a dark woman with an accent Clyde had never heard, a few retarded people. Yeah, I see it, everybody's Walmart, we're all in this together, quack quack quack. "Through our commitment to low prices," one of them said over shots of people from all over, "we are bridging the global gap and bettering the lives of millions. Congratulations. You are a part of that effort now," someone else said, then everybody who'd called themselves Walmart showed up again. "Welcome to our family," they shouted, all of them smiling like it hurt. Then it cut to static.

The noise washed over Clyde. What a load of shit. He made no move to shut it off. He'd been very fortunate to get on at Mr. Longarm in his senior year in high school. That was very clear now. Even though he'd had to join the union to work there, nobody had ever confused workplace with family. He hadn't been somebody's corporate kin, he'd been a highly skilled worker, paid accordingly. That stint at Longarm had allowed Clyde to witness the end of an era that would never happen again in America, he suddenly realized, looking around this room built out of the cheapest materials—gray cinderblocks; brown linoleum; white dropped tiles; buzzing fluorescents. He tried to read one of the inspirational notes pinned to the corkboard by corporate and couldn't from where he sat. Probably best, given his frame of mind. Clyde had never been in prison before, but he figured this was what it felt like. The static surrounded him, he shut it off; he needed this goddamn job and decided he'd better try to get along.

In the manager's office Wilson was at his desk. "Finished?" he said, eyes down.

"Yes sir."

"Good, good," Wilson said. "Interesting, isn't it?"

"I'm Walmart," Clyde said. That made the manager look up.

Wilson paraded his new hire around for introductions before bringing him to Pets, where Esther was singing to a bagged goldfish, sunglasses covering her from hairline to lip. She had a sweet voice, actually, and for a moment neither Clyde nor Wilson said a thing. Then the manager cleared his throat and Esther practically jumped into Clyde's arms. "You hired him!" The bag rolled in the aisle behind her.

Mr. Wilson blinked and marched off and Esther rested her head against Clyde's shoulder. Her hair was rough and smelled of cigarettes. "Be gentle with me, Clyde. I ain't slept a blink." She asked him to run to Starbucks for a venti drip. He was worried about leaving so soon after getting there, but Esther assured him that Wilson wouldn't even notice. His ass was planted in his chair for the next half hour while he worked on the morning's "challenge."

Clyde checked his wallet. He had four bucks. He'd never gone into a Starbucks before and crossed the lot with the low sun on his face, waited behind a dozen people, some who'd brought their own mugs from home to be filled here. Clyde wondered about the effort of bringing an empty mug to a coffee shop. He ordered Esther's cup and said, "You're shitting me," when the woman in green gave him the price. He did not think the whole pot he made for his uncle every week cost three dollars. When he went out he couldn't help but bleat like a sheep at the people in line.

"I love you long time," Esther said, blowing across the coffee, fogging her glasses. "You didn't get one?"

Clyde shrugged. "Couldn't afford it."

"Clyde," Esther whined, her mouth hung open. "I woulda given you some money." Clyde dismissed the idea with a gesture. She held the cup out. "We'll share it."

"Nah," he said. "You have it. I don't really drink coffee anyway." Though this morning he would have, happily.

While he worked to make Pets presentable, Esther nursed the coffee and entertained Clyde with tales of the party she'd been to the night before. Deep in the woods, it had ended near five when the bonfire spread to the trees and she'd failed a three-way in a mound of damp hay. "I'm so humiliated," she said.

Before opening, Wilson came on the P.A. with the morning's challenge. It was, Esther said, a team-building exercise. Employees cheered, and Esther yelled, "Brownnosers!" She deflated immediately. "I think I'm gonna barf." Someone yelled from another aisle wanting to know who'd said that and Esther got behind Clyde. "Protect me, Clyde."

"Nobody here but us fishes," Clyde said in a pinched voice that made her laugh.

Today's challenge came from a personal conversation Wilson once had with Sam Walton, "the nicest, decentest, most down-to-earth man you could ever know." The challenge was to define the spirit of Walmart. A few minutes later Wilson appeared in Pets with a clipboard. "So?"

Esther raised an imaginary gun and said, "Low prices! Take *that*, high prices. Ka-blooey."

Wilson smiled stiffly. "That's a great point, Esther, and I like your enthusiasm, but it's not what Sam Walton said when we talked. I hope you're not wearing opaque lenses when we open." He turned to Clyde and waited.

Clyde tried to remember the terrible video. "Community," he said.

Wilson's face flushed pink. Clyde could tell that he'd hit a home run. "I'm gonna have to keep my eye on you, boy," Wilson said. "But. It's not *exactly* correct. What Sam Walton said when we spoke is that people think of us . . . as an old friend." He spread his arms. Clyde thought that "community" and "an old friend" were, more or less, the same damned thing. He also thought that nobody in a million years would guess "an old friend," so the challenge had been set up to be unwinnable. Bullshit.

"Weird," Esther said.

"No, not weird, Esther. Use your cabeza. Who do we call in our times of need?"

"Ghostbusters!" Esther said.

"You call on your old friend."

"Jesus is my old friend."

"And I bet you call on him in your times of need."

"He's not my emotional tampon, Mr. Wilson. I call on him in *all* my times," she said. That was all Wilson needed to march off with his head in the clipboard. Clyde felt worn out and the store hadn't even opened yet. Barely there two hours and he'd already been screwed. Esther must have sensed his mood; she slipped her arms around him from behind. "Ciggie break?"

Outside she said, "Watch me smoke," and French inhaled, looking up with bedroom eyes. "Is it sexy?"

Clyde nodded and took the cigarette she offered him. He didn't smoke, but one wouldn't kill him. Esther dragged hungrily on her Marlboro Light, burning an inch of paper, closing her eyes and resting her temple on Clyde's shoulder. When she finished she waved her hands in front of her face and looked at the sky. "I'm sorry, darlin, I swear that'll be my last one." She slipped her arm through Clyde's and waited for him to finish. A sick sweat rose to the surface of his skin. The lot filled with cars sliding around each other silently, rocking side to side as drivers sprang out. Clyde wasn't sure he was ready for human interaction. Maybe he wasn't made for work of this sort, with the public. He did not think, no matter how hard he might try, that he could buy into this "we" team-building crap, but Wilson, you could tell just by looking at him, bought it all hook, line, and sinker. Anyone who wanted to climb his corporate ladder would have to do the same thing.

Esther held her hand up in Clyde's face and fingered a gold band on her thumb. Clyde sank with disappointment. "Who's the lucky sum'bitch?"

Esther laughed. "My dad," she said, slipping it from her thumb to her ring finger. "I promised him I'd remain pure till my wedding night." Clyde looked at Esther for any sign of a grin but none came. Obviously Mr. Hines didn't know the first thing about his daughter.

Before they finished their cigarettes a black couple drove into the lot, got out, and made their way to the entrance. Esther squeezed Clyde's arm when they went in. The doors jerked shut behind them and she shook her head. "Wonder how long it's gonna take them to realize they're in the wrong Walmart?" she said. There was an older one across town, where all the black people lived.

When Clyde's shift ended around three he went in the back and wrote down his next shift—not until Thursday, and only four hours—and asked Wilson when he could expect his first paycheck. "You've only worked one day," Wilson said, laughing, and explained that Clyde had just missed the pay period. "Should be around the eighteenth," he said finally.

"Great," Clyde grumbled, going out. Three weeks of labor before I see a penny. Typical.

Esther told Clyde that she'd be out cruising Main Street after work and hoped he'd be there. He couldn't afford to waste gas; he had to get to Independence tomorrow morning. But he figured he could park and wait for Esther, maybe ride with her a while. He drove halfway down Main and pulled into the empty lot of a bunch of empty storefronts, *For Rent* signs in every dusty window, and parked nose to the street. With his engine ticking, Clyde ran back in his mind through his experience with the fairer sex. It didn't take long. It had been four years since he'd had a girl, and that girl—a woman, really—had been his one and only. When it came to women, Clyde had never been much good. In school, he'd paired off with Cindy Teagarden two weeks into their sophomore year. They'd both begun and ended that three-year relationship as stone-cold virgins; that whole time Clyde had turned down offers from other girls, he'd been a baseball player, in great shape and so popular that students, when he wore his number in the halls, shouted it like a cheer. No one knew that Clyde had graduated high school with his cherry intact and had only lost it in his first year at Mr. Longarm, to one of the secretaries up on the second floor, a married mother of two in her thirties who'd fucked Clyde four times and stayed in his bed until five in the morning, making Clyde almost sick with worry. Clyde picked up *The Turner Diaries* to take his mind off sex. As soon as he'd read a paragraph, his thoughts jumped to Jay and training. The funny thing was, the moment he put the book down so that he could try to remember how to execute a certain technique, Jay's name appeared on his phone. Clyde wasn't planning on going to class tonight, so he let the call go to voicemail.

"Osu, Clyde-san," Jay said in his message. "Hope we didn't scare you off yesterday, hope you're feeling good and strong after a morning of hard training. Get your mom to work all right? If not, I'd be happy to talk to her, smooth things over," Jay snickered. "Hope to see you at class tonight. Dale's coming out, couple others. We'll pick up where we left of yesterday. Six o'clock at the house. Let me know if you can make it. Osu."

Clyde checked the time, almost five thirty. From where he was parked he could see the start of the hill that ran to Liberty Ridge, he could be there in no time. Just when he was thinking about going, Esther's tiny mustard-yellow car turned into the lot, tires and power steering squealing. She backed in beside Clyde, rolled down her window, and smashed her cigarette into a large black spot halfway down her door. Clyde saw that she was slowly making a smiley face. "Like my car?" She spread her arms, one across the passenger seat, one in the air outside. "I call it the Honeybee." She pointed off. "I ran into some friends who want us to join 'em in a truck-bed party."

"Oh, yeah?"

"Yeah, they're cool, and they got like five bottles of wine. What do you think?"

The clock on Clyde's dash read 5:45. He could still make class. "You know what, you go ahead. I think I might just take off."

"What!?" Esther said, throwing her door open. She hooked her hands to Clyde's window and hoisted herself up. "Don't be crazy," she said, her smoky voice choked by the effort of staying off the ground. She let herself down and flapped an arm. "Give me five minutes. I'll go say hi and come back and me and you can cruise to our hearts' content." She jumped. "Okay!?"

"Sounds good," Clyde said, and Esther hopped in, tore out, and disappeared into the flow of traffic.

Clyde watched the clock. 6:00 became 6:15, then 6:30, finally 6:40 before he saw Esther again. She was in the back of a truck that had been raised twice as high as Clyde's with a lift kit, music was blasting, the back was full, Esther right in the middle, cigarette in her teeth, sunglasses on, a Big Gulp in hand that Clyde knew wasn't full of soda. She was sandwiched between a thin guy with a beard and a girl in a tube top, dancing. Clyde cranked his engine.

It took ten minutes just to nose out of the lot, the traffic was so heavy on Main, and fifteen more to pass under Highway 50, only a quarter of a damn mile away.

B y the time Clyde got to the house, it was twenty after seven and he was seriously questioning what the hell he was doing. Fucking Esther! There were a couple cars in the street and the front door of the house was standing open. Clyde could hear the TV on somewhere downstairs and women's voices. He knocked and Jan came up. When she saw Clyde she shook her head and laughed.

"I know," Clyde said.

"Half hour left?" Jan took him down through the TV room and opened a door in the back that led to the basement. Noise rushed up: Jay keeping count, people shouting *kiai*.

Tina said, "You are *not* coming to class an hour and a half late." She was sitting on the floor with a box of Amway products between her legs and a black binder in her lap.

"He gonna be pissed?" Clyde said, and Tina nodded deliberately. Then, he thought, she winked at him.

Jan said, "When you get to the bottom of the stairs, say 'osu' and just kneel down until Jay says otherwise."

Clyde saw J.D. first when he got down there. He was in his street clothes, sitting in a folding chair in the corner holding a spit cup. When J.D. saw Clyde he laughed.

"Well well well," Jay said, and Clyde saw the look of exaggerated surprise mixed with real disappointment. "Class starts at six p.m., white belt," Jay said.

Clyde said, "Osu," and knelt with his fists pressed into his hips like they'd done Sunday.

There were three men from Tina's Amway event and J.D.'s scrawny little brother Dale. They paired up and Jay said, "Little conditioning," which Clyde saw meant punching each other in the chest, forearms, and stomach while Jay swung a bamboo stick into their legs that made a loud *whap*. "Ain't gonna know what it feels like to be hit by slapping each other like girls." Jay finally said, "Clyde, get changed." He hurried into his workout clothes and then stood there. "Sit in seiza again," Jay said. Clyde knelt watching the men kick each other in the stomach, shins, and thighs.

From his position he could see the door open at the top of the stairs and Tina sneak down a few steps. She sat with her chin on her hands. Clyde tried not to catch her eye, but he did, and she held a finger to her lips. He couldn't help but smile. Jay yelled, "Tina!" without even looking at the stairs. "This ain't the goddamn *Dating Game!*" She ran up giggling and slammed the door. "Clyde, if you're done flirting with my daughter, you can bow in," Jay said, then, "Git back down in seiza." He knelt before Clyde. "Look how I do it." He came up on his right foot and then rose to standing, knelt again, and pretended to grip a sword on his right side. "This why we do it this way," he said, getting to one foot and pretending to draw the sword. "Always ready. We direct descendants of the samurai, Clyde, part of the warrior class." Jay ended class right then and Jay said, "Good spirit, everbody, see you all tomorrow. Everybody but Dale and Clyde free to go."

It was already after eight, but Clyde followed Jay and Dale to the front yard. Dale stood in a karate outfit that was yellow, grass- and blood-stained, with his hands in fists near his hips. Clyde stood to his left. Jay said, "Little light *kumite*." Dale bowed and turned to Clyde, raising his fists and yelling his *kiai* like he was furious. Clyde raised his fists and wondered when Jay would give instruction. All Jay said was that he didn't believe in wearing gear or padding when they sparred, thinking that protection was a barrier to truth. He made a noise that must have meant start fighting, because Dale kicked Clyde in the stomach, hard.

Clyde tried to get his breath as Dale came at him throwing kicks at Clyde's thighs and punching him in the chest and stomach. All of it hurt and Clyde flushed with panic. What the fuck? Dale drove him across the yard and Jay ran up behind Clyde and physically kept him from backing up. "There's no retreat in training!" he yelled, shoving Clyde at Dale. The picture window at the front of the house framed the women, cheering silently behind glass. It was like Dale wanted to hurt. "You gotta enter the *mai*, Clyde!" Jay yelled. "Can't win a fight if you ain't in it."

"Osu," Clyde grunted, his heart fluttering like a rabbit's. Clyde had never had a father to teach him the fearlessness a boy needs if he wants any respect at all.

"Heaven's found an inch beneath the blade," Jay said.

Clyde landed his only good punch when Dale turned before running into the street. "Hey!" Jay said. "We ain't done!" Clyde saw where Dale was headed: a group of boys were crossing the Ridge. "Ahh," Jay said. "Dale don't like them Molasses Gap boys." Clyde's chest heaved, the lungs struggling to take air. Blood rushed in his ears like he was being dragged underwater. "My nephew's about as sharp as a turd, Clyde, but fierce." When the boys saw Dale coming they scattered like catfish, leaving three who stuck to their course. "They like to cut through here to get to the Colonel's down the hill." Jay gave Clyde a little shove. "Think he needs backup." Clyde huffed. He thought Jay was kidding. "Fight's over there, Clyde-san," Jay shouted, shoving him again. Clyde had never been in a real fight in his life, and he hardly ever encountered black people. Jay shoved him from behind. "We still training, Clyde-san, I train at work, when I'm driving, watching TV. Anything can be training, whatever I say is training is training."

"Osu," Clyde grunted.

"Look," Jay said, and Clyde saw Dale surrounded, swinging arms and legs. "Sempei needs assistance."

Clyde said, "Osu," but the vicious beating Dale had just given him didn't make him too eager to help the guy out.

When those boys saw Clyde and Jay coming, they bolted, leaving Dale with a black eye. "This our property, niggers!" Dale yelled, throwing a rock.

They flipped him off and started down the hill. One of the boys yelled, "We gonna come back with a nine millimeter!"

"Good!" Jay yelled. "It'll be a fair fight!"

Dale said, "Thanks for the help, white belt," and walked back to the house touching his face. "I got to get to work."

Clyde watched Dale stomp off touching his face and felt what Jay had seen in him the other day—anger. What he felt right now *was* fury. He did not think he'd ever hated another human being as quickly or completely as he hated Tina's fucking cousin. Clyde had hardly trained at all and Dale had shown no mercy, and called him "white belt" like it was pathetic. Clyde's ribs were sore to the touch, his left thigh hurt bad enough from a kick that he had to limp, a wrist was strained, both ankles, the bones where his thumbs came off the hand were twice their normal size. If this was the way everybody learned karate there would be only one tough fucker at the top of the mountain and everybody else gone home.

Jay wrapped an arm around Clyde's neck, hot and sweat-slick. "In Japan," Jay said, "uchi deshi guard the training ground. They live at the dojo, train, keep the bad guys from getting in. Back then students would go around challenging your karate. Uchi deshi was the first line of defense. If they let a challenger beat 'em, challengers got in the dojo." Jay shook his head to indicate how bad that was. Ahead, Dale entered the yard, the house. "People who don't train, Clyde, they don't understand. This." Jay made a fist. "What it's all about. Outside this, nothing but distraction. Job, friends, even family, whatever it is people worry about. Money, sex, religion, none of it matters when it comes to this. You tell other people the way we train? They gonna question you, think it's brutal. Too macho for our modern times. But let me ask you, when the day comes to defend yourself or your way of life, and it *will* come, only a matter of time, what gonna matter then? Shit goes down, I mean *really*, all them doubters are the ones suckin pee-pees for a slice of bread. And that's the lucky ones with their pussies still ripe." Jay sniffed the air like a dog and slapped Clyde's chest. "But you and me, Clyde-san, we's warriors. Five hundred years ago we woulda been respected, part of the warrior class. I've trained with you only twice now and I can tell how strong you is." Jay tapped Clyde's sternum. It was also sore, bruised from a punch. "I train every day. Door's always open to warriors." They were in the yard now. The sod felt good on Clyde's bare feet. The sun was down, but a few hundred street lamps around Liberty Ridge laid hard shadows around everything.

Dale came out of the house in his tattered poncho. Tina followed in a gray Mickey Mouse sweatshirt that ran to her knees, an enormous glass in both hands. Jan stood behind the screen door. "Osu, Uncle Jay," Dale said, getting in his car, a twenty-year-old, dented, rusted Chevy Nova, and drove off, belts slipping under the hood.

"Did he know this was my second class?" Clyde said to Jay, low enough that Tina wouldn't hear him.

"Every action has an equal and opposite reaction. You don't like it? Hit him back. This how real men communicate, Clyde." Jay looked at Tina and said, "Cigarettes." She threw a pack that he caught without hardly looking. He slipped out two, handing one to Clyde, and lit them. "Just like after a good fuckin, nothing like a smoke after hard training." Jay sucked deeply and said, smoke leaving his mouth with every word, "Karate men built different than normal men. Stronger lungs. Better blood cells, scare the shit out of cancer."

Clyde nodded and took a drag. His second cigarette in two days. His throat burned, already raw from class. Jan came into the yard and lit her own cigarette and Tina sipped her drink. Clyde wondered if it was a clean version of what her parents drank, or if Jay and Jan let their sixteen-year-old daughter drink booze.

"He do good?" Jan said.

"Yes, he did," Jay said, winking at Clyde. Then Jay slapped Clyde's stomach. "We leave you two lovebirds alone," he said.

"Dad!"

Jay snickered, went with Jan into the house. Tina dropped her face into her hands and shook her head, Clyde stood in the grass and finished the bitter cigarette. When she looked up, she said, "Want a margarita?"

He'd never had a margarita before. Tina went in and fetched another big glass, salt around the wide rim, full of phosphorescent mix.

"Cheers, buddy," she said, clinking his glass carefully. He sat beside her and she said, after a minute, "You're warm." He nodded. "Try that shampoo yet?" He shook his head. "You'll like it. It smells real good." Tina launched then into a steady stream of words about her business dreams, telling Clyde about trying to start a publishing company when she was fourteen, selling Herbalife when she was fifteen, studying for but never taking her real estate license exam. Amway was a new thing, and she thought it was going good.

"I never done nothing like that," Clyde said.

"My dad thinks you're gonna be really good, by the way."

"Hardly done anything yet," Clyde said.

Tina shrugged. "Just telling you what he said. Says you're like really good clay. Got tons of raw potential." Clyde used to hear that word pushed his way back when he'd played baseball and it hadn't amounted to anything, so he didn't get too excited. It was usually more about the person who saw the potential than the one who supposedly possessed it. Tina smiled at him in a girlish way, folding over her legs. "Do you have a girlfriend?" she said. It was funny, a question that a little girl might ask on the playground. But he had to admit that there was something sexy about a female being that direct.

"Huh uh," he said, thinking about Esther.

Tina grinned with all her little teeth and pushed into him with her hip, she dropped her head. "Do you think I could be your girlfriend?"

Without really thinking it through, Clyde answered her. "You want to?"

Tina put her glass down, took Clyde's glass and put it next to hers, leaned in, and kissed him with a sticky, cold, open mouth. Her tongue pushed in, running across Clyde's teeth. She stroked his face. After kissing a while, she nibbled at his earlobe and whispered, "I'm gonna blow your mind," before returning to the mouth, then the other ear. "You ain't never had nobody like me." Her cold, wet tongue filled his ear.

"Hands on your heads!" Jay yelled, and Clyde and Tina jumped off the porch, spilling drinks.

Tina covered her face and stood with her back to the house. "Oh. My. God," she said, about ten times. Clyde pursed his lips and flushed red.

"Clyde and Tina, sittin in a tree," Jay sang, his arms and legs moving in the doorway in some kind of loose-limbed jig.

C lyde drove home from Liberty Ridge with a boner. He played a CD called *A Night in Tunesia* that Troy had given him; it was all clanging drums and shouting. The light in his mom's room was out when he got in, and he unlocked the house quietly. He still had the hard-on, that thing had held tough for twenty-two miles. In his room he took out a *Penthouse* he'd found by the railroad tracks behind the house and flicked past the dumb costumed pictorials to the pages he liked.

In the bathroom, a Post-it was stuck to the mirror. *Troy called*, *he'll be back tomorrow*. Clyde made a jug of rocket fuel and put it in the fridge.

Even though he made it to Independence early the next day, Leon still asked about the radiator. "You want me to have a properly working vehicle," Clyde told him, "you're gonna have to pay me more than eight bucks an hour." Clyde had never been this direct to Leon before and Leon, it seemed, didn't much like it, because he signed Clyde out with a Prius, quiet as the night and twice as boring. It had been wrecked and repaired but the front end still put up a fight on the highway.

All day Clyde waited for a call from Tina or her dad but his phone buzzed only once, when Troy hit city limits. Growing up, Troy had spent so much time at Clyde's house that Clyde's mom thought she'd had half a hand in raising him. Before Clyde had made it home, Troy's car, an early '80s Camero that had been shedding parts since high school, rushed into his rearview swerving and honking. Clyde tapped his brakes and Troy swung past with his middle finger in the open passenger window. Then he slowed to a crawl. Clyde laid on the horn and got close enough to tap bumpers. In a burst of smoke, Troy rattled off and beat Clyde home.

Getting out of his truck Clyde said, "I think you left your tranny back on 58."

"I think you left your tranny in Thailand," Troy said, moving his tongue in his cheek and jerking his hand near his mouth. "With a serious case of blue balls."

They shook hands, half hugging, and already Clyde thought Troy looked different. He couldn't tell what it was, only a couple months had passed. It unsettled him but he tried not to let it show. Troy had a brand-new Graceland T-shirt on and Clyde wondered if he'd brought one home for him. "Mom ain't come out yet?"

"Guess she didn't miss me."

They walked to the door. "She practically cries herself to sleep every night," Clyde said. "Truh-huh-huh-hoy . . . my favorite suh-huh-huh-hun . . ."

In the house Clyde's mom gave Troy a hug that lasted so long Clyde had to stick his hands between them and say, "All right, Mom, break it up."

"Well, I missed him," she said.

"He missed you too," Clyde said.

They had leftover cake and warmed coffee at the table. Troy looked around the way a person does who's left, studying the things that those who stayed behind don't notice anymore. Clyde guessed that Troy was seeing him the same way. His mom asked all sorts of questions about Nashville, saving Clyde the effort, then Troy and Clyde drove to the general store in Grain Valley for a six-pack. As they passed Strasburg on their way to Ekland Field, beers between their legs, they tried to find the rhythm they'd always had. It didn't come easy and Clyde started to feel like his best friend had changed. Looking out, Troy said, "God*damn*, I do not miss this place."

Clyde wasn't sure why, but he didn't like hearing it.

There was a time, and not so long ago, when Clyde would have chosen the perfect spot to park his truck, so people could admire it. Then he would have climbed the stands, heard the comments. "Wish you were out on that field tonight, Twitty," that sort of thing. He might have stood up for somebody on the field, his modesty wrestling with an ego that wanted people to notice him. There was a time, that year or two right after school, when Clyde Twitty and Troy Hoffman would have been in these stands three, maybe four nights a week. But after Longarm shut down, after Strasburg died, people saw less and less of Clyde Twitty. And since Troy moved away, Clyde hadn't taken in a single game, hadn't wanted to spend the night answering questions. Tonight he could see how happy they were to see them again, Clyde Twitty and Troy Hoffman, the way it always was.

Clyde had never much liked playing baseball and had quit with no regrets when he got the Longarm job senior year. Coach hadn't tried to hide his disappointment. "You broke your promise, you made a commitment to me and your team," quack quack quack. Suddenly it's my team, suddenly it's a promise. Of course Coach had brought out the big guns, then: "potential." He could win a scholarship, make the minors, he could blah blah blah. Clyde just didn't buy it, a guy will say anything to get his way. Coach wanted to keep his pitcher, he didn't want the inconvenience of finding a new one mid-season, that was all "potential" meant.

The air up top was still and cool, the bugs plaguing the lights up high. Troy shook hands with half the people in the stands and Clyde watched their faces. He knew almost all of them. He knew them from high school, grade school, work, his mom's business, baseball, FFA. Strasburg was the smallest of towns, so small that it had to share a high school with Grain Valley. When Clyde saw Coach at the fence, he pretended he hadn't. He suddenly felt funny being here with Troy again, just like old times. All these familiar faces made Clyde understand why Troy had left. Clyde's phone buzzed. A text from Tina read: *Dad says class, 6 p.m., stay for supper.*

Troy sat down. "Got yourself a girlfriend, Twitty?"

Clyde recalled the language Tina had used on the steps and said, "I guess I do." He told Troy about Tina and her dad. He pointed out the bruises on his arms. Troy had taken karate in Harrisonville once, for a few months, just long enough to instill fear in his fellow sophomores. But the more Clyde told him about the way that Jay trained and what Jay talked about, the more concerned Troy looked.

Clyde said, "You think it's crazy?"

Troy stared at the field. Then he nodded once. "Uh, yeah, dude. I fuckin do. He even got insurance?" Troy said. That made Clyde laugh. "You sign anything?"

"Jay," Clyde told Troy, "teaches traditional karate, not *sport* karate." He didn't even charge for classes. There wasn't gonna be any *paper*work. When Clyde repeated what Jay had said about the uchi deshi, and that he thought that Clyde, in a different age, would have belonged to the warrior class, Troy nearly choked on his beer.

"I know you don't wanna hear this," Troy said, "but he sounds like a fucking nutcase. Like the bad sensei from *Karate Kid*." Troy made his voice into a husky growl: "There's no fear in this dojo, is there? No, Sensei!"

Clyde didn't even smile. He wrestled a cold beer from the tight plastic hold. "Yeah," he said, taking a sip and turning his eyes to the field. "Most people don't get it." Clyde checked his watch. If he left right now he'd be only ten minutes late for class.

"Come on, dude," Troy said, bumping Clyde. "Oh, I'm sorry, I'm sorry I fuckin *care* about what happens to my best friend." Troy wrapped an arm around Clyde's shoulders. "Let's get drunk and go watch the planes take off. Fuck fucking baseball."

Passing the dugout, Coach called Clyde over. "Troy back?" Coach said.

"Visiting." Clyde turned to watch Troy walk to the truck. "Says he's done with this shithole."

Clyde saw Coach narrow his eyes. He wasn't used to this attitude from Clyde. Clyde wanted to say something even worse just to throw him off.

In Raymore Peculiar Troy bought another six-pack and they parked on the gravel strip that ran along the high cinderblock wall surrounding Richards-Gebaur AFB. Clyde felt his phone buzz on the way. His mom, his uncle, Tina, or Jay; those were the options. Now parked, he saw Tina's number. She'd called twice, no message. Clyde and Troy settled in with the new beers. Troy took Clyde's .45 off the dash and held it out the window. "It's loaded," Clyde said.

"Motherfucker," Troy said in a growl, pointing the gun gansta-style. "You talking to me?" They were into their third beer before the truck shook. They stuck their heads out howling like they used to, trying to spot the jet, but it was lost to a starless gray sky. Troy crouched in the seat with his knees on the dash, balancing the beer on his chest. It rose and fell. The gun was back on the dash in its holster. "You know," Troy said. "I've been pretty pissed at you," he said.

"Yeah," Clyde said. "I figured."

"Me and you, man. Way we were supposed to. Me on drums, you selling merch." Troy shook his head. "I woulda gone a fuckin year ago if I'd known you never meant it in the first place."

"Really?"

"Maybe." Troy shrugged. "Don't matter."

"My mom," Clyde said.

The wind picked up and moved through the truck, disturbing the wrappers on the dash. "Your fifty bucks make a big difference?" Troy said.

Clyde resisted the urge to correct Troy's too-high assessment of his earnings. "Still got the house," he said.

Troy grunted. "So," he said, adjusting his position. "Fucking." He squirmed again. "What." He finished the beer and chucked the can. Clyde heard it land with a hollow scratch in some brush. "You two own that house? Or does the house," Troy poked a drunken finger at Clyde, "own you?"

Clyde laughed. "That don't even make sense," he said. "It's a house. We live in it. We either pay the bank, or we pay somebody else who pays the bank. Ain't that complicated."

"Only words you said twice in that statement were 'pay' and 'bank.' Just sayin."

"You go to Nashville and you get all . . . " Clyde's thoughts petered out. Troy could fill in the blanks if he wanted to.

"What about you?" Troy said. "Longarm's gone. Strasburg's fucking dead. You gonna marry this chick? Work at Walmart your whole life? There are Walmarts in Nashville, you know."

"There are Walmarts in fucking China," Clyde said.

Troy scrunched up his face and said, "The row plice reader," and they both cracked up. When they settled down, Troy said, "You got any, you know, plans? For like, the future?"

The future had always been a sore subject for Clyde. "I don't know. Right now I'm just taking it day to day."

"You in AA now?"

"What?"

"Takin it day to day, goin with God," Troy said in a pompous voice. "You could take some classes at Longview."

"In what?"

Troy grinned. "Music production. You can learn how to mix an' shit, move down to Nashville next year. That'd be perfect, man, give me time to get something going."

Clyde drank some beer and looked at a blinking light beyond the high stone wall. He would never enroll in college, he would never move to Nashville. "Maybe," he said.

"Look into it."

"I will."

Troy groped around, got another can open. "You know, man, I actually can't believe you still buy all that bullshit after Longarm and everything else that's happened to you. How many times you have to get fucked in the ass before you buy a pair of pants?"

"What bullshit?"

"That if you just," Troy slipped into a presidential voice, "work hard and play by the rules, you can be one of them."

"One of who?"

"Whoever, man. Successful. Middle-class. Last few years have made it pretty fucking clear that there's the bankers, the CE-fuckin-Os of the world, and they're up here." Troy raised his hand high, then dropped it below the seat. "And everybody else is down here."

Clyde laughed.

"What?" Troy said.

"Nothing, it's just, you think Jay's crazy but he said pretty much the same thing to me the other day."

Troy raised his eyebrows, his hand was still up near the ceiling. "Maybe he's actually pretty smart," he said. "Anyway," he moved his hand up and down, down and up. "There's no *honest* way to get from here to here no more."

Clyde guessed that Troy had a point, but he didn't like to embrace this hopeless attitude. "So what are we supposed to do, then?"

Troy shrugged. "Own nothing." He spread his arms across his lap. "Be free."

C lyde made a point of getting to Liberty Ridge half an hour early on Wednesday. Troy was busy with family the next two days and Clyde had no obligations except a four-hour shift at Walmart the next day, for which he would make $31 before tax. Tax would take fifteen, twenty percent, say, $5. So, $26. Just to get there and back would take four gallons of gas. At $3 a gallon, that was $12. Subtract $12 from $26 and you're left with $14. How much money will Walmart make in those same four hours? Clyde wondered. In Liberty Ridge, he waited in his truck until Tina came out in her bare feet. "You here to see me," she called across the street, "or my dad?"

"Both," Clyde said. It was enough of an answer to bring Tina across the remaining ground. Even though no one drove in the Ridge but the Smalls, Tina looked both ways before she made it to Clyde's door. "Thought I'd kill two birds with one stone," he said, but Tina didn't laugh.

"I thought I was your girlfriend," she said.

Clyde didn't say anything for a moment, then told her, "You are."

Tina shook her head. "You didn't even call me back."

"You leave me a message?"

Tina shrugged. Her fingernails, bright pink, clung to the last inch of Clyde's window. "Didn't think I'd have to."

"A friend came up from Nashville," Clyde said.

"A friend?"

"Yeah."

"What kind of friend?" Tina said.

"My best friend. Troy."

"Troy."

"Yep."

"Troy a girl?"

"A girl?" Clyde said. "Uh, no. Troy's a dude. Ain't seen him in two months, either."

Tina nodded and looked out at the street. "I guess that's all right," she said, bringing her gaze, those bright emerald eyes, to his face. "Wish you'd called me back, though."

Clyde had had about enough of this. He hoped Tina wasn't one of those feminist types, wanting to keep his balls in her bedside drawer. He saw on his watch that it was close to six and grabbed his gym bag. He bowed out the window so that his forehead fell upon Tina's knuckles. "I'm so solly, belly belly solly," he said, and Tina cracked up and stepped back so he could get out.

They kissed in the middle of the street and Jay, who obviously had some kind of radar for catching these moments, yelled from the doorway, "No kissy face in training, Clyde-san. Class starts in four minutes."

"Osu!" Clyde yelled, hurrying into the yard.

It was Clyde's first full class, and he was the only one there. The first hour he faced Jay doing *kihon*. When they were done, Jay said they'd thrown a thousand reps. "We train until we're exhausted, then the real training begins," Jay said. They did conditioning drills next, and the swollen middle knuckle of Jay's hard right hand tormented the exact same rib every time. Push-ups and sit-ups and squats followed, until Clyde's arms and legs wouldn't stop shaking and he had to use the railing to pull himself up the basement stairs after they'd bowed out. When Jay asked Clyde if he could stay for supper, he didn't hesitate. In the kitchen, Jan and Tina were at the table. Tina smiled at Clyde. He ran a forearm across his face and felt sweat pooling around his bare, dirty feet on the linoleum floor. "Tina," Jay said, slipping a cigarette out of his pack of Winstons on the counter, "Get Clyde a towel and show him where he can shower."

Tina jumped up and pulled Clyde by the sleeve of his gi. In the bathroom she kissed him and wiped her nose. "Sweat much, buddy?"

Clyde had made the drawstring of his gi pants so tight he thought he was going to have to cut it to get them off. Finally he worked some give into it. Just as he was reaching into the shower, Jay yelled, "Tina Louise," and Tina squealed right outside the door.

Before supper, Jay read Clyde the letter he'd written for him to the IRS.

I have received your angry notice informing me of a debt you claim I owe for mistakes which originated in your own office. As a law-abiding, tax-paying, hardworking citizen of these United States, I have chosen to execute my inalienable right to liberty—in this case financial liberty—by refusing to pay you another red cent. In fact, you should pay me $862 for the emotional distress and turmoil your letter has created in me and my family, which is sizeable and could be documented through the proper medical and legal channels. Furthermore, you should be ashamed of yourselves for pursuing honest, hardworking tax payers to cover clerical errors built on government corruption and inefficiency. I for one refuse to take part in your many global wars and other criminal efforts being perpetrated by the New World Order AKA the United States of America AKA the plaything of the Fed. Feel free to do your evil work, go ahead and send a collection agency to seize my assets; they are few, and easy to defend, as I am legally armed and will act in a manner accorded by law when an unlawful person trespasses and attempts to steal that which is mine.

Sincerely,

Clyde Eugene Twitty, citizen

Jay dropped the paper, a big grin on his face. "Pretty good, huh?"

Clyde had no idea what to say. Part of him would have loved to send a letter like that to the goddamn IRS. But he worried that if he did he'd get in trouble. He didn't think he was prepared, as Jay seemed to think he was, to enter into a shootout over his truck.

"Dad!" Tina said. "Clyde ain't ready for your craziness."

"Daughter-san," Jay said, holding up a finger of warning. "You ready for my quote-unquote craziness, Clyde, or aren't ya?"

"Well, that's not the way I'd put it . . ."

"See?" Tina said. "He ain't ready."

"Let poor Clyde fight his own battles, Jay," Jan said.

Jay balled up the letter and said, "All right, mama." He lit a cigarette and chucked the pack at Clyde who took one out and lit it with Jay's lighter. Jay pointed the cigarette at Clyde then. "Write your own letter."

Clyde huffed.

"I mean it," Jay said. "This part of training. Write your own letter, and let me see it 'fore you mail it."

"Osu," Clyde said.

During supper Jay opened the first bottle of Rebel Yell. In the front room an hour later he opened the second. Pouring from that bottle, he raised his glass and said, "To the new couple!" Everyone but Tina shot the whiskey down. Tina sipped hers, making a face and giggling. It seemed that the Smalls didn't give two shits about laws of any kind. Tina, at sixteen, drank alcohol every single night. By ten o'clock, the whole family was sharing cigarettes and telling jokes, their shoes upturned on the carpet. A little later they split into two couples, Tina and Clyde in the front room by the wall of bookshelves stuffed with decades of *National Geographic*, *Playboy*, *Penthouse*, and *Black Belt* magazines, Jay and Jan in the TV room, kissing so wetly that they sounded like two dogs licking themselves clean.

Pressing Clyde into the floor, Tina whispered for him to keep his eyes open while she touched them with her tongue. She filled his ears with slobber and sucked it out in loud snaps that made him flinch, ground her pubic bone into his sore pecker and freed her bra with a springy snap beneath her sweatshirt. She lifted the shirt to her neck, grabbed one of her boobs, and shoved it into his mouth. Clyde had never had a girl's tongue in his ear, and he'd sucked on some titties only once before, the night with that married woman, who'd fucked Clyde again and again on his bed, her pale pink nipples swinging just above his nose.

Just then Jan hollered up the stairs, "Y'all keepin it clean, ain't ya?"

Tina giggled. "Yep," she said.

"Clyde?" Jan said.

"Uh, yes ma'am," he said, Tina's cold, wet nipple against his temple.

"Clyde-san?" Jay said.

"Yes, sir, absolutely."

"Better be."

Tina stared at the top of the stairs. Without turning to Clyde, she smashed her enormous bare breast into his face. For a moment, he was drowning in tit.

Sometime later she jumped up and released a sob that sounded like she'd been punched in the neck. She ran out of the house. Clyde had no idea what had happened.

"Tina?" Jan said from downstairs.

"Uh," Clyde said, wiping his mouth and trying to hide the erection pressing tight and hot against his zipper. "She, uh," he said, as Jan climbed the stairs.

She came into the room dragging her sweatshirt over her naked breasts. "What happened?"

"She just," Clyde said, getting unsteadily to his feet. The bottle of Rebel Yell lay on its side, a stain on the carpet around it. "Uh, jumped up."

Jan looked out the screen at the yard. "Tina?" she called. Tina didn't respond. Clyde could hear her sobbing out there somewhere. "Here we go," Jan said.

For the two hours that followed, Clyde sat with Jay on the frozen cement step with an afghan over their legs. Whiskey, cigarettes. Clyde worried about what the Smalls would think had happened, what Clyde had done to upset their only daughter, but there seemed to be no judgment at all. He got the feeling that he could have gone to his truck and driven off without Jay or Jan thinking it was a bad move. Twice in that first hour, Jan returned to the porch for a drink and a smoke. "She's never had a boyfriend before, Clyde," Jan said. "She's afraid you're gonna hurt her." Jan smiled sweetly, smoking her cigarette, and went back out. The next time she returned she said, "Clyde, you are either the loyalest son of a bitch the world's ever seen, or the dumbest!" Drunk, exhausted, blue-balled, and confused, he didn't know what he was.

"He in too deep to git out now, mama," Jay said. "*Way* too deep."

Jan looked at Clyde in a way that he would come to learn only she ever did. "I think you're right," she said. "Clyde is here to stay."

That night Jay told Clyde about how the Smalls had ended up alone in Liberty Ridge. Technically the house belonged to Jay's parents. What had happened was, after laying the macadam grid, lighting every damn street, and punching half the basements, the developers had tilled up relics from Civil War times. A whole mess of important shit, some lawyer said. At that point, they'd finished and sold exactly one address, the model house, bought by one Curtis Duane Smalls of Grandview, Missouri. The Liberty Ridge Development Corp. had tried to buy it back, but Jay, acting on his father's behalf, said no, thank you. Since then the whole thing had been stuck in the courts. According to Jay, it was typical government bullshit and made as much sense as a dog in a whorehouse. The developers had even threatened to sue, backed by the city council, and Jay had written a letter to the council quoting Patrick Henry and citing the ever-increasing power grab of the United States government. Fifty open basements had since filled with standing water, mosquitoes, and garbage thrown in by the trespassing boys of Molasses Gap. There was a dark line of trees in the distance that Jay pointed out to Clyde, the border between the two communities. "Slavery," Jay said, "were the worst and dumbest thing to ever happen in this country, you know that?" Clyde nodded. "If the goddamn Europeans had had a decent fuckin work ethic they wouldn't a needed to pilfer Africa of its babies and the Negro would never have set foot on American soil. Ever since they have, their presence is a fuckin cancer, just spreads and spreads, from the south to the north, from the city to the country. They only eleven percent of the population today but they're about a hundred percent of the problem." Jay jumped up then, disappearing into the house. When he came back, he had an AR-15.

"Damn," Clyde said. He'd seen assault weapons at gun shows but never held one.

Jay handed it over. "Ain't loaded," he said, nodding at a clip on the step. The gun was light as hell. Clyde sighted at a distant piece of machinery and gave it back. Jay slapped the clip in and pointed it at the woods. "Pow," he said. "One of these days they get the idea." He lowered the gun and got a new smoke lit. "Hell." He sighed and rubbed his face. "They only the tip of the iceberg."

By the time Jan talked Tina in, it was after three and Clyde was drunker than he'd ever been. He'd never drunk whisky before—only beer—and he had no idea how mean it could be. He and Tina made up in the yard and then Clyde puked into the mulch around one of the saplings and lay down on the damp, cold ground. In the light of day he woke on the sofa in the front room with Jay crouched beside his face, whispering, "Cryde-san . . . Cryde-san . . . "

"What time is it?" he said, pushing the blanket down. He was in a clean pair of karate pants and a T-shirt he didn't own. His throat burned, stomach threatened, a headache began at the base of his skull, crawled around his temples, and dug in behind the eyes. It would have been easier to throw up than not to.

"Time for work, Cryde-san . . . time for work." Clyde had forgotten all about Walmart, but Jay hadn't.

As Clyde got ready to go, Jan made coffee in a pair of sagging panties and a torn T-shirt, no bra. She handed Clyde a cup and held his face when she kissed his cheek with warm, smoky breath. Clyde liked Jan and he liked Jay, a lot. He wasn't sure about Tina. He'd never known a girl like this, sweet and sexy one minute, shithouse crazy the next, like Jekyll and Hyde. But Jay's words from last night came to him: in too deep, that's what he was.

"What time's your shift over?" Jay asked him.

It took Clyde a moment to answer. His brain felt like potted meat. "Eleven thirty, I think."

"See you in class tonight?"

Clyde groaned. "Osu. Might need to recuperate a little bit."

Jay blew across his coffee mug, steam shaking across the top. "Mm," Jay said. "You know what 'osu' means?"

Clyde realized he didn't.

"Comes from 'oshi shinobu,'" Jay said. "'Oshi' means to persevere and 'shinobu' means while being tested. If you ain't gonna do that, then don't use the word."

Clyde felt his chest tighten. "Oh," he said. Jay had told him to say "osu" for everything.

Jay waved a hand. "Guess I see you when I see you."

"No," Clyde said. "Sounds good."

"Clyde-san," Jay said, getting close enough that Clyde could hear him breathing. "Don't do me no favors. I'll train with you or without you. Don't matter to me."

"I'll be here."

"Strength through repetition, Sosei said. Sosei said it takes a thousand days to master your basics. I don't believe in part time, Clyde. Part time is half-assed."

"Osu," Clyde said.

"Oh, and, uh," Jay said, "just use my computer to write that letter after class."

Clyde nodded. The truth was, he figured he'd just have to pay the fucking IRS. They seemed serious. But he didn't have a fraction of what they were asking for, even with two jobs. But Jay seemed pretty set on it, so he'd give it a try.

After punching in at Walmart, Clyde went to Pets, walking with a minor limp and carrying a general air of abuse. When Esther saw him she hugged him and said, "You poor kitty, what happened?" She inspected his bruised forearms and made the run to Starbucks herself, without asking for money. She came back with two venti cups, hers black, his sweet and light, and slipped her arms around Clyde's waist, laid her cheek between his shoulders and said, "Sorry about the other night." Clyde nodded and Esther squeezed him harder. It made his stomach lurch. "You know what I bet'd make you feel better?" she said.

"Huh uh."

"A blow job."

Clyde's breath came out in a cough.

Esther split away, picked something up from one of the shelves. "I'm serious," she said, looking in a murky tank. "Whenever you want, okay? Just come up to me and say, 'Why don't we go out and sit in my truck a while.' I'd love to do that for you." Clyde nodded and Esther smiled like he'd just made her day.

By the end of his shift Clyde didn't feel much better. He'd accomplished almost nothing. Pets was still a ruin. Just before the shift ended, Tina appeared in the mouth of the aisle. "Found him," she said. Her eyes skipped to Esther the next aisle over and narrowed. Tina's mom came around with a shopping cart. Clyde had been trying to put a fish tank together and Esther was pricing chew toys.

"Mrs. Smalls," Clyde said, looking from Tina to Esther and back. Tina didn't like that, didn't like that at all. "What are you guys doing here?"

"Well, Tina's working," Jan said with a crooked grin.

Tina flapped a notepad and said, "Brand strategy stuff."

"And I'm getting groceries. You like Mexican food, Clyde?"

"Uh, yeah," he said.

"I was thinking about making tacos tonight," Jan said. "How'd you feel about that?"

Clyde scratched his eyebrow so he could glance at Esther. She was pretending not to watch. "Sounds good," he said softly.

"Figure you might be hungry after class," Jan said.

"And after last night, thanks to you, we need more whiskey," Tina said, all her teeth showing. Clyde couldn't tell if she was joking. But then she took a bunch of little girl steps in his direction, as if her knees had been bound with electrical tape, and kissed Clyde on his cheek. "I better not see you flirting with that little blonde slut," she whispered in Clyde's ear. "Don't forget who your girlfriend is, buddy." She leaned back and smiled. Loudly, so that anyone close by could hear her, she said, "Okay, honey, see you tonight."

Tina and Jan went off in search of taco shells and Clyde returned his attention to the tank. Esther didn't say anything until he'd removed his name tag and punched out and wandered back to Pets for reasons he didn't entirely understand. "Wow," she said when she saw him.

"What?" he said.

Esther shook her head, her mouth tight like she'd rather not say.

"What?" Clyde said. "Come on."

"Just," Esther said. "Kinda pushy, right?"

"You think?"

"Uh, yeah. Showing up while you're at work asking you what you want for dinner?"

"Huh." Clyde knew she was right and looked between aisles for signs of them.

"Pretty," Esther said.

"What?"

"Your girlfriend's pretty." Esther stamped a chew toy with a tag.

"Mm." Clyde looked around. Tina and Jan were very likely still in the store. "She's, uh . . . "

Esther was watching him. "If she's not your girlfriend, you better tell her, like, tonight, because as far as she's concerned, Clyde, the two of you are a done deal."

"It's complicated."

"Guess so. I, on the other hand." She splayed a hand near her throat.

"Are about as complicated as it gets!" Clyde hadn't meant to say it and cringed now that he had. But Esther burst out laughing, and her face, when laughing like that, relaxed, her blond hair tumbled, her eyes drifted shut, and those long white lashes touched the tender skin of her cheeks.

E very time Clyde thought about Tina his mind shifted immediately to Jay. He could not have one without the other, he realized, kicking himself for letting that happen. Leaving Walmart, Clyde turned up the hill to Liberty Ridge.

It was a warm evening. Jay met the class—Dale, a nice dark crescent in the thin skin beneath his eye, and Clyde—in the yard, then walked them to one of the open foundations. He told them to climb down. The pit held a foot of slick and frothy orange water that stank of fart gas and hummed with insects. At Jay's words, Clyde and Dale bowed in. Then Jay said, "Good technique, now, keep it clean." He shouted down, "*Hajime!*" Start fighting.

The first thing Dale did was sweep Clyde's legs. Clyde didn't even know you could do that and his back and head smacked the water with a giant splash. Dale was suddenly on top of him, driving one hard punch after another into Clyde's chest. Beyond Dale's head, Clyde saw the streetlamps blink on in a line.

"You just gonna let Dale murder you in that pit!?" Jay yelled down from the edge. "Get off your ass, Clyde! Ain't no lyin down in training!"

Now that he'd been given the idea to do it, Clyde pushed Dale off. He was a mean bastard, but he was light as a kite. The rank water sloshed around them, staining their clothes and adding weight.

Back on his feet, Clyde choked down the vomit he felt pushing up and kicked an empty milk jug out of the way. Cigarette butts, the beige plastic ends of Swisher Sweets, empty fifths of cheap bourbon, and chicken bones pooled at his feet. Mosquitoes stood on his face. Dale circled. His thin purple lips held a sadistic grin. Clyde wanted to punch the fuck out of that ugly mouth. Dale jumped at Clyde, driving a knee up into his stomach that forced the air from his lungs with a cartoony *ooff* sound. With no breath and his body flushing with panic, Clyde just shut down. Dale drove a punch. Clyde felt it in his lungs and didn't care if he died.

Jay shouted, "*Yame!*" and Dale hit him one more time before backing off. As Jay climbed down, Clyde grabbed his knees, barfed into the water, and tried to breathe.

"Stand up, Clyde." Jay helped him to standing and put his own arms behind his head to show how to suck air. He put a hand on Clyde's shoulder and looked him in the eye. They were close, Clyde could feel Jay's heat. "You okay," Jay said.

Clyde tried to say "Osu," but couldn't. He didn't think he had it in him right now to fight Jay. At the far wall, Dale was climbing out. Clyde wanted to yank him down and drown him. Jay said, "Don't know where you's going, white boy."

Clyde knelt in seiza in an uncluttered corner in the filth. Jay and Dale squared off, Jay said, "*Hajime!*" and proceeded to give Dale a fierce beating, pushing him back and back and back, getting him against the wall and driving punches into his gut. He kicked him in the head, stomach, thighs, he swept Dale's feet. When Dale finally started blubbering, Jay said, "No crying in training, faggot." Clyde grinned but Dale didn't see it. Jay winked at Clyde and told them to line up. For the next hour, standing in that pit, they did *kihon*, arms and shoulders burning. When class was over, and they were walking slowly on wet bare feet in the road, Clyde realized he felt better, he'd got the liquor and sickness out. Nearing the house Jay told Clyde, "Stay for supper." It wasn't a question.

After showering, Jay asked Clyde if he'd written his letter yet. Clyde hadn't, so Jay led him downstairs and opened a blank document for him on the computer. He stood over Clyde's shoulder and said, "Dear IRS bastards," snickered, and went back upstairs. After a few false starts, Clyde wrote:

> *To Whom It May Concern,*
> *I was surprised to receive your notice demanding payment of $862 due to a mistake made three years ago by you, the IRS. If I'd been the one in the wrong, I'd gladly pay you what you say I owe you. But since it was*

you, I don't see why I should have to suffer. Why should I pay to cover your accounting error? It doesn't make sense. If this was the way corporations were run today, we'd be in even worse trouble than we are already in. And believe me, if you stepped outside the comforts of those pearly gates, you'd see that most Americans are suffering now as much as they were during the Great Depression. In short, I simply DO NOT HAVE this kind of money. Nor do I know anyone who does. Since the plant where I'd worked since high school (Mr. Longarm, Inc., my employer during the year that this mistake was made) closed for good, I've been unable to find good work. This was three years ago, by the way, and I have looked. I work two part-time jobs today and my combined earnings are not enough to cover even room and board. Forget about luxuries like telephone, cable, and gas, which seems to only go up and up despite the fact that no one here has "bounced back" from the economic collapse.

When Clyde finished, Jay grabbed his Winstons and a book from the shelf in the front room. "Let's take a walk." In the street, he lit two cigarettes. "You read that book Jimmy gave you?"

"Mm," Clyde said, inhaling the cigarette. He liked smoking now. "I'm reading it."

Jay looked disappointed. "Finish it," he said. "When you're done I wanna give you *Protocols of the Elders of Zion*, *Behold a Pale Horse*, and *Unintended Consequences* because them four books one hundred percent predicted what the United States government is up to right now." Jay's eyes bugged out and he shook his head, his lips making a funny sound.

"What's the, uh, protocols, uh," Clyde said.

Jay huffed. "It's actually just a record of a meeting these old important Jews had a hundred some years ago."

"About what?"

"Oh," Jay said, "nothing much. They just laid out their blueprint for how Jews could control the economy and media and rule the world. Supposed to be secret but somebody leaked it. Oops. Some people think it's fiction but, uh, let's see here." He used his fingers to tick things off. "Disney. Run for twenty years by Michael Eisner, Jew. Disney owns ABC-TV and radio, and Radio Disney, targeted at: children. Get 'em while they're young. There's a reason why young people today overwhelmingly support shit like gay marriage and miscegenation. Ain't evolution. Disney also owns enough daily newspapers to reach a hundred million people. Then you got Viacom, run by Murray Rothstein, a Jew who changed his name to Sumner Redstone. Viacom owns MTV, Nickelodeon, BET, TNN, CMT, and a shitload of publishing companies." He took a drag and spat. "Time Warner. Largest media company there is. Originally founded by Polish Jew brothers Hirsch, Aaron, Szmul, and Itzhak Warner. About ninety percent of the top brass today is Jews, and they run Time, Warner Bros., CNN, AOL, the biggest Internet service provider by far, HBO *and* Cinemax, and Warner Music, where most of that fuckin gansta rap shit comes from and which is run by Edgar Bronfman, Jr., big fuckin Jew whose dad—" Jay said, stopping. "Take a guess what Edgar Bronfman, Sr., does?"

Clyde was stunned. How was it that he'd never heard any of this before?

"He's president of the World Jewish Congress!" Jay stomped in a circle around Clyde, wagging his head. "Hell, Clyde, I could go on all day. And don't even get me started on *Behold a Pale Horse*. Chapters of that book are just scary, they're so accurate. Once you read 'em, this shit'll make a lot more sense."

"Osu," Clyde said.

"In Japan, part of an uchi deshi's training is reading. Couple hours a day set aside for betterment of the mind, learning all the history and philosophy associated with the physical. Body's just a machine, but part of that," Jay tapped his temple, "is the mind. Can't ignore the mind. Uchi deshi gotta remain ever vigilant, and acquiring knowledge and a deeper understanding of your mechanics is a big part of that struggle. Reading ain't no different than stretching, doing push-ups, fighting. If you're gonna read, read hard," Jay said, reaching into his back pocket and waving a little book. *The Art of War* was its title. "That book right there's been very influential in my thinking. You ever heard of Mishima? Big Jap in the '60s? They made a movie about him." Clyde had not. Jay tapped the book. "He didn't just read this, he *studied* it. Committed it to memory almost. He trained." Jay made a hard fist. "Tough fucker. Came to believe—and he was right, by the way—that his government was overextending its power, that its reach went beyond what was for the good of the people. This always happens, Clyde, always happens." Jay shook his head, almost sadly, Clyde thought. "A government might form for all the right reasons. Escape from tyranny. Practice a different religion." He shrugged. "But you give them fuckers too much power and 'fore you know it they no longer actin in the interest of the people. They acting in their own interest, period. You ever read the Declaration of Independence?" Clyde was sure he had in school at some point but he was damned if he could recall a single word of it. "When in the course of human events," Jay began, "if the government becomes destructive of its original purpose after a long train of abuses et cetera et cetera, and it becomes necessary for people to dissolve the political bonds that connect them, it's not only their right, it's their *duty*, to throw off that government and provide new guards for our future security." Jay nodded. "Good shit. That's what Mishima tried to do in Japan." He fished more cigarettes from his pack.

Clyde could smell the pit they passed. He flicked his cigarette into it and took another one of Jay's.

"Revolution," Jay said, smoke hovering in front of his mouth before trailing past his ears. "Overthrow the government."

"Did he?" Clyde said.

Jay shook his head, lower lip flipping out, wet and shiny as a slug. "He stormed some official building, held it a couple hours. Made speeches from the balcony." Jay raised and shook a fist. "Tried to get the masses off their asses."

"They arrest him?"

"Nope." Jay pretended to draw a sword and run it into his guts. He grunted and jerked both hands up to his chest, sticking out his tongue and crossing his eyes. "Right in that building," he said. "Ritual suicide, the most honorable, and difficult to execute, death there is. No groveling before the state, Clyde-san. No 'I'm sorry.' Them Japs don't fuck around. Pearl Harbor, Rape of Nanking." They walked on and Jay said, "Ol' Mishima had the right idea, he just didn't think it through good enough. We a lot alike, now that I think on it. Both train karate. Both of us assembling an army of warriors."

Clyde smiled. He thought Jay was joking.

"We don't train so that we can feel good when we take our shirts off. We train so that in the event of war, we're ready."

"What war?" he said.

Jay's head floated up and he patted Clyde's chest with his free hand. "That right there is the question, ain't it? You ain't just a perty face, Clyde-san. No sir-ee." They made another turn that put the house in front of them, in the distance. "Know why I push you so hard?"

Clyde was happy to hear this. "No sir," he said.

Jay squeezed his shoulder. He'd appreciated the show of respect. " 'Cause you got natural ability. Natural physical ability. That's the difference 'tween you and me. I ain't got no natural ability. I had to learn everything. Had to learn how to make a proper fist. The mechanics of the punch, how to kick. *Your* body, Clyde-san, already knows all that. Ain't fair." Jay snickered. Nobody had ever put it like that. "And that's the problem. The natural takes what he was born with for granted. You was born with the ability to do and it don't mean shit to you. Never had to work for it." Jay pulled him in tighter. "That's why I push you, Clyde-san. I ain't gonna let you throw it away."

No one had ever seen into him so clearly before. Not his uncle, not his mother, not his coach, certainly not Troy. They walked on, Clyde's head weightless with their talk.

"More and more, Clyde, our status as white men counts against us. Reverse discrimination's everywhere once you start looking for it. Affirmative Action, talk about an unlevel playing field. Bull. Shit. I was born in a house with a dirt floor. And hell, look at you, Clyde-san."

"Look at me?"

"Look at you. If I went on TV and cried about my friend's upbringing in a broken home, raised by a single working mother, a hairdresser, who's behind on the mortgage and can't afford the basic necessities, who lost his job at the plant and ran through his unemployment checks, they'd assume I was talking about a black man. And they'd do something to help him out too, lift him up. And the moment I told 'em, 'But my friend's white,' they'd be all, 'Hold up now, hold up. He white he's got an *advantage*.' " Jay shook his head and spat in the road. "If that ain't discrimination I don't know what is."

Clyde had to admit what Jay said made sense.

Jay handed him the Mishima book. "Read this one too. And don't take forever. I wanna talk to you about what they all say about where we're at."

"Where who's at?" Clyde said.

Jay touched a finger to Clyde's chest, then his own.

"Me and you?" Clyde said.

They'd reached the yard, the windows of the house burned brightly. Jay took to the cement steps. "The white man."

C lyde made Strasburg by eleven and got in bed with *The Turner Diaries*. Troy had called twice from a bar in Harrisonville. "There are chicks here, Clyde," he'd yelled against the country music and smacking pool balls, "who want one of your famous moustache rides." Clyde didn't call him back. He wanted to train the way Jay insisted so he pushed himself to read quickly and in two hours had made it halfway through the book. It reminded him of a book he'd had to read in school, *1984*. In this case, a man named Earl Turner had joined a resistance movement in a version of America where the white man had no rights. Clyde stopped for the night at a scene where Turner committed his first illegal act:

> *My inclination was just to walk into the first liquor store we came to, knock the manager on the head with a brick, and scoop up the money from the cash register.*
>
> *Henry wouldn't go along with that, though. He said we couldn't use means which contradicted our ends. If we begin preying on the public to support ourselves, we will be viewed as a gang of common criminals, regardless of how lofty our aims are. Worse, we will eventually begin to think of ourselves the same way. Henry looks at everything in terms of our ideology. If something doesn't fit, he'll have nothing to do with it.*
>
> *In a way this may seem impractical, but I think maybe he's right. Only by making our beliefs into a living faith which guides us from day to day can we maintain the moral strength to overcome the obstacles and hardships which lie ahead.*

*Anyway, he convinced me that if we are going to rob liquor stores
we have to do it in a socially conscious way. If we are going to cave in
people's heads with bricks, they must be people who deserve it.*

Clyde had never thought in these terms before. Like Jay and people
at some of those gun shows, Turner said that America was in the hands of
Jews and blacks, and whites had lost their basic rights. It was illegal to own
a gun, the Second Amendment had been repealed, and it wasn't unusual for
the police to show up and search your house. And you just had to stand aside
while they did it or face incarceration. Jay said America was only one small
step away from that already. Earl Turner had become so sickened by how far
America had fallen from its promise that he'd decided to fight back. Clyde
saw why Jay had wanted him to read this book; what Jay Smalls believed
and what Earl Turner believed weren't so different. They were both men
who lived by a code. You had to respect that, you really did. Most people
just walked through life with one eye closed. Most people these days didn't
believe in much of anything. Except for the rich. They believed in making
money at the expense of everybody else. Poor people were too overworked
and tired to believe in anything beyond surviving.

The next morning, Clyde finished the book in bed sipping rocket fuel
from the cold mason jar he'd made it in. Earl Turner and the movement, which
had spread across the country now, went around destroying major American
cities and then, getting their hands on some nukes, blew half the people off
the face of the globe, reshaping Earth into an all-white planet. Clyde didn't
buy it, but the points the book made about the erosion of freedoms in America
had got him thinking.

That afternoon he went over to Troy's house to watch TV. Troy had a
hangover, his voice an octave lower than usual. During commercial breaks
Clyde showed off what he'd learned in training. Troy watched with his eyes at
half-mast, nursing a bloody beer. Most people, Jay had said, never know how
to throw a good punch; if you can throw a good punch, most fights will be
over before they start. In a very short time Clyde had already figured that out
and so much more, and he could tell Troy knew it, that look on his face was
envy, he was impressed. Clyde went outside and drove his fists into the cement
steps at the front of the house until the pattern held in the hardening skin of

his knuckles. In front of the TV he did push-ups on his fists and fingertips while Troy complained from behind his sunglasses. The skin peeled off the first two knuckles of both hands, Clyde tore it away and craters of dirty raw flesh formed where the calluses had been. He covered them with bandages. "Looking pretty tough, Twitty," Troy said. He'd been kidding, but Clyde, seeing his fists covered in bloodied bandages, thought he was right.

Just before he left, Clyde asked Troy if he'd ever read a book called *The Turner Diaries*. Troy hadn't, so Clyde went out to his truck and got it. He sat watching television while Troy leafed through it, making sounds. After about ten minutes, Troy said, "Jesus, dude, this is some crazy racist shit."

"Really?" Clyde said, puzzled. "That ain't what I'm reading it for. It's what it says about gun rights. That was written like thirty years ago and it's predicted half of what's happened. There are other books that predict other stuff that's happened too. The eurozone and the New World Order and all that."

"Like the band?"

Clyde didn't know about the band, but he thought he'd heard enough to get it more or less right. "One government for the whole planet. One currency. Single military, you know, stuff like that."

"What's that got to do with the euro?"

"Well. Few years ago Europe had like a dozen different currencies, right? Now there's just one."

"Yeah, it's probably pretty fuckin convenient."

"You yourself said the banks were the enemy."

"Did I?" Troy said, laughing. "Was I drunk? I mean, yeah, you know I went to P. Hill Bank to try to get another loan before I left? I didn't think the Camero was gonna make it to Nashville. They'd given me the first loan, and I'd paid it off, a hundered and fifty-six dollars a month for three years, right on time. This time, though, they looked at me like I'd come in there with my cock hanging out." Troy shook his head, shifted position. "So yeah, guess I'm not a big fan of the banks right now." He shrugged. "Camero's still goin strong, so fuck 'em."

"Jay says this is how big changes are sold to the public. Like privacy? They make you afraid so you don't mind losing your rights."

Troy stared at Clyde waving the book. "I don't know, dude. All I know is this Earl Turner guy and his, uh, 'comrades' are going around braining Jews and blacks left and right. They want to eradicate the planet of anybody but white people. This is like the Holy Bible of racist craziness. Where'd you get this? That sensei?"

Clyde said, "Nah, Walmart," without thinking. He hadn't meant to lie.

"Sheesh," Troy said, tossing the book back at Clyde and twirling his finger at the side of his head. Then he groaned and leaned into the couch. "I can't wait to get back to civilization."

Clyde thought, Don't let me keep you.

Jay didn't hold classes on Fridays. "Even warriors got to relax," he liked to say, but Tina called to ask Clyde over for "family night." Family night at the Smalls' wasn't much different than other nights. Jan made dinner and blended margaritas. Then Tina and Clyde went out to the video store. Jay liked kung fu and karate movies, no matter how old or shitty. Tina liked comedies and horror.

They returned with one of each and Jay turned off the comedy after half an hour but the kung fu movie they watched through, the room thick with smoke. When the credits ran, Jay said, "Clyde-san, you're sleeping over."

"Oh," Clyde said, trying to sit up.

"No argument," Jan said. "Look at you. I don't wanna have to explain to your mama why we let her son drive home drunk and kill himself and a bus full of babies. You can sleep in Tina's room."

"Thanks, Mom," Tina said.

"Door open," Jan said, going up with Jay. "See y'all in the morning."

As soon as their legs disappeared at the top of the steps, Tina climbed onto Clyde's lap. They kissed wetly and Clyde wiped his chin when Tina was busy tonguing his ears. "Tonight's the night, buddy," she whispered. "My cherry's so ripe and ready." Tina sat up pulling her sweater over her head. She reached back and freed her bra, cupping her breasts in one arm while she peeled the shoulder strap down one side, then the other, before finally slipping the cups from her breasts. She stood up then and took Clyde to her room. With the door open four inches Tina shed the rest of her clothes. The door to her parents' room, also open, was right outside. Lying on the floor on his back, Clyde could see a few feet into their room where light from the hall spilled over the carpet, if he and Tina stayed still, he thought he could hear her father breathing. Tina, completely naked now, sat on the floor beside Clyde, taking her time to pull his shirt over his head, unbutton his jeans. He kicked out of them and Tina stripped off his socks, then his underwear. "I'm on the pill," she whispered.

For all her wet-eared promises of craziness, Tina only climbed on top and moved slowly against him. Clyde tried his best to hold out but could have counted the strokes she'd made on two hands. She seemed all right with it; she sat there grinning, pinning him to the floor, staring into his eyes. There was so much wetness that Clyde worried about the noise when they started again a few minutes later. All the while, Tina smiled sweetly, her little teeth gleaming in the dark, her hips moving in slow, even loops. Clyde thought about what Jay had said about power, how it comes from the hips. This time he lasted longer. He heard nothing from Tina and she never broke her smile. In the silence after, Clyde listened for Jay's breath. Much later, Tina got off and lay down, inviting Clyde to her this time. There was a hint of light in the window when Tina finally crawled into her bed, giving Clyde a pillow and a thin blanket for the floor.

Then there was Jay in his ear. "Time for work, Cryde-san . . . time for work . . . " The room reeked of sex.

In the kitchen, Clyde sat with a cup of Jan's coffee across from Jay, everybody was tired. "Read your letter," Jay said after a while.

"Oh," Clyde said. He felt a little funny that Jay hadn't asked or anything.

"Was good," Jay said, nodding at his cup. "Made a few changes."

"Right," Clyde said. "I'll take a look and mail it."

"Don't bother," Jay said. "I already did."

Clyde thought about saying something but could see that Jay wouldn't want to hear it right now so he decided to let it go. He channeled his anger into Walmart, having to get up at seven in the morning only to punch the clock for four hours to make a lousy fourteen bucks. It didn't make a man feel good about himself, that was for sure.

"Ever work construction?" Jay asked him.

"Assembly line, but not construction."

"Well, if you can manage an assembly line you can clean up after a rough-in crew. Pays shit, eight an hour, I won't lie to you, but unlike fuckin Walmart, it ain't part-time. Monday through Friday, Clyde-san, workin out of doors all day long the way God intended, shoulder to shoulder with Sensei."

"Sounds pretty good," Clyde said. He'd almost forgotten what it was like to work every day.

"Good. You can start Monday."

"Oh." Clyde didn't realize that Jay had actually been offering.

"Yes, Cryde-san? Somesing wong . . . ?"

"I should probably give notice."

Jay blew across the top of his cup, his eyes suddenly distant. "You's a good boy, Clyde. Responsible and fierce. Wanna do the right thing, wanna pay the IRS what they say you owe 'em. I get it. But you can't let that keep you from seeing the big picture. The warrior, Clyde-san, is a lone wolf. And the lone wolf should not align himself with multinational corporations or plutocracies."

Clyde didn't know what a plutocracy was but he nodded.

"Lone wolf needs to remain autonomous," Jay said. "What sort of paperwork you fill out when Sam Walton hired you? Social security number, home address, phone, next of kin?"

That pretty much covered it.

"Thought so. That's okay. You's learning. The warrior needs to be able to drop everything at a moment's notice and walk away with no paper trail," Jay grinned, "with nobody trying to track him down, so he can set his sights on a greater calling than, uh, lining a fat cat's pockets and, uh, paying the mortgage on time."

Clyde thought about his mom's house. "Don't pay the mortgage on time, lose the house."

"Do you?"

Clyde shrugged. "Don't you?"

Jay shook his head slowly. "What does that even mean. 'Lose the house.' " Clyde remembered when Troy had said the same thing. "You know how long it takes the bank to dispossess someone from their house? You know that they cannot legally remove you unless you step outside your property?" Clyde didn't know that. "Most people, they hear the federal marshal banging on their front door, they git scared, lose their cool. I knew one sum'bitch stayed in a house he'd stopped paying on for two *years*, Clyde-san. Two fuckin years. You know how much money he'd saved up in that time? Twenty thousand."

"Wow," Clyde said.

"Remember the dojo koan? 'Look upwards towards wisdom and strength, not seeking other desires'? Ain't just words, Clyde. Let me tell you something you may not know. You don't owe Sam Walton, billionaire, a goddamn thing. You did him a fuckin favor showing up to work with an hour's notice. They needed a warm body, no offense. Sam Walton got this down-home image so people think he gives two shits about his employees, or about, uh, bringing lower-priced goods to communities or some shit, but take it from me, Clyde-san, all Sam Walton fuckin cares about is money, and if he runs other companies out of business 'cause his prices is so fuckin low, while paying his employees the legal minimum—and that's here in America; ask me about what his fucking chink employees make over in Bee Bop Boop—guess what? He gonna make money, a lot of money. When all the other companies is gone, guess what happens to Walmart's everyday low prices? And the working man is, once again, screwed. Why would you wanna show Sam Walton the courtesy he wouldn't show you, Clyde Twitty, warrior? One thing you must not be, Clyde, is a fool. The foolish warrior loses more than just his head." Jay finished his coffee, put the mug on the kitchen counter with a clank, and clapped his hands. "All right," he said, grabbing Clyde's shoulders, his face contorting into a grin. "Here's my offer. Should you choose to accept it. When your shift's over today, quit. That's all the notice you give. Go home, git your clothes . . . move in here. I want you to be my uchi deshi, Clyde. Think you can do that?"

Clyde's chest swelled with pride. After years of nothing but worry and sitting still, so much was happening so fast it was overwhelming. Jay's grinning face was inches away, his eyes burning. Clyde saw the moment Jay realized he was struggling with this. "Big decision, Clyde, I know. But let me tell you this. I like to think I know you pretty well. You do this," Jay held up a finger, "you won't regret it, that much I know. I also know you *need* this, Clyde-san. This the only thing that will allow you to realize your potential, perfect your fierce character." Jay stood nodding, his eyes glazed over with some far-off thought. "Take today to think it over." He turned from Clyde then, looked out the window into the backyard. "Offer's on the table twenty-four hours. If I see you at class tomorrow morning, I take that as a yes. If I don't . . . " Jay trailed off, then he nodded, said, "well," and left the kitchen.

Esther was out sick so Clyde was on his own in Pets, and the department was worse than ever. All morning as he cleaned up he thought about his character. Never in his life had he thought about his character, training really was like holding a mirror up to your soul. You had to be strong to even look at what it revealed, let alone try to fix it. Even in this short time Clyde had learned a few things about himself, knew that as much as Jay saw potential he also saw deficiencies that would need hard work to correct. Clyde could either stand before the mirror by accepting the uchi deshi post and training with Jay, doing whatever Jay said, and, in time, maybe grow into the warrior Jay thought he saw. Or he could back out now, never truly examine himself, surely not reach the potential everyone had always thought he had, and live the sort of life that most men lived: dull, filled with regrets and struggle, and just enough pay to keep you alive, a completely forgettable life.

At supper that night Clyde told his mom the whole story. The girl, the karate master, the uchi deshi post, the first full-time job in years. Before meeting Jay, Clyde had never had much to say, but tonight he could tell that his mom saw how he'd changed for the better already. He tried to see himself through her eyes: a young man who suddenly sat up straight at the table, spoke with authority, held himself with confidence, saw the way the world really worked. This was not the son she'd come to know in recent years, and it had everything to do with Jay Smalls. When Clyde finally broke the news that he was moving, that this move was in fact the meaning of uchi deshi, one fat tear rose to the surface of her lower left eyelid, hovered there, and then spilled quickly down her lined pink cheek. She nodded for a while then, holding back tears; she hadn't uttered a sound since Clyde had started talking. Then she rose from her seat, Clyde tensed. "My baby," she said, her voice breaking, wrapped her arms around his neck, and kissed the top of his head. She held him like that for a solid minute, then she cleared the table.

Watching her do the dishes, and wipe her face with her shirt sleeve, all the excitement he'd felt telling her about Jay drained right out of him. Where were the questions, where was her anger, her worry? This response of hers threw Clyde for a loop. What the hell was she doing, hugging him that way, saying nothing but a couple words? "My baby," what was that? Watching her upper body rock in a small circle as she washed a plate in the sink, he thought he began to understand. To leave her now was to do the worst thing he could have done to her. She knew this, of course, but had chosen to sacrifice herself for the good of her son.

When a stream of questions followed the dishes, Clyde was almost relieved; this was more like her. Would he still drive her to the Omega on Sundays, would he still keep her *Pretty Lady* sign clean, could she call him when she needed help moving something heavy, or a trip to the bank or the post office or the store, what about his room, his things, what about cleaning out the garage like they'd been meaning to do, would her new uchi deshi be able to make the time for all that? She had so many questions that Clyde ended up laughing at her. "I'm not going to prison, mom. I'll be free to come and go." He knew that most of his days, from dawn to dark, would belong to Jay, but after dark was a different story. Those hours were his. Of course Tina would have her own demands, but as Clyde saw it he would still have plenty of time to help out around the house like he used to. Nothing had to change.

He packed his guns and some clothes and stayed up late with his mom watching television, their feet touching on the sofa. She smoked beside him and Clyde, even though he wanted to smoke, didn't. He thought his mom had seen enough change in him for one day.

It was only seven thirty when he got to Liberty Ridge Sunday morning. Training didn't start for a half hour but Jay was in the doorway like he'd known Clyde would arrive early. "Welcome home," he called out, holding open the door. "Think you called it, mama," he said into the house.

Jan appeared in the doorway and they watched Clyde cross the street with his gym bag. There were a couple other bags in the back of his truck. "Yep," she said, giving Clyde a warm hug. "You can stay as long as you like. Tina is gonna be *thrilled*."

"Clyde Twitty," Jay said. "First uchi deshi."

Jay changed his Sunday class to allow Clyde a big break in the middle so that his mom wouldn't miss work. He'd burn through gas, he knew, but the money he'd make working with Jay would cover it. Now training ran from eight to noon and picked up again from four to seven. In between, Clyde drove to Strasburg, dropped his mom at the Omega, and waited at Troy's house for her to finish. Clyde asked if Troy wanted to come with him, watch the rest of the class, maybe then he could decide whether Jay Smalls was a bad influence or not. "He might even let you train," Clyde said, hoping he would.

When Clyde pulled to a stop in front of the house with a passenger, the look on Jay's face made his guts clench up. Of course! He should have asked for permission before bringing a total stranger to class. Clyde sheepishly introduced Troy to Jay, then Dale, Tina, and Jan. Tina asked him immediately how he liked living in Nashville, probably, Clyde figured, to see if Clyde had lied about it. Troy's hair was maybe a little long but there was no mistaking him for a girl. Jay was impatient to get back to training. Clyde and Dale bowed in on the lawn while Troy sat down on the porch next to Tina. "Troy, was it?" Jay said.

"Osu," Clyde said.

"Yeah," Troy said.

"Wanna join us? We keep it civilized." Jay snickered.

Troy laughed. "Thanks, but I'm not really wearing the right stuff."

Jay shrugged. "I got a spare gi. Tina?" She ran inside.

"That's okay," Troy said. "Thanks anyway."

Jay waved a hand at him, "Don't worry about it. We fix you up." Even Troy was caught by Jay's insistence.

Tina came out with a stack of white cloth. Reluctantly, Troy went around the side of the house and changed. The gi was way too big, the sleeves ran past his fingertips and the pant legs swallowed his feet. When he walked awkwardly up to Jay, Jay waved him over and rolled the sleeves to his elbows. "You never trained before," Jay said. It wasn't a question.

"No, I have. I took karate in Harrisonville."

"Did you?" Dale grinned and spat in the grass. Troy nodded as Jay tied the old ratty white belt around his waist, snapping it tight. "What kinda karate was that?"

"Shotokan," Troy said, and Jay laughed. "What?" Troy said.

"Nothin," Jay said, pushing the bottom lip out wet and dark. "We'll see if we can reverse *that* damage."

Jay stepped back and Troy got in line next to Clyde. "I thought it was fine," he said.

"No talkin in training, white belt," Jay said, winking.

Jay started them off with the basics, going slowly so that Troy could keep up. They got into a simple stance and threw hard, slow techniques. Punches, strikes, blocks, then kicks. Then they did drills where they slid across the yard throwing various techniques, turned, and did it all the way back. The whole time Clyde had Troy in his peripheral vision and Jay in front. Troy was keeping pace with Clyde and Dale and throwing techniques with power and the right kind of breath. Clyde was impressed, but when Jay watched him his face was sour. "Keep up, white belt!" he yelled. "Watch Clyde," he said, "see how he does it?" Hearing that, Clyde pushed himself harder, faster, tried to snap his techniques like an arrow hitting its mark. *Thwack.* "Lookin good, Clyde-san!" Jay said in response to the new effort, and Clyde heard a noise from Dale that made him want to look over. But he didn't. When they all turned at the end of the yard, though, Troy was watching Clyde's feet, trying to get it right. "Turning's hard," Jay said, "people wanna be doing jump-spin kicks after one class but the hardest things to master are the quote-unquote simplest. They also the most important, by the way." Clyde, Troy, and Dale moved back across the yard, throwing punches, blocks, kicks. "I git in a dark alley, give me a whirling dervish any goddamn day over a chunk of stone knows how to throw a good punch. Ain't that right, Clyde-san?"

"Osu!" Clyde yelled.

When they crossed the yard and turned back, Jay had his hands on his hips and his head tilted. His eyes were on Troy and Troy alone. Jay blinked and shrugged as if to say, No good, white belt, no use. Troy had trained for three months, but Clyde could see that he was better than Troy, and Clyde had hardly trained at all.

Near the end of the day Jay paired off with Clyde and had Dale face Troy. "Light *kumite*, now, keep it clean," he said, then he stepped aside and grabbed Dale's gi. "Take it easy on our guest, Dale," he said. "We want people to come back for seconds."

"Uh, gloves?" Troy said, raising his hands like a hold up.

Jay gave him a hard look. "We say 'osu' when we ask a question, white belt."

"Osu," Troy said, halfheartedly, Clyde thought.

"We don't hit that hard," was all Jay said, again winking at Clyde. Dale grinned but Troy just stood there blinking like a baby in the sun. He was worn out, Clyde could see. His hair hung wet as a shower and his cheeks burned bright red. Clyde worried that his buddy might collapse. Jay yelled, "*Hajime!*" and everybody, even Troy, raised their bare hands. Jay kept coming at Clyde so he couldn't see what Dale and Troy were up to, but he heard all of Dale's sounds, every 'shhh!' and every 'hushah' and all the breathy 'fffps' that went with a punch. He heard Troy's uneven breathing and, more than once, a whimper. Then he heard, "Jesus, what the fuck, dude!?"

Jay said, "*Yame*," and Clyde watched Troy stomp down the yard and into the street.

He walked half a block before turning and yelling, "You're fuckin nuts, you know that!?"

"You hurt our guest?" Jay asked Dale.

Dale's hands went up and his eyes were wide, the picture of childlike innocence. "I barely tapped him, Uncle Jay."

"Barely tapped me!?" Troy yelled. Now he was crying and Clyde felt terrible. He shook his head and crossed the grass to the sidewalk.

"You all right?" he said.

Troy paced in the road on his bare feet, one hand rubbing his stomach where Dale must have hurt him. "No," he said, dropping his head.

Clyde turned back to Jay and Jay sighed and waved him over. Clyde ran back up the yard.

"Sorry, Uncle Jay," Dale mumbled.

"There's no sorry in training." Jay grabbed Clyde by the shoulder of his gi and said, "Give him your truck."

"What?"

"Give your friend your truck so he can go home. It's obvious he's done with us."

Clyde watched Troy pacing in the street, trying not to cry, rubbing his stomach. Dale had punched Clyde there the first time they sparred and it hurt, Clyde knew how much. The fear, the panic. It was a lot to take. "Um, osu, maybe I oughta just take him back."

Jay shook his head. "I've thought this through, Clyde-san, and I gotta be honest with you. It worries me. I know he's your buddy," and here Jay lowered his voice, "but I don't trust him. On that drive home, he's gonna pollute your mind. His point of view is dangerous to you right now, Clyde. To where you're at in your training."

It made Clyde feel good to know how much consideration Jay had given his well-being. "Osu," Clyde said, nodding.

"Good boy," Jay said, squeezing the shoulder meat. "I'll take you to fetch your truck tomorrow."

Clyde grabbed his keys from inside the house—both Tina and Jan asked him what had happened—and went to Troy in the street.

"Jesus, dude," Troy said. He wasn't crying now, he was just pissed. "You know both of 'em are fuckin crazy, right?"

Clyde grimaced, hoping Jay hadn't heard.

"That tattoo on that fucking guy's head," Troy said. "You know what I think that is?"

"No." Troy was watching Dale from the street. Clyde looked, caught that black window's peak.

"A fucking swastika."

Clyde didn't think Dale had covered his skull with a swastika but he didn't want to get lost in a bunch of meaningless details with Troy, pissed off and not thinking clearly, while Jay waited for a quick key exchange so they could get on with training. He handed Troy his keys. "I'm just gonna finish this class and . . . " But he had no idea what came after the "and." It seemed that Troy did, though. His face tightened and he snatched the keys out of Clyde's hand.

"Whatever," he said.

"Hey, man, don't be mad at *me*."

"I ain't," Troy said, heading for the truck. "Will you get my fuckin clothes, please?"

Clyde ran over to the side of the house and got Troy the clothes he'd come in. "I'll call you," he said at the side of his own truck.

Troy nodded, cranked the engine, and jerked away. He raced down the block, squealed the tires on the first turn.

"One of the bigger pussies I've met," Dale said when Clyde got back in the yard. "Sorry, white belt, I know he's your butt buddy and all."

Clyde wanted to tell Dale to go fuck himself but he didn't. Jay was right there and class wasn't over. What upset him the most, he guessed, was that Dale was right. They all watched Clyde's truck squeal from one turn to the next, circling the house to get the hell out of Liberty Ridge. Even after the truck was gone Jay's eyes remained pinned to the entrance, to the ridge that gave his home its name.

That night before bed, Jay told Clyde that being an uchi deshi came with all the responsibilities he'd already told him about, and some that he hadn't. Training would only get harder and more intense, and training didn't have to mean what you thought it meant, training could be almost anything. Punching, kicking, reading, thinking, testing oneself in the real world, challenging friends, family, the status quo. He wanted Clyde to know that if he told him one day to jump off a house, as uchi deshi, Clyde would be expected to shout, "Osu!" and jump off the damn house. In normal training, Clyde already knew, there was no room for questions. An uchi deshi's training went beyond normal training, and uchi deshi knew better than to ever, *ever* question Sensei. Teacher knows best. Only teacher sees the big picture. From his uchi deshi, Jay expected nothing less than total faith, allegiance, loyalty, and commitment. Jay offered Clyde his final chance to leave. "Uchi deshi," Jay said, "or Joe Nobody?"

"Uchi deshi," Clyde said.

The next morning Clyde rode to work with Jay, a jug of rocket fuel between his legs. When they passed Walmart Clyde said he felt bad about not telling his coworkers he'd quit. Jay said, "There's plenty I've done in my life I could feel bad about. You's done with Walmart and everything associated with it. Anyone works in that building is as bad as Sam Walton his self. They do not have Clyde Twitty's best interests at heart. A person doesn't have to actively work against you to keep you from reaching your potential, Clyde, remember that." Clyde could see that Jay had strong feelings about this; though Jay hadn't said it outright, Clyde knew that stopping in to see Esther would not be allowed. "You need to focus on your training," Jay said, "and your family, your *kenka* family. Forget that place even exists."

"What place?" Clyde said, and Jay did a double take, then laughed.

Working with Jay, Clyde got to be outside all day, strengthening his body. He picked up scrap and drove it to the dump. At lunch, while the other roofers slept, Jay led Clyde on half an hour of *kihon*, just to get the blood flowing. He told jokes from the roof and always had something deep to say about life or training. Driving home Jay told Clyde that the family was taking a trip in a couple months and Clyde was coming. Every few years Jay taught self-defense at "the whack." Dale sometimes helped, and this time Clyde Twitty, new uchi deshi, would too. Hot damn. Other than Kansas, which didn't much count as he'd only gone there to buy beer after turning eighteen, he'd never left Missouri.

When they got home from work that first day, a secondhand trailer was parked across the street. It had *American Dreamin'* printed in sunset script across both sides. Tina and Jan were standing next to it in bare feet despite the cold. "What do you think?" Jan said.

Clyde figured it had something to do with the trip to the whack. But the thing didn't look road ready upon closer inspection. The door hung at a hurricane angle, and there were holes in the walls large enough to pass a beer through. Jay kneed Clyde in the ass and Jan said, "When you showed up yesterday, you looked like a puppy who'd been kicked out of the pound." It didn't make Clyde feel good knowing his homesickness had been so apparent.

"Uchi deshi live where they train, Clyde-san." Clyde opened the trailer door carefully and poked his head inside. It was a shit heap, but Jay had bought it especially for him, and that meant a lot. Jay jerked his head at the house. "Tina's room ain't big enough for long term," he said, "and we need to start thinking long term."

The First Uchi Deshi

Five weeks later, Clyde negotiated with Jay and Tina to spend a Saturday with his uncle. Since he'd moved to Liberty Ridge, Clyde hadn't had as much time as he'd thought he might for anything outside of training and working with Jay, reading Jay's books, and attending to Tina's needs nights and weekends. He imagined that Willie and his mom thought he'd thrown them over for another family. He guessed he had, though he didn't like to think of it that way. Jay had turned the direction of his life, and he was afraid to do anything to alter its new course. He had a good job now, a girlfriend, an exciting new family, a growing sense of purpose; suddenly he had a future. Neither his mom nor Willie had said anything outright since he left, they weren't the types to moan about when you gonna visit. But he could feel their disappointment. What Clyde did not tell his mom was that in Jay's view the wolf cub eventually needed to break from his mama wolf. Warriors had to cut ties, had to harden themselves against life's nostalgias. And at the most basic level, no self-respecting man should be taking advice from a woman, even if it was his mother. Behind every good warrior is not a woman, but another warrior. In order to fight, Jay said, a warrior has to commit himself a hundred percent. *Budo*. The warrior who kept one foot in the past and one in the present ended up cut in two. Clyde was coming to believe more and more of Jay's philosophy. What Jay said about feminism made sense to Clyde because of how he'd been raised. The women's movement had not been the great leap forward most people thought. It had been a big step back, dealing a serious blow to society by taking an important influence out of the home. In turn, it was easy to see why so many young people these days were reckless, lost.

At his uncle's, Clyde mowed the grass and trimmed the bushes and threw the trash into the back of his truck while Willie sat on the porch sanding pieces of a new chair he was making out of cherry wood. Watching his uncle these last few years, Clyde was amazed by what a person could do if they set their mind to it. Maybe it took Willie a month to make a single chair, but in the end, he's got a chair to hold him up. When Clyde was done he climbed the steps and drank a glass of ice water, leaning against the railing. He'd been doing chores four hours straight. His shirt was off and he caught his reflection in the window glass. Though he'd actually gained ten pounds, the wobbly flab around the middle had been replaced by a hard, defined stomach and a thicker chest. His arms and shoulders had blown up.

Willie said, "Looks like you just returned from boot camp."

"Ain't too far from the truth," Clyde said.

The sun and the exertion had made all the bruises and abrasions from training stand out clearly on Clyde's chest, arms, and stomach. He pointed out spots saying, "kick," "punch," or "I don't remember." Unlike how his mom would have reacted, Willie watched grinning. Clyde got into the *san chin dachi* stance and executed techniques, moving slowly at first so his uncle could see the mechanics, then hard, shouting the *kiai* and feeling that already, already after only six weeks, the muscles remembered. He told Willie the name of each thing in Japanese and went out to the yard and ran through the *kata* Jay had taught him. After that, chest heaving, he rooted around inside the shed and came back to the porch with an old broom handle, Jay had said that it was a good idea to condition the nerves of the shin with a dowel, and Clyde sat down beside Willie's old dog to do it. It hurt like hell, raising a ripe ache from the swollen lumps where he'd clashed shins with Jay or Dale. Willie's dog watched, eyebrows up. Clyde took the pain—"Pain's just information," Jay would say—and kept count until he reached a hundred. Then he set the handle aside and got into push-up position on his knuckles. The skin of those knuckles had ripped off three, four times, but now it held. Since Willie was watching, Clyde pushed himself to do fifty straight.

Clyde threw a few kicks, a few combination punches—right, left, hook—making the noises, the breaths, grunting like they did in class. Willie watched until it was over. "Lookin good, Clyde."

Full of Willie's approval, Clyde made two whiskey and sodas in the house and sat down beside his uncle in the low afternoon sun. Willie's property faced west and that front porch was a great spot come early evening. Clyde didn't mind smoking in front of Willie, he had his own brand now (Winston). He thought about telling his uncle what Jay had said about karate men and cancer but decided to keep quiet since Willie smoked up a storm and couldn't exert himself any more.

"Troy didn't stay too long," Willie said.

"No," Clyde said. He sipped his drink and dried his lips so he could take a drag. "And he left without saying good-bye."

"Did he?"

"I don't know, Uncle Willie, he was kinda a dick when he was here."

"More 'n usual?" Willie said.

"I think he's changed. It was like he's all of the sudden too good for . . ." Clyde was thinking "me" but he said, "Strasburg, that's for sure. Couldn't wait to get back to Nashville."

Willie nodded with his top half and drank. He dragged deeply on the cigarette and fired the smoke out the one nostril. "Well, I wouldn't pay too much attention to it."

Clyde grunted.

"He's lonely. Misses his ol' buddy Clyde. Might even be thinking he was stupid for moving. Young men tend to say about the direct opposite of what they actually mean." Willie's working arm roiled the air as he searched for a word. "A place is . . . nothing. One spot's just as good as another, objectively. Grass, trees, buildings, cars, electricity, all that. What matters is who you know in that place. Your friends, family. Troy know anybody in Nashville?"

"No."

"Well."

Clyde nodded a while and said, "He thought the way I'm training with Jay was crazy."

"It is crazy," Willie said, which surprised Clyde. When he looked over Willie's eyebrows were up and he'd turned to look at Clyde. "So what?" he said. "You gonna get yourself hurt?"

Clyde said, "No. I mean, not bad."

"That's what I mean. Hurt bad."

"No."

"Then so what? That man Jay's got my vote, let me tell ya. If Troy'd stuck around long enough to see what he's done for you he'd be singing a different tune."

Hearing that from his uncle, Clyde felt a lot better. He went back in the house to refill their drinks and when he sat back down said, "You ever been to Idaho?"

"Can't say that I have," Willie said, sitting back, eyes closed against the red sun, his GPC smoldering between fingers.

"I'm goin in a few weeks. I'm not even sure where it's at. Jay wants me to help him at a fight-training seminar. The WAC."

"Sounds like it's gonna hurt." Willie laughed, thinking, like Clyde himself had when he'd first heard it, that it was spelled different than it was, that it was just another word for getting hit. Clyde didn't want to tell him yet what those letters really stood for.

Willie tipped the last of his drink; ice clanked against his teeth and his breathing went ragged and dog-like. "Idaho's a funny state," he said, into the glass, his voice distorting. "Potatoes comes to mind and that's about it."

That Sunday night at the Smalls' residence, the WAC, the World Aryan Congress, despite being weeks away, was on everybody's mind. For Jay, it was a chance to teach killing techniques to like-minded men. It was a unique forum for the exchange of ideas and information about all sorts of topics important to the patriot movement today. What made it even more exciting was that there hadn't been a Congress for the last eight years, due to a rift in the Aryan Nations organization that saw defections to Montana, Alabama, and Pennsylvania. This one was sure to see a record attendance.

But to Tina, the WAC meant something altogether different—opportunity. She sat everyone down before dinner around a bowl of the barbeque sauce she was planning on selling there. She and her mom had perfected the recipe (it was mostly ketchup) and already had a case in the garage; the plan was to make five more. While Jay taught skinheads close-fighting drills, Tina, from her own booth at the Congress, would make a splash with what she said was a "superior product." But the sauce was still nameless and she was worried. Choosing the right brand was even more important than the quality of the product, according to Tina, who flipped through her books and made notes in her pad while Jay, Jan, and Clyde sat with cigarettes and beers around the bowl. "Okay, let's get started," Tina smiled at them. "If this sauce were a person who lived on your street . . . "

"Nobody lives on our street," Jay interrupted.

"Right, Dad, but let's just say for the sake of argument we're normal people, living in a real neighborhood. If this sauce was a person who lived on your street, how would you describe them?"

"Ah, right," Jan said. "Smoky, spicy."

"No, Mom." She consulted a book. "Human qualities. Is this person trustworthy, for instance? Is she funny? Would you go to him if you needed help? Would you steer clear of his house on the way home?"

Jay gave Tina a death stare. "You have got to be shitting me."

"It's brand strategy stuff. Y'all don't understand it like I do."

All Clyde wanted to do was eat it, he was hungry as hell these days. After half a dozen clunkers, everyone was about to settle on *J.J.'s Smoke Sauce*, named after Jay and Jan, when Jan slapped the table and said, "I got it. Smalls *Big Flavor* Sauce." Even Tina liked that one. She said now they had to work on a label. "A good logo," Tina read from one of her books, "is the first step toward establishing a commanding brand presence in the marketplace."

At work those weeks before the Congress, Jay said more than once that Clyde would soon be tested in a way he hadn't been tested before. This was the evolution of his training, it was important, Jay said, for warriors to leave the safety of the dojo and put what they've learned to the test in a real-world situation, where the stakes were high. This was the only way to know how far your training had taken you, how far you still had to go. Most important of all, it was the only way to know yourself. The more they trained, the clearer Clyde's spirit had become to Jay. All that natural ability Clyde had taken for granted his whole life worked against him when it came to fighting; it kept him from entering the *mai*. The *mai*, Jay had explained to Clyde, was an imaginary circle around each fighter. In order to win—in order to even *fight*—you had to break your opponent's *mai*, get in close. Reading *The Art of War* and the other books and talking them through with Jay on the way to and from work, Clyde felt that he was starting to understand. Whatever this real-world test ended up being, Jay told Clyde that in order to pass it, he would have to look hard at himself and make a decision. Do you master your character or do you let your character master you? Jay made Clyde nervous with a warning, the last thing he ever said about it: "If you don't, you gonna get hurt. In the real world, not in the basement."

Willie's words—"That's what I mean, hurt bad?"—flashed into his head.

Two weeks before the WAC Jimmy-Don and Dale both renounced their citizenship and began referring to themselves as "nonresident, nonforeigner strangers to the current state of the forum." Clyde didn't understand what it meant, but J.D. explained that it was the same thing Terry Nichols, Timothy McVeigh's right-hand man, had once told a judge to get out of paying child support. Jimmy-Don and Jay spent hours in heated debate. They'd heard talk out there of raids on gun owners' houses, new attacks on the Second Amendment, they called the Fed a criminal organization, the dollar a worthless currency. One day Jay unfolded a big map of U.S. government land holdings and almost cried at all the blackness indicating what the government owned. From the East Coast across the Midwest there were only pockets, like ink blots from a busted pen, but most of the West, and almost the entirety of the Northwest, was pure black. "Like a cancer," Jay said.

There were times when Jay and J.D. were debating something too important for any other ears. When that happened they walked off across the ridge, making it clear that nobody else was invited. Sometimes Clyde or Dale trailed after them, but if they got too close, Jay would stop and wait for them to get their asses back to the house. Just being near them those days and nights, Clyde heard enough to know that there was more to these conversations than just talk, they were planning something, weighing their options.

Then one day Dale showed up at work. The three of them rode in Jay's truck, pulling out from the lot in the opposite direction of home. They drove west, and had soon breached the ruined outskirts of Kansas City. On Troost, a street that Clyde had heard horror stories about his whole life, they kept a constant watch for trouble; the only thing to do as a white man in this part of town was stomp the gas and load the chamber. Jay noted the proliferation of tire shops, burned-out storefronts, liquor establishments, and fast-food relics packed to the rafters with dark faces and their French-fry-eating welfare babies. When Jay hit his blinker and Clyde saw a familiar roadside red and white bucket, he said, "We're stopping here?" He'd been thinking since they left Boonville that his real-world test had begun, but now he wasn't sure.

"Just 'cause we's white boys don't mean we ain't entitled to some chicken and biscuits, Clyde-san. The Negro may think he invented good eatin but he be wrong. White people was eatin good when the Negro was still in chains."

Jay wasn't scared of anything, anyone, anywhere. Clyde was relieved to walk in his shadow. They pulled into the lot and parked between two low-riders and Clyde told himself to relax, this was just supper.

They stepped inside and Jay raised an eyebrow. "We lose a war I ain't been told about yet?" The menu was in Spanish. Iceboxes were crowded with Mexican beers and fluorescent sodas and TVs blasted their shows.

"This ain't no fuckin KFC," Dale said.

The girl at the register said, "No," and some other words nobody could make out.

Jay leaned on the counter. "Hola," he said.

"Hola," she said.

"Mexicans lost the War of Independence, darlin."

"I sorry," she said.

"Don't be sorry," Jay said. "We had better weapons." He snickered and this girl, despite everything, smiled. Jay nodded at her and said, "You is one pretty Mexican. All right, what's good?"

"Tacos," she said, blushing. Clyde didn't know a Mexican could blush but this one was.

She pointed at the menu above her. "Conchinita pebil, carne asada, carnitas?"

Still leaning on the counter, only half a foot from her face, Jay stared at her while she talked. When she finished, she smiled sweetly and dropped her eyes. Jay looked back at Clyde and Dale grinning. "I might just have to take this one home with me." He turned back and said, "We take six steak tacos for here, and, uh, one sweet little mamacita to go."

She giggled and covered her mouth with a hand and rang in the order.

They sat in the last booth so Jay could have his back to the wall. When the tacos came they were soft and bare; tiny bits of chopped steak and a few onions on tortillas no bigger than a palm. Dale said, "Fuck, I'll be starving."

Jay looked at his plate a long time before picking one up. On the TV, a Mexican in a bikini was holding a monkey. "Where's the lettuce?" Dale said. "Where's the cheese? Ain't even no goddamn salsa."

Jay grabbed a bottle of hot sauce from the holder and slapped it down in front of Dale. Dale unscrewed the cap and sniffed. "Woo!" he said. "I think I just burned my fucking nose hairs off."

Jay took it and dribbled some on both his tacos. He took a bite. With his mouth full he grinned. "Might have to git that cutie pie to make us a couple more." He finished each taco in three bites and sat back chewing.

"Give me Taco Bell any day," Dale said.

Jay had Clyde go up and order four more. Dale sat in the corner rolling a smoke. When they finished eating, they all lit up. Dale's foul stink brought stares. Jay took something from his jacket pocket and put it on the table. It looked like shoe polish. Next to it he dropped two store-bought black moustaches on cardboard that said *Bandito!* "You ever see that Richard Pryor movie where the white guy robs a bank like he's a nigger?"

Clyde didn't remember seeing it. Dale said, "Yeah."

"He blacks his face and wears a ski mask and goes in all, 'Git yo white ass down on the flo fo this niggah shoots it!' " Jay laughed. "Time to embrace your inner beaner." A nearby Mexican turned around in his chair. Dale stared him down.

"Is, uh," Clyde said, lowering his voice. "This part of the test?"

Jay didn't give anything away. "No questions in training, uchi deshi."

Dale dabbed some polish on his face. "Hey mang, ju seen my rice an' beans?" he said, contorting his right hand into something like a gang sign.

Jay laughed so hard his cigarette tumbled. "Get it in close to your eyes." He nodded at the door behind them. "Go in the baño and come out bandito."

Dale took the tin into the head. Ten minutes later he came out.

"That some funny shit," Jay said. Dale's face was as brown as a new shoe and the moustache made him look like a '70s porn star.

Clyde went in then, making sure to get his neck and hands; Dale had only done his face. Jay nearly pissed himself when Clyde came out, but after sitting across from him and Dale for a while, he said that to anyone not too close or bright, they passed for something other than strictly Caucasian. Clyde's face felt tight. Diners talked and stared. Dale said, "What?" to a few of them. Going out, he yelled, "Ai yai yai!"

All the Mexican words and the gang signs made Jay crack up and swerve into the next lane. The car coming past honked and Jay lost it. He got behind them and stomped the gas, riding right up on their ass, flashing his brights, and laying on the horn. The car sped up, swerved, then hit the brakes, and the whole time Jay kept on them, the hand that wasn't on the horn at the windshield, middle finger up. "Motherfucker!" he yelled out the window. "Cocksucker!" Clyde held on, gritting his teeth, waiting for the impact, but the car finally swerved wildly into a side road and Jay sat back and let go of the horn. He turned snickering to Clyde and Dale. "Scared the bejesus out of them, didn't we?"

Under a huge cluster of freeways Troost went dark. They passed a storefront topped with a Mohammad's mosque sign in both English and some sand-nigger language, and Jay shook his head. Clyde, resisting the urge to scratch his face, kept quiet and grew increasingly nervous. He tried to breathe the *nogare* way from class to slow his heartbeat, doing it quietly so no one would know he was the only pussy in the truck.

Dale pointed at something they passed and Jay went another three blocks, hit the blinker, pulled off, and executed a slow, legal three-point turn. They sat facing Troost on the side street and Jay leaned over and opened the glove box. He tossed a piece of cloth onto Clyde's lap. Dale dug something out of his coat and worked it over his head slowly. It was a white sport sock, with lopsided eyeholes, so tight that it smashed his nose. The soiled end flopped limply to one side of his head like a dog's ear, red and orange stripes hugged his chin where it ended, smeared brown with polish. Jay could not stop laughing.

He pointed at the cloth on Clyde's lap and said, "Put it on."

Clyde took it up. A ski mask, store-bought. "What, uh, what we doing?"

Without moving his head, Jay looked at Clyde, shook a cigarette from his pack, and fingered the truck's lighter. Until it popped, no one said anything. Jay lit up, blew smoke, and said, "Dale's in charge, Clyde-san. You his second. This your test. Don't fail me."

Clyde knew it. He rolled the mask carefully down over his head.

"Get out," Jay said. "Dale," Jay said. Dale looked at him. "Jesus, you scary," Jay said. "This your deal. You in charge."

"You got it, Uncle Jay."

Jay jerked a thumb at the glass behind his head. "Shit's in the back." Dale reached over the lip and felt around until he came up with two homemade blackjacks, socks stuffed with big bars of soap. In *The Turner Diaries*, they called this an "Ivory Special" and used it to brain a liquor store owner. Dale handed one to Clyde.

Jay jerked the truck into drive and it lurched. "Now," he said, "you boys can find your own way home." He tore out. Clyde and Dale stood at the dark intersection watching his taillights float down the street, the plastic cover on one was busted, popping a floating white pupil into the corner of that crimson eye. The truck disappeared up the freeway exit.

"Shit," Dale said. He looked side to side and stepped back off the sidewalk into the shadow of the building on the corner. Clyde followed. Down the street, a cluster of black men stood in the spill light of a liquor store, old-timers with nothing to do and all night to do it.

Clyde didn't want to stand in a slice of shadow on one of the most dangerous streets in Missouri much longer. What the hell kind of test was this? What would he have done, he wondered, if Jay had told him from the start that his real-world test would involve breaking the law? Jay didn't believe in the law. He thought the whole system corrupt, from the very top to the bottom, but Clyde had never broken the law before, though he knew he came from bad blood and had often wondered if it was inevitable, like having blue eyes instead of brown. The year after Clyde's dad left the family he reappeared in Blue Springs with a CB repair shop in a little rented storefront. He kept it open long enough to get a bunch of suckers to drop off their busted gear, then left town with twenty-five CBs in his trunk. No one had seen him since. Clyde knew about this only because his mom liked to complain a couple times a year, usually on holidays after drinking too much Franzia.

Without realizing he'd done it, Clyde had wrapped the loose end of the blackjack around his fist, tight. His heart was fluttering. Jay thinks you're a warrior, he told himself. Be one.

"All you gotta do is take care of them sidewalk niggers," Dale said. "I handle everything else."

"What everything else?"

"Don't worry about it," Dale said. "What two know one can tell." He started out of the shadow, and Clyde grabbed his arm. Dale yanked it away with more karate flourish than necessary. They stared at each other, Clyde embarrassed by how hard he was breathing. "I be goddamned if I get what Jay sees in you," Dale said, and Clyde flushed with anger. He wanted to punch Dale, but he knew that it would probably be the only punch he landed, he'd trained long enough with Dale to know that a street fight between them would not end well for him. Clyde had at least twenty pounds and a few inches on Dale, but Dale had something more important than size or skill: he had natural aggression and intent. "Why are you here?" Dale said, the grin big enough for Clyde to see it through the sport sock.

"This is my test," Clyde said. "I'm the fuckin uchi deshi." Dale bent over, hands on knees, laughing so hard that his noises became pained and the men down the sidewalk looked around for the source of the distress. Clyde yanked Dale back into the shadows and Dale slapped his arm away with a *soto uke*. "Just fuck off," Clyde said. Dale calmed down and they stood watching the men. "What's the fuckin plan?"

"The guy sells drugs out of that liquor store," Dale said. "Crack. We gonna take his dirty money, save some kids. You're just crowd control."

Those men were old, busted up, lives of loitering and brown-bag liquor. Clyde figured it would be easy enough, maybe they were all on crack right now. He remembered the scene in *The Turner Diaries* where Earl Turner was going to rob a store. But one of his comrades found out it was white-owned, so they changed the target to one owned by an old Jew. Remembering that made Clyde feel better, these people sold drugs and liquor, they polluted their own neighborhood. They deserved it.

Swinging his blackjack, Dale stepped into the light. "Time to enter the *mai*, white belt." At that moment Clyde knew that this test had been created specifically for that reason: to force him into the fight.

Soon they attracted attention. One of the men said something and laughed. Another pointed at Dale's head. Dale shoved Clyde in their direction and jerked the door of the liquor store, making the hollow bells explode with noise. "Damn! Broad daylight," one of the men said, even though it was dark out. As soon as Dale went in, the door burst again and three or four people scattered out cussing. Clyde looked around, he was surrounded. There were, in a blink, a dozen black men on the sidewalk. He started swinging the Ivory Special. "Ho!" one man said, dropping his bottle and running. The two with him backed away, but one said to the other, "Get around that side." Clyde could almost hear Jay yelling. *Enter the* mai, *goddamn it!* Someone was trying to sneak around, so Clyde scooted at him like they did in class, pushing off the back foot and sliding forward to cover a lot of ground without taking an actual step, and hit him with the blackjack. The man's arms jerked his jacket up around his head and he ran off. The other followed, his big feet slapping the sidewalk with a long-legged lope.

The others who'd left the store were shouting at the door. "Call the cops!" one said. Another, a woman, slapped the door with her palms and said, "You okay, Marvin!?" Clyde went at them screaming his best *kiai* and they burst, reassembling farther down the sidewalk. Clyde remembered that he was supposed to be Mexican at the same time he saw Dale inside the door, pinned to the ground by an enormous black man whose sweaty face was shaking with the effort of choking him. Dale's sport sock was on the floor and most of the polish on his face was gone. His yellowy eyes were rolling back in his head.

As soon as Clyde was inside, the big man looked up, making his wide face a perfect target. Clyde stood there like a dummy, trying to figure out what technique to use as this man choked Dale to death. He heard Jay's voice— "*chusuku mai geri!*"—and threw the kick. It didn't feel like he connected with anything but the man's head snapped back and he fell onto Dale so fast and hard that his forehead bounced off the floor.

Outside, everyone was shouting and stomping their feet. Clyde was ready to fight them all. He'd put his training to the test in a real-world situation and it had worked. Maybe he'd hesitated, but there was no denying that he had entered the *mai*. Jay would be pleased.

Dale coughed, rolled over. He was crying. A bottle shattered against the door and Clyde said, "You all right?" Dale didn't answer. Beside them, the owner of the store groaned, his face wet, cheeks as pocked as the moon. Dale didn't look good. Maybe his trachea was crushed. If it was, there wasn't anything Clyde could do to save him. If he ran out of there and left Dale, he might stand a chance of getting away. Dale would either die or go to prison, which would keep him out of Clyde's sight for either a few years or forever. Another bottle smashed against the door and the owner got himself onto his hands and knees, keeping his forehead on the ochre-colored linoleum, its surface disturbed by years of scuff marks and cigarette ash. Outside, they were going nuts. Thanks to Dale, Clyde had managed to get himself into an impossible situation: two white boys surrounded by an angry mob of black people. Clyde lifted Dale and marched him into the door, hard.

The mob scattered, and Clyde's legs and feet fought with Dale's to keep them both standing on the sidewalk. A bottle flew over their heads. Clyde marched them back to where Jay had dropped them off, only then remembering that Jay wouldn't be there. Someone rushed up on them and Clyde let go of Dale and spun with his arms up yelling his *kiai*. Goddamn if it didn't work. The man's eyes popped and he stumbled off like he'd been stung. Clyde felt real power for the first time in his life and for a moment considered taking them all on. He would stomp the bony asses of every last one of them. Instead he gathered up Dale again and ran into the street, bathed in bright open light. They went quickly down the opposite side until he was sure no one was following, though he could still hear them complaining.

After a few blocks, Dale shook Clyde off. Clyde let go with a shove and Dale fell, trying to roll the way they do in class, to break fall, catching the ground with an arm and tumbling with grace back to standing. It didn't work. What you deserve, Clyde thought. Dale lay on his side looking at his bloodied hands. After a while he got to sitting. He kept snorting in his throat and spitting on the sidewalk. "That nigger wanted me *dead*." Clyde took a cigarette out of his pack and passed it to Dale. Dale coughed and spat. He smoked sitting on the sidewalk. Clyde watched out for trouble. Dale got up and they walked. They reached the highway on-ramp where Jay had last been seen, its cement curb busted, the dead grass in the dirt cluttered with cardboard and bottles and butts, strips of truck tire shredded off the rim and two soiled mattresses stacked sloppily against the embankment. Clyde had no idea how to get back to Boonville. He'd never taken a bus in his life. And he didn't think hitchhiking was a good idea. No driver, no matter what color they were, would stop to pick up two men who looked the way they looked right now.

"How much money you got on you?" Dale said.

"Why?" Clyde said.

"How much?"

Clyde looked around and took out his wallet. He checked and returned it to his pocket. "About a hundred."

Dale made a gesture for Clyde to hand it over. Clyde didn't move. Dale yelled, "Goddamn it!" Clyde gave him the money. "Hundred and *twenty*," Dale said. "Can't trust no Twitty. I got about the same. Almost three hundred, that ain't bad."

"Ain't bad for what? A taxi cab?"

"Jesus, Twitty," Dale said, folding and pocketing the money and looking off at something moving down the street before turning back to Clyde. "Nigger-run liquor store in the 'hood. Ain't gonna have more than that in the fucking register, I bet."

When Clyde understood what Dale was up to his lack of respect hit a new low. "You gonna lie to Jay?"

Dale ran across Troost and tried the handle of a parked car. Clyde went after him, tried the passenger side. They moved down to the next one. Both were locked.

At the third car, Dale said, "How many chances you think Jay's gonna give you before he decides your sorry ass ain't worth it? Not every dog can be trained. Some are just . . . " Dale spat and looked around. "Useless."

"I just saved your life."

"The fuck you did."

"Wish I hadn't," Clyde said.

Dale went around the weeds, bent over. When he found a stone he didn't hesitate in throwing it through the back window of a rusted old Lincoln leaning at an angle to the curb. He groped around the floorboards and glove box and popped the trunk. Clyde stood on the grass, watching. Dale jumped back in and jammed a screwdriver into the ignition. After a bit of fighting the wheel, the car groaned to life.

The Lincoln lurched into drive and Clyde tried the passenger-side handle even though he'd tried it before and knew it was locked. Dale leaned over, his middle finger up. "Motherfucker!" Clyde yelled, hitting the roof with his fist. Dale pulled out, tires squealing. Clyde looked around the curb for something to throw. He found a bottle and threw. It smashed against the trunk and Dale flinched, yanking a U-turn, and sped up the freeway on-ramp. Then the fucker honked.

Within five minutes Clyde had smashed the windows out of four cars. It made a hell of a racket to explode glass on a quiet street and he found no screwdrivers or anything else to jam into the ignition. He was worried about attracting attention, so he crossed the road and followed Jay's and Dale's path up the on-ramp, vehicles blowing past him not two feet away. When he reached the freeway above, its shoulder was littered with tire scraps, broken glass, splintered wood, and trash. Clyde stuck close to the battered railing. The look of the metal barrier and the many skidmarks under his feet didn't give him much confidence that he'd make it home alive. He hadn't paid attention on the drive and didn't know the way back. He just hoped that whatever freeway it was that he was on right now would eventually connect with 50.

Dale would be pulling into Liberty Ridge any minute now. He would drive in there in that stolen Lincoln and walk into the house waving money and boasting. Jay would tell him he'd done good, he was proud of him. At what point would he ask where's Clyde? Uncle Jay, Dale would say, I don't know what you see in that guy. His heart's not in it. He doesn't care about the movement. I would've been better off without him tonight. Dishonesty, to Jay, was about the worst offense there was. His whole purpose in life, with training, with family, even with the movement, Clyde could see now, was to get at truth, the real truth beneath what most people thought was the truth. This was unforgivable.

Head down, hands in his front pockets, Clyde walked the shoulder as cars and big rigs blew past disturbing the dirt and dust; a chalky, bitter cloud roiled over him and pebbles bit into his legs and back. Clyde thought of what he'd say when he got home. He could anticipate Jay's reply. You gonna let people push you around your whole life? What about a firm, unshaken spirit? Why didn't you punch the window in before Dale could drive away? Why didn't you perceive the threat? Why'd you let him pick the getaway car in the first place? Why are you so content to walk in the shadows? You can't be the second your whole life; one day you gotta become the samurai. Where's that anger, Clyde? Where's your rage? You're so used to being fucked over you don't even feel it anymore.

What Clyde didn't want to accept was that Dale might be right: maybe lying *was* the way. In a short time Jay had become the most important person in Clyde's life. What Clyde feared more than anything else now was the moment that Jay would give up on him.

It was twenty miles to Boonville, he figured. Walking, he'd be lucky to make it home by dawn. But, thanks to the training, he could run it in probably three hours. He kept to a steady pace on the shoulder and in time saw signs for

435. Off to the left, Kauffman Stadium glowed against the black sky and even with the traffic screaming past he could hear the Royals game. His dad had taken him when he was little, but he didn't remember much: a foul ball had come close to their seats; his dad had argued with somebody over something, the ball, the price of beer. The music that filled the stadium now crossed the roofs of all the industrial buildings in the low asphalt grid. America's pastime, he remembered Jay saying, with his grin, at the auction that day. Now that Clyde knew him better, he got what Jay had meant. Like a lot of what America said about itself, it was bullshit. Baseball was invented to sell hot dogs and beer and to keep the American public from thinking. 'Cause if we think too hard about what's happened to our country, the only rational thing is to rise up. Instead, we drink beer while men chase a little ball around the dirt. What had started out, Jay would say, as a good way for boys to develop hand-eye coordination and community and character had become, like everything else in this life, corrupt.

Clyde had already jogged, he figured, three, maybe four miles, and he wasn't even winded. At the liquor store, he'd done well. He himself hadn't committed any illegal acts. He'd done only what he'd been told to do. He had kept that angry mob at bay. Just by trying to rob it they had likely hampered the illegal drug operation going on in there. Clyde had also saved Dale's life and would make sure that Jay knew it. Breath and body taking on a good, steady rhythm as he jogged, Clyde saw clearly now how his life had shifted from the pursuit of selfish endeavors. If he was part of the warrior class, he was part of something greater than the pointless desires of one man.

Interstate 435 connected with 350 and he knew that 350 led to 50 just a few miles outside Boonville. By the time he got onto 350, he'd been running somewhere between one and two hours, he figured; his inner thighs were raw from his jeans and burned. His shirt was soaked under his jacket, and stained down the front from the face paint his sweat had washed off. Clyde kept the pace through Raytown, even when people yelled from their cars. At the steep hill to Liberty Ridge, he pumped his arms hard, sprinting the final stretch. The Lincoln Dale had stolen was nowhere in sight. Some lights were on in the house even though it was late. Clyde went into the trailer. It was just after midnight. He heard Jay crossing the yard. "Get your gi on," he said.

"Now?" Clyde said in the open door.

"That's right," Jay said.

C lyde was exhausted. His feet were so sore he had to stand on their outer edges. The muscles of his legs burned and his inner thighs were raw and hot. The gi hadn't been washed since the last class, it was dirty and stiff as cardboard. When he came out of the trailer Jay was looking into a pit down the road. He walked to the next one. Maybe he'd murdered Dale and wanted to show Clyde where the body was. He followed in the street as Jay went from pit to pit. Standing beside him, he smelled ammonia and decomposing animals, but Dale's corpse was nowhere in sight. A busted cement mixer lay half submerged in the middle of a pit, crowded with food wrappers, disintegrating boxes from KFC, McDonald's, Long John Silver's. Something hissed; a possum crawled over a pile of bricks, its pink-rimmed eyes blank and crazy.

"Damn," Clyde said. Jay punched him in the stomach.

Clyde doubled over, he covered up but Jay didn't hit him again. Speaking was impossible, his voice wouldn't work. Jay took a step. Clyde braced himself but Jay only grabbed his gi and jerked him upright. It looked like he was about to say something, his lips were tight and dry and his nose puffed with breath like a bull's. Jay stared into him with deep, wet eyes. With his left hand he held Clyde at arm's length; with his right, he punched him twice in the mouth.

Clyde felt an odd moment of peace before he blacked out. When he woke, he was drowning. He coughed and thrashed. The brown pit water was two feet thick. Clyde pushed himself off the cement mixer to get on his feet. Filth stung his eyes; he rubbed them with soiled fingers and blew bitter snot from his nose and looked at Jay, above, at the edge. It would have been disrespectful to meet Jay's eyes so Clyde kept his down. He tried to slow his heart. It was as if he had no control over it. He made fists with his hands and said, "Osu!" His abdomen ached where Jay had punched him.

"Osu?" Jay said, the first time Clyde had ever heard him say it that way. "You lucky I don't come down there and hold your fuckin head underwater. Make Dale take you out to Lick Skillet, dig a grave. Nobody ever fuckin know. 'I got no idea, Mrs. Twitty, he was disturbed.' "

"Osu," Clyde said.

"Shut up. You don't git to use that word no more."

Clyde nearly said, "Osu" but stopped himself.

Jay said, "Think I'm fuckin stupid? Two hundred sixty dollars?"

Clyde was just at the edge of controlling his breath. He kept his eyes on his own reflection on the opaque water in front of a quivering streetlamp. It took him three tries to get out, "What did Dale say?"

"And you don't git to ask the fuckin questions either. Askin questions a privilege only warriors got."

"Can I say something, then? 'Cause I think I know what Dale told you."

"No, you cannot say something," Jay said.

"He fuckin told you it was my idea."

Jay made a fist and it looked for a moment like he was about to leap in and make good on his threats. Watching his reaction, Clyde knew he'd been right. Dale had swapped the blame, told Jay that it was *Clyde* who had screwed up, that *Clyde* had ruined their robbery, that *Clyde* had got the idea to deceive. Dale had probably even said that it was *Clyde* who would have died had *Dale* not saved his sorry ass.

"I hope you like it down there, boy," Jay said, " 'cause that is where you's spending the night. I'm gonna come out every hour and check on you. I wanna see you standing, just like that, all night. I catch you sittin down I will fuckin shoot you, Clyde, I shit you not. You are about this close to a shallow grave in Lick Skillet." Jay spat. Clyde heard it, then saw the gob fleck the water. Jay walked off.

Clyde tried to keep it together. The water was so ripe it made him nauseous. He splashed the possum in the corner and it hissed and crawled in a circle. Bugs floated around Clyde's legs and he disturbed the water to get them away. An hour passed and Clyde, already exhausted, stayed in the stance, mosquitoes all over him, one eye kept on the possum, the pants of his gi leeching water the color of dried blood up his thighs. He heard the screen door, and voices, and then Jay, Jan, and Tina appeared.

"There he is," Jay said, kicking some dirt from the lip of the pit. Clyde closed his eyes and felt it pepper his head.

"Pee-yew!" Tina said. She pinched her nose and leaned over to spit. Clyde heard her hock loudly in her throat and hated her. She missed, cursing. Clyde heard Jay's zipper and Tina said, "Yeah, Dad, do it!" Clyde finally looked up. "We oughta *all* piss on you," she said. "Lie to my dad. I don't know about you and your stupid mom, buddy, but in this family we don't sneak around lying to each other!"

"Tell that to Dale," Clyde said, and Jay made a noise and grabbed a handful of dirt and threw it at Clyde's head. After that, they all walked back to the house. Tina hadn't even asked if what Dale had told them was true. They'd just trusted him completely, because he was family and Clyde wasn't.

For a long time Clyde kept his eyes on the possum, worried that it would make a move if he wasn't watching it, slip under the surface, swim over, and attack. The more he watched it the more afraid of it he got. He grabbed a brick, waded over. The possum reared back hissing, gray mouth wide, teeth bared. Clyde inched in, the water broke around his knees, scattering garbage. The possum bobbed like it was going to jump and Clyde brought down the brick, hitting something hard in its back. The possum screeched and disappeared underwater.

Hours passed before Jay returned. Clyde fought to stay awake. The pit sheltered him from a strong wind blowing dirt and garbage overhead. It kept up half the night, dusting Clyde's face and shoulders, and then stopped suddenly, the noise replaced by a thousand bugs and, from the direction of Molasses Gap, a dog. Clyde's tired mind raced across time, settling again and again on the past. Clyde remembered watching Troy's karate class in Harrisonville. Troy had had a good loud *kiai*, Clyde knew now, he'd seemed fierce then, to Clyde, who didn't know any better, and had carried himself different enough that nobody ever challenged him. Clyde knew for a fact that Troy had never been in a real fight in his life. The way they'd faught in that class in Harrisonville, all padded up and any contact earning you a point and stopping the fight before it even began more often than not, hadn't prepared Troy for Liberty Ridge. That image of Troy, hurt and trying not to cry, his cheeks flushed red, returned to Clyde. "Both of them are fucking crazy. You know that, right?" Those words had made Clyde mad at the time but standing in this stinking pit in the cold of night, they circled back, as a mosquito would, sounding less and less like a question.

It was deep into the night and Clyde hadn't heard Jay come out, he was suddenly just there, above. But Clyde was in position. His body, if not his mind, had stayed in position. The brick he'd used on the possum balanced on the cement mixer. He hadn't seen any sign of the animal in hours and he'd convinced himself that it had gone off in search of a private place to die the way animals seemed to do. "Somethin different," Jay said, and Clyde flinched.

He didn't offer any explanation.

"What'd you do?" Clyde kept quiet. "I'm asking you a question."

"I tried to kill the possum."

Jay nearly fell over laughing. "With that brick? Jesus, better keep an eye on Clyde Twitty." Jay walked around the pit. Clyde heard him moving and felt sick with frustration at this injustice, what did Jay want from him? He wouldn't even allow Clyde to give his side of things, he'd accepted Dale's bullshit without question. Clyde had thought of Jay as different, but he'd starting acting like everybody else who'd mistreated or bullied Clyde over the course of his life: his dad, his coach, Mr. Longarm, the unemployment office, the IRS. It pained Clyde to think that Troy had been right, and that Jay might belong in this category. Clyde searched the rough walls for the rebar holds; he could climb out, there was nothing stopping him. To persevere while being challenged, to prove how hard you were, to endure the worst the family could throw at him, that was what stopped him from leaving. When they later realized that Clyde had been wronged, they'd be ashamed of themselves.

The next time Clyde saw Jay was at dawn. Jay reached the edge of the pit holding his coffee mug and stood looking down. Clyde was still in his spot; he'd determined to show Jay just how hard he could be. He was the very embodiment of osu. There were a few moments in the night when he'd fallen asleep on his feet, but each time he'd jerked awake before going under. "You still standing," Jay said. "Time to git to work."

Clyde climbed out. "Can I take a shower?"

"No," Jay said. "You ain't welcome in the house."

As the orange sun crept across the ridge, Clyde dragged his sore, bloated feet through the grass in the yard, searching the picture window for any sign of Tina. He wanted to meet her eyes. Skin hung off the sides of his feet in gelatinous white globs. In the trailer he put on two pairs of socks, it hurt to stand. His upper lip, he saw in the mirror, was split, purple and swollen.

At work he had a hard time keeping up. More than once Jay saw him and said, "Pain's just information. Ain't no different than 'I'm hungry' and just as easy to ignore."

Scrap and trash rained down from the house all morning, and just before lunch a busted shale tile slapped the ground only about a foot away. "That one nearly got me," Clyde said, backing up until he could see Jay. The other roofers kept hammering. But Jay, puffing on a cigarette at the very top, swung a tile. It landed near the other. "Oops," he said.

The rest of the day Clyde stayed on his toes. It got so that he could tell the sound of Jay's hammer from the others. Tiles still flew, but none hit.

After work, when Jay made a right turn up Liberty Hill, Clyde made a left and went to the KFC at the far end of Main Street. He kept to the drive-through and sat with his meal in his truck in the bright parking lot watching the black families inside. He didn't hate them the way Jay or Dale did but they had made it pretty clear that he wasn't welcome. Reverse discrimination, Jay might have said. Then Clyde realized that he wasn't welcome anywhere right now. Clyde wondered about the people who had been in his life before. He'd never explained to Esther why he'd quit without notice and he'd always felt bad, no matter what Jay said about the warrior breaking from the old life. He'd done that to the extent that was humanly possible, he thought, breaking with Esther, barely seeing his mom, not visiting with his uncle much at all anymore. When Clyde got back to Liberty Ridge, he put a folding chair in front of the trailer and made a call.

Picking up after the eighth ring, Willie said, "Howdy, stranger."

Clyde said, "I know, sorry."

"I don't want you to ever worry about your Uncle Willie. You don't got to check in, touch base, or drop by if you're too busy with work and Tina and training."

Work and Tina and training. That was pretty much it. "I'm not. I'm just saying hi."

"How you been keepin?"

"Mm," Clyde said, watching headlights sweep the entrance to the development. A car—not Dale's—pulled in. "Not bad."

Willie laughed. "Sounds more like not great. What's up?"

"Nah," Clyde said. "Nothin. Training's just, uh . . ." Another car entered. Clyde stood up. It looked like Dale's. "Sorry, just hard lately. I'm tired's all." Clyde stared at the car as it made the first turn. It was Dale.

"Well, you stick with it you won't be sorry. Can't say the same if you give up."

Clyde went up into the trailer and said, "You're right, yep. Speaking of training, I gotta get changed. Class is about to start."

"See you soon?" Willie said.

"Yep," Clyde said, and hung up. Dale made the last turn and pulled to a stop in front of the house. He was wearing his gi and hurried across the grass to the door. "Hey!" Clyde yelled, and Dale jerked, surprised. "Fucker!" Clyde ran after him. Dale went quickly in and shut the door. Clyde stood in the street.

Jay came out to the porch and waved Clyde off. "You ain't welcome," he said.

"Dale is? This is fucking bullshit!"

Jay spat and eyeballed him. Clyde braced for a beating. But after a second, he just went back inside.

Clyde would wait for Dale. He would make that son of a bitch tell Jay the truth if it was the last thing he did. All evening Clyde watched the door. The other students left. Three hours passed with no sign of Dale and Clyde fell asleep in his folding chair. When he woke up around midnight, Dale's car was gone. He'd slipped away in the dark, sneaky as a possum.

C lyde thought about what he'd been through and what he was dealing with now and came to see this new turn in a different light: it was a test, just another test, the robbery, a test of Clyde's character. The idea to endure whatever hatred the family heaped on him in order to punish them later with guilt gave way to deeper thinking. What he was being made to go through now, no matter how fucked up it was, would be good for his character. He'd be smarter than everybody, he'd not kick the shit out of Dale, because to kick the shit out of Dale would be to fail two tests. He would endure it all in order to develop his warrior spirit. Clyde felt better having broken free of the petty thinking and pushed through to something more philosophical. It made him think that the last few weeks had changed him for the better, no matter how he felt on a given day, not unlike a difficult tour of duty. Once he was back on Jay's good side, Clyde would chip away at Dale's trustworthiness, bit by bit by bit, until the doubts that Jay had previously held for Clyde shifted onto Dale, his own flesh and blood. To win Jay's allegiance away from Dale would be to beat Dale completely.

When Clyde drove past the house that night after supper at Long John Silver's, Jan was out on the step with a margarita, a cigarette, and a magazine. Clyde watched her, but she didn't look up once. Had even she turned against him? Why would she make herself so visible if she had? She'd never sat outside with a magazine the whole time he'd known her. He decided that even though she hadn't looked up, she'd come out to let him know that she was on his side, maybe nobody else was but she was. He went in the trailer and filled its small sink with two gallons of water from the Sinclair station. He washed himself in the sink, the first real bath he'd had since the pit, and sat outside in his lawn chair smoking and thinking about his dad. It occurred to Clyde that the image he'd held of his dad since the age of six had been created and reinforced his whole life by his mom. The man was a failure, the man was reckless and lost their farm, he was selfish and abandoned his family, cheap and never paid child support, proved his true nature by stealing CBs. No matter how Clyde felt about Jay right now, the man had taught him to think beyond the bullshit that people wanted you to believe was the truth.

Maybe Clyde's dad had worked his ass off and still lost the farm. Maybe he'd tried everything possible before realizing that he had no power against the goddamn bank. Maybe he'd failed back then in the same way that Clyde's mom was failing now, and the way that Clyde had been failing before he met Jay. To work hard and still not make ends meet, to do everything in your power as the water rose around you. Clyde imagined how hard that might be on a marriage.

The next day after work Jay followed Clyde on his way to return the dump truck to the office. He'd never done that before; maybe he was going to put an end to all this. Clyde had paid his dues, had endured all punishment. Jay must have seen his warrior spirit by now.

Clyde parked and returned the keys to the office. Jay lingered at the gate outside his truck. It was after six and the place was empty. When Clyde came back outside, Jay was gone. Clyde got in his truck, backed up, and only then saw that the gate had been shut and padlocked. Goddamn it. He thought about ramming it, but ramming it would surely get him in trouble, maybe fired. He'd have no job and Walmart wouldn't take him back the way he'd quit. But there was no way he was going to spend the night in this lot; the only thing to do was climb over.

The chain link hurt Clyde's fingers. The toes of his boots wouldn't fit in the spaces between links so the hands had to do all the work. Pain's just information. Damn straight it is. When he reached the top he held on by one hand and tried to push the razor wire flat. He wondered if he had anything like a blanket in his truck and decided he did not and to climb back down to look around, only to remain empty-handed, would just make this worse. With a handful of razor wire, he threw a leg over and straddled the top. He lay flat for a moment to get his breath back. The sun was low in the sky and the bugs in the ditches on the roadside were making noise. Flies bothered his temples.

He started down the other side, gripping the razor wire with one hand and searching for a hold on the chain link with the other. He got his legs over and fumbled the grab, starting to fall. The smart thing would have been to let go of the razor wire but that was all he had hold of, and he hung there by one hand for a moment as the wire sliced into the meat of his palm and fingers until he had to let go. He fell the length of the fence, hitting the ground hard and having the wind knocked out of him. "Fuck!" he shouted, rolling onto his side.

Like Christ, he was suddenly bleeding from his palm. He pressed it flat to his jeans and left an almost perfect print on the thigh. It hurt to make a fist but he made one, blood dripping out the bottom as if he'd crushed a small bird. It was four miles home and he thought, I could die from this. That would be a dumb way to go—bleeding to death from wounds to one hand. He started walking. The hell with my character, Clyde thought, finally. What I could use right now is a little comfort, a little peace, a little kindness maybe. When the lot opens, I'll get my truck and just go back to Strasburg, lie on the bed watching TV, no one to bother me. I'll drink beer and drive around in the dark playing one of Troy's crazy albums. Even after contributing to the mortgage, Clyde had some money; thanks to the job he had a few hundred in cash. If he returned to Strasburg under normal circumstances, Jay would have been on his doorstep in no time. His phone would have never stopped. But the way things stood now, Clyde didn't think he'd call once.

Before long Clyde was standing at the mouth of the Walmart parking lot. He paced in the dry shoulder off the road, fighting with himself about going in. He kept a low profile inside until he saw her, Esther, back on register duty. He almost missed her, she had a straight line of bangs just above her eyes and her hair was raven black. Clyde hid behind a fat woman in line, not wanting to be seen until he was right there. When she finished with the woman, Esther turned a bright smile at Clyde that dropped immediately. Her face was a complicated mix of signals that Clyde found impossible to read. Raising his red right hand, Clyde waved and smiled. Esther's mouth dropped open and she threw her *next register please* sign on the belt. "Come on," she barked, dodging slow-moving shoppers. The last thing Clyde wanted was to run into Wilson, but he tried to keep up. In the employee break room in the back corner of the store she dug through the first-aid kit and told Clyde to run his hand under cold water and asked him what he'd done. He said only,

"Cut it on a fence," wiping away the blood that had splattered the sides of the white enamel sink. Esther ruined a cloth napkin drying his hand, sprayed it down with something that stung, and wrapped it to twice its size with a tight ribbon of gauze. By the time they got to the McDonald's up front, blood had made its way to the surface. Esther handed him a giant cup of soda and went out through the automatic doors. They finished their first cigarette in silence as the automatic doors jerked open and shut, Clyde watching Esther smoke in that sexy way, Esther watching Clyde with her beautiful shaking emerald-green eyes.

"I," Clyde said, taking a deep breath. "Am. Sorry."

Esther dug the toe of her shoe against something on the cement. "For what?"

"Uhhh," Clyde said. When it came to Esther, there was a lot he was sorry for. "Disappearing on you. I wanted to come tell you."

"What happened?" she said. "That family lock you up?"

"Not really," he said.

She French inhaled. "Thought you'd died or something."

Clyde put an arm around her neck and pulled her in. "I didn't."

"Holy crap, Clyde," she said, squeezing his arm. "When'd you get so big?"

"Been training karate." He let her go and rolled a tight fist with his good hand that made his bicep bulge. "And working construction."

"Dang." Esther pulled the arm back around her neck and, squirming against it, squeezed his pecks and stomach and said, "Yummy." She lit new cigarettes with her old one and they watched the last of the sun drag a line across the roofs of the cars clustered in small groups. With her head resting on his shoulder and smoke drifting over her upper lip, she said, "Where'd you park?"

"I didn't."

"How'd you get here?"

"Walked."

"Yowzer. Come on." They made their way to Esther's car. Clyde kept quiet. She let him in and sped through the lot to the side of the store, stopping near the last loading dock at the very back. She lit more cigarettes and they sat with their arms out the windows. "I'm done for the day, thank goodness." She nodded to a tattered Bible on the dash. "Would you please put that in the backseat?"

Clyde flipped it open. On the inside page was written, *Property of Esther Hines, don't take or you will burn in hell!* Esther put her cigarette so deeply into her mouth that only an inch remained before the glowing orange end. "I shouldn't be smoking cigarettes," she said. "But I love it." She clamped it in her teeth. "I gotta be home in like twenty minutes," she said, unbuttoning Clyde's jeans.

He jimmied his pants down and his pecker sprung free. "I hope I don't smell too bad. Just got off work."

"I don't mind." When she saw all the bruises marking Clyde's thighs and hips she said, "This from karate, or you into S and M, you naughty boy?"

Clyde grinned. "Karate."

"Does it hurt?" She pressed and Clyde flinched.

"Yeah."

She leaned across and said, "Say something if you see anybody coming. Besides you." She laughed, so did Clyde. He rested his head on the seat and smoked the rest of his cigarette and then finished Esther's, listening to the wet rhythm she made under the shroud of hair. He'd never had a woman do that to him before and it was over in no time. When she was sitting up again, she looked at the sagging brown lining of her roof and put her hands together to pray. Halfway to Liberty Ridge, she said, "By the way, where's your truck?"

Clyde told Esther what Jay had done. Before he knew it, he'd relayed some of what had happened since the robbery downtown, a detail he left out entirely. He didn't know how much to tell her. He hardly mentioned the movement or the way the government was working against people like him and the Smalls, honest Americans. He knew that even *talking* to Esther was to betray Jay— again, and this knowledge made him even more mad. He couldn't get Jay out of his fucking head, Jay telling him how a distraction like Esther was gonna hurt his training. Esther didn't say a word while Clyde talked, she just watched with a look of concern that spread across her face until it became something else, maybe it was anger, anger at what Clyde had been put through, or maybe it was something else, like fear. That was what it looked like to Clyde, and he said, "Looks like you're afraid of me right now."

Esther nodded. "I am."

"Why?"

"You're shaking."

"No, I'm not."

"You are, Clyde. You're shaking because you're *pissed*."

Now Clyde wished he could just take it all back. "I'm probably overreacting," he said, watching for the top of the hill.

"Uh, your karate teacher locked up your truck and made you walk home from work. He's *trying* to *hurt* you."

When they got to the top of the hill Clyde told her not to pull into the development. "They're liable to shoot you."

Esther yanked the break on the side of the road. "You can call me, you know."

Clyde nodded.

"I mean, not just for blow jobs. If you need to talk or anything."

"Thanks."

Esther shook her head. She looked sad. She leaned across the seat and pulled Clyde into a kiss with her soft palm on the back of his neck. She tasted of cigarettes and Juicy Fruit and sweat and semen. "I ain't like Tina," she said. "And my dad would be *nice* to you, which you deserve, 'cause you're a good person."

Clyde got out, faster than he'd intended because he'd started to cry and didn't want Esther to see it. He blew the snot out of his nose to cover the sound.

"You know where to find me," she said, pulling away, and Clyde wondered if he'd ever see her again.

T he front door of the house in Liberty Ridge was standing open. Clyde went up to the porch, three cement steps with four square holes intended for railings. The railings had never come and the holes had filled with cigarette butts and rain. He could hear the TV and tried to make out what they were watching.

Clyde stayed on the porch for half an hour, laughing once along with the family. He went around to the side of the house and crawled to the window well, his bandaged hand aching. Jay was on the sofa in his gi, balancing a whisky on his black belt, a handgun was on the table next to him. Tina and Jan were on the floor surrounded by jars of barbeque sauce, making notations in Tina's books. He hadn't seen Tina since that night in the pit; she slept in the house now, in her old room. Clyde crawled around to get a look at the TV. They were watching one of the nine o'clock dramas.

To keep the spring from squeaking Clyde took his time opening the screen door, stepping through, and easing it shut. Now he was only three feet closer to the TV but it seemed so much louder. Jan said something and Tina said, "Make mine a double." Clyde hurried up the steps to the upstairs bathroom and shut the door. He hoped the TV would mask the noise of the shower. If not, there'd be some sort of confrontation. He almost welcomed it.

The water around his feet ran black and red. The warm shower felt so good he wanted to linger, but he didn't dare. He got as clean as he could with only one working hand and then washed the Lifebuoy bar clean of his hair. When he finished, he got back into his clothes and opened the door. Downstairs the show was still on: shouts, gunshots, music.

The TV snapped off as he reached the door. Clyde jumped into the dirt that ringed the house and someone came to the door, smoking a cigarette. He could hear breathing, a belch. The door opened and Jan stepped out, flicking her cigarette all the way to the sidewalk. "Jesus!" she said, and Clyde jumped. "What the hell you doing, Clyde?" she whispered. "You sneaky thing. I thought I heard the shower. Figured I was losing my mind."

"Sorry."

Jan lit a cigarette for Clyde and another for herself. "You better hope Jay don't wanna come out and join me," she whispered. They smoked for a moment in silence and Jan said, "I'm sorry about all this."

"Oh," Clyde said. "Nah."

"I figure it can't go on forever, though, right?"

Clyde wasn't sure what to say. He didn't know if he'd ever feel the same about Jay, and he didn't think he could forgive Tina for her part in it. He'd never seen that side of her; now that he had he worried he'd never be able to see anything else. "I know he's your nephew," Clyde said quietly, "but whatever Dale told Jay, it ain't true." Jan didn't say anything. "I told him I didn't want to lie to Jay."

Jan kept her eyes on the street, lit up and humming. "Where'd he get the money?"

Clyde sighed. "I gave him what I had before I knew what he was gonna do with it."

Jan turned her head. "Really, Clyde?"

Clyde almost said, "Yes!" but stopped himself. He didn't want to dig a deeper hole than he was already in. "No," he said, sadly. He saw now that he could not honestly claim complete innocence. The shift from soldier to traitor could be so slight. "But it sure as hell wasn't my idea and I only did it 'cause he said Jay was about ready to give up on me."

"Well that just ain't true," Jan said. "Jay won't tell you this himself 'cause it's not his way, but he thinks you're pretty damn special, Clyde. Wouldn't treat you so bad if he didn't really care. Take it from me. I know right now it don't seem like it, but he's got *huge* hopes for you." Clyde felt a rush of relief. "Maybe," Jan said, crossing the remaining distance. It was as close as he'd got to any of the Smalls without a fight in some time. She looked past him. "I don't know, I was gonna say he likes it when you take initiative." She shrugged and brought a hand to her mouth to bite her thumbnail. Her nails were all short, a man's hands, hard and thick and in no way pretty. The cigarette between her fingers smoldered over her eyes and she didn't blink. "Maybe there's something you can do."

"Like what?"

She pulled the screen door open. "That's for you to figure out, honey."

Clyde set his alarm for five. When it went off, he used his teeth to cover the cuts on his hand with Band-Aids, using seven. He got dressed, snuck into the back of Jay's truck, covered up with a heavy blanket, and woke with a start when the screen door banged shut. Jay put something in the cab, said, "Yeah, all right," and walked toward the trailer. "Time to get to work!" he yelled.

Clyde resisted the urge to jump out of the truck and shout, "Here I am!"

Jay banged on the trailer. "Clyde?" He came back to the truck. "Guess he got an early start."

"He woulda had to," Clyde heard Jan say.

A dull smack and Jay's snaggletooth laugh, a kiss not two feet from the truck, a door pulled shut. The truck backed to the road. Clyde's shirt was soaked and it wasn't even seven, he watched the sky and welcomed the breeze. Black clouds pressed at the trees.

They rolled under the construction office gate and parked. As soon as Jay went in, Clyde ran out to the road. He turned and walked casually back. His truck was in its spot. He was just coming through the gate when Jay saw him. "You come that way?"

"Yeah."

"Ain't that longer than this way?"

"Is it?"

"Think so."

"It's how I got home, so I just figured I'd stick to that."

"Stick to what you know," Jay said, tossing him the dump truck keys. When Clyde caught them, Jay said, "Cut your hand?"

Clyde studied his hand like it might answer for him. "Yeah, I did."

At work that day Jay didn't throw a single tile Clyde's direction. Ominous clouds crawled overhead but never broke. When five o'clock came Jay walked his tools to the metal box in the back of his truck. "We leaving six a.m. tomorrow for the WAC," he called back to Clyde.

"See you when you get back."

Jay huffed, dropping his head. "You're coming," he said, looking at the ground. "Don't mean nothing's changed. You still on probation."

Clyde said, "Okay."

"It's just too good a opportunity to miss." Jay got in his truck and pulled out, then stopped and waved for Clyde to come. "Do me a favor, this all I ask. When we're there, do not speak unless spoken to. Got it?"

Clyde nodded.

"And leave the beef you got with Dale at the door. I catch one moment of shit 'tween you two and you can find your own way home."

That ain't gonna be easy. He nodded.

Jay pulled away and Clyde took his last run to the dump, returning the truck to the lot. He went in to exchange keys and got in his truck and backed out and headed home.

Only Clyde was up and ready and waiting to leave for the WAC by five, even earlier than Jay had suggested. Only Clyde was as disciplined as Jay. An hour or more would pass before there was any sign of Dale or the others. When Clyde opened the trailer's door to the frigid morning air the house was dark.

Later in the day than Jay had wanted to leave (it was the women's fault) they finally pulled away from the house. Jay, Jan, and Tina sat up front in Jay's truck, with Clyde alone in the back, and Jimmy-Don, Dale, and Jay's sister Missy stuffed into the Bronco riding Jay's bumper. Clyde hoped they would give him a little more space than this on the long ride to Idaho. At the last turn, Dale yelled something, pointing. One of the Gap boys was walking through the Ridge, maybe even the one who'd given Dale the black eye. The boy had a big bag from Dunkin' Donuts in his hand and hugged the edge of the pavement with his head down. Jay inched closer to the roadside, finally jerking the wheel and going off the road entirely just before the boy, who ditched the bag and dove into the dirt. Jay yelled, "Dropped your breakfast, boy!" J.D. jerked his wheel to get the bag under his tire, smearing it fifty yards down the road.

"What an idiot!" Tina said, jumping in the seat in front. She hadn't said anything to Clyde since the pit. He wasn't sure he wanted her to, didn't know what he'd do if she did.

Leaving Liberty Ridge, he watched the boy get up and walk toward what was left of the bag, his arms hanging loose at his sides. The boy was maybe twelve or thirteen, and Clyde felt bad for him for a moment. But he shook it off. You can't be a warrior if you're oversensitive about every little thing. Warriors had to have hard hearts.

It was dusk when they entered the Bighorn National Forest campground and everyone was so tired they ate cold hot dogs and potato salad out of plastic containers passed around. They made a circle with folding chairs while Clyde and Dale separately gathered firewood in the very last light of the day. It was September and dark fell fast, bringing a painful high-altitude cold with it. The women were shivering under blankets.

Tina sipped at a bottle of peach Schnapps. "If anybody's getting sloppy drunk tonight," she said, "it gonna be me." She took a gulp and smacked her lips for effect.

With the fire burning well, the men started talking about the WAC. More than once Jimmy-Don mentioned "the ten percent solution."

Clyde had read about the ten percent solution in *The White Patriot*. There were a lot of people in the movement who believed that it would be possible to attain enough power politically through the proper channels for Idaho, Washington, Oregon, Montana, and Michigan to secede from the union and become a whites-only independent territory. It would have lots of resources, including ports, and beautiful land right next door to Canada, a sympathetic nation. They'd develop their own banking system, their own currency. Like-minded whites from the other states or Northern Europe would be welcome.

"I'd move there in a second," Dale said.

"Well, don't start packin, 'cause it ain't gonna happen," Jay said. "I take that back. In my lifetime. In the lifetime of my children and their children and probably their children it ain't never gonna happen. I think since the idea came up maybe five sympathetic people been elected to office up there?" Jay huffed. "I personally don't got the patience to wait two hundred years. Maybe if I was immortal."

"I thought you were," Jan said.

Clyde was beginning to understand the movement. Jay Smalls wasn't just some charismatic dreamer with big plans that may or may not ever see the light of day, he was part of a far-reaching assemblage of patriots working, one way or other, to preserve a culture that was under attack. Those in the movement were aware of the increasing tyranny of the U.S. government, overstepping its power with increasing impunity and turning America into an overtaxed police state that crushed any threat—real or perceived—under its iron heel. Some people were actively fighting it now. More often than not, these fighters were white, because, contrary to popular belief, white people were being targeted and oppressed on their own soil by their own government right here in the twenty-first century. The well-funded anti-gun lobby was aggressively targeting the Second Amendment and it was only a matter of time before a deal was struck with the devil. A couple dozen more toddlers gunned down would be all it took, especially if it was caught on video. The Patriot Act had weakened privacy laws, and thanks to Section 215, the NSA collects in a single year more phone calls, emails, and Web site visits of law-abiding American citizens than the Stasi collected during the entire Cold War.

"Over five million names of 'possible and suspected subversives and terrorists,'" Dale said, making air quotes, "currently in the United States are on the Cray supercomputer in Brussels, Belgium. Ranked according to threat."

"I bet we's near the top," Jay said, raising his hand high. "Osama bin Laden." He lowered the hand an inch. "Jay Smalls." He snickered.

The conversation went on and on. Habeas corpus was a historical footnote and most Americans didn't even know they no longer had the right to a fair trial; Obama had tried to take Clinton's "political socialism big-government trend" to a new level. It was a trend that would, Jay predicted, run for at least the next quarter century; "What we's dealing with today is just the goddamn beginning." Then there was, as Clyde already knew, the Jewish-controlled media, pumping the lie of multiculturalism into American households day and night. To explain even half of the ways that the American government has overextended its reach to touch almost every single citizen would have taken hours. This was the Zionist Occupational Government, "a cabal of Jews and niggers," as far as Jay was concerned, that made this once-great nation nothing but a puppet of Israel. The officials elected to office every four years were nothing but puppets of a different sort. With the hand of ZOG up their asses, they made speeches on TV and talked about change. As soon as the cameras were off, they went back to doing ZOG's bidding, and the average American idiot was none the wiser.

With the fire raging, Missy passed around fresh beers. Everyone but Tina and J.D. smoked and stared into the flames.

Jay said, "Woo!" and clapped his hands. "I cannot *wait* for tomorrow!"

Jimmy-Don said, "Me neither, Uncle Jay."

The fire shifted the shadows around Jay's face as he watched his family, making it hard to see where exactly his eyes had landed. "I'm tired of fucking *talking* about taking action."

Jan turned her head. Clyde thought she looked scared, an emotion he'd never seen on her before. The Smalls were not familiar with fear.

Jay said, "I been thinking either *way* too big or way too fuckin small."

"Here here," Jimmy-Don said. "The Smalls. Small hearts, small minds."

Tina said, "Small pee-pees," and fell over laughing.

Jay grinned. "Problem is it ain't so easy anymore to, say, walk up to the POTUS with a wheel gun."

"Tell that to Loughner," Dale said.

Jay huffed. "That's different. What'd it accomplish? Even if she'd died." Dale shrugged. "Unless we put a bullet in POTUS himself, assassinations ain't a big enough wake-up call. One dead congresswoman ain't gonna bring the government to its senses. And unless it's captured on video, it'd be a missed opportunity, photo-op wise."

"What about the Fed? We assassinate him, that'd get noticed."

"True enough, little brother. But say we did pull off something like that, it'd be a supermax or K.I.A." Jimmy-Don pointed at Dale, then Jay, then himself. "For you, you, me, and maybe a few others."

Clyde thought "K.I.A." meant "killed in action" and felt a tug in his belly.

"Hell, if we wanted to, we could get Jay Nixon a lot easier than Tim Geithner. Politicians is stupid, they ain't learned yet how risky it is to stand around in parking lots. I ain't saying that's what we oughta do. I'm just saying we could. Killing the governor's within the realm of what's possible, and that's the way we need to be thinking right now."

Clyde felt Jay's eyes on him. He tried his best not to show the growing alarm he felt upon hearing words like "assassination" and "supermax" batted around a campfire as casually as talk of beautiful women.

"We always have to ask ourselves," Jimmy-Don said. "What would it accomplish?"

"Yes, we do," Jay said.

"Every one of us sitting here is an unlawful enemy combatant, as far as the United States government is concerned, am I right? As stipulated in the

Military Commissions Act, a person who engages in hostilities or supports hostilities against the United States or," Jimmy-Don paused, raising a large finger. "Or, I tell you, *or* a person who before, on, or after the date of the enactment of the act, which is to say *anytime* in *all* of human *history*, am I right? Has been *determined* to be an unlawful enemy combatant, determined to be one, by the authority of the president or the secretary of defense. A broad canvas, I'm thinking. That Cray supercomputer, little brother, is like a Commodore 64 compared to what's on a single thumb drive at the NSA. And they've got something on you, me, Jay, Jan, and probably even little Tina Smalls."

"What about me?" Clyde said, forgetting that Jay had told him to speak only if spoken to.

"Oh, Clyde Twitty, how you tickle me. I wish I had your innocence. If I had your wonderful innocence, Clyde, I would grease it up and fuck it raw against a fence."

"Jimmy," Jan said.

"Sorry, Aunt Jan!"

Dale said something and Clyde said, "What?"

"I said you oughta already know this shit."

Clyde stared at Dale and Jay said, "What I tell you?"

"Osu," Clyde said quietly. He finished his cigarette and let it drop, resisting the urge to flick it at Dale's face. The men returned their attention to the fire.

Jimmy-Don said, "I for one, call me crazy and stick a pin in my eye, but I for one, Uncle Jay, would rather not pursue a plan whose natural and obvious outcome is death or incarceration unless that plan is seen, later, after the fact, I'm saying, upon further reflection and in the cold backward glance of history, as advancing our cause in a big, big way. And by 'big,' Uncle Jay, I mean of truly exceptional size and stature. Bigger than what Tim accomplished."

Jan said, "We've had lots of shit-brained ideas that didn't make a whole lot of goddamn sense if you stopped to think about it." Clyde hadn't known she was listening, but of course she was. "How can you even know what something accomplishes, you know?" Jan said. "In the long run."

Jay said, "True enough, mama." He pushed out of his chair and walked down to the edge of the lake unzipping his pants. "True enough." He pissed into the water. "Half these idgits got no idea what the world's come to they're so fuckin wrapped up in their own day-to-day shit. The ones who *do* know is worse. They know and don't fuckin care!" Jay yelled across the lake, "Wake up, white man!" Clyde heard the call cross the lake and repeat. *Wake up, white man!* Jay snickered and zipped. *Wake up, white man!*

Back at the fire Jay lit a cigarette. Once or twice J.D. or Dale or Jay would start to speak and stop. Clyde wondered what was wrong with him that his own mind wasn't racing with ideas about how do we help the movement? Maybe he just needed more time. Jay had said once, a while back, that there was a steep learning curve to this life.

Jimmy-Don said, "It's going to take harsh, decisive action, not just assassinating one governor, to kick-start the kind of race war that becomes a brush fire, Uncle Jay, know what I mean? Civil war does not come easy, otherwise we would have had more than one by now. Don't get me wrong. I think we're close. Closer every four years, but the average Joe's gonna need some motivation."

"J.D., Dale," Jay said, waving them and Clyde to draw closer. They circled the fire with their chairs and the four of them sat, apart from the others. "We can't get to the White House."

"No," Jimmy-Don said.

"We can't get to the House of Representatives, the Senate."

"No, we cannot," Jimmy-Don said. "Though we could, I imagine—and why don't you imagine with me?—get to some congressmen and senators, pick 'em off one by one, two by two, Noah's Ark style, but I doubt we could get to the actual chambers of which you speak, to the, what the kids would call bricks-and-mortar establishments, no, we can't get within spitting distance of their learned foundations."

Missy said, "Jimmy, half of what comes out of your mouth is fuckin gibberish, you know that?"

"Ooga booga," Jimmy-Don said. Missy dismissed him with a wave.

Jay's eyes were pinned to the fire. He chewed a thumbnail and shrugged. "I don't know what the answer is yet. I'm just dreaming." He raised his head and held up a finger. "I tell you this, though." His voice dropped. "I think it's time to move in with y'all for a while. Lick Skillet's a better base of operations than Liberty Ridge."

Jimmy-Don clapped his hands once, sitting back in his chair. "Whatever you need, Uncle Jay."

Dale poked his chin in Clyde's direction. "Him too?"

Clyde wanted to get up and kick Dale in the face, break the nose, bloody the mouth, knock out some teeth.

"You heard your brother," Jay said. "Clyde's the only one of us whose name don't set off the NSA computers, for one. Think about it, dummy." Clyde felt good being singled out by Jay. "Far as ZOG's concerned, Clyde Twitty don't even exist. If you pulled your head out of your ass for a second you'd see what kind of advantage that gives us."

Clyde thought back to one night after supper not long ago when Tina had searched the Internet for "Clyde Twitty" and found nothing but a few hits about some guy in Arkansas. There'd been nothing at all about Clyde Eugene Twitty from Strasburg, MO. Jay had been in the room then, eyes on the TV, but he'd been paying closer attention than Clyde had thought.

Jay moved his chair so it was facing Clyde. "Trust me, Clyde?"

Clyde nodded. Despite everything, he did. His rage at everyone else had focused and fell mostly now onto one person: Dale. Clyde couldn't stay mad at his teacher. Teacher knows best, even if it hurts.

Jay turned to Dale. "He trusts Sensei. More than I can say for you."

"That ain't true," Dale said.

"Then fucking act like it."

Dale eyeballed Clyde in such a way that Clyde inched up out of his chair. His forearms flexed, he clenched his teeth, he felt like an animal and it felt good.

Jay laid a hand on his forearm. "You two gonna have to git along, god-damn it. Leave. Your shit. At the door."

Clyde nodded. He wasn't happy about it but he knew he had to obey.

Dale said, "You ever asked Clyde if he actually wants to be involved? I'm not just saying this just 'cause I don't trust him."

"You got balls not trusting *me*," Clyde said.

"What I tell you?" Jay said, looking right at Clyde. "I don't have to ask Clyde," Jay said to Dale. "And you don't fuckin lecture me, neither. But just to humor you, Clyde-san, let's see here: last year the three of us broke from WAR, a national group, White Aryan Resistance, 'cause of politics and endless chitchat. Since you become uchi deshi, I've been considering you for membership in our new thing, which is just us, the four of us." Jay flicked a finger at J.D. and Dale and Clyde and his own chest. "We don't need no goddamn overseers. No fuckin national support. Unlike everybody else, we ain't gonna wait around for the revolution to come to us, we gonna bring it to them, on our own terms, not on their terms. You may not have known this was what it meant to be uchi deshi, but unlike my nephew, I have faith that you ain't gonna run for the hills now that you do know. United States government don't give two shits about you, Clyde Twitty, think about it. The way they've treated you, your dad. All they care about's the banks and the bankers, and the banks don't give two shits about you either, in case you ain't figured that out yet. Where's the fuckin mortgage payment at, that's all they care about. To take the second piece of property your family has ever owned would get some banker a fuckin bonus. And I think you's starting to figure that out. Which is why, Clyde-san, I came down on you like I did after what happened down on Troost." Jay looked at Dale and Clyde saw Dale lower his eyes and felt good that he at least had some shred of guilt over what he'd done. "That test wasn't just for shits and giggles, it was to see if you was ready." Jay stared at him a moment, breathing out his nose loud enough to hear. "You weren't. Now we know." Jay leaned back, spat, and held his arm up, his finger pointing at the road they'd come in on. "There the hills. If you wanna run, run."

Clyde wasn't sure what he should do. A part of him did want to run, to just get the hell out while he still could—*if* he still could—and return to his old life. But whatever part of him wanted to run lost to the stronger part of him that told his ass to stay in that chair. But it wasn't fear that kept Clyde in the chair, it was the realization that his old life had been a lie, a lie told to him by his own government. From the White House to the city council, like the bankers they'd bailed out, they were all actively working against the interests of people like Clyde Twitty. He felt ashamed that it had taken him this long to see the truth.

"I'm not a superstitious person," Jay said. "But I like to think that Clyde left his wallet in that Firebird for a reason."

"Y'all about done over there?" Jan said across the fire. Jay ignored her. She didn't ask again. Clyde remembered Jay saying, "Be with women, but don't let them rule the roost." Jan seemed content to be subservient to a man as powerful as Jay.

"What I tell you? His brain done blew a fuse." Dale made a fuzzy farting noise.

"No," Jay said, studying Clyde's face. "Ain't what you think it is, Dale. We just witnessed the resurrection of Clyde Eugene Twitty. Welcome to consciousness." Jay clapped Clyde on the back. It was the first time they'd touched without pain since the robbery. "You ain't out of the woods yet, Clyde-san. Gotta get outta probation, clear a few more hurdles 'fore you're all official."

"Osu," Clyde said.

"All right," Jay said, casting a glance at the women across the fire. "For now, this shit stays between us. No pussies allowed."

That night, when Clyde was sleeping, Tina unzipped the tent and climbed into his sleeping bag. He woke and rolled away but she pressed into his back and wrapped her cold hands and feet around him. She was shivering. Clyde turned to face her and rubbed his hands on her until her teeth stopped chattering. Neither of them said anything and then Tina slipped out of her clothes and dragged the sleeping bag with her to the dock. Clyde ran after her. She left the sleeping bag on the wood and slipped into the water like a seal, breaking the reflection of the half moon.

Tina was a natural in the water; she swam ahead and stopped where the lake was deep. Clyde reached her and they dog-paddled facing each other. She cupped water into his face and he splashed her back. She said, "Shhhh," and swam to the black shape of a floating dock farther out. She used the ladder getting out but Clyde didn't; he wanted to show off his upper-body strength. Then he did eighty push-ups on the dock, creating a rhythmic slap-slap-slap of water that made Tina giggle. "They're gonna think we're porking." She started shivering again and he lay on top of her. "Let's just stay like this," she said.

"Just one more set," Clyde said, and pumped out forty more right on top of Tina, touching his chest to hers with each one. His triceps felt warm and tight when he finished and he let most of his weight settle onto Tina. He breathed into her hair. In the moonlight her skin looked bronzed, like a statue in a town square. Softly Tina said, "I do feel bad, you know, buddy?"

"About what?" Clyde said, even though he knew what she meant and didn't want to think back through that night or the days since.

"That I didn't stand up for you." She looked into Clyde's eyes. The darkness made it easier. "I don't got any experience at being a good girlfriend."

The water lapped at the dock and a woman laughed somewhere across the lake. *"You ridiculous fuckwit,"* she said. Clyde looked into the blackness.

Tina said, "I treated you really bad and I'm really sorry. I'm actually, uh, ashamed of the way I treated you. I'm a bad person."

Clyde wanted to say, You're right, but he didn't because Tina was crying. She lifted her head and kissed him and lay back on the dock, turned away. Tears ran across her temples. "That was," Clyde said, thinking.

"Shitty," Tina said, and a bubble formed and burst in her mouth. She shut her eyes and tears darkened her eyelashes. "I know, I'm sorry."

"The last couple weeks," Clyde said, shaking his head. They'd been the worst of his life.

Tina squeezed him with her legs and arms and repeated "I'm sorry" about ten times in his ear. Clyde got tired of hearing it, told her it was all right, settle down. Her teeth started clacking and her whole face was slick, shiny. "I love you," she said, her jaw quivering. Tears shook in the small pools of her skull. Neither of them had said that word before and Clyde resisted saying it back without thinking it through.

For the first time in a while, Clyde felt good. He was in the back of Jay's truck, on his way to the WAC, the wind in his ears, Tina's head in his lap like a puppy dog's. When they reached the Aryan Nations compound in Hayden, Idaho, mid-afternoon, he was surprised to see all the armed guards, in dress shirts and ties, patrolling the fence. Tina and Jan went to set up shop and Jay took Clyde to find somebody in charge who was over the age of sixteen; there were plenty of pale, skinny A.N. teenagers in tan button-downs, up on the tower and wandering around with clipboards, but Jay said he didn't think any of them looked like they knew the big picture. They were low-level infantry, foot soldiers. Finally he procured a hand-drawn map of the grounds that showed him where his demonstration would be held. On the way to it, they passed the Klan's official table. They were selling White Power T-shirts. Jay bought four.

Clyde had never seen anything like the WAC. Rows of booths set up for people to give demonstrations, hold court, or sell everything from turkey calls to handguns to Hitler wall clocks. Clyde passed a woman draped in a Nazi flag. Kids ran around with temporary tattoos of swastikas and lightning bolts on their cheeks. Two fat girls, probably a little younger than Tina, were wearing "runner nigger" Obama shirts, gun targets with the generic black profile usually in the crosshairs replaced by Obama. Fathers carried young kids on their shoulders and more than one woman walking around was pregnant; talk was, there might be a WAC baby this year. The armed guards and a lot of other men were hard and rough-looking, most of them ex-cons, J.D. said, men that Clyde feared in his gut, no matter how much he trained. There were a lot of families at the Congress this time, and Clyde heard people commenting on how good it was to see this sort of turnout. The movement was the strongest it had been in years. There were a few newspaper reporters and they didn't try to hide.

Jay was in heaven. He got into his White Power shirt and said when they got home he was wearing it to work. If the blacks at the next site can go around with Black Power on their chests, Jay could do the same. It was reverse discrimination, a goddamned double standard. "No," Jay said, correcting himself as they walked, "it's actually *worse* than a double standard, Clyde, 'cause when a nigger goes 'round in his Black Power T-shirt, it don't just mean 'Black Power.' It means 'Black Power, motherfucker!' " Black Power, Jay explained, was a threat, whereas White Power was just a reminder.

By the look of it, Jay's demonstration had more attendants than any of the other events. He talked from the stage, making people laugh and cheer and move their limbs, echoing his techniques. Dale helped him and Clyde watched from the sidelines, fighting jealousy. Dale wasn't even doing a good job. He wasn't focused, Clyde could see; he was easily distracted, waving at girls and making an ass of himself.

About forty-five minutes in Dale grabbed Jay's shirt to show a common start to many conflicts, and Jay overdid the technique, wringing a loud *pop* out of the arm. Dale went down groaning and Missy ran off for ice and Clyde wondered if Jay had done it on purpose. There was only fifteen minutes left and everyone stood around waiting for the verdict while Jay inspected Dale's arm. Dale had ruined the whole thing. This would be all that people remembered of the seminar. Then Jay announced that it was just a strain and people applauded. Jay looked for Clyde and said, "You ready, uchi deshi?" Damn right.

Even better than being called to help, Clyde learned some grappling techniques they'd never done in class. Some of it hurt; a choking move cracked his neck, threading a sliver of pain through his head that wouldn't go away until he was back in Missouri. But he was excited to learn such practical techniques. When time was up, Jay pointed in the direction of the watchtower, dark and flat against the late afternoon sky, its two long crimson and black swastika banners nearly lost in the dusk. Jay said, "Be sure to pick up a jar of Smalls Big Flavor Sauce at booth forty-three. It's homemade and, like its maker, packs a hell of a kick." Jay threw a front-snap kick and a dozen men stayed behind for one-on-one instruction. A man as big as Jimmy-Don went to one knee when Jay took hold of nothing but a finger.

A line fanned out from booth 43; the sauce was really moving.

Tina yelled, "Jay Smalls's Big Flavor Smoke Sauce, ladies and gentlemen, all the way from Missouruh! Add some power to your white! Add some kick to your lick!"

"Goddamn entrepreneur, ain't she?" Missy said.

"When we get back I'm seriously gonna look into retail," Tina said. "If I could get this into Walmart?"

"Fuck an A right," Missy said.

"Fuck a B, it's got more holes," Tina said, slapping her thigh.

"Tina!" Jan said, trying not to laugh.

"Sorry, Mom. Aunt Missy started it."

Jimmy-Don showed up to take Dale off to meet somebody, and Jay manned the stand so the women could take a breather.

A half wall behind the guy the next booth over held prints of outdoor scenes and a banner that read *Hitler the Artist*. "Adolf Hitler was more than just a great dictator," he yelled out. "Get to know the Hitler the establishment doesn't want you to know."

Clyde manned the sauce so Jay could take a look. "Jay Smalls," he said, shaking the man's hand. "Barbeque sauce and, uh, self-defense."

"Frank Sheehan," the man said.

"Ol' Adolf wasn't half bad," Jay said.

"Though he was never able to go to art school," Frank said. "He was following the artistic path before the war. Few people know that of course, with the Jews controlling the media and the publishing industry. But he lived in Vienna from 1909 to 1914 and painted over a thousand paintings there."

"No shit?" Jay said, thumbing through the smaller prints in a cardboard box on the table. He held up the occasional picture for Clyde.

"Lot of people are pretty surprised by that. 'When'd he have time to sleep?'" Frank chuckled.

"Paint a picture a day, in three years you got a thousand," Jay said. Numbers didn't impress Jay. He pulled a print.

"That one's Vienna. Those are ten dollars each. They make a good and, I reckon, fairly unique Christmas gift."

To be neighborly, Jay purchased two prints off Frank Sheehan. Reconciling with Tina made Clyde want to do something nice for her, so he bought one of Hitler's dog paintings. She came back with a half-eaten funnel cake and Clyde took her off to the side to give her the print. "Aww," Tina said, and she kissed him, white powder exploding across his cheek.

The Lone Wolf seminar wasn't officially taking place. On the other side of a rusted barbed-wire fence, in a sloping field patrolled by armed guards, a group of about thirty men had gathered in the failing light, and Clyde, Jay, Jimmy-Don, and Dale were among the last in. When one of the men standing beside a stack of hay bales forming a makeshift podium saw Jay he nodded. "Glad you could make it," he said.

"Buggy," Jay said.

Buggy was small, bald, and constantly fingered the beaded strands of his goatee. From the end of one long, thin hand hung a Big Chief pad. A man next to him—Ski—spat into the grass. He'd either shaved the top of his moustache or it didn't grow there, but around the sides of his wet mouth it grew dark and ratty. "There some faces I don't recognize, all right?" Ski said, walking among them and grabbing one man's shirt. "Anybody know this asshole?" The guy covered up and someone vouched for him. Ski marched over to the guy who'd done the vouching. "I don't know you either, fucker." He slapped the ball cap off his head and the guy shot up and punched Ski in the face twice with the same hand.

A grin pinched Ski's muscular face and somebody he trusted yelled that the guy was all right. Their hands went down, Ski walked backward to where Buggy was, his nose was bleeding, he didn't even bother to wipe it. "Always fuckin undercover pigs here," Ski said. "ZOG watching our every move. Anybody else hops that fence I don't see, speak up 'cause chances are they're a pig."

Jay leaned over to Clyde and whispered, "I wish Ski lived in Missouri. Hell of an asset, boy."

Ski sat on a hay bale and Buggy consulted his Big Chief pad, said something to an enormous man heaped in the grass, sweaty, swollen bands of skin drooping from his knees, triceps, chin. Except for ovals of pink flesh around his eyes, his face was a tattooed green-black mask. "All right, listen up," Buggy said. "Found this on the Internet and I think it'll be useful. Ten rules for dealing with the police."

"Make sure your gun's bigger than theirs," someone said.

Buggy grinned, nodded, and said, "Which brings me to number one. Don't talk. I cannot stress how important this rule is. If all anybody remembers today is rule number one—don't talk—you will be in better shape than ninety-nine percent of the idiots out there. Don't try to convince the police of your 'innocence.' Every one of you is innocent, not a one of you sodomites deserves arrest or incarceration, I get it, I've heard all your sob stories. 'I'm innocent' is all the police ever hear and they're fucking tired of hearing it. A cop doesn't give a crap if you're innocent and couldn't do anything about it at this point in your arrest if the bastard wanted to. Any time you speak to the police you say something that makes your situation *worse*. There will be time to talk later, to somebody that fucking matters, and it won't be a cop." Buggy consulted his pad and sped through the next three—don't run, don't resist arrest, and don't believe the police. "The po-lice," he said, "are trained to lie to you in order to get you to admit what you fucking did. They'll separate you from your buddy and say, 'Hey shithead, your pal just told us it was you that planned that whole thing.' Your buddy, drunk and not too bright to begin with, let's face it, rats you out and the police have what they came for. Easy as candy from a gork. 'It'll be easier if you talk to us now,' they might say. It's B.S.! Don't believe it. It'll only make it easier for them to prove their case against you later."

Don't let the police search your house, car, or person; don't look at the exact thing you don't want them to search; and don't talk shit were Buggy's next three rules, and a groan went up. "I don't care if you've been wrongly arrested and the true culprit is standing right in front of you fucking your wife in her cherry ass. Don't talk shit! Police have a lot of say in the charges against you. They can change a misdemeanor to a felony. Just don't do it. Eight: If the police come to your home, do not let them in and do not, *do not* step outside your abode. If they are confident that you've committed a felony, you can be damn sure they're coming in, because they don't need an arrest warrant if they got probable cause. Make it very clear to them. 'No, you may not come in. You need a warrant to enter my home.' Nine, we're almost done, then we can get on to lone-wolf tactics. Say you're arrested *outside* your home. You're in the front yard, working on your truck. This one fucks many people up. Do not accept," Buggy made air-quotes, " 'offers' to go inside your home. The kind officer may say, 'Wanna freshen up, talk to your ol' lady?' Then they'll graciously escort you in and, guess what? Once inside they can search. Same goes for your car. The cops are lying to you. They don't give a fuck."

Clyde wished he'd brought something to write with; this was all new to him.

"The best bet is to not say a fucking word," Buggy said. "Pretend you've just swallowed a donkey dong. It's incredible how many people think they can convince a cop that they're not guilty. Your case is not decided by cops, dick-heads. Wait to speak to your lawyer! All right, you shit-for-brain losers, follow these ten easy rules and many of your rights, such as they are, will remain intact. I don't care how nervous, scared, drunk, high, or whatever the fuck you are, follow the rules. Commit them to memory." Buggy nodded and dropped the pad on the ground and sat down.

It was Ski's turn.

He paced the grass, popping knuckles and rolling his head on his neck like a fighter. Clyde wondered how many years he'd have to train before he lost the fear of guys like Ski. "Most people are pathetic faggots," Ski said, holding up six stubby fingers. He whined, "I want a new car. I like my job. I love my ugly wife. What will my queer neighbors think? Bull. Shit. None of it means anything, all right?" He pinched the skin on his arm and said, "This is the only thing that means anything. You think you're the majority, white man? Think again, all right? We are fucking losing. The niggers, the Jews, the faggots, the nigger-loving traitors, the apologists, the goddamn illegals, and the fucking suicidal sand niggers are winning this war. Our movement might be enjoying bigger numbers than ever, but it is still stalled like a rice burner on the side of the road. Nobody's willing to commit. Sacrifice. If you're not willing to give yourself one hundred percent to the cause of the white man then get up off your lazy ass and get the fuck out of this field right now!" Ski threw his arm at the fence.

Clyde held his breath. Nobody moved. In a silly voice, Jimmy-Don whispered, "Scaaa-wee," and Clyde worked very hard not to smile.

"Six points for the lone wolf," Ski said. "One. Act alone, and I do mean *alone*. There's no goddamn need for a 'cell,' all right? What two know, one can tell." Hearing Ski say the same thing that both Jay and Dale had said made Clyde flinch. It was a big thing with the movement, and he realized that there was more communication going on between people than he'd thought. "Don't let *anyone* in on what you've done or what you are planning to do. Don't tell your wife, your buddies, your priest, *no one*. And be careful what you write down. Dear diary, today I burned down the mosque over at 35 Towel Head Lane." He shook his head. "Remove yourself as much as possible from human proximity and contact so that no one will be able to notice anything about you. *Any*thing." He paced the trampled grass, unfolding another finger. "Do not rob banks. Or Pizza Huts or Circle Ks to obtain funds for your activities. The kind of thing you will most likely want to do is not expensive and you can, here's an idea, get a job, preferably one that's seasonal and flexible so you can engage in your revolutionary acts rather than punch Uncle Sam's clock. Cutting trees, driving trucks, flippin patties, cleaning shitters, whatever the fuck. All right? And keep collateral illegality to a minimum, like stealing license plates or, if you must, vehicles, though I don't recommend it and I'll tell you why: every illegal act you commit is another piece of the puzzle they are assembling right now about your clueless white ass. You might end up wiping out the entire liberal elite of your community but get pulled over for driving a car with stolen plates. Well done. Make sure all vehicles you drive are legal and in good running condition, with inspection and registration and tags and all that shit up to date. Check your lights, check your lights, check your lights. Do not let a goddamn burned-out taillight be your undoing. And don't speed, run lights, or adorn your bumper. *I love Aryan Nations! Jews suck!* The white warrior's worst fear is the routine traffic stop. Just ask the Kehoe brothers. Oh, wait, you can't. Executed by the state."

Ski looked down and kept quiet long enough that Clyde thought he was finished. Then he unfolded another finger. "When you act, act *silently*. Don't send letters or make phone calls to Fox News. If you communicate publicly, your communication is a link between your dumb ass and the thought police. They'll digitize it, analyze it, dissect every aspect of it and from that they will find you. They will. You're not smart enough," he said. "None of you motherfuckers is smart enough to beat their taxpayer-funded technology. Your only hope of evasion lies in giving them as little to work with as you possibly can. And you know what's really little? Nothing! Nein. And think about this. Think about the psychological impact of silent action, action without fanfare, quiet, deadly, unexpected, and best of all, unexplained. You don't have to explain that you're a foot soldier of the white resistance. Believe me, they'll know." He unfolded another finger and laid his hand on the fat man's head. "Do not deface your body with tattoos. Joseph Paul Franklin was nailed by a nurse who remembered his ink. Placing a permanent identifying mark on your body, especially your face, is about the most nigger-brained thing a young white man or woman can do." The fat man grinned and Clyde looked over at Dale and J.D. Their arms were practically covered. Jay's were bare. "If you already got one, get yourself a second job so you can get it lasered off." Ski swiveled the fat man's head, shaking it "no." "This is only meant for those of you who are considering the life actions of a lone wolf, unlike Pork Chop here."

"I'm too fat to be a lone wolf," he said.

"The one thing our society can never forgive is direct resistance to the iron heel," Ski said. "They don't mind us sending nasty little leaflets to each other every so often, but we all know they keep an eye on us, all right? And any time it even looks like we might be getting together to form some sort of effective resistance, action is taken, believe you me." He raised a finger. "An actual federal agent told me that, all right? If you strike a blow that causes genuine damage to the real enemy they'll never, ever stop hunting you. Eric Rudolph. Five years, all right? And that was just a stupid abortion clinic. They can't afford to let anyone get away with actually hitting them where it fucking hurts. The other peasants might start to get ideas, all right? Ask Sam Bowers or Byron De La Beckwith or some of those other fucks they're dragging off to torture to death. Ask that poor motherfucker Walter Moody, whose ass they framed for sending package bombs in 1990 to that judge in Alabama and that NAACP nigger, all right? Moody was victimized because the feds couldn't afford to let such a bold blow be seen to go unpunished. I personally think the real bomber is still out there and was smart enough, unusual I know, to knock that shit off once he realized the fucking feds had handed him a get-out-of-jail-free card."

Ski made his hand into a gun and pretended to shoot every single man in the field, one by one, making *puhh* sounds. Some men laughed; one fell over. But as Ski kept it up, the men turned serious, defiant. When Jay's shot came, he shook his head as if to say, "I'd never give you the chance." When Ski finished, he said, "In our society, at present, to seriously resist is an act of suicide. You have to accept this in your own mind. You are all expendable." He touched a finger to his temple. "Before you begin this life, you must accept that you are committing suicide as effectively as if you put a bullet in your skull right here in this field. A lot of us hold on to this idea that it's possible to *dabble* in racial politics. This freelancer's approach is behind most of our goddamn problems, all right? Direct, active resistance is not a Hollywood movie. Once you begin active resistance, you won't be able to say, 'Let's take a time out.' All right? It sucks that I even have to say this, but that's life today. All the real men are fucking dead and buried. Whatever you do, don't grovel. Take a cue from Timothy McVeigh. I would much prefer that you spend the rest of your miserable life sitting in front of the shitbox swilling beer than attempt something radical, get your dumb ass caught, and grovel to the media in a hopeless bid for mercy that you will not actually receive. All right? I of all people know how difficult it is to get Generation JewTube to think about anything beyond their own fucking shallow lives. I would rather no white man ever raised his hand in resistance than to go through another one of these disgusting spectacles. If our race is going to die, all right, at least let it die with dignity!"

Jay raised a fist and yelled, "Dignity!"

Clyde raised his and yelled the same.

Everyone in the field came to their feet shouting, "Dignity! Dignity!" and Clyde shouted right along with them, pumping his fist. It was full dark now; the sky directly overhead was thick with stars, clusters and clouds of them, chunky and powdery and smeared across the blackness. Down on earth, the men were fired up, committed to the cause. You had to admire that. Most people never got excited about anything. And very few were willing to commit the way these men had, with their whole beings, no matter what. Clyde could see that these men looked at him and thought he was one of them, a man committed. Here stood, they thought, another white warrior ready to lay down his life in the fight for his race.

ost of the men left the field, hopped the fence, and disappeared among the tables and stands in the grounds. A few stayed behind, smoking and talking. Clyde hung back as Jay and J.D. huddled with some of the men. Dale walked a slow circle around them, rolling a stinky smoke. Clyde's phone buzzed. He answered, walking uphill to a wooden post circled with barbed wire. "Hi, Mom."

"Clyde?"

"Uh, yeah. You called me."

"Is this Clyde?"

"Yes, Mom. It's me, Clyde."

"Am I bothering you?"

Clyde took a breath. "Well, I can't really talk right now. Everything all right?"

"They need me half an hour earlier tomorrow at the Omega. That's why I'm calling."

Shit. Clyde watched Jay and J.D. and the men. Their heads were only inches apart.

"Clyde?"

"Yeah. That might be . . . tough."

"Rough?"

"Tough. Hard."

"Oh. Why? Jay won't let you out of class thirty minutes early?"

"I'm in Idaho."

"You're in what?"

"I'm in Idaho. Right now, I'm in Idaho. The state."

"You're in Idaho."

"Yeah. Yes."

"You moved to Idaho?"

"No, we came up yesterday. For a karate seminar."

"Oh."

"It's sort of a big deal. To get to come to this. At the level I'm at."

Jay and the others were shaking hands and parting. Dale moved in and shook some hands. Clyde wanted to be in there too, and he saw Jay looking around for him. "I gotta go, Mom."

"Who's gonna drive me to work tomorrow?"

Clyde started down the field toward Jay and the others. "It's only four miles, mom. You could walk it in an hour."

"*Walk* to the Omega!?"

"Be good for you. I'll call you later." Clyde snapped his phone shut and said, "Sorry," to Jay.

"FBI?" a man Clyde didn't know said.

"My mom," Clyde said, and everyone nodded knowingly.

The next morning Clyde went with Jay and Jan to hear Eric Zweibe speak at the A.N. church on the grounds. Jay had told Clyde about Zweibe's show on Storm Front Radio. The show was boring as hell, but Zweibe made important points, Jay said. Behind the pulpit he went on in the same nasal monotone and Clyde watched the heads bob. Clyde had expected some fire up there, some real hatred, like in those old videos of Hitler holding his rallies. With boring men like this in charge, no wonder the movement was stalled. When Zweibe finished, Jay made a snoring sound and said, "Nothing we don't already know."

Afterwards, Zweibe invited everyone to the annex for coffee. When they entered the hangar-like building, Zweibe pointed out two enormous new paintings, a gift from a young member of the congregation. He said they formed a diptych and Jan laughed. In one: a triumphant blonde boy holding a sword above a sea of slaughtered Negroes, Jews, homosexuals, and Mexicans. In the other: a pubescent girl, her long golden sword stuck in the ground between her legs; from her outstretched hands dangled the severed heads of a Negro and a Jew.

Jan and Dale started up a ping-pong game in a corner. Jay introduced Clyde as "my uchi deshi" and looked around for Tina; she was at a

Ms. Pac-Man machine, jerking her arm and cursing. Zweibe took Clyde's hand. The handshake was limp, not what Clyde had expected.

"Welcome to the patriot movement," Zweibe said.

"Thanks."

"What do you think of all this?"

"It's pretty interesting," Clyde said.

"It's a lot to think about," Zweibe said. "And the more you dig, the deeper the hole gets."

Zweibe wanted to know what was happening with the movement in Missouri. He'd heard that the Smalls had broken with WAR. From the ping-pong table, Dale said, "War my ass," and slapped the ball over Jan's head.

"We got something big in the works," Jay said, winking. "I'm not sure you'll be seeing us next time."

Jay wanted to get on the road to miss traffic, but Tina had discovered her new favorite band, the Racist Redneck Rebels, so everyone watched a set. They were funny as hell, and finished with a song called "Dropping the Kids Off in Harlem" that made Tina practically piss herself.

The singer was wearing a T-shirt with a big tombstone on it that read *The United States of America. Born 1776. Died 2008. Cause of death: suicide.* The guitar player's T-shirt had a sniper's rifle and said, *Vote from the rooftops.* During their break, Jay and Dale went after those shirts and Jimmy-Don put his arm around Clyde and walked him with great purpose to a crowded table where a man was reading from a book.

Posters on easels held blowups of *The Turner Diaries* and *Hunter,* Andrew MacDonald's follow-up. A sign hung on that one said, *Inspired John Allen Muhammad and Lee Boyd Malvo's actions in D.C.!* A third easel held up a large black-and-white photo of an old man. *William Luther Pierce,* it read. J.D. nudged Clyde and said, "Pierce is the actual author, Clyde. Former head of the National Alliance. He's dead now. R.I.P. Andrew MacDonald is just a pseudonymenem."

The man at the table said, "I want to read this bit near the end. It's . . . I think Pierce wraps up his whole point right here far better than I could do just talking. Let's see here, uh, this is, yeah, page 218."

Clyde slipped Jimmy-Don's copy out of his back pocket.

"No," the man read, and Clyde found the page. "Talk of quote-unquote innocents has no meaning. We must look at our situation collectively, in a race-wide sense. We must understand that our race is like a cancer patient undergoing drastic surgery in order to save his life. There is no sense in asking whether the tissue being cut out now is quote-unquote innocent or not."

As the man continued to read Clyde looked at the margins, at all the notes he'd never read. Near the bottom, J.D. had written in letters so bold they'd torn through the pulp: *THE TRUTH!!!* The man went on, reaching the paragraph that J.D. had indicated. "The fact is that we are all responsible, as individuals, for the morals and the behavior of our race as a whole. There is no evading that responsibility, in the long run, any more for the members of our own race than for those of other races, and each of us individually must be prepared to be called to account for that responsibility at any time. In these days many are being called."

The man stopped reading and everyone broke into applause. Clyde put the book under his arm so he could clap.

"Many," Jimmy-Don said, walking Clyde away. "Many are being called. Many are being called, put that in your peace pipe and smoke it, Clyde Twitty, fatherless son of America."

Much of the ride back, Clyde thought about the WAC. He'd never given much thought to his government before. Upon turning eighteen, he hadn't registered to vote because he'd never believed all that "one vote counts" bullshit. Look at fucking W. Votes didn't count for shit in that election; the Supreme Court put him in office, grossly overstepping their reach, something Jay had said proves the New World Order is alive and well; ZOG was not about to put an anti-petroleum activist upon the throne. So much of what Clyde was learning about the way the government *really* operates—and the shadow government—made sense to him now. Why was this knowledge in the hands of so few? Why wasn't this on the nightly news? The answer: Because it took courage to speak the truth; it was much easier to live in denial. If you actually accepted the state of the world today, you'd probably just kill yourself. Clyde thought about how training was to stand before a mirror that saw beneath the surface. Not many people are strong enough to handle what that mirror reflects. Or to do something decisive with what they see.

Behold a Pale Horse had said that it was inconceivable that people with power and wealth would *not* band together with a common interest and a grand plan to direct the future of the world. Unless we can wake the people from their sleep, the book said, it will take civil war to change things. That's what Jay and J.D. hoped to start. The book said that we've been taught lies; a New World Order is beating down the door. No surprise that the writer of that book was murdered by police in Arizona. The overwhelming majority of the most wealthy and powerful men were Jews, not just in America but the world over, and anyone who has actually read *The Protocols of the Elders of Zion* will know the long-standing plan behind their ascent to power. The state of the world today is no accident. It's by design.

Many are being called, the book said. Clyde was being called, he saw now that the call had really begun with the loss of the Longarm job. He'd just been too ignorant then to hear it.

Failing that test had set him back badly, and the realization of this, so slow to sink in, only added to Clyde's growing anger. Jay was *considering* him, this whole time he was only considering him. Clyde's involvement had never been sure, never, every single step he'd taken, since day one, had been watched, judged, his successes weighed against his fuckups. After experiencing the WAC, Jay's perspective made more sense. Clyde couldn't fault the man for his strong reaction. It wasn't about whose fault was the failure. Even if Dale had acted badly, assigning blame was the work of ZOG. If Jay was planning to take revolutionary action of some sort, they had to be a hundred and fifty percent sure of Clyde's character and commitment. This new perspective made Clyde disappointed in himself for the way he'd let things go down on Troost. He knew he could waste a lot of time hating Dale, plotting revenge, looking for an opening, or he could stand before Jay's harsh mirror and accept what he saw reflected back. He thought, he hoped, that he was man enough now to do that.

It must have been somewhere in Nebraska that he got the idea to do something big, something bold, something that would prove to Jay that Clyde Twitty, uchi deshi, was ready to be called.

T hey got back to Liberty Ridge late and everyone went right to bed. Tina slept in the house, as she had since the robbery. She wanted Clyde to spend the night in her bed but Jay hadn't extended the offer so Clyde stayed outside. It was better that way for more reasons than one; he could hardly concentrate, and sleep was a long time coming. Half the night he lay in the trailer with the door open to the cold air. The WAC had set his thoughts to overdrive. He felt like the first twenty years of his life had been a waste. He looked back with regret at the willful ignorance, the selfish goals, the naïveté of buying into the American Dream. Now that he'd decided to take action, it couldn't come fast enough.

Work was torture the next day, every minute dragging on. When Jay got in his truck after five he said, "You're welcome in class tonight, Clyde-san."

Clyde flushed with relief and shouted, "Osu!" He returned the dump truck to the lot, got into his own, and pulled out in the direction of Kansas City.

Driving the route that he'd run on foot made Clyde intensely aware of everything he'd seen that night. He reached Troost earlier than he had with Dale and Jay that time. He drove slowly, looking for the right store. Every block looked the same; neglected, closed, burned down, dead. The whole strip of road seemed to be sick, and patches of old black men sat or stood around on the sidewalks drinking, smoking, and complaining. "Porch monkeys," Dale had called them. When Clyde saw the same three on the same corner, he spun a U-turn and parked. From the glove box he got the face mask and Ivory Special. A few bits of soap had splintered off and sticky bluish powder was coming through the stitching. Clyde raked the mask on and wrapped the weapon in his fist. He left his keys in the truck, in the ignition, and left the truck unlocked.

He knew what they'd said at the Congress about collateral illegality. But he had to prove himself. He had to prove himself to Jay and to J.D. This was important to them, to their plans, to the movement. But more important still, Clyde had to prove to himself that he was committed. That he could enter the *mai* when the stakes were real. That he was, as Jay had said that first time, a "damn warrior."

Between his truck and a parked car he crouched, working his breathing. This time things had to go off without a hitch. Initiative wouldn't mean shit if he ended up dead on the floor. He had to do what Dale could not do. No wavering or uncertainty, not even the slightest pause once he'd opened that door. He wanted Jay to be impressed, proud even. "All right," he said, picking up some rocks. He stepped out.

"Again!?" one of the black men said, and another banged on the liquor store door. Clyde threw a rock and they scattered. He threw another and one man yelled, "Dah!" The sleeves of his baggie gold shirt fluttered like wings. Clyde yanked the door and marched in with intent.

A man behind the milky partition ran from one side to the other. Clyde looked for a way around or through that Plexiglas. In the middle, between two counters, it stopped halfway up. Behind it was the register. The man was shouting to someone in back, and Clyde knew he was losing time. He ran for the glass and jumped, grabbing it and getting his upper body through. He put a hand on the register and heard, "God*damn!*" A gun went off before he could get down.

Clyde let go of the glass, touched the floor and his legs buckled. He fell backward and saw above him a cloud of blue smoke hanging in the air below the filthy drop ceiling. Fluorescent lights flickered through brown clusters of dead bugs. The man moved behind the partition. Clyde got up, he couldn't hear a goddamn thing but his own breathing. His shoulder hurt and he didn't know why. An arm snaked out the top of the partition, a gun in the hand. The barrel exploded with bright, silent flashes and Clyde knew he was being shot. It felt almost exactly like a kick, and he tightened his stomach the way they did in class, but found himself hitting the door, jangling the noiseless bells. He had enough sense to take the momentum the rest of the way out. The black men were halfway down the block now, driven away by the shots. "Serve you right!" one of them said, punching the air. Another fastballed a rock. Nobody tried to stop Clyde, but a crushing fatigue dragged him to the ground not fifteen feet from the store. He smacked his face off the rough sidewalk, his right hand landed in a clump of sun-baked dog shit. The truck was just ahead. With the men cursing behind him, Clyde crawled, dragging himself up onto his seat.

Behind the wheel, he felt a little safer. Maybe the damage wasn't so bad. People survived being shot all the time. His eyes flushed with water he had to wipe away again and again. He got the engine on and tore away from the curb with rocks and bottles bouncing off the truck. The passenger window shattered but didn't fall in on him. He took the on-ramp he'd walked the other night, hitting the guardrail and nearly going over, putting into his head the odd image of running himself down. On the freeway he focused on *nogare* breathing. A hand pressed to his chest came back with so much blood that it ran off his palm. He coughed and blood splattered the backs of his fists, he tried to say, "You're okay," but couldn't. "Osu, godddamn it," he tried to say. His racing heart pumped blood into his clothing.

When he saw the 350 turnoff he was pleased, so pleased. He'd made it this far, just like the other night, when it had taken him an hour or more. Then he realized that he was headed for Liberty Ridge. He needed an ER, not Jay Smalls, but he had no idea where to find one. Fighting the wheel, he looked dumbly off both sides of the interstate for the bright red-and-white cross. He started battling unconsciousness.

Clyde remembered trying to shout when he ran off the road, because Jay had once told him that more people would survive car wrecks if they knew to *kiai* on impact. The passenger window finally fell apart on the floor mat, and the tires slipped into the grass, yanking the truck off the road as fast and deliberate as a roller coaster. The median flipped that deep blue Ford F-150, bought five years ago by Clyde Eugene Twitty who, without a seat belt on, was thrown clear of it the third time it tumbled.

The Death of Clyde Eugene Twitty

Six shots were fired inside the liquor store. One entered the chest and exited the upper back, shattering ribs that splintered into the meat of the left lung. Slowly the lung collapsed. Another round lodged in the shoulder muscle below the clavicle, nicking bone. A third ate into the stomach before embedding in the lower intestine, flushing the blood with bacteria. This bacteria, more than anything, resulted in Clyde's death. The last round that hit Clyde bore a hole through his right forearm.

The two other rounds missed. Clyde was unconscious when he was thrown, when he met the ground with his shoulders, when the truck tumbled over him groaning. Freed of it, Clyde's body slid across sixty yards of damp grass and dirt. After Clyde stopped moving, the truck came to rest bent, broken, and hissing. The thighs, knees, and ass of Clyde's jeans were grass stained. His pockets, ears, and mouth held dirt.

Clyde slipped into cardiac arrest before the ambulance reached St. Luke's. The EMTs administered CPR and epinephrine and radioed their status to the ER.

When Clyde didn't show for class, Jay called him at six and said, "Clyde-san, we are bowing in without you. Where you at!?" When class ended at eight, and Jay saw that Clyde hadn't returned the call, worry took over. Jay tried the phone again, got voicemail. Another hour passed, with Tina trying Clyde every few minutes. So when the phone hanging on the Smalls' kitchen wall rang around nine, Jay snapped it right up. "Mrs. Twitty," he said, looking at Jan and Tina, his eyebrows up with questions he wasn't asking. He nodded, wrote down her words on the pad on the counter, told her, "My wife'll be there in twenty minutes."

Jay and Tina broke all the laws getting to Raytown. When they arrived at St. Luke's, Jay had to raise a stink to get anybody who knew anything about Clyde Twitty to talk to him. Finally they were led out of the waiting room and told in a hallway what had happened. Three minutes thirty-four seconds after Clyde's heart had stopped it had been revived in ER 2. The doctor said that when cardiac arrest goes beyond two minutes, brain damage is a factor. He said that they wouldn't know anything for some time.

Jan came in later with Clyde's mom and Uncle Willie. Jay shook Willie's good hand and hugged Mrs. Twitty harder than she'd been hugged since Clyde's father. He said, "Clyde's told me a lot about you," which wasn't strictly true. Jay told them their boy was in surgery and led them into the open air so he and Jan and Willie could smoke it up. Out there he relayed what he knew.

"Why would somebody want to shoot *Clyde*?" his mom asked.

Jay shrugged and shook his head. "It don't make no sense, I know."

Tina said, "I bet you anything it was a carload of niggers."

Jay didn't sugarcoat the situation, but he did say, "I don't know anything about medicine, Mrs. Twitty. But I do know Clyde. Your boy's as tough as they come. Fierce and determined. That's gonna get him through this."

Willie said, "I think we got you to thank for that."

"Well," Jay said, laying a hand on Willie's shoulder. They smoked cigarettes, watching people come and go—on foot, in wheelchairs, on crutches, in the backs of ambulances—and Jay offered, "Clyde gonna be just fine," more than once. The surgery moved into its seventh hour.

Half the night they stayed at St. Luke's, moving from the waiting room to the parking lot outside the entrance to Emergency so they could smoke as they pleased just downwind from where the medical staff smoked. Finally a new doctor found them in the waiting room and told everyone that Clyde had made it through surgery. Due to the heart failure, his body temperature had been reduced in the hopes of arresting brain deterioration, putting Clyde in an induced coma to help his body heal. Probably half a dozen times the doctor said how lucky Clyde had been. He was in intensive care and it would be a few days before anyone could be in the same room with him. The doctor suggested that they all go home. The hospital would contact them if there was any change.

Jay himself drove Clyde's mom and uncle back to Strasburg. He helped Willie up his steps.

For the next four days, Jay called the hospital every few hours until someone finally told him that Clyde had been moved out of intensive care, but there'd been no change to his condition. Jay left work and got Jan and Tina. He thought about calling Mrs. Twitty but wanted the family to have some time with Clyde before letting anybody else get their hands on him.

Even though the nurse warned them before they went in, no one was ready to see Clyde laid out on that hard bed with a milky two-inch tube punched through a hole bored into his sternum with a surgical drill. Gray, patchy skin and a constellation of abrasions made Clyde resemble a cadaver on a slab. A drip was taped into the back of his hand. A pulse monitor hid a finger, an array of machines made noises that were reassuringly steady, if not plain annoying. Clyde's face was bruised, his upper lip split and purple, swollen to three times its size, either from the impact or Jay's abuse or both. Gummy, yellow sores had taken root in the corners of his mouth. The eyelashes were caked and sticky. A thick purple scar cut through an eyelid and crossed the forehead. His shot arm was wrapped with a big bandage gone rust brown. Being thrown from the truck hadn't broken a single one of Clyde's bones. This was less a miracle, a nurse said, than the blessing of unconsciousness.

After a fit of sobbing, Tina settled in a hard, cold chair next to the bed and studied Clyde's face for a sign that his brain hadn't been bludgeoned into pudding. She ran her fingertips lightly in the hair of his forearm and said that if this was anybody's fault it was probably hers. Jan took to a chair on the other side of the bed and Jay paced the room. They all talked, to Clyde and to each other, telling him just go on sleeping, take your time getting better, you're gonna be all right, and it don't matter how long it takes. Hours later Jay said, "He ain't waking up today," and took the family home. Jan called Clyde's mom to make arrangements to bring her and Willie in for a visit.

WHILE CLYDE RESTED IN THE HOSPITAL FOR HALF OF NOVEMBER, JAY AND J.D. made plans. Jay was damned if he was going to allow what had happened to derail things. There was a pressing need for action. If anything, this turn had only strengthened Jay's resolve. He and J.D. had settled on three possible action scenarios: one, a full-borne assault on the First AME church in Kansas City—while in service—to start a race war; two, assassinating on the same day the Missouri governor, lieutenant governor, and secretary of state, effectively cutting off the hydra of leadership; or three, taking their cues from Timothy McVeigh, bombing a high-casualty federal building in Kansas City, Jefferson City, or St. Louis. Jay feared that it was only a matter of time before federal agents were on his doorstep. Men at the WAC had warned him of this. None of them—Jay, J.D., or Dale—were strangers to the FBI. If the feds came with a warrant, they'd have a standoff on their hands, and the last thing Jay wanted was to defend himself on the wide-open plateau of Liberty Ridge, nowhere to hide, streets wide and flat enough for a hundred Humvees, helicopters, SEAL Team Six, Seven, and Eight. The Smalls would relocate to Lick Skillet, off the power grid, unreachable by road, ASAP.

Jay was sure he'd get a fight out of Tina. This was a girl who did not like change and had never been a hundred percent on board with her father's ideas in the first place. But revolution was bigger than the disappointments of a daughter. The standing buyback offer from the Liberty Ridge Development Corp. would make things easy. Whatever Jay walked away with would be converted to gold and buried at Lick Skillet. Out there already were stashes of gold, weapons, cash, and food in a number of hidden spots. Jimmy-Don believed that, when society collapsed, the country would return to the gold standard or a barter economy. It was likely that guns would become a new currency. What was hidden at Lick Skillet would make the compound the Goldman Sachs of the new age.

TWELVE DAYS AFTER DYING, CLYDE LEFT THE COMA. THOUGH HIS MOM AND uncle had visited, twice staying all night, they weren't there when Clyde opened his eyes. Only Jan and Tina were. Jan called for a nurse and the nurse found the doctor and the doctor said that this was a good sign. "Ya think?" Jan said, and the doctor explained that the length of post-hypoxia coma is a good indicator as to brain damage. Jan said, "What?" The doctor explained that a twelve-day coma was not such a long coma, the damage may not be as extensive as it could have been. For several minutes, Clyde's eyes opened and closed, but he could not seem to focus on any one thing, even when both Jan and Tina leaned over him and said his name softly into his face again and again. Jan called Jay and Jay rushed in fifteen minutes later with a crisp blue belt in his hand, the next color in Clyde's promotion cycle. Promotions didn't have to run like clockwork and weren't always in recognition of hard training. Some were about commitment and perseverance and guts.

They all stood over Clyde, watching him work his mouth like a fish without water. Jan feared that they were witness to a broken brain, a river trout stupor that would be poor Clyde's life. An inability to talk or badly slurred speech, amnesia; the doctor had said any of this was not just possible, but likely. Physical incapacitation, partial or complete, trouble with simple tasks; this too could be expected. Worst-case scenario: a persistent vegetative state, the patient forever needing care. Jay would not let that happen; one day Clyde would simply vanish. But the doctor had explained that brain damage can take many forms. It can even manifest itself in a reduced emotional capacity, a change in the ability to feel or express oneself that can lie dormant, like a sticky bomb slapped unknowingly upon the skull, awaiting a trigger that may never even come. The doctor leaned over Clyde and called his name several times, the third person in twenty minutes to do so. Then Jay pushed past and said, "Let me do it." His grinning, expectant face took up Clyde's field of vision.

What Clyde said then, when he saw Jay and forced himself to make sounds in his horribly parched throat was, "I'm sorry," and this made Jan and Tina sob.

The doctor said that this was all a very good sign, very promising indeed. The patient must be very strong, a determined young man, and Jay said, "You got no idea." To Clyde, he whispered, "The hell you sorry for?"

There was some slurring in what Clyde said and Jay had to run the possibilities before settling on "I fucked up." But minor slurring Jay could accept. He would by God learn how to listen.

"No, you didn't," Jay said. "No, you did not."

"I did," Clyde said.

"What's he saying?" Jan said.

"Nothing, mama," Jay said, squeezing Clyde's arm and leaning in. "I am truly sorry I doubted you, son."

Clyde cried then, embarrassed and unable to stop, the wetness pooling uncomfortably in his ears. But he felt good, as if things had been put right again. He wouldn't know that nearly two weeks had passed until Tina told him.

In the days that followed, split around the Smalls' last Thanksgiving in Liberty Ridge, Clyde was tested every which way for lasting damage. There was lost coordination on the left side, some slurring. There were certain words that didn't seem to make sense to him now, or that he didn't seem to even hear. With help, Clyde could walk, slowly at first and with a limp. He had full use of his arms and hands, though the tingling from nerve damage in his right arm was annoying and he quickly developed a habit of flexing his fingers. He was heavily medicated against what the doctor said would be severe pain in the first weeks. Broken ribs, severed stomach muscles, a compromised clavicle. He would not be able to move in any way that did not bring pain for at least five weeks. But after that, and certainly within a few months, with physical therapy, the pain would subside, and Clyde could start training again, build the muscles he would lose, work on getting back coordination and balance. He would return, if not exactly to normal, to something that everybody could live with.

It helped Clyde that Jay did not believe what the doctors said about what Clyde could expect. He told Clyde that those quacks all stuck to the script, written for the average American man. Life wasn't about scripts, and Clyde was anything but average; life was about what a goddamned fierce individual could do when he set his mind and spirit to it. A warrior like Clyde, who embodied the meaning of osu? There'd be no stopping him.

Clyde knew he was lucky to have someone like Jay overseeing his recovery.

The day before Clyde was released, two police officers, both black as tar, arrived with questions. By then Jay had seen Clyde's F-150 in the impound lot. He'd taken a good look at the bent and broken doors and had decided that not even the *po*-lice could have said that this wasn't a random drive-by. So that's what Clyde told them, and they wrote it down like it was gospel. They weren't going to do a damn thing, they weren't even going to go see the truck. Let the gun-toting niggers loose on our highways.

He was released twenty-three days after the accident. With his mom and Uncle Willie and Jay and Jan and Tina all at his side, he emerged from the hospital into the cold open-air feeling like a new man, a different man. The end of the year loomed, like a sign. Surrounded by everyone he knew and loved, Clyde felt safe. Now he knew the meaning of "heaven is found an inch beneath the blade." No one experiences such a thing, and lives through it, without being altered.

With his vehicle broken for good and no income, Clyde was more reliant than ever on the Smalls. His mom wanted him to move back in with her and recover at home. But Jay talked about all the "withouts" of this scenario: two people in the same house without transportation, Strasburg without a single store where the basic necessities could be procured, Clyde without his physical therapist, Jay Smalls. Jay drove Mrs. Twitty to work that Sunday, and told her that if he or Jan or Tina couldn't do it the next week, he'd pay somebody who could. He was sorry about the oversight that weekend they'd all gone to Idaho without arranging for someone to drive her.

That first week outside the hospital Clyde slept more than anything else, despite spending half the day working his way through a liter of rocket fuel. When he wasn't sleeping, he watched TV and videos, dozing off and finding that his afternoons just bled out, a wash of pain and heaviness and drunken slumber. When his mind dulled from too much television he took up Jay's pamphlets and books, feeling good because he was already aware of most of what he read. He called his mom every day, talking twice to his uncle, who offered wise words about recovering the body from a major trauma. When Jay and Dale and the others trained in the basement or front yard, Clyde watched, moving his arms and hands in slow motion, eager to return to the physical world. Evenings he let Jan and Tina tend to his needs. Jay showed him some stretches he could do that shouldn't hurt too much and would keep him in the game. Jay didn't think much about sedentary people and was concerned about Clyde's lack of mobility. Clyde spent his first few nights in Tina's room but slept so poorly she banished him back to *American Dreamin'*. Out there Clyde attached a flagpole and a yellow flag with *Don't Tread on Me* printed on it. He'd seen those flags at the WAC and asked Jay to buy him one from the army-navy store in Boonville. Tina came to the trailer late one night starting something that Clyde couldn't finish. He blamed it on the pain and the pills that kept his pecker cotton-soft no matter how much Tina slapped at it. She wasn't happy but told him they had all the time in the world to get back in the saddle. What he didn't tell her was that since waking up to the truth he had as little interest in fucking as he had in returning to Strasburg.

One night at the end of that week, Clyde was jerking in and out of sleep when he heard somebody laughing. He didn't get up right away, but then he heard it again. There were people in the street. Someone yelled, "I bet you can!" and a few others laughed and Clyde hauled himself out of bed, got his .45. When he opened the door, a pack of Molasses Gap boys scattered. Clyde fired the Colt into the sky and those boys disappeared into the night. He stepped down stiffly from the trailer, each move hurting, and saw that half the letters had been painted away on one side. Now it read *me can ream*, which Clyde didn't find funny at all. *"I bet you can."* Fuckin pricks. And then Jay was laughing in the yard.

Jay held class for Dale and two others in a pit one night in December and Clyde sat at the hard, cold edge, legs dangling over, hands rolling into fists. Down there Jay was tougher on Dale than he'd ever been, punching and kicking him with the full force of a back-alley beating. With Dale pinned to the wall, Jay drove punches, then knees, into him, and Clyde growled to himself, "Get him!" As Dale folded over like a hinge on his hips had just snapped, Jay grabbed his hair and kneed him in the face. Dale broke the water and Jay walked off, letting the others rescue him. Clyde hadn't talked to Jay about Dale and his lies but watching this he felt that Jay had come around to believe him, Clyde, over his own nephew. As much as he enjoyed seeing Dale suffer in this way, he hoped Jay's punishment would be more than a few beatings in the pit.

After class, Clyde sat on the porch under a blanket while Jay paced in the yard, sweating. He kept glancing over, Clyde knew something was coming. "You went back to that liquor store, didn't you?" Jay said.

Clyde wasn't surprised that Jay knew what he'd done. He nodded.

"That's some lone-wolf shit right there." Jay hollered into the house for somebody to bring them some whiskeys. Jan came out a minute later with three. Jay said, "Thank you, mama," and stared at her until she said, "Oh," and went back in.

"I got inspired at the WAC," Clyde said.

Jay said, "Me too." He looked out at the darkness and sipped his drink.

"You know when you were talking at that campsite?" Jay looked over. "About taking action." Jay nodded. "You know what I think would be cool? Rob banks," Clyde said. "Like that Bonnie and Clyde movie. They were heroes."

"They were," Jay said, sipping. "Briefly. The Depression helped. Half the country out of work, bankers on the shit list."

"Don't sound so different to now. The same bankers that fucked us four years ago are getting record bonuses this Christmas. The Smalls Gang could go around doing what the government didn't have the balls to do. We could shoot some fuckin bankers too. Or hang 'em from a lamppost on Main Street." Clyde grinned. "People would love us."

"People might."

Clyde shrugged. He could tell Jay didn't like it as a real plan.

"Wall Street ain't the problem, Clyde-san. It's *a* problem, but it ain't *the* problem."

Clyde nodded. He guessed he agreed. The banks and the government had got about as incestuous as you can get but they were still operating on different levels, toward different ends. He said, "Yeah."

"Speaking of public executions." Jay turned to Clyde and made his finger into a gun, aimed at Clyde's guts. "I take it the robbery didn't go, uh, as planned."

Clyde shook his head and went through his attempt to rob the liquor store again and before long was shivering so much that his teeth began to clack. Jay told him to take it easy, to breathe. Clyde sucked in five *nogare* breaths and felt calmed; he'd controlled his heart, he hadn't let it control him. He downed his whiskey—alcohol helped the pain more than any fucking pills—and finished the story. "Guess I'm lucky to be alive," he said.

"Luck favors the prepared," Jay said. "You and me, Clyde-san, this what I mean when I say *super*human. The normal man takes four bullets, drives his truck off the road, gets chucked out, heart stops workin . . . the normal man, he slips into death from which he does not return." Jay put an arm around

Clyde. Clyde welcomed his heat. "You ain't normal now. Maybe there was a time when you was, but you ain't no more. That time is over. We's done with normal, me and you. We're on to extraordinary."

NEAR THE END OF THE YEAR, WHEN THE DEAL WITH THE LIBERTY RIDGE Development Corp. went through, Tina announced that she planned to stay right where she was, thank you very much. She'd lately directed all her energy into her sauce, hoping to build on the success of the WAC. Lick Skillet, remote and isolated, hard to reach and hidden, would be a poor base of operation for the Smalls Big Flavor expansion she had in mind. Her stubbornness brought on scenes similar to what Clyde had seen that first night and, like then, he sided with the family, which Tina didn't like at all. Just when they'd got back to fucking again, her boyfriend had betrayed her like everybody else.

Getting shot, dying, and being reborn had taught Clyde what does and doesn't matter in this life. Tina was still young, she just didn't know any better, she hadn't experienced anything nearly so profound as Clyde had and he hoped she never would.

Their last day in the house Tina bounced wildly between moping and shouting, as Clyde and Jay and Jan, with J.D. and Dale's help, packed up. They would leave much behind, the hell with it, people need a lot less than they think, and the Smalls needed even less than that. After Dale and J.D. left, Clyde and Jan sat in the kitchen while Jay, upstairs, threw Tina's things out her bedroom window. Clothes, makeup, yearbooks, stuffed animals, all that she owned grew into a large, sloppy pile. Then, outside, Jay kicked the mound into shape and unzipped. "I'm a-pissin on your past, Tina Louise!" he yelled at the house.

Tina, still in her room, stomped her feet and screamed through the window, "I am *done* with this family!"

Clyde could see that she meant it but with nowhere else to go and no one in her life besides family, Tina rode later that day with her mom to Lick Skillet, her new home.

After Clyde and Jay made their last walk-through of the house, Clyde got Jay's clippers and worked on his appearance. He'd been thinking since the hospital that he wanted the profound changes he'd gone through to be apparent on the outside. When he finished and came down, Jay flinched. "Shit!"

Going out, Jay told Clyde that there were some things hidden around Liberty Ridge that they'd need in Lick Skillet. Clyde was excited to finally get to see the compound he'd heard so much about; he'd started to think it didn't even exist, that the whole thing had been a silly game the family had played on him. Jay drove his truck three lots down, took a shovel out of the back, and started tapping the dirt. Clyde heard the shovel hit wood and watched Jay uncover a four-by-six slab of plywood flat on the ground. He dropped the shovel and lifted the board on one end, uncovering a set of rough stairs leading down into darkness. Jay told Clyde to light the oil lamp that was in the back of the truck and they descended into a thin, damp tunnel dug at the outer wall and cut ninety degrees to run along the other foundation wall to its end. The opposite walls were rough mud, two-bys, and chicken wire. The uneven ground had been covered with wooden planks. Jay turned the corner and put the lamp down, illuminating a wall of metal shelving packed with handguns, assault rifles, shotguns, and other weaponry, both legal and not, and large metal ammunition boxes. "Holy shit," Clyde said.

"Holy something," Jay said, snickering.

"You been holding out on me."

Jay handed Clyde a breech break, a sawed-off, a bolt-action rifle, an AR-15, a rocket launcher. Clyde took the weapons like firewood until his biceps strained and Jay told him to go put them in the back of the truck. Before the accident, Clyde, bet he would have been able to carry twice as much.

Clyde had seen weaponry like this only at gun shows. He knew he was looking at $20,000 or more and there were some things here he'd never encountered. He went to the truck and back and when he came into the light Jay handed him a set of headband earmuffs. Clyde hung them around his neck and Jay took two Hi-Points off a shelf. He released the mag of a .40 S&W and handed the gun to Clyde, empty. He fed ten rounds into the mag and Clyde slipped it in. "You know about Delta Force?"

"The movie?"

Jay grinned. "Delta Force is real, although officially it don't exist. Unlike the SEALs who are writing books and making fuckin movies. J.D. knows some guys, they taught him how to shoot. Counterterrorism special forces shit for urban situations." Jay dragged his earmuffs on and walked the lamp down the tunnel until it cast its shifting light on a runner nigger target hung against the far mud-packed wall. There were already some dark holes in the paper. Clyde put his earmuffs on and Jay came back to where he was standing. He spoke too loud now. "This how a normal person shoots a gun," he shouted, raising the gun head high, extending the arm, and sighting. He pulled the trigger, a new hole popped in the target. It was a good shot. With the gun down, he said, "This how Delta Force shoot." He bent his arm so the gun was waist high, took a few steps firing three times. All three hit the target. The blasts were loud, even with the protective gear, and the tunnel filled with smoke that smelled like Independence Day. Clyde had always liked that smell. He remembered shooting Roman candles over the railroad tracks behind the house with his father and his uncle and his mom in July. "It's called run 'n' gun," Jay said. "You try it."

Clyde held his gun the same way. He made minor adjustments with arm and wrist until he thought he had it right. He tried to breathe normally and walked firing, expelling five shells and a lot of smoke. The impact rocked his torso but not in a terrible way. Jay went to the target. "Not bad a'tall. Got the sucker right through the neck, looks like."

"I'm surprised I hit it at all," Clyde said. "How many times I hit it?"

"Uh, one." Jay snickered. "One's all you need, though. Took me months, Clyde-san, to learn how to shoot this way. Don't get discouraged. You a warrior. This just another tool in the tool box."

It was dark in the cramped tunnel with the lamp flickering behind Jay, casting shadows on the paper target and making the slick edges of weapons gleam. Now that the smoke had thinned, Clyde could smell damp earth. "You still think I'm a warrior?" Jay's face skipped with light as he stepped closer and wrapped a hand around the back of Clyde's neck. "I thought I entered the *mai*," Clyde said softly. "But."

"You did enter the *mai*," Jay whispered. "At that moment, you did, I have no doubt, but I can't say the same thing in a . . . " Jay searched for the word, blinking. "Being in the fight's about more than just getting in close when you perceive a threat. It's a way of life. A way of living your life. Like Ski. You ain't there yet. Still got one foot in this, one foot in that. Still a dabbler."

Clyde couldn't believe what he was hearing. He *had* committed, he really had, especially since the WAC. When it came to the course of Clyde's life, Jay had jerked the wheel, but the WAC had stomped the gas. Clyde saw clearly now how ZOG worked actively against the interests of the white American male. Since the WAC Clyde had even developed his own theory about the American Dream: it was no different than the stories in the Holy Bible; it existed for the same reason, to give hope to the hopeless who produced the goods that made their masters rich. Clyde felt like a sucker for ever having believed it in the first place. He had no idea why Jay couldn't see in him what he saw in himself—a committed warrior—and he wondered what else Jay had missed. Casting suspicion over Jay brought his thoughts to a dead end. The only way out was to recall his many failings and flaws, all the ways in which he'd disappointed Jay since being welcomed to this family, to this movement, with open arms. Of course Jay was right, Jay was always right when it came to Clyde. No one had ever seen into him so clearly. When you really looked at it, if you studied it the way Jay had, it was clear: Clyde had not committed to this life, not really.

"You wanna be a lone wolf?" Jay said. The Hi-Point was in his hand again. Clyde didn't have to think about it anymore. "Yes."

"I believe you," Jay said, pointing the gun at the target again but not firing it. "Remove yourself as much as possible from human contact. Ski said that."

"I know."

"That's lone wolf, Clyde, or uchi deshi, call it what you want, it's having only one thing to focus on, *ichi*." Jay held up the gun like a finger. "Taking decisive action against an imminent threat—and it *is* imminent, believe you me. Can't do what we're gonna do and, uh, go to mama's house every Sunday for biscuits and gravy."

"No," Clyde said, his intonation falling somewhere between question and a statement.

"No," Jay said. "Can't mow your uncle's yard and chitchat about current events. Know why?"

Honestly Clyde did not know why. But he saw how Jay was right, he'd got shot because he hadn't let go of his connection to the past, to the life of the normal man. It made sense.

Jay said, " 'Cause the longer you keep them involved in your life, the closer you bring them to danger. Think your mom, or your uncle, for that matter, could take ten years in a supermax?" The idea was so ludicrous that Clyde laughed. "That's about what Fortier got for helping McVeigh and all he did was rent a storage locker. Hang on," Jay said, and fired a round, Delta Force style. The air went blue and Clyde's ears stung. Jay stripped his earmuffs off, popping the clip. He laid it on the shelf. "These good guns, boy. Made in Ohio."

"I know. I almost got one myself." Clyde's chest ached. He knew what this pain meant. Maybe it was just information, but it told a tragic story. "So what's the plan?" he said to change the subject. He did not expect Jay to tell him what action he was planning to take but he was growing annoyed at the fact that he hadn't. "If we're not gonna rob banks like the Barrow Gang, what is it? I know while I was in a coma you guys talked about it. You were talking about it in that field in Idaho."

Jay's face, Clyde could see now that his eyes had adjusted completely, was soft, relaxed. "Soon," was all Jay said.

Clyde stared at him. He'd never challenged Jay before but now was the time. "I went back to that liquor store to prove I was fuckin ready. It didn't work, I know, but I got shot, got thrown, and went in a coma. I took all that and fuckin died and I'm still standing here. You think after all I been through—not to mention your punishment for the thing, which was Dale's fault and I never even complained. And he lied, to your face, unlike me. You think after all that that I'm still somehow not committed enough?" Now Clyde was pissed.

Jay nodded. He spoke softly, with great deliberation. "You right. We talked about three things and settled on one."

"What?"

"We gonna attack the state capitol."

"Attack," Clyde said.

"Attack. Jefferson City."

"Like, with guns?" Clyde said.

Jay's moustache curled. He shook his head. "Boom."

Clyde laughed in his nose. He'd thought Jay was joking. Jay's stare remained on his face and Clyde felt the impact sinking slowly in, a force filling his body with dread, with excitement, with worry, wonder, and purpose. This was inevitable. Even though he'd known Jay Smalls only a matter of months, he believed now that some unseen hand had been guiding him in Jay's direction for years, maybe even since birth, without his ever being aware of it.

Jay said, "Gonna be a high body count, I can tell you that much. We need a high body count. High body count's the only thing that might make ZOG think about what they're doing. Wake-up call. Blood will run in the streets, and I pray that it won't be yours. Know who said that?"

"McVeigh," Clyde said, and Jay nodded. McVeigh had said it in a long parting letter written to a childhood friend who'd questioned his beliefs. Clyde decided right then and there that he'd write a letter like that to Troy. "How high?" Clyde said.

"Hundreds."

"How many people died in Oklahoma City?"

"Hundred sixty-eight, I think."

"So this'll be bigger?"

Jay nodded. "You wanna be part of the warrior class? Now's your chance. This what it means, means building a firewall between yourself and the world."

"Right."

"No visits, no phone calls. In fact I'd say get rid of your phone altogether. No friends, nothing outside of this." Jay pointed at the ground. "Nothing but a hundred and fifty percent to the cause. You a warrior, we about to go to war. This what you've trained for."

Clyde was ready. Jay and the WAC and dying had prepared him for this.

"All that matters is the mission. Collateral damage? Doesn't exist. Everybody in, near, lookin at, or even thinking about that building is as guilty as the president. What happens to us? We get caught? We get killed? Don't matter. All that matters is the mission. The mission's all there is."

"The mission's the capitol."

"Yep."

"Will there be politicians in it?"

"On the day we hit it, there will be."

"The politicians that bailed out Wall Street?"

"For starters."

Clyde spat. "Good," he said, with real hatred. "They fucking deserve it. We'll be doing people a favor. People will fucking *thank* us."

"I'm with you on that," Jay said. He started to fill Clyde's arms with the weapons. "One more visit with your mom, one with your uncle. Soak 'em up, 'cause that's all she wrote."

Clyde felt a clenching in his chest at the thought of never seeing his family again. But he fought it.

Jay loaded him up: shotguns, assault rifles, bolt-action, wheel guns. "And this goes without sayin, but you can't tell them shit."

"Duh," Clyde said, using one of Tina's words to make Jay laugh. He rounded the corner, walked into the light. By the time he reached the stairs tears were dripping from his chin. He took longer than he needed laying the weapons in the truck bed and then got a hold of himself. Warriors do not cry. He made dozens of trips that day, the bed was a foot thick with carefully stacked weapons and ammunition boxes and crates. The last item Jay added was an RPG launcher and a plastic bucket of rounds, then he laid the plywood back on the stairs, covered it. They dragged a blue tarp over the weapons and hid the tarp under dirt. In the truck Jay lit cigarettes with black hands. Out the windshield, *American Dreamin'* sat bright in the low sun, *Don't Tread on Me* fluttering on the wind. "Your uncle home right now?" Jay said.

"He's always home," Clyde said.

"Then let's get him over with."

B y the time Jay turned into Willie's drive thirty minutes later, Clyde hadn't come up with any last words for his uncle. "I'll wait here," Jay said. The unfamiliar vehicle brought Willie out of his house. Clyde threw open the door and waved and called his uncle's name as he walked up the gravel drive. He made sure to keep his winter hat on.

"Well, howdy stranger," Willie said. "Get yourself a new truck?"

Taking the porch with a bit of a limp Clyde shook his head. "It's Jay's." He wasn't sure if Willie could see Jay sitting in it from here.

He reached his uncle and hugged him. "That's an interesting choice of moustache," Willie said. Clyde grinned, shrugging, and they went inside. It was cold in the room and Willie had grouped his chairs around the wood stove. Clyde went into the kitchen and washed the skin of burned coffee from the bottom of Willie's pot, ignoring Willie telling him not to. Then he made a fresh pot and brought two hot cups to the stove. Willie's dog lay on a soiled rug matted with his hair. "How you feeling?" Willie asked.

Clyde said, "Been better." He dragged a clawed hand diagonally across his torso. "Pains come out of nowhere. Literally like I'm committing seppuku."

Willie nodded, watching Clyde. "Still slurring a bit."

"What?"

"I say you're still slurring your words a bit."

"Oh."

"Not bad," Willie said. "I didn't know you I wouldn't notice."

"I don't hear it," Clyde said.

"Jay got you doing your exercises? Physical therapy and whatnot?"

Clyde wagged his head and took a sip of coffee. "A little. Says I gotta let the wounds heal before I try anything too hard or I'll injure myself all over again. So, I'm just getting fat again."

Willie grinned and made a noise. "I'm sure Jay knows what he's doing."

That was all Clyde needed to dive into a turmoil of warring thoughts. While his uncle slurped up coffee, sucking it from the tips of his yellow moustache, bad thoughts in Clyde's head were beaten into submission by the good. Jay does know what he's doing, like nobody else. Willie opened the stove door and added some logs to the fire with fingers so hard and worn he didn't need the lid lifter. "Got enough wood for the winter?" Clyde said.

Willie nodded. "Oh, yeah."

"Do you?" Willie gave Clyde a thumbs-up with the hand not holding his cup. "Sorry I didn't help this time."

"A little near-death experience don't mean you can shirk your chores around your uncle's house."

Clyde laughed. The dog stood up and walked a few circles. Clyde patted its gummy fur and it leaned against his shin. "What about food, how you doing for food?"

"I been getting my provisions from Suddeth's in Grain Valley. Fine."

"Suddeth's? They got everything you like?"

Willie stared at Clyde a moment and changed the way he was sitting, the chair groaning under him. "I ain't got extravagant tastes."

Clyde took up his cup, saw that it was empty, and stared into it. "Merry Christmas, by the way. Sorry I didn't call."

"Same to you," Willie said, raising his cup, and Clyde felt sad hearing it. "Don't you worry about your Uncle Willie."

Clyde stared at the fire through the dark glass of the wood stove. He hadn't prepared, didn't know what to tell Willie. "I might not, uh . . . " A log shifted inside the stove, bumping the door and settling. Willie's feet shifted and the dog raised its head. Clyde said, "I might not be seeing you for a little while." He wanted to look up, to see his uncle's face, but he feared if he did that he'd lose it. His eyes and the angle of his head remained downward.

Willie pushed himself up out of his chair and Clyde reached out to help but his uncle shuffled past. He entered the kitchen and returned with the coffee pot clanking against his aluminum cane and refilled their cups. Clyde let Willie use his arms as leverage to get back in the chair without sitting down too heavily. The muscle he'd built training with Jay helped him hold his uncle's body; last year, before training, Clyde had ended up falling on top of his uncle once, less than no help. He put the coffee pot down, the dog sniffed at it, he sat. Neither of them spoke while the full cups warmed their hands. Clyde wrapped his around it, the warmth clammy on his fingers, not as rough as Willie's but rougher now, on both sides, than they'd ever been. Willie hooked his cup with a pointer finger and sat it on a thigh, either the thick fabric of his work pants or the death of feeling in his leg insulating him from heat. Clyde had told himself coming here that he was not going to cry in front of his Uncle Willie, he'd convinced himself of this by tricking his mind into believing that this break from his family would be temporary and brief. Once they'd gone through with Jay's plans, they would all enter into a new period of life, and who was Clyde to know what that might be? In the years to come, it was very possible that Jay, his family, and Clyde would be able to pursue whatever dreams they chose. This was what Clyde told himself as he sat across from Willie, who, Clyde saw, had been staring at him intently for some time.

"Goin somewhere, are you?" Willie said.

Clyde shook his head. Then he said, "Yeah."

"Where you goin?"

Clyde reached down and patted the dog. "It's just a training thing. Happens all the time in Japan. Karate guys go into the mountains for a while, a year, year and a half, focus on training."

Willie stared into Clyde. "You planning on being gone that long?"

"No, no. That was just a, an example, a dumb example."

Clyde could tell that Willie wanted to question him a whole lot more than he was. He could see that he could hardly keep still so many questions were filling his head. Clyde leaned back and left the dog alone. Willie's eyes, when Clyde met them, were wet. He blinked and Clyde looked away. "Don't worry," he said to the dog.

Willie got out of his chair and Clyde reached out again. This time Willie pulled his arm out of the way, he limped to the other side of the room on his cane. "I don't know," he said. "I just don't know . . . I do not know if that Jay is as good a influence on you as I mighta thought. I gotta be honest." If he could have moved his head it would have been shaking.

Clyde nodded at his lap. He hadn't expected this.

"Look at what's happened since you met him. You got shot, you came this close to pushing up daisies."

Clyde said, "Nothing to do with him," even though it had everything to do with him.

"The way you're looking at things now, I'm not so sure it's for the good. And now you give me this 'won't be seeing you.' You're about the only person I see."

Clyde's heart sank. Selfish, everybody's so selfish. Here he'd thought his uncle had been concerned for his well-being. Turned out, he just didn't want to be left alone. Clyde didn't want to argue right now. He wanted to have a nice time that he could remember later, something for the reserves. But he didn't like being attacked either, and he didn't like his teacher being questioned. "All Jay's done is open my eyes to the way the world really is."

Willie leaned on his cane. "How's that then? The way it really is."

All right. Why not? Might as well let him have it. "ZOG," Clyde said.

"What?"

"ZOG. The Zionist Occupational Government," Clyde said. "ZOG."

"What's that. I don't know what that is."

"Nobody outside the movement does."

"The movement," Willie said.

"The patriot movement. The resistance," Clyde said. "Since the creation of Israel, Uncle Willie, no matter who's elected president every four years in Washington, it's a secret group of Jews who really run the country, the world, really, 'cause the U.N. and the U.S. and the eurozone are all in it together. Why do you think England went along with Iraq? ZOG is powerful, wealthy, and the American people are nothing but puppets working themselves half to death to fund ZOG's interests. Which are," Clyde used his fingers to tick them off, "Military industrial. Which leads to profits, which leads to economic disparity, which leads to global unrest, which leads to terrorism, which makes it easy for them to take away our rights, attack the Constitution, repeal the Second Amendment, and that's just, that's just what's happening *today*. Don't get me started on what they got planned for the future." Clyde shook his head but he wasn't looking at Willie. "One thing I know now without a doubt, Uncle Willie, and I wish I'd known this a long time ago, and I hate to say this to you because you work hard and don't ever complain, but the greatest lie, the greatest joke, really, that's been played on the working people of this nation is the American Dream."

Willie opened his mouth, held it open working up a word, then he shut it, grunted, and turned away. Suddenly Clyde was sorry he'd been so honest. Most people didn't understand—didn't want to understand—the complicated workings of the New World Order because most people would not want to admit that they too were one of ZOG's soulless puppets. It had taken Clyde weeks of study just to have a basic grasp of it all, and he knew there was still so much to learn. Willie shifted his weight, the floor groaned below him, and he leaned so far into his cane that Clyde got up, thinking his uncle was about to fall. "Well," Willie said, shuffling back into the kitchen and disappearing from view. "I guess you've given the matter a lot of thought."

I have, Clyde thought. "I really have," he said, loudly. "There are books."

"I don't care to see them," Willie said from the kitchen.

Clyde took that as his cue. He got up, went into the kitchen to put his dirty cup in the sink, and saw Willie leaning against the counter looking out the window. The temperature in the kitchen was ten to twenty degrees cooler than in the front room. Clyde washed his cup. "Don't worry about that," Willie said, his face bathed in light from outside.

Clyde ignored him and set his clean cup on the drying rack. He washed the plate and knife that was in the sink too, and said, "Do me a favor." Willie didn't look at him but he shifted his weight. "Tell Mom for me."

"Tell her what?"

"That I won't see her for a little while."

"Won't see her neither?" Willie said. "Ain't just me, then?"

"Course it ain't just you. It's . . . " Clyde almost couldn't say the word: "everybody."

Willie took a quick breath in through his one working nostril and stiffened his pose in the window light. "No, thank you," he said.

"Willie."

"I think it'd be best if you told her whatever you got to tell her yourself," Willie said, softly. "Might regret it."

Clyde wasn't sure Willie meant that he, Uncle Willie, might regret it if he was the one to tell her, or that Clyde might regret it if he didn't tell her himself. He dried his hands and ended up standing behind his uncle. He could see, out the glass, what his uncle could see, the lawn in need of cutting, the neglected berm. Clyde studied the back of his uncle's head; the hair, blonde streaked with gray and long enough to gather in the collar of his shirt, was thinning against a large pink, liver-spotted skull. The shoulders were held in that permanent shrug. Clyde put his hands on top of them. Willie moved when he did, shifting his body with an impulse to look in a way that he no longer could. Clyde felt him take a deep breath.

"Heard from your dad lately?" Willie said.

Clyde laughed in his nose. "No," he said. "Have you?"

"Nah." Willie raised his right hand and gave a thumbs-down.

Clyde patted his uncle's shoulders once and left the kitchen. When he yanked the front door open, he waited a moment watching Willie's shadow on the kitchen floor. By the stove Willie's dog raised its head. "See ya, John Wayne," Clyde said. By the time he hauled himself back up into Jay's truck, where he belonged, he'd managed to control his heart and seemed just as calm and collected as anybody. "Good?" Jay said.

"Good," Clyde said.

On their way to Lick Skillet, Clyde watched his side mirror and worried about all the dust clouding the air behind them. Jay told him to relax, there were Hi-Points on the dash. To their right, the stone walls of Richards-Gebaur AFB rushed by, and Clyde started composing his letter to Troy, who needed to know about the state of the nation, about ZOG and the New World Order, the struggle that every working white man should participate in, the strength of his own commitment. *Look upwards towards wisdom and strength, not seeking other desires.* Desires like friends or family who defend the status quo, question your passion, stand in your way. A break from the old life completely. Clyde would be one of the few who acted in a way that truly mattered. If he sacrificed himself, which Jay had said could happen, it would be so that others like him would have a chance at a better life. This was a noble cause.

Clyde had stumbled across something on the Internet about air force bases around the Midwest being decommissioned and turned into something called smart hubs. He hadn't read enough to understand why it mattered. Looking at Richards-Gebaur he asked Jay if he knew about this.

Jay pointed at the high stone wall. "See them blue flags in there?"

Clyde craned his neck. He wasn't sure but he nodded. "U.N.?"

"Yep. Governments of America, Mexico, and Canada conspiring to dissolve all the borders in the name of free trade. When that happens, and it's already happening, we'll need smart hubs."

Clyde knew that the U.N. was behind the push for a single currency. A single police force would follow, the New World Order, guided by the United States and Israel; everybody else would fall in line like they always did. It wasn't just a paranoid belief. It was already underway. U.S. military was spending ten times that of any other nation. It was more than all of Europe combined. A single superpower to lead the world into a new age? Well, now that Jay mentioned it, that *did* sound a tad bit familiar.

"Picture a map of North America," Jay said, "from Canada to the Panama Canal. Now, if you was to point to the city that would be closest to the dead center of all that, what would it be?"

Clyde saw it, plain as day. "Kansas City."

"Ding ding ding ding," Jay said, fishing his pack off the dash. "Smart hub. Everything, and I mean every goddamn thing, will pass through Kansas City. The United States of North America, that is what they intend to call it, by the way, USNA is gonna need spots like Richards-Gebaur for inspections, transfers, shipping connections. Smart hub. And you know what Missourah gonna look like about two weeks later? Fuckin Guadalajara. There will be such a fuckin mud flood into our state it'll make your cabeza spin." No borders, no border control, nothing holding them back. Hell, as it was, Mexicans had already made their way to small towns all across the Midwest, it wasn't just California and Texas anymore, they were working in restaurants, driving without insurance, clogging up hospitals, and increasing the danger of death for hardworking white Americans. Pretty soon, a living wage for the white man would be just another relic of the past. The dashboard lighter popped and Jay left the highway for a gravel road. "Don't worry, Clyde. *We* ain't gonna wake up in no Guadalajara."

"No, we ain't," Clyde said.

"You ever hear that saying, 'The meek will inherit the earth'? It's from that book, what's it called, the Holy Bible?" Jay snickered. "I been thinkin about that. I think people think it's supposed to be a good thing, like, 'Don't make a fuss and everything gonna be all right. Don't rock the boat.' But that ain't what I think. I think it means the meek, those who choose not to fight, will inherit the earth they goddamned deserve to inherit. And it won't be pretty."

At a T-stop ten miles down, Jay went straight through a break in the fence, the truck bucking into a grassy field. On a distant hill, a red brush hog made a wide turn. A farm track ran into the woods and Jay folded in his mirror. Clyde did the same with his. Trees whispered past. The track ended at a big metal gate, fire-engine red and taller than the truck. Old slate tombstones were clustered on the other side. Jay got down with a big ring of keys, worked a lock the size of his hand, and jerked the gate open, tearing vines. Clyde heard the mud sucking at his boots on the way back. The canopy was dense. Everything here was dark and damp.

"Ain't the only way in, but I wanted to show you this," Jay said, climbing back up. A thin, overgrown path wound through graves nearly lost to weeds, their old stones pitched at odd angles, like an Arab's teeth. "Welcome to Lick Skillet cemetery," Jay said. Out Clyde's side they rolled slowly past a cluster of headstones chipped at their God-ends. Most of the etchings were lost to time and overgrown with moss. "That's one whole family right there," Jay said, brushing the top of a stone with his hand. "Half their kids died before they was ten. This is all from the Civil War. This whole town bought the proverbial farm."

"Nobody ever comes here?"

"You give somebody half a chance to forget something, they will."

Jay's truck crawled steadily through the overgrown cemetery. Clyde had never liked being around the dead. Off the narrow path, the ground rose and fell in soft mossy mounds around sunken graves that pooled black water thick with rotting leaves and bugs. In the elbow of a curve in the path, a small tomb had collapsed as a knotty tree grew through it, pushing the masonry apart until it tumbled. It was almost impossible to tell the difference between the ground and the stones that had disappeared under grass and lichen. Clyde looked into the tomb's opening but couldn't see anything beyond darkness.

The path straightened near an open gate and Jay accelerated through to a dirty gravel road that curved downhill, thick forest all around. An old iron sign spanning the road above the truck read *Lick Skillet Village* in sharp cursive letters. The road turned to cobblestone and Jay slowed down. "This the High Street," he said, the truck shaking. He pointed past Clyde at a long sloping field and said, "That's the village down there, where the houses are." They reached the first of half a dozen buildings built close to the road, small single-story structures with center gables rising about twelve feet. As they rolled slowly past, Clyde saw a wooden door, rotted through, framed by eight-sash windows on either side with most of their glass panes busted out. A brief porch had long ago collapsed, though balusters remained to hold up a rotted roof spilling joists like a burst ribcage. All the hitching posts had lost their rings. On the brick wall beside the door Clyde picked the word "tobacco" out of a faded ad. Inside, shelves were crowded with dusty bottles of dark green, brown, and clear glass.

All the buildings were on one side of the road and much the same as the first. A tree had grown through one of them and out the top, roofing tiles and lumber stuck in branches thirty feet above. Beside it, a dirt road ran downhill, cutting the sloping field in half. Jay parked at the end of the High Street, right outside an old milking parlor, open to the road and filled with a dark jumble of boxes and barrels, leaning stacks of five-gallon paint buckets and truck tires, coiled rope and copper wire, tool cabinets, and car doors, quarter panels, hoods, bumpers, and other parts stacked in piles. Near the front a large sheet of clear plastic covered an assortment of chainsaws, the biggest one with a four-foot guide bar. Jay got out of the truck and said, "Come on."

A large lean-to draped with camouflage netting was built onto one side of the milking parlor. Jay pulled the netting around the back of a beat-up cargo truck, twenty-four feet long, its sloppy white paint job tagged all over with graffiti. The cargo door read *Case Hauling*, with a Pleasant Hill address, painted by a shaky hand. Jay squeezed his way between the truck and the wall and Clyde followed on the other side until they were at the back of the milking parlor, standing on a farm track that began at the front of the cargo truck and ran downhill a quarter mile to an apple orchard. Jay pointed off. "Connects with the paved road we come in on, about a mile closer to 291."

"J.D. and Dale own the orchard?"

Jay shook his head. "Neighbor."

Clyde took in the cargo truck. A headlight hung out of its socket by a wire like a dislocated eyeball. "So this is it," he said.

"We git her in shape, Clyde-san, don't you worry. Dale used to do body work."

"Where'd you get it?"

"Blue Springs. Bought it for a thousand bucks off some Mexican," Jay said. "No title, no questions asked." He stepped up and kicked the bumper. "Jimmy's got plates to put on there."

"Stolen?" Clyde said.

Jay shrugged. "A cop gets interested? That's the last routine traffic stop of his life."

Staring at the truck Clyde said, "Who's gonna drive it?"

Jay said, "You tell me. Jimmy-Don Smalls, six years in Leavenworth? Dale Smalls, two felonies, four misdemeanors? Yours truly, whose perty mug is loved and adored by the boys at FBI, NSA, and NAACP?" He snickered. "Or Clyde Eugene Twitty, whose record is so virgin clean it sparkles."

A part of Clyde did want to be in that driver's seat.

"We's still working out the details, Clyde-san. Don't worry, you'll be an integral part of it."

"Long as it's not Dale," Clyde said.

Jay nodded and clapped Clyde on the shoulder. It hurt.

Walking the cobblestones back to Jay's truck, Clyde was hit with a strange feeling, like he'd been here before, and he knew that he couldn't have. Then he remembered a school trip he'd taken to a ghost town outside Joplin. That trip stood out because it was the day Clyde and Troy had become friends. They'd been forced to, really, because they'd worn the same Incredible Hulk sweatshirt on the trip. Their classmates had noticed before they did, shoving them together and laughing at them, and Clyde and Troy had remained side by side because anytime one of them tried to walk off, kids wouldn't let them. At the end of the trip they'd been shoved into the same seat while the kids near them, and then all the kids on the bus, made up songs about the Incredible Hulk twins. Had Clyde not got a best friend out of it, he would have forgotten that day's humiliations a long time ago.

Now he couldn't recall what it had been that drove those people away from that Joplin town, or killed them off, but the place had looked an awful lot like Lick Skillet, one street of collapsing old buildings that had once been important to a thriving community. Clyde had always thought that the towns people built would last forever. They would always grow, ever expanding until their borders finally met. But towns could die. It might take a hundred years, or more, but any town could die.

They took the road that led downhill to the village and Jay pointed out the copses of trees planted strategically in the open field. He told Clyde that this field had been bare as a baby's ass when J.D. and Dale bought the land. He'd personally helped them dig up two dozen Douglas firs and relocate them for strategic purposes. You just never know. J.D. was not the type of man to get caught with his pants around the ankles and no Vaseline within reach. Jay pointed off at boulders placed near the edge of the field as it rose to the tree line. On the other side similar rocks were arranged in the same way, a short sprint from the woods, big enough to hide two men. "More cover," Jay said, accelerating down the hill. J.D. and Dale had spent their lives at Lick Skillet hoping for the best but preparing for the worst.

J ay passed an old broken greenhouse full of tree-trimming machinery and rusted farm equipment. The hill bottomed out at a narrow intersection with half a dozen small green cabins built right to the edge of the road. Jay turned left and parked. Fifty yards on, Tina's Firebird sat beside a cherry picker near where the road came to an abrupt end with a mound of dirt and junk at the edge of the woods. In the opposite direction, just past J.D.'s Bronco and Dale's Nova, the road ended the same way. It was silent but for birds and bugs. The air held the scent of wood smoke, pine, and rotting grass; Clyde liked that smell. The cabins around the intersection and the intersection itself were cast into darkness by a cluster of old-growth trees, reinforcing in Clyde the feeling of abandon and ruin.

"Hundred fifty years ago, this road had eight, ten, maybe more houses. Most of 'em fell down." Looking closely along the road Clyde could see remnants, a few foundations almost lost in the grass.

Between the cabins a footpath of pallets ran into the trees and circled a bright mossy pond in the back, a real mosquito factory by the look of it. Down the road sat a high pen with three ostriches. Clyde had never seen an ostrich before. He stepped onto a pallet and it rocked underfoot, squirting mud. A pack of dogs tore out of the trees barking for hell. "Don't worry, Clyde," Jay said. "They only bite a little. And it only hurts for, oh, about a month." Clyde stood still, trying to show no fear. If he couldn't intimidate a few mutts, what kind of warrior was he? The dogs circled him in a wide arc, growling and eyeballing him. Jay flapped his arms. "Go on, git!" They skulked off with lowered heads and canine worry. Clyde followed Jay to the cabin on the corner.

Inside, Jimmy-Don sat at a folding table near a brick and iron fireplace that took up most of the wall and looked built for heating and cooking both. A mound of gray ash hugged the grate and fanned out onto the old terra cotta floor tiles. Pushed against two walls were a pair of army cots sagging with clothes, books, extension cords, newspapers, and weapons. A *Penthouse* centerfold hung above one cot, the woman's face scratched off with a pen; a *kanji* scroll from Jay's basement and a poster of a wolf baring its fangs had been taped above the other. The floor was covered by overlapping skins of animals that smelled wild and damp. Built into the wall that held the front door and the room's only window were rough plywood shelves packed with tools, books, magazines, ammunition, weapons, and food. The windowsill was three feet deep. The walls were built thick to protect inhabitants from the elements, but J.D. liked to say it would protect them from other things too.

"Welcome to our humble abode," Jimmy-Don said, getting up. An AR-15 hung from the back of his chair. "It's not much, Clyde, just eighty acres of forest, a street with half a dozen standing structures, a greenhouse, a chicken coop, an ostrich pen, and a few modest homes down here for rest and relaxation. Not much at all, not much for the working man to have to live with, but I suppose you could say we make do." When Clyde stepped into the light streaming through the window, J.D.'s eyes lit up. "Well well well," he said, coming closer so he could better see. "What has become of Clyde Twitty? My son, my son, what have ye done? I don't know but I know this: I like it. I'm man enough to admit it. Uncle Jay? I am, I confess, semi-erect right now." J.D. held Clyde at arm's length, shaking his head. "As our coffee-skinned cousins to the south like to say when they're not cutting off each other's heads in the street, ai carumba." This was the impact Clyde was hoping for when he'd decided to modify his appearance.

A toilet flushed and Dale came out of a raw-wood door in the back wearing his six-shooter in a shoulder holster. He left the bathroom door open and Clyde could smell his shit. Dale said, "Uncle Jay," and sat at the folding table, buttoning his pants. Clyde went to the fire to warm his hands. "Check it out," Dale said. The table had been covered with a piece of butcher-block paper, onto which they'd drawn an unfinished map of downtown Jefferson City. In the middle was a thickly lined circle with *capitol bldg* scribbled inside almost illegibly. Roads were represented by parallel lines and one circled the building, splitting into four roads leading off in different directions marked by question marks. More question marks were scribbled where those roads connected with the circular one. A few inches from the capitol building, some wobbly lines and a fish, a piranha by the look of its teeth, represented the Missouri River. Fanning out from the capitol building were squares and rectangles filled with more question marks, including one that read *gov. dickhead's house we think.* Hot Wheels cars and trucks were scattered around, gray and green army men stood in for the general clueless public or collateral damage, the metal Monopoly dog lay next to three squiggles drawn beside one of the Capitol's walls marked *main entrance we think.* A dotted line ran from the capitol building to the road that circled it and into one of the four connecting roads. In the hand-drawn "legend" in the corner, someone had written *represents possible escape route.* A compass showed north, south, east, west. An arrow near the edge of the paper reading *to Lick Skillet* pointed east.

Jay didn't say anything for so long that Dale and J.D. both looked up at him, waiting. "It's a start, I guess," he said.

"Based entirely on crystal-clear memories of a school trip to our state's capitol." J.D. closed his eyes and smiled with whatever memories he'd called up. "Ah, yes, I sat in the back of the bus, next to little red-haired Sally. What was her last name again? That's right, I remember now. Rotten Crotch." J.D. took a big breath in through his half-clogged nose.

"I think I was on that same trip," Jay said.

Clyde ran a finger along the road that circled the capitol building. There were too many goddamn question marks. "Do we know how far the building's set back from the road? Or how big the curb is? Aren't there steps on both sides of the building? That's the way I remember it from my school trip, and unlike yours mine was in this century."

"Look at Clyde Twitty," Jimmy-Don said, sitting back with his hands on his knees.

"Can you Google it?" Clyde said.

Jimmy-Don shook his head. "The World Wide Web has not made its humble way to Lick Skillet. And even if it had, Clyde Twitty, even if we had wires coming out of our asses and Google for breakfast, lunch, and dinner, don't you think typing 'Missouri State Capitol Building' into the search engine would set off the NSA's alarm bells?"

"Oh, it would," Jay said.

"I know it would. What I'm curious to know, Uncle Jay, is if Clyde Twitty knows it would."

"I get it," Clyde said. "Do it at the library or something."

"Not if you got a library card, you won't," Dale said without looking at Clyde. Clyde stared at his black wooly hat but Dale never raised his gaze. "NSA can search membership like that," Dale snapped his fingers. "Cross-check names till 'Clyde Twitty' gives 'em something to go on. This is all they're doing these days."

The men slipped into silent contemplation of the map and Clyde felt like he could read Jay's mind. It was almost too rudimentary to be of any use at all. They needed firsthand accounts of Jefferson City, that was obvious. A few days spent observing the building would fill in most of those question marks. How easy or difficult would it be to drive a big, white, twenty-four-foot cargo truck through downtown en route to the capitol building? How easy or difficult would it be to get onto that road that circled it? Was it a two-way or one-way road? Were there any checkpoints? Once on that road, could a vehicle continue to circle indefinitely, or did it have to pull off? How many roads connected to the circle, exactly, and where did they lead? To maximize the blast, the truck would have to be placed right against the building. It couldn't be left on the street. If it was left on the street the capitol building would be scarred, but not destroyed, and the symbolism of that would be seen as a failure for their cause, worse than if they'd done nothing. Were there any service roads? Any loading docks? Or was there a two-foot curb preventing vehicles from getting that close? Clyde turned to Jay. "Why don't I spend some time in Jefferson City?"

Jay's eyebrows went up and he held his face frozen like that so J.D. and Dale could see it. Then he said, "*That's* the fuckin spirit, Clyde!"

"Osu," Clyde said, watching Dale, who never looked up.

Jimmy-Don slapped the table. "I think we can learn from the mistakes Tim made and come out of this in better shape than he did, which is to say, oh, I don't know, alive? Still of breath, as the Victorians called it. Notus currentus mortus. Free of worms eating our flesh as we rot away to nothing in the cold, cold ground."

Clyde hadn't spent enough time looking into Oklahoma City to know much about any mistakes that might have been made. Before getting close to the Smalls he'd always thought that McVeigh had just been unlucky when he got caught. Now he knew better, now he knew that no matter how much time and effort went into a revolutionary action like that, the iron heel would pool all its resources to hunt you down. No matter how clever you were, the successful revolutionary would be found and brought to justice before the American public.

"First off," J.D. said, "we're already ahead. Tim *rented* his truck. From the Ryder Truck Rental Company. Even though he used the Tuttle alias. This wasn't as dumb as it sounds, since he'd done research that led him to believe a Ryder-brand moving truck in downtown Oklahoma City wouldn't stand out. But on the other hand, the hand other than this hand," J.D. held up and wiggled his left, "it gave them a starting point, even if it was to an alias. We, on the other hand, which I guess would be a third appendage that I'm not at liberty to present just now, maybe next Tuesday, come back then for a big surprise. We on the other hand *own*. Ownership, I'm told, has its privileges, and I don't know about you but I personally think that being able to fill what you own with enough high-explosives to level a small city is one of them. Priceless."

"They trace the truck they gonna arrest one clueless Mexican in Blue Springs," Jay said. "Who sold it for cash to a guy never even gave him his name."

"Exactly, Uncle Jay. Tuttle may not have led the feds to anything had Tim not spent the night in a nearby motel, the Dreamland Motel, where, wait for it, wait for it, wait for it . . . "

"Goddamn it, just say it," Jay said.

"Wait for, okay, he signed the register as, that's right, Timothy McVeigh." Jay shook his head.

"After the blast, and half of downtown disappeared into pixie dust and blood, Tim got in the car he'd parked several blocks away a few days earlier and drove calmly away like a good little revolutionary. Highway patrol stopped him in Kansas, ninety minutes later, and I bet if I gave you fifteen million guesses you'd never ever guess why."

"I know why," Jay said, picking up an army man. He looked at Clyde with his eyebrows up.

Clyde asked, he didn't know why.

"He didn't have plates on the car," J.D. said, and Clyde laughed. What a dumb mistake. "He'd removed them when he parked the car in an alley three days before the bombing. They were in the car. He could have put them back on before driving away, or, I don't know, gone a few miles, pulled off, and put them on there. But he didn't. He just kept going. On the highway. Headed back to Kansas. Where he was arrested and kept in jail for three days waiting to see a judge about driving without plates before they put two and two together."

"What an idiot," Dale said, and J.D. shook his head.

Even Clyde would have known better than to drive away from the crime scene in a car without plates. He was excited to be part of this conversation, and the larger one, within the movement. His mind was starting to work like a lone wolf's. This was how things changed. Study the actions of those who came before you and learn from their mistakes. "It's like he wanted to get caught," Clyde said.

"He did," Jay said.

"Before we get to psychology, and I think Uncle Jay's right, by the way, I always do, don't I, Uncle Jay?"

"Do you?"

"I do, yes. But I think we should follow the trail the feds followed to find Tim before we get into Tim, as you say, wanting to get caught."

"Go for it," Jay said.

Jimmy-Don shifted and the wooden chair groaned under him. Dale took out his tobacco and began filling some papers. "As we've already covered," J.D. said, "Tim rented his truck, the ka-blooey two thousand model, if I'm not mistaken, using the Tuttle name. When the feds found the Ryder's axle in a parking lot two blocks away, which was all that was left of it, by the way, they traced the CVIN back to the branch. There are CVINs on axels, ladies and gentlemen. There are CVINs on everything. There's probably a CVIN on your eyeball. And what follows such a discovery in the case of a national act of terrorism that results in the mass murder of women and children and the wholesale destruction of government property? A little sit-down between the rental branch manager and the FBI, of course, during which time their talented sketch artist scribbles up a pretty fair likeness of our demon to be pasted on fence posts across our great nation. Names and fake IDs mean a lot less than eyewitnesses and feds who can draw."

"It's a fucking miracle he managed to get the bomb to go off at all," Dale said, putting two army men on top of each other in the 69 position.

"You can't dip a toe in the waters," Jay said. "He fucked up, but Tim sure as hell entered the *mai*."

"Heaven's found an inch beneath the blade," Clyde said, and didn't even look up to see if Jay had heard him.

"So what," Dale said. "He just wanted to get caught?"

Jimmy-Don nodded deliberately. "He knew they'd get him, sooner or later, and he was, dare I say, depressed. Saddened by the state of the country, just like us. To him Murrah was everything. There was nothing else beyond that one action. But I for one am a hundred percent certain that if he hadn't made those mistakes he'd still be with us and the U.S. of A. would have fried some guys named Akbar in his place. Hell, his own defense team spent millions trying to prove al-Qaeda was pulling the strings and Tim was nothing but a patsy." Jimmy-Don feigned getting shot in the belly, smiled, and continued. "But, *but*, I tell you, when it comes to the device itself, the death blast, it was peccadillo-free. Tim rigged that thing to go off no matter what, even if it meant he went with it, worst case." J.D. made a gun with his hand. "And unless there's some objection you'd like to offer, Uncle Jay, Dale, Clyde, speak now or forever hold your burner, I don't see a single reason to build a substantially different bomb this time out. If it ain't broke, am I right?"

Jay nodded. He smacked Clyde's arm. "We gonna have to rob a quarry or farm store. That's next."

Clyde said, "What about keeping collateral illegality to a minimum?"

"You gotta show ID to buy more than five hundred pounds of ammonium nitrate these days, Clyde, thanks to Tim. So."

"How much we need?" Dale asked.

"Tim used five thousand pounds," Jay said. "A hundred bags, give or take. I wanna use a little more than that."

"Won't five thousand fuckin pounds of ammonium nitrate gone missing sorta alert the feds?"

"It definitely will, little brother," Jimmy-Don said.

Jay shrugged and said, "We'll just burn the place down."

They left the greenhouse and entered the forest with Dale in the lead and all of them carrying supplies. Dale had assembled a miniature version of the bomb that would fill the truck and they were going to blow a stump with it. The path turned steep and rough and Clyde had a hard time. He fell behind and hurt something awful. His body had lost so much of what he'd gained. They finally reached a plateau and left the forest for an open field. Dale ran ahead through high grass, excited. He stopped at a tree stump, setting down a Folgers can full of ammonium nitrate and nitromethane. He ran back to the others and took a coil of fuse cord from Jimmy-Don that had been crimped into a blasting cap. He ran back to the tree stump.

"What all do we need?" Clyde asked.

"A few hundred pounds of Tovex, shock tube, fuse cord, couple hundred blasting caps," Jay said. "All of which we already got enough of, right?"

"That's right, Uncle Jay."

"Am I forgetting anything?"

"How much liquid nitromethane we have?" Jay asked J.D. "Tim used seven or eight hundred pounds."

Dale secured the cap through the plastic lid of the Folgers can, unwound the fuse, lit it, and ran back, arms and legs hopping.

J.D. said, "We don't have eight hundred pounds, that much I can tell you right now, Uncle Jay. But anyone can buy liquid nitromethane at racing supply stores without a license, unless the law has changed and I'm pretty sure it hasn't, though I'm not, as you may or may not be aware, an elected official, so I don't have the breaking news on everything in the whole wide world. We're going to need about fifteen hundred pounds. But nitromethane's the least of our problems, and by problems I mean challenges, really, obstacles, call them what you will, hurdles which we will leap like gazelles in a field of golden wheat, much like this one here, though I believe that rather than wheat we are standing in ragweed."

"All right. You two handle the nitromethane. I wanna have everything else we need soon as we can git it," Jay said. "Goddamn politicians only work in Missouri January to May. I'm reluctant to just piggyback McVeigh and Waco but whatever date we pick needs to send the same message."

Jimmy-Don nodded. Dale bounded up to them, breathing hard, and turned around, crouching.

"What fuse you use?" Jay asked.

"One minute," Dale said.

Jay checked his watch. "Then are we ready, ladies and gentlemen, to witness what we've come to witness?"

"I think we are," Jimmy-Don said.

"Here . . . we . . . go," Jay whispered, and a moment later, it blew.

The ground shook, a shower of dirt and dead leaves fell across them. Starlings and blue jays burst screaming from the trees and circled while everyone waved their arms and covered their faces. Dust, grass, and leaves hung above the clearing. Jay yelled, "Hot damn!" and hugged Dale. They all ran to the crater. The stump was gone entirely—obliterated—and the black-earth hole where it had just been was twenty feet across and a few feet deep. Clyde stood blinking as dust settled gently upon their shoulders. "That was two pounds," Jay said. "Two fuckin pounds! We gonna drive up to that goddamn building with eight *thousand!*"

Clyde could not even imagine what sort of damage that would do.

"It gonna shear that fuckin building off the hill," Jay said.

"It will, Uncle Jay, be substantially *larger* than Oklahoma City, if I do say so myself."

"It'll be the biggest revolutionary act this state's seen since Governor Jackson seized the St. Louis arsenal, 1861," Jay said.

They stood around the circle of disturbed earth. If they were right, all of downtown could disappear, not just the capitol building, but the governor's mansion with the governor in it and every other building within two blocks. Cars would be totaled for half a mile. Hundreds of people would die, not just

168, and the entire Missouri government would be wiped out in the time it took to spit. What followed would be chaos and unrest. Martial law, curfews, the usual stripping away of human rights. Thinking whites across the state, maybe the nation, already pushed to the limit by an overaggressive government, would rise against the ZOG power grab. The well-armed militias that had swelled in the wake of 2008 would fight the National Guard part-timers in a war that was as bloody as anything seen since 1859. The militias would win, because they would be better trained and more motivated and better armed than the fat, lazy Guard troops who would rather be at home watching TV. First Missouri, and then other Midwest states with it, Kansas certainly, Arkansas, Nebraska, and Oklahoma, would undergo a radical shift. The beating heart of the country would break free and move into self-rule, a period that would no doubt be as tumultuous and violent as the years around the shaping of this nation. There had already been one Missouri Compromise that changed history's course. It was time for another.

Clyde saw clearly enough now to understand how a series of events like this could occur, though what would ultimately happen would unfold very differently than what any of them had imagined. It didn't matter either way, because for Clyde it wasn't about who would die or how many or what would come in the weeks or months after the bombing; it was about making sure the action was planned and executed in a way that would make Jay proud to call Clyde his uchi deshi. Clyde intended to show Jay that whatever difficulties the old Clyde Twitty might have had with entering the *mai* died with the old Clyde Twitty in the back of that ambulance.

When they got back to Lick Skillet village, J.D. and Dale went back to their cabin leaving Jay and Clyde to wander the property. Jay wanted to give Clyde the full tour, and they made their way up the road, past the greenhouse, to where it ended at the High Street. From here, Lick Skillet village spread out below, a long sweeping field full of gold dead or dying grass. The cabins, clustered around the intersection in the flat, damp brake below, were mostly hidden by trees from here. Whoever had planted those copses on the hill had done so with protection from this street in mind. Only a few bits of tiled roof poked out, the glass of a single window shaking in the sun. Jay stood beside Clyde at the lip of the hill. "Which one's Tina in?" Clyde said.

Jay pointed and Clyde followed his finger. "That one, I think. Jan says soon as they got here she slammed that door and ain't come out since. Well, she ain't got nothing to eat and I don't think she even knows how to light a fire, so she be out soon enough. Much to everbody's delight, I'm sure." Jay snickered, but Clyde knew he was hurt by Tina's behavior.

"Maybe I oughta take her with me to Jefferson City."

Jay flipped out his lower lip and blinked. He said, "Maybe you oughta." Jay wrapped an arm around Clyde's shoulder and they walked on the cobblestones, looking into buildings.

"I'm gonna need a vehicle though," Clyde said. "Firebird won't take a tail hitch."

Jay grinned at Clyde and said, "You can have Dale's."

That was what Clyde had hoped Jay would say. "I tell him you told him to give me the keys he ain't gonna like it."

"Frankly, my dear, I don't give two shits," Jay said. He winked. "I'll have a word with him."

After a dinner of summer sausage and canned okra in J.D.s' and Dale's cabin, everybody but Tina sitting with paper plates on their laps, Clyde took the end of the whiskey and some food out to her. While she ate, shoving in slice upon slice, he sipped Rebel Yell, welcoming its slow migration through his chest. Then he made a fire in the wood stove and they sat in front of it wrapped together in a smelly wool blanket covered with bits of dry leaves.

Clyde was on the road in Dale's Nova early the next morning, imagining the look on his face when Jay ordered him to hand over the keys. Tina followed in the Firebird. In Liberty Ridge, he got *American Dreamin'* onto Dale's hitch while Tina went in the house and walked from room to room saying things Clyde couldn't hear. The Nova wouldn't want to pull that thing up steep hills but Clyde didn't think there were any mountains between here and Jeff City. He could see that Tina was sick about not living in Liberty Ridge anymore and he tried to distract her. He stripped off his wool cap and grinned, causing Tina to stumble away. "Holy. Crap," she said, a hand up to her eyes as if Clyde were emitting a harsh light. "You look like a crazy person." Clyde put his hat back on and showed her how to connect the line for brake lights, thinking that she enjoyed learning something new and practical. Before they left, he took down the yellow Gadsden flag so the wind wouldn't shred it.

For two hours on Highway 50 he had Tina in his side mirrors. The last thing he needed right now was the unpredictable emotions of a woman. He wondered if an unpredictable woman had been lost somewhere in Jimmy-Don's detailed analysis of Timothy McVeigh's screw-ups. Clyde remembered at least one woman involved in one way or another. He wouldn't have been at all surprised to learn that the fatal mistake, the one that put Tim away, had involved her. He'd be damned if he'd let it happen to him. He thought he could use this time in Jefferson City to draw Tina back into the fold.

At the capitol, they pulled off and circled the building without even intending to. Clyde didn't know which of the roads to take so he drove around the building three times, already filling in a couple question marks. He took a road uphill to a high vantage over the river. As predicted, the Nova's chassis quivered and groaned. Tina followed in her Firebird, honking, her music blaring and her hair leaping. At the top of the hill Clyde pulled over. The capitol dome was visible from the street, which Clyde thought a good omen. Tina stayed in her thumping car, some loose part vibrating with every beat, while Clyde unhitched the trailer and leveled it with cinder blocks and wood. He stopped the tires and hooked up the propane. It was late in the day and Tina stuck her head out the window. "I'm hungry, crazy person, feed me!" Clyde got in with dirty hands and they drove back down the hill to look for a McDonald's.

Over dinner Tina said, "While you're off doing whatever it is you're doing here, I'm gonna go to the library."

"What for?" Clyde said.

"R and D," Tina said. When Clyde stared at her dully, she said, "Research and development."

Clyde picked up one of his hamburgers and ate a third of it in a single bite. Outside, Jefferson City was dark. Aside from the area around the capitol, the place was a real shit hole. Black and brown faces outnumbered the white ones, and Tina whispered, "Now I know what it feels like to be a mi-nor-ity." She popped a fry in her mouth. "I mean, I've got a lot of experience with Amway and self-publishing and real estate but I'll admit," she said, grinning with all her little teeth. "I do not know the first thing about starting a small business, mofo. I figure the library's about as good a place to figure it out as any."

Damn. Clyde had hoped that by now Tina would be talking more about throwing in the towel again, moving on to her next project. She'd given up on self-publishing and real estate; surely it was only a matter of time before she gave up on barbeque sauce. But she sure seemed determined. "Just be careful," he said.

"Uh, okay."

"Don't give nobody your real name is what I'm saying. Especially on the Internet."

"Um, officer," Tina said, raising an eyebrow. "How am I supposed to get a library card without giving them my name?"

"You don't need a library card to be in the library."

"No, but I do if I'm gonna check out any books."

"Do not, I repeat, do not check out any books. Read 'em there. Or photocopy the passages you need."

"Oh, Jesus, buddy," Tina said, shaking her head sadly. "You've gone just as crazy as my dad."

Clyde took time to think about his response while he ate his third hamburger, watching the other diners. Almost every one of them was obese. He was the only man in there who knew how to control himself. When he was finished, he said, "I know you're pissed at your dad right now, but let me ask you. You so pissed that you want him either dead or incarcerated for the rest of his life?"

Tina sat back, like the thought had never occurred to her before. "Uh, what do you think?"

"I honestly don't know."

"You don't know?"

"I'm just saying, you go around typing 'Tina Smalls' all over the Internet, or you check out books, you know, a couple blocks from the capitol when your actual address is in Boonville? That's the kinda shit that gets noticed."

"Jeez, paranoid much?"

Clyde said, "If you deal a serious blow to the system they'll never stop hunting you."

Tina's mouth practically fell open. Her eyes were wide and damp. She shook her head and sucked soda through the straw. Clyde thought that her silence meant that she finally got the seriousness of the situation, so he let it go.

That night, after lying in bed in the cold trailer a while, Tina crawled on top of Clyde. He felt conflicted; he was a soldier now and soldiers had to have higher ideals. Soldiers knew how to deny the body. After weeks of denying pain, he found it easy enough to deny pleasure.

The next morning Tina drove off in search of the library. Clyde made a jug of rocket fuel and went down to the capitol. School buses were parked on the road circling the building. Clyde figured it was a span of about a hundred yards between that road and the capitol walls. A bomb would dissipate much of its charge in that wide-open space. Students were clustered on the steps and around the statues, teachers trying to maintain order. It reminded Clyde of when he'd done this, years ago, and he checked the bus names for Strasburg or Grain Valley. He circled the building on foot and filled in another question mark. The curb was of normal height and there were no pylons or other obstructions to prevent the truck from leaving the road and crossing the lawn. On the side of the building that didn't face the river, the lawn was as flat as a parking lot and ran all the way to the façade. They'd be able to put the truck flush with the building. Clyde was shocked that a decade after 9/11 a major government building could be left so vulnerable to attack.

Out front, Clyde got in line behind one of the schools, wearing a wool hat. The building was so noisy and chaotic that nobody asked him anything. They just checked his face against his license and let him through. He hugged the back of the group for most of their tour. The ceilings were so high you could hardly make out what was written up there. There was marble everywhere and brass, polished to a million-dollar shine. In the gift shop, Clyde bought a notepad with a picture of the building on it and sat out on the steps in the cold sun recording his impressions. He walked around the building again and then sat down and drew a map more detailed than what J.D. and Dale had attempted. Later he would drive each road and record whatever they led to. On the front flap of the pad he wrote *Notes for a novel*, just in case he lost it and it ended up in the wrong hands. Inside, he put the name of a guy he'd worked with at Longarm but his own cell phone number. Anyone calling for "Jake Boher" would be calling about the pad, so he'd know how to handle it. Clyde was learning.

When he'd recorded everything—including the note about the backside of the building being their best option—he put the pad in his pocket and went inside again. He asked the security guard by the door what time the politicians usually worked there and whether their schedule was posted anywhere. The guard wasn't interested in talking to someone like Clyde. He mumbled something about a Web site. Clyde said, "I don't have a computer," but the guard looked away. Po' white boy without enuff money fo' technology. Two members of the cleaning staff—both Mexican—came out of the back with pushcarts. Maybe that was the answer, a job, like that guy who'd worked at that federal building in Oregon so he could steal a bunch of plutonium. People at the WAC had talked about him. If the capitol was willing to employ a team of uneducated Mexicans, half of them probably illegal, surely they'd jump at the chance to put a hardworking white American male on the payroll, especially one who didn't care how much he got paid.

T hat night Tina was in good spirits. She talked about the library, or "booksico," as she called it, since everyone in it was either an illegal Mexican or homeless and smelly. She said she'd already learned a lot about starting a small business. She showed Clyde forms for establishing a DBA and Clyde said, "What's a DBA?"

"Doing business as, silly," she said. "It's the first step. Gotta have that to even sit at the table with the legit mofos."

Clyde didn't know what she meant and asked to see the forms she'd printed out. They were blank, printed from government Web sites. She intended to fill them out with all her personal details and mail them in. Either she had no grasp of the bigger picture or she was actively working against her own family's interests. Or she just didn't care. She was selfish, putting her own desires above all else. There was no "not seeking other desires" in Tina. Clyde knew he had to put a stop to her craziness. But Tina was happy again, for the first time since Liberty Ridge, and her being happy made his life easier. He didn't want to go to war in a trailer. Instead of confronting her he decided to hide the forms when she went to bed. He'd hide the next ones too if she was dumb enough to bring them home.

When Tina was in the cramped bathroom brushing her teeth before bed, Clyde's phone buzzed. It was his mom and he let her have the voicemail, imagining the various possibilities of her message. None of them made him feel good, so when the "new message" indicator appeared, he deleted it without listening.

In the morning Clyde left Tina sleeping and went down the hill again. You never know what you might discover with simple observation. He'd been thinking more about how good it would be to spend time on the inside, to get access to secret shit. Jay would be impressed by that initiative. Clyde circled the building and entered a lot overlooking the river, parking right up against a sign that read *Employees Only*. Fuck 'em. He sat with the engine threatening to stall. It was just after six and there wasn't much activity. Then two capitol police officers rode by on bicycles and Clyde reached for his pad. He watched them pass and noted their radios, sidearms, billy clubs, cuffs. He wrote it all down. He hoped that they weren't assigned to permanently loop the building. When they disappeared around the far side, Clyde's eyes moved across the building at bicycle speed, waiting to see them again, but, to his relief, he didn't.

Glass at the top of the steps blinked the sunrise into Clyde's eyes. People were leaving the building. Some of them crossed the road and entered the parking lot. They were all Mexican, every last one of them. They got into their old vehicles and started fogging the air with exhaust, except for one guy who stood smoking a cigarette and throwing glances Clyde's direction. When all the others had driven off, and this suspicious-looking Mexican lit another cigarette, Clyde got out of the car, lighting one of his own. Sitting in a car was a bad defensive position. He didn't know what this one wanted but it was obvious he wanted something. Clyde leaned against Dale's quarter panel, looking casually at the building so he could keep half an eye on his potential attacker. The Mexican nodded and Clyde said, "How you doin?" The Mexican came closer. Clyde made sure his feet were evenly spaced on the ground. A solid base was important in a fight. He took his left hand out of his jeans pocket and let it hang, ready. "Work here?" Clyde said.

The Mexican looked back at the building as if there were any other possibilities around. He said, "Yeah."

Clyde gestured with the cigarette. "I asked a guy in there yesterday if they were hiring but he was less than no help."

The Mexican took another step. "So you no cop."

"What?" Clyde said. He couldn't understand half of what he was saying. "You a cop?"

"A cop?" Clyde came off the car. "I look like a cop?" The Mexican shrugged and took yet another step closer. "Couple of 'em went by a few minutes ago," Clyde said.

The Mexican kept inching closer. Closer closer closer. Clyde prepared himself. Why was it you could never trust a Mexican? Whatever happened to having a normal conversation? Hello, how are you? I'm good, how about you? Honestly Clyde didn't see much of a threat. A head shorter than Clyde, his skin was such a funky shade of brown it looked like he'd smeared dirt all over himself. Like all Mexicans, his hair was as black as electrical tape and stuck up all over, probably to remind him of all the cactus he missed from the home country. Pulpy bunches of acne hugged the shiny hairline around his temples. He dug at it now with long yellow fingernails, inspected what he'd found, and said, "What you want, man? Reefer, crystal, X?"

"What?" Clyde said. "I. Can. No. Understand you." He thought that Tina would have got a kick out of that.

The Mexican jerked his arm. "Chinga tu madre," he said.

Every Mexican wanted to live here but not a one gave two shits about learning the language. "Speak English, amigo?" Clyde pretended to scratch his moustache so that his hands were in a better position.

"I speak English. Habla usted Español, maricón?"

"Uh, you just made my point. No idea what you're saying."

"Cabrone," the Mexican said with more force. "Reefer? Crystal? Ecstasy? I give you good price."

Drugs! Clyde should have known. "I don't want drugs. I want a job." Clyde pointed at the building. "You got that? You get me a good price on a *job*?"

The Mexican looked behind him. "You want work aquí?"

"I want to work there." Clyde pointed again.

"Why?"

"I need a job, just like you."

"Just like me?"

"Yeah."

"Okay, man."

"I didn't go to no college. I got shot and crashed my truck and didn't have insurance. I got medical bills."

The Mexican stood where he was between Dale's old Nova and a twenty-year-old Toyota that sagged almost to the ground in the back. "Pues," he said. "Talk to boss."

"You'll talk to your boss?"

"No, man, what the fuck?" The Mexican pointed at Clyde.

"What's his name?"

"Featherstone."

"Featherstone?"

"Yeah man, what the fuck wrong with you? You repeat everything? Señor pinché Featherstone."

Clyde jerked his head at the doors. "That guard, he's a dick. I already tried." They stood quiet for a moment and then the Mexican headed for his car. "Shit, all right, hold up," Clyde said. The Mexican stopped but didn't turn. Clyde dug in his pocket. "Twenty bucks. What'll twenty bucks get me?"

The Mexican turned back, but he didn't look happy. He came right up to Clyde and said, "Couple joints."

"Couple joints?" Clyde said, and the Mexican made a face. "Joints are ten bucks a piece?" The Mexican shrugged. Clyde sighed. "All right." He started to hand the Mexican the bill but the Mexican jumped back.

"Vamos a la coche," he growled. "Chinga."

Clyde followed him to his car. Inside, he held out the bill and the Mexican reached under his seat and dug two perfectly rolled joints from a bag of what looked to Clyde like two dozen. He held them out and Clyde took them delicately in his fingers. "Gracias," the Mexican said.

"If I come by here tomorrow, can you get me in? To see the boss?"

The Mexican sat staring at Clyde a minute. "Okay."

Clyde got out and the Mexican revved the engine. Clyde knocked on the passenger window. "What's your name?" he said.

"Chetto."

"Cheh," Clyde started.

"Chetto, mafufo."

"Chetto," Clyde said, shaking his head. What kind of name was that? "Clyde."

Chetto pulled away and drove around the building, engine sputtering. Clyde was hiding the joints in his glove box when his phone buzzed on the dash. Jay wanted him back in Lick Skillet. Clyde didn't mind the two-hour drive. It gave him a chance to collect his thoughts. But lately what he was thinking about was the past, the good times he'd had with his mom, his uncle, his friend, even his dad, what he could remember of him: being under the truck when he changed the oil; getting yelled at when he lost control of a wheelbarrow and dumped the cement. His dad had always been the one getting the Christmas tree, untangling the lights, wrapping the gifts. After he left, that first year Clyde rememberd his mom staying up all night trying to get it right, and then falling asleep on the couch as soon as Clyde unwrapped his presents. He'd taken his favorites—a yellow dump truck and a yellow backhoe and a red tractor—out to the yard where he could make noise. After that, Willie had taken over, teaching Clyde to shoot, drive a car, throw a knife at a tree so it stuck with a satisfying *thunk*. Clyde was halfway to Lick Skillet by the time he realized that his mind had spun out of control, the last sixty miles passing in a fog. He cursed himself and shoved the past away by saying the dojo koan out loud, repeating it for the next several miles with more and more force—*all our lives!*—until he was shouting it across the wheel and attracting concerned stares from the drivers he passed.

When he parked Dale's Nova on the High Street, the dogs lying in the sun jumped up barking and Jay, at the back of the cargo truck, the camouflage netting pinned to one side and the truck up on risers, yelled, "Clyde-san!" Jimmy-Don was under the truck. Dale was lying in the back talking to his brother through the floor. The dogs circled Clyde on the cobblestones, he offered his hand. Maybe they were getting used to his scent. Some wheel guns and one of Dale's Parker-Hales lay scattered on the floor of the cargo hold beside Dale, along with a dozen cans of beans.

"We's making progress, ain't we, boys?" Jay said.

"That we are, Uncle Jay," Jimmy-Don said from underneath. "Boucoup progress, as they used to say in Vichy France."

Jay grabbed Clyde and showed him the fuses. "Gonna have two like Tim did, a five minute and two minute. Fail safe." Jimmy-Don lay on his back on a big piece of cardboard in the grass below the truck, Dale feeding him plastic fish tank tubing through a hole in the hold's floor near the driver's seat. Another hole, two inches wide, had been bored through the metal near the rear. Clyde touched one of the cans and said, "Lunch?"

"Configuration," Jay said, and slid the can Clyde had moved back into its place. Now Clyde saw that they made two backward *J*'s. "This way," Jay said, "the blast's directed out the right side. So we're gonna wanna park with that side against the building."

"Huh," Clyde said. He didn't know that by simply arranging the barrels in shapes you could control the direction of the explosion. He was impressed by all the little details that seemed to come naturally to Jay.

"Come on," Jay said, and Clyde followed him down the street, their breath visible on the air. One of the dogs trailed them halfway before stopping. The winter sun was directly overhead, making small shadows. Jay walked to the old bar and kicked the door in, which made the dog who'd come halfway turn and trot back to the others. Jay's foot went right through the rotted boards; he laughed and wiggled it out. He said, "Why don't we just use the window," and crawled quickly through, helping Clyde in. "Careful, this glass sharp as shit." Clyde still had trouble moving in some ways and sliced through the shoulder of his coat. He didn't know if the new clumsiness had to do with getting shot, getting thrown, his heart stopping, not training, or drinking too much. Jay helped him get steady and said, "Longer you wait to get back into training the harder it gonna be to get back what you lost."

Clyde knew he was right.

Jay lifted two old stools from the floor, wiped off the dirt, and sat. The stool creaked. "They don't make 'em like they used to." He faced the bar, arms on the rough wood. A hundred and fifty years ago, two men had sat here like this.

Clyde took out the pad and flipped through. There were the notes about the cops, to which Jay said, "They won't be on their lil trikes for long," and three pages of other observations, about the date the building was made (Clyde had seen it etched in a stone), the better lawn, the lack of barriers, how many roads there were off the circular one, the employee parking lots, even the number of steps to the main entrance. Clyde didn't know exactly what he was looking for so he'd decided to note everything, thinking Jay might find something of interest that Clyde himself had hardly considered. "Keep it up, Clyde-san," Jay said. "This important work you're doing."

"Osu," Clyde said.

"How's Tina?"

That caught Clyde off guard. He thought about telling Jay what Tina was up to down there, but he decided to let it play out. He still thought she'd give up on her dream without any help from Clyde or Jay. "Good, I guess. Don't like living in a freezing-cold trailer in Jefferson City too much though."

"What's she doing with her time? 'Sides driving you crazy."

Clyde's thoughts raced. He took a drag to buy some time, shrugged with the exhale. "Just sittin around."

Jay shook his head. "She's not exactly what you'd call, uh, active, is she?"

"No," Clyde laughed.

"She even feeding you down there?"

"It's easier just to get McDonald's."

"Goddamn. Well you won't be there long. Keep an eye on her, Clyde. Don't let her do nothing stupid."

Clyde looked at Jay. "I will do my best." He really meant it.

Jay freed a new cigarette. "Weren't so long ago that a young Jay Smalls had to keep a young Jan Cox from doing something stupid."

"Jan?"

Jay nodded. "Believe it or not, she was once just like her daughter." He blew smoke into the shelves across the bar. "Jesus, we had problems. Screamin and yellin, carryin on. We used to argue till I wanted to shoot myself—or her. All the fucking this and that. Ultimatums up the wazoo." Clyde had thought about giving Tina an ultimatum, but he figured she'd just laugh if he tried. "Ultimatums, conversations, negotiations. None of that shit means a goddamn thing, by the way. In case you ain't worked that out yet."

"No?"

"No," Jay said. "Ultimatums don't mean shit. Talk don't mean shit. Only thing that means anything is this." He brought his fist down on the bar, splitting the old wood. "Oops," he said, snickering.

"But," Clyde said. He shrugged.

"Yes, Cryde-san?"

"I mean, you didn't." He made a fist.

"Hit her? You bet I did. Course I did. More than once too. You cain't hit a woman just once. You hit a woman just once you never see her again. This what men got, Clyde, muscle, the ability to generate power. To have, what is it? Dominion over women, and to protect 'em. From other men but most of the time from themselves." Jay looked Clyde in the eye. "Jan ain't subservient 'cause she's just naturally subservient. She's a goddamn pit bull. You back her into a corner, you better watch out, boy. I *made* her subservient. For her own good, and if you asked her right now she'd say the same thing." Jay smashed his cigarette into the bar top. "Women are like dogs, Clyde. Ain't nothin wrong with that neither. But you ever see an untrained canine? Shittin on the floor, chewing up your shoes, humping grandma's hip. Chaos. They work best when there's rules. You need to lay down the law in your own home before it's too late. Told her not to get a card or use computers? Good. Why not tell her to just stay the fuck home in that goddamn trailer and get your dinner on the table? You know what they say: can't teach an old dog new tricks? There truth in that."

"Osu," Clyde said. He knew that Jay was right. Tina had turned her back on her duties as a woman. What she was doing with all this business stuff was trying to act like a man and all it had done was cause problems, disrupt the natural order of things. If Tina spent her time at books-ico pumping the Smalls name across the Internet, Jay would flip his lid in a way Clyde had never seen.

A curse shot down the street. Dale hopped out of the truck sucking on his thumb. "Motherfucker!" he shouted, jerking it before putting it back in his gray maw.

"Dale," Jay said, sighing. "I talked to him, by the way. About what he did."

Clyde said, "Give him an ultimatum?" and cringed. Jay slipped off the stool and kept both hands on the bar, head low, breathing heavily. "Sorry," Clyde said, bracing himself.

Jay watched Dale, his shoulders rising and falling with the burden. "That night you were in the pit? The whole fucking time I sat in seiza in the basement repeating the dojo koan. I must have said it a thousand times. Look upwards towards wisdom and strength. All our lives! Never forget the true virtue of humility." Jay sighed. "I was looking for guidance. I was hoping Sosei would speak to me."

"Did he?"

"No. No, he didn't. He did not. I wish he had, but." Jay shook out another cigarette and lit it. With smoke streaming from his nose and mouth, he said, "Dale's been a problem from the get-go, long before you showed up. I won't lie to you. Don't think 'fore he acts. Got no understanding of anything outside of this fuckin moment. If I end up incarcerated, first tattoo I give myself's gonna say, 'It was Dale's fault.' Right here." Jay saying that made Clyde realize that he'd already won. Jay trusted him more now than he trusted his own blood.

Dale got back into the truck, the dogs following. "If our plans weren't as far along as they is," Jay said, "I'd probably just have you . . . " He turned to Clyde and shrugged. "Take care of him."

When we're through with Jefferson City, Clyde thought, killing Dale will be the first order of business.

lyde got to the capitol early the next day to make sure he didn't miss Chetto. He sat in Dale's shitty car watching the rising sun warm the building's façade, a scene somebody else might have called tranquil. Since the accident, mornings had been the worst for Clyde. The body hurt and his head was clouded, which he figured was mostly due to all the drink. Clyde shoved the door and leaned out retching more than once while waiting for his Mexican drug dealer to come out. Nothing but spit came up. Finally, just like yesterday, Chetto left the building with the other Mexicans, laughing and carrying on the way Mexicans always seemed to. Chetto nodded at Clyde and walked right up to the car this time. Clyde rolled down his window and offered him a cigarette.

"Gracias," Chetto said.

"What'd he say?" Clyde asked.

Chetto half nodded and half shook his head. It was a perfect picture of confusion. He took a piece of paper from his pocket with Featherstone's name and room number on it. "He say fill out application," Chetto said.

"Oh, yeah? When?" Chetto shrugged. "Is he in there now?"

Chetto nodded and smoked and squinted at the river. Clyde rolled the window up and got out, locking the door behind him and smoothing his shirt with both hands. After about three steps, he had to stop and put a hand on his car. His stomach this time churned up the rocket fuel he'd drunk this morning. He cursed and hacked in his throat and let his spit drool from his bottom lip to the pavement. "Coño borracho," Chetto said, laughing.

"What's that mean?"

"Um, like drunk fuck."

Clyde laughed. He wiped his mouth and stood still until he felt better. Then he pushed off his car again. Chetto said, "You go in now?"

"Yeah, why?"

"You no look, uh, too bueno. You no *smell* too bueno, coño."

Clyde stopped. He felt awful. "I used to be in good shape," he said. "Five hundred, thousand push-ups, I could run ten miles like it was nothing. Got shot, rolled my truck." Clyde jerked his thumb. "Got thrown out."

"Cabron," Chetto said. "You like a kitty cat? Nine lives?"

Clyde was going to talk about how he'd technically died, but didn't think the Mexican would understand specifics like that. Chetto went to his car. Clyde thought, here we go again with the cartel drugs. But Chetto came back with a stick of gum.

Clyde got back in his car and looked at himself in the mirror. He thought he looked okay and chewed the Juicy Fruit walking up the steps. Mr. Featherstone was a busted-up old Negro, someone who liked being able to order the white man around like he had power over him, which he did not. He had no idea what true power was. Clyde let Featherstone condescend to the Caucasian who had to work like a Mexican. You give a black man the slightest whiff of superiority and he gonna run that shit to the top of a mountain and plant it like a flag. Clyde could almost hear Jay snickering in his ear. Clyde kept his mouth shut, listened to a stream of bullshit, said, "Thank you, sir," and got Featherstone's okay. All that remained between that and full-time employment in the Missouri State Capitol building was a drug test and a mandatory criminal background check. Clyde was informed of his rights and signed the forms, worrying for a moment that Jay wouldn't be happy about this. He'd bitched about Tina using the library and here he was handing his name to the highway patrol and heading to a doctor's office to piss in a cup. Personally he felt like he knew what he was doing. The potential good would far outweigh what bad might come of this move. Jay was right; Clyde's record was spotless.

He drove across town and pissed in the cup. Two days later, Featherstone called early and told Clyde to show up that night for work. Clyde went into the street to call Jay. When he told Jay that he'd managed to get himself hired onto the Capitol's cleaning crew, Jay's yell nearly blew the speaker on Clyde's phone. Clyde thought that maybe, at some future WAC, he'd stand next to Jay in a field surrounded by men and talk about how easy it is to get access to a federal building.

The job was full-time, six nights a week, no benefits, minimum wage. Chetto would train him. How do you like that, being trained on the job in America by a Mexican? Clyde would have preferred to be on his own so he could wander more easily into intel, but he didn't want to draw attention to himself. It was a good thing that Clyde didn't need this job to feed a family, a good thing that this was not the old Clyde Twitty trying to make his way. What a state this country was in. He was more certain than ever that Jay's plan was just.

Within an hour of being on the payroll, Clyde scored his first big victory: a copy of the year's legislative calendar lying unattended on Featherstone's desk. He didn't hesitate to snatch it. At work that first night, Clyde trailed Chetto, who seemed happy that Clyde had got the job. Any chance Clyde got to slip off on his own for ten seconds he made notes in his pad. The height of the ceilings, width of the halls, marble, mahogany, brass, which doors seemed to be locked all the time, which weren't. But two hours of steady walking on those hard floors brought up pain that was so crippling Clyde started having trouble breathing. Chetto had already seen him limping along like a fag, and now here he was struggling for breath. Some warrior.

"Chinga," Chetto said when Clyde stopped and splayed himself on the floor like a starfish. Chetto said some other things in Mexican, sitting down a few feet away. "You okay?"

Clyde wasn't sure he was going to be able to tolerate this—any of it, the pain, the job, the wetback. He was used to drinking whiskey or margaritas anytime he wanted to take the edge off. He said, "Pain's just . . . information."

"Yeah, information that's, like, pinche importante," Chetto said. He just sat there, in no hurry, trabajo be damned. The floor was cold and dirty—they hadn't polished it yet—and felt good against Clyde's body. "You gonna die, man? I need to call, like, nine-eleven?"

Clyde laughed. He'd never known a Mexican with a sense of humor. "Sometimes . . . I just gotta . . . lie down."

"Pues." Chetto said. "De nada. Sometimes I got to lie down too. I like to lie down with my wife, you know, but if she not around, man, like if she go shopping or something? I lie down with my girlfriend instead." Chetto grabbed a ball of hair off the floor and blew it away. "I tell you, man, I were you? Pain like you got? Chinga, I be smoking mucho marijuana, like every day."

"Dude," Clyde said, "I do not understand Mexican."

"No comprende Méxicanos?" Chetto said it the way Jay did sometimes when he was joking around. "I talk good, mafufo."

Lying there looking at the ceiling, Clyde thought about what he needed. He was happy that he'd already answered some of Jay's questions; he'd already gone further with this than Jay had expected him to. A bolt of pain tore through him violently enough to make him jerk. When it passed, he said, "I never smoked those, uh, you know." Clyde pinched his finger and thumb near his lips.

Chetto laughed. This he got without any trouble. Clear as a Taco Bell.

"What you wait for, amigo? Let's take a break. It help."

Clyde considered it, but heard Jay in his head and pushed himself up off the floor. Warriors don't wallow in their aches and pains. "Nah," he said. "I'm good."

Two short hours later, the pain was back. Clyde hugged the floor again, Chetto watched. He didn't seem bothered.

"How you say . . . it fucking hurts . . . in Mexican?"

"Pinche duele."

"Pinche duele," Clyde said, and Chetto's shoulders shook with laughter.

"Mafufo, you accent fucking terrible."

Clyde went with it. "Hola, amigo," he said. "Qué pasa? My back-o hurt-o."

"Speak Spanish, it more than, like, adding 'o' to the end of shit, mafufo."

"Si," Clyde said. "I see-o."

Chetto laughed.

"What's that word you keep saying?"

"Qué?"

"Maf, uh."

"Mafufo," Chetto said. "Is like, uh, person who, uh, smoke mucho marijuana."

"Ah," Clyde said. "That ain't me."

"Marijuana bueno, man, but no what you need."

"Not what I need?"

"No. Crystal what you need. Crank." He dug a fingernail into his temple, looked under the nail. "With crank, man, nada mas importante." Crank had been a dark cloud hanging over Northwestern Missouri Clyde's whole life, but not once had he wanted to try it. "Crystal make you feel . . . " Chetto made a fist. "Pinche invincible, man. Pinche, uh, like tough."

"That's some serious shit."

"Si. That why, like, soldiers take it with them into war, man."

Clyde had never heard that and figured it was just something Chetto said to get dumbasses to buy his drugs. But his curiosity was up. He wanted to feel invincible. "Does it mess you up?" he said. "I heard it can really mess you up."

"I look messed up?"

"You're on crank now?"

Chetto laughed. "No man, but I do all the time. No te preocupes, mafufo. You just got to do it right. You do it right, that shit heal your wounds. Take away you pain. Make you wanna fight, man. Make you wanna fuck too."

As soon as he could stand, Clyde followed Chetto to the lot and got in his car. Chetto pulled a pack of Marlboros from under the seat and dug a small bag full of damp-looking beige powder out of it. From his pocket he retrieved what looked like a .22-caliber shell. He stuck the shell into the powder. Watching the rearview mirror, he put the shell up his nose. "Muy bien," he said. Tears ran in streams down his cheek. "Is call a bullet," he said, handing the shell over. It was flat on both ends and had a small cylinder that trapped powder. Clyde held it up and a cold sweat rose on his skin. His heart raced and he hadn't even done anything yet, what a pussy. A few quiet *nogare* breaths got that muscle under control. Is this the point of no return? Chetto's head lay back, his eyes still shut. Clyde worked it into his right nostril and sniffed.

Chetto made another bump for Clyde and he thought about how McVeigh had gotten into crank for a while without getting hooked. He'd been fine, he'd done it right, he'd handled it. Clyde felt the drug's current spread through his head and into his meat. All of his pains flared like he'd palmed a set of jumper cables. Then they faded, near to nothing. His heart pounded but he didn't care. Chetto took another bump and so did Clyde, three his first time, and then he smoked a cigarette fast, feeling pretty fucking fearless. Most of his nasal passage was numb. His senses dialed things in and out, his mind fractured thoughts. His focus was so intense that he knew immediately that crank would help him in fighting, would plunge him fearlessly into the *mai*. Chetto loaded a small glass pipe with weed that smelled like skunk even before it was lit. He sucked and held his breath, passing it to Clyde. "Jesus," Clyde said. "Anything else we gonna do tonight?"

Chetto laughed and coughed smoke. Clyde tried to suck on the pipe. This was another first. Troy had smoked pot a few times and had tried to tempt Clyde but Clyde had always resisted. He'd believed in the slippery slope, maybe he still did. Coach had once said that marijuana led to heroin and few men had the power to stop it.

"Maricón," Chetto croaked. "Do like me." He showed Clyde how to smoke.

Clyde tried it Chetto's way and coughed. It felt like he'd burned his lungs. Finally he managed to hold some in. He let it out with a *nogare* breath.

Chetto said, "Whatever, man." Clyde felt funny and cotton mouthed and went to his car for the thermos of margaritas he'd made the way Jan used to in Liberty Ridge. Chetto took a gulp and nearly spat. "What you make these with, mafufo, fucking gasoline? I got tequila from México," he said. "Reposado. Y Controy. Good shit. Mañana, I bring you margaritas from México. Polishing floors de nada if you fucked up."

Chetto turned on his radio, filling the car with Mexican music. Clyde laughed, but Chetto didn't seem to take it personally. Jay always said most minorities went out of their way to show you the size of the chip they've been shouldering since birth. Clyde and Chetto drank the terrible margaritas for five minutes and Clyde felt unsteady but fierce. He hadn't felt this good since getting shot. If McVeigh, and the United States Marines, used crank as a weapon, there was no goddamn reason why Clyde shouldn't too. He was as much a soldier as they were. *More.* Maybe warriors who weren't born with a killer instinct needed this kind of help. Outside Chetto's grimy windshield, the building was lit up, the dome's high orange windows shaking against a flat black sky. In two hours it would slowly turn blue. Another day closer to oblivion. "How long you think it's been around?" Clyde said. The building had never looked better.

"No se, mafufo. Like a hundred years?"

"You think it was here when the Civil War happened?"

"In school we study history Méxicana."

"You go to college?"

Chetto laughed lazily. "College, mafufo? I go to school till I was nine."

"Nine?" Clyde sat up.

"Si. Nine-year-old."

Clyde had never heard of such a thing. "What'd you do after that?"

Chetto spat out his window. "Try to cross border couple times . . . one time spent like nine month in Texas in this place for niños Méxicano. Then," he whistled. "Bus me to Guadalajara, man, where I don't even live." He shrugged. "I rode train back to Algodones, sell hats, T-shirts, leather belts to fat Americanos like you. Almost free today, amigo." He laughed.

Back inside, Chetto took Clyde up winding stairs to a door that led into an enormous room: the inside of the dome. Jay would be pleased that Clyde had got in. "This where, like, the Senate do they thing," Chetto said, walking around the perimeter on squishy green carpet. The Senate, Clyde thought. They were the target. This room would be turned to fire. Desks and chairs were everywhere; it was nothing like Clyde would have thought. Just a bunch of cubicles, really, littering the floor. Chetto put Clyde against one of the walls and said, "You stand there," jogging to the wall directly opposite, a hundred yards away. "Hey, mafufo," Chetto said in a whisper, "wanna smoke some reefer?"

Clyde could hear him like he was a foot away. "Whoa," he said. "Is this the crank?"

Chetto laughed. "Nah, man, this way the dome designed." Clyde looked up. The painted ceiling rose and rose. "So, mafufo, you ever go to jail?"

"Huh uh," Clyde said. "I know somebody who did though."

"I do five year, man." Chetto raised his hand, fingers splayed. "Cinco años."

"What for?"

"Nada, man, fuckin nada. I do five year for some maricón I no even know."

"Where?" Clyde said.

"Mexico."

Clyde had heard that Mexican jails were about the worst on earth. He wondered if Chetto had been raped, tortured, damaged in some other way. "How old are you?"

"Thirty-four, man. Ever married, mafufo?" Chetto was so far away that Clyde couldn't see his mouth moving.

"Huh uh."

"I got two wifes. One here and one in México." Chetto laughed. His shoulders jumped but the sound in his mouth didn't match up. "So no niños?" Chetto said.

"Nope."

"Kids, man. I got four in México and two here. I take you to my house, man, I show you."

The Turner Diaries had said that the other races were winning the war. Clyde hadn't thought much about it but here, standing right across from him, was living proof. Chetto had six children and Clyde had zip. Statistics had the browns overtaking the whites already, a mud flood rushing ever north. But Clyde knew that he'd taken the more radical path. If he'd wanted to repair the white race like a normal man, he could have married Tina and kept her pregnant for ten years.

"I got Juanita," Chetto whispered, counting on his fingers. "Erendira, Aimara, y Solymar in Algodones still, y here I got Rosa y Pitina, six girls, man. All I make is las chicas." Andrew MacDonald would have been plenty upset to hear this.

Clyde could see all of Jefferson City spread out below through the windows behind Chetto. The view was to the east; directly below were the steps and the wide, flat lawn that they would cross with their truck. Clyde went to one of the windows and leaned his forehead against the glass. He thought he might be able to see the exact spot where they'd leave the truck before running away, but he couldn't. He took the pad from his pocket, checked to see that Chetto wasn't watching, and recorded everything he'd seen. The crank and weed and tequila made his writing fast and loose.

On the way up the hill after work, Jay called. "Meet me at the old house at four o'clock. Liberty Ridge. Old MacDonald needs a few things for his farm."

lyde and Jay sat in the truck across the road from the Orscheln's farm store in Mexico, Missouri, two loaded Hi-Points on the seat between them. The store was closed, the parking lot dark, it was after eight. The sign at the roadside read *Make us proud, Miss MO!* in uneven black letters. Jay had looked into hitting one of the quarries near Independence, but the rent-a-cops on their payroll made for a messy getaway, so here they were.

Jay passed Clyde a can of Busch from the cooler, poured spicy V8 into his own, and studied the legislative calendar Clyde had stolen from work. "I don't fuckin believe it," he said, stabbing the paper with a finger. "Those bastards scheduled a vote to erect a monument commemorating the Missouri con-con of 1861."

"Con-con?"

"Constitutional Convention, Clyde-san. You wanna change the constitution you gotta hold a con-con."

Clyde had never heard of that. The longer he spent around Jay the more he wished he'd paid attention in history class. "Why's a vote about a monument matter?"

"It matters, Clyde-san, 'cause on March twenty-first a hundred and fifty years ago the government held a con-con to vote *down* a proposal to secede from the Union. And then they elected a pro-Unionist fucker and changed the course of the state into the Civil War." Jay's mouth twisted into a half grin. "We hit the capitol the day of this vote it gives our action . . . " He roiled his hand in the air, searching for the right word. "Resonance."

Clyde touched the Hi-Point nearest him. It was cold.

"3/21," Jay said. "That's our day. Everbody else doing April sixteenth,

April nineteenth, Waco, Murrah, Patriot Day. Hell with that. We claim 3/21 as our own, we create a new goddamn day to celebrate."

"3/21," Clyde said, thinking about what it would take to finish a truck bomb once they had the fertilizer that lay across the street. It wouldn't take no eight weeks of work, that was for sure. How strange would it be passing the next two months like a normal person knowing that on this day a city would fall, so many would die? He watched the wide-open road. Since they'd parked they hadn't seen a single vehicle; this town was quiet as the dead. "How long before we go in?" Now that they had their day Clyde could hardly sit still.

"Patience, grasshopper." Jay snatched his cigarettes off the dash, lit up. They filled the cab with smoke. Outside it was full dark and only about ten degrees. Jay wiped the fogging windows with a pale red rag. This was the perfect opportunity to tell Jay about Tina. She no longer believed, she was jeapordizing their plans. They finished their cigarettes. Jay started the engine, crossed the street, and entered the lot. When his headlights swept a trailer behind the store, he pounded the wheel. "Shit! Dale, goddamn you, I'm gonna fuckin kill you."

"What?" Clyde said.

"He didn't say nothing about no trailer."

"I thought *you* cased this store."

Jay shook his head. "Sent fuckin Dale." He shut the lights, leaned down to slip the breech break from under the seat. By the time he'd snapped it, the trailer's door was open, an enormous man standing in the light.

Clyde thought, Why don't we just leave? Find another way. The plan was obviously flawed. "He's lookin at us," he said, resisting the urge to say, "Just go."

"I don't give two shits," Jay said. He put the shotgun on the seat between them and picked up a Hi-Point. "Hide your piece. Follow my lead." He shoved the driver-side door. "You Daryl?" he yelled.

"What's that?" the man said.

Jay rounded the truck shaking his head, breath coming out in gray puffs. The handgun was in a pocket. Clyde put the other one in his belt and got out. Jay said, "They told me to talk to, uh, well I thought they said 'Daryl' but I could be wrong, I usually am." He came to rest about eight feet from the trailer, hands on his hips. He spat. "I was supposed to pick up an order but." He shook his head. Clyde stayed back, near the front bumper. "We had a blowout on 50."

"No kiddin," the man said. "Well, I don't know Daryl. I'm Calvin."

"Calvin," Jay said, snapping his fingers. "That's right, that was it."

"Yes sir. But." This man Calvin rolled his arm to check a watch, and when he did, Jay took another step, slipping the Hi-Point nice and easy from his pocket. He returned his hands to his hips, pivoting at an odd angle to put the gun hand in shadow. Clyde tried to spit so he might seem as relaxed as Jay, nothing wrong here, but it came out dry. This was supposed to be a normal break-in. No witnesses, no cameras, no trouble, candy from a baby. That's what Jay had said. "Per' near eight thirty," Calvin said. "I'm afraid you and your son'll have to come back tomorrow."

Jay dropped his head and let it hang. "Damn it." He rolled his eyes Clyde's way. "We come all the way from Independence, didn't we?" Clyde nodded, playing his part, adjusted the grip on the gun. He wanted to wipe his palm on his jeans but didn't. Jay said, "All right then," and took a big whirling step. The gun was out, up, and Jay marched the three metal steps into the trailer, shoving Calvin back so hard that he fell against a small floral-patterned loveseat, banging his head into the cabinets mounted above it and breaking glass. Clyde stood watching, his feet frozen to the ground. Jay looked out. "Git in here!" he said.

Inside, a woman said, "Calvin?" from behind a set of heavy brown curtains in the hall.

"Don't come out here!" Calvin yelled, trying to get up.

Jay stomped his chest to keep him down. The trailer rocked on its springs. "What's your wife's name?" Jay said. Calvin shook his head.

Jay laid the explosive end of his handgun against Calvin's forehead. Calvin's eyes clamped shut. "April," he said.

Jay told Clyde to cover Tiny and went to the curtain.

Clyde showed Calvin his gun—it was the same gun that Jay had, he wanted him to know that. Calvin tried to wipe the tears from his face. "Don't hurt her," he said as Jay flattened himself against the wood-paneled wall, poking the curtain.

"April?" Jay said. "You in there, sugar?"

"Frank?" she said. "Who's that?"

"Come on out here a minute," Jay said. "Nothing to worry about. We just got a little misunderstanding here."

"Is that Frank?" she said. "Calvin?"

"It is *not* Frank, honey," Calvin said.

"Who's here?" April said.

"Uh, well," Jay said. "That ain't important. What's important is Calvin needs your help."

"Just leave her be!" Calvin hissed, and Jay motioned at Clyde. Clyde thought it meant "shut him up" but he wasn't sure what to do so he kicked Calvin in the shin. Calvin yelled and grabbed his leg, face pulled into tight folds. "I just had a knee replacement, you son of a bitch."

"Sorry," Clyde said.

"You kick him in the knee?"

Clyde shrugged.

"*Kensetsu geri,*" Jay said, which Clyde knew meant "kick to the knee," though not the way he'd done it.

A short round woman pulled the drapes aside. Buried in her fluffy purple bathrobe was a little girl no older than two. Jay's face dropped. He recovered before anybody but Clyde noticed. "Well well, what do we got here?"

"Who's this, Calvin?" April said. She didn't look directly at Jay.

"He's here to rob us," Calvin said loudly. "Sir, she can't see."

"What?" April said.

"Can't hear neither," Jay said. He leaned in. "We're—here—to—rob—you!" He waved the gun in front of her face.

April's swimmy eyes slid this way and that. "I don't understand," she said, her mouth starting to quiver.

Jay put a hand on the little girl's head. "This your granddaughter?"

"I'd kindly ask you to take whatever it is you want and leave us be," Calvin said.

Jay moved April to the sofa, put her down gently. She was shaking now and the girl she was holding on to started to cry. Watching her face, Clyde felt awful. Calvin plucked the pieces of broken cabinet glass from the loveseat and dropped them in a little blue trash can attached to the wall with a metal bracket. He held his arms out. The girl climbed up, burying her face in his polo shirt.

"Calvin!?" April said.

"I'm right here," Calvin said, a hand on her thigh.

"Don't move," Clyde said.

"We didn't," Calvin said.

"I thought you did."

"Well, maybe I did. If I did, I apologize."

April's head swiveled from Calvin to somewhere between Jay and Clyde. "Are they still here?"

"Yes, dear," Calvin said.

Jay sighed. "Where's your phone?" Calvin nodded at the counter below the microwave. A flip phone in a black leather belt clip lay atop a *Sportsman's Companion* catalog. Jay put the phone in his pocket, rolled the catalog, and put that in his pocket too. "No, uh, landline or nothin?"

"No sir."

"What about weapons?" Jay said. "Y'all Orscheln's security, you gotta have some weapons."

April said, "Weapons?" She rubbed at her face with both hands. "Who has a weapon?"

Into her ear Calvin said, "Nobody has any weapons. There are no weapons, honey." He pointed at the counter behind Jay. "In the drawer you'll find my six-shooter. That's all I got." Jay opened it. There among the bills and papers was a Colt .45 with a pretty pearl and turquoise handle. He gave it to Clyde, it wasn't unlike Clyde's own gun.

"Check it," Jay said.

"It's loaded," Clyde said.

"What we gonna do," Jay said, "is we gonna tie y'all up a while. We gonna take care of some business, then we gonna go on our way. How's that sound?"

April shot blindly off the couch but Calvin yanked her back down. Snot popped from her nostrils and her arms flailed like she was being attacked by bees. "Get out!" she screamed. "Get the hell out of here!"

Jay told Calvin to calm his woman before she made him do something he didn't want to do. Calvin sat up on the edge of the loveseat, hugging his granddaughter, turned his upper body with his arm up, and backhanded his wife across the face. "Oh!" she cried, falling back into the couch with her hands on her face. Her ratty pink slippers slid against the carpet.

"Damn," Jay said.

Calvin said, "We just want whatever you want."

"I doubt that." Jay sidled up to Clyde. "In the truck behind the seat's a toolbox. In there's a roll of twine."

Clyde went out. The air felt much colder than before. The enormous building put everything behind it in a thick black shadow. All the high lamps in the front were dark. Out in the country they didn't see the need to light up everything all night long. Maybe now they would. Clyde found the twine and took a minute to gather his courage. His chest ached and he felt sick; he wanted to tie them up, get in the store, load the fertilizer, and get the fuck out of there. Jay had expected this job, from the time they got there to the time they left, to take under an hour. Any more than that and they'd be risking their necks. Twenty minutes had already passed and they were nowhere.

In the trailer, Jay had everyone face down on the floor, the little girl sandwiched between her grandparents. They both had their arms on her. She was crying, but not like April was crying. She was shrieking and hysterical. She was only two, she was afraid. She hadn't learned the impulse to hide the fear, hadn't developed the impulse to negotiate or escape. Calvin rubbed her back with one of his big swollen hands. Jay left the trailer and Clyde got to his knees. He grabbed April's wrists, just bone and skin, making her shriek so loudly it hurt his ears. Everything in the trailer was an assault: the girl, his own breath in his head, he couldn't stand it. He bound her wrists and Calvin said, "Is that necessary, young man?" Clyde ignored him. The knot wasn't tight, he didn't want to hurt a little girl. When he was working on Calvin's wrists, Jay came back, the trailer rocked. He slapped a roll of duct on the counter, started opening drawers.

"What you looking for?" Clyde asked.

"Ah hah," Jay said, waving a box of freezer bags. He put one over his own head, sucked a breath, the plastic hugged his face. "Where the keys to the store, Calvin?" Jay said through the bag, garbled. Calvin squirmed to get a look at him and didn't understand what he was seeing. Jay took the bag off his head. "The keys."

"Hanging on a hook under the microwave."

Jay found a heavy ring, two dozen keys. He knelt. "Which ones open the back?"

"That one."

"There just one or more?"

"There's more."

Jay went through the keys until Calvin nodded. "What's the alarm code?" Calvin didn't say anything. "You don't tell me, I'm gonna tape freezer bags over your heads. Y'all be dead in ten minutes."

"Pound-six-four-one-one-three-off," Calvin said.

"Where's it at in there?"

"Inside the door on the right."

"How far?"

"Just right there."

"Thank you," Jay said. He looked in the drawer where he'd found Calvin's revolver. He got a pen, wrote the code on the inside of his forearm, then took up the duct tape. Jay had Clyde hold onto April's head so that he could get it on her mouth, then he ran it around two times. The girl was easy, she went quiet when they did her. Calvin was the hardest, Jay had to punch him in the head and kneel on his back while Clyde pulled his arms back to get him to stay still enough. Jay said, "Jesus," when they were done. He handed Clyde the freezer bags. "Put those on. Tape 'em up."

"I thought," Clyde whispered, but something in Jay's face told Clyde not to question him right now. Jay went out again.

Clyde pulled a bag on April. Calvin yelled at him through the tape but April didn't struggle much, unlike Calvin, who bucked, thrashed his head, screamed into the tape. The little girl hardly moved at all. Clyde told them it was gonna be all right, they were going to make it through this just fine. He ran tape around the bags at the neck to make a seal. When he finished, they lay there. The bags crinkled, puffing and contracting.

S lowly April and Calvin squirmed together until the girl was hidden between them almost completely. All Clyde could see was hair. It was such a light blonde color that it was almost white, like the feathers of a baby bird. They turned their faces toward each other until their foreheads touched. Clyde remembered someone at the Congress talking about freezer bags as a great way to calm somebody down in a tense situation. You put a bag on somebody's head and they git how serious it is. You're not someone to be fucked with. You are not Joe Robber. April and Calvin understood the situation now, they would go along with any plan. Clyde did not know how he had ended up in this trailer, with this handgun, watching this family breathe into bags.

The door opened and Clyde almost jumped out of his skin. Jay said, "You do it?"

"Yep."

"You tape 'em 'round?" He ran his hands over all three bags, turning heads this way and that like he was inspecting cabbages at the store. He stood up nodding. "Now, y'all be good and we'll be back to take those off 'fore too long," he said. "Or, go ahead and try something stupid, in which case we won't be back at all. We'll just drive on out of here and forget we ever knew you. How's that sound?"

Only Calvin nodded. His bag crinkled. Clyde and Jay went out, pulling the door. In the cold air Clyde tried to stop his jaw clacking. "How long can they breathe like that?"

Jay shrugged. "Half hour?"

"You said ten minutes."

Jay waved a hand. "That was just to scare 'em."

The back door of the Orscheln's stood open, some lights on inside. Jay marched right in. Clyde hung back, watching the trailer. "Clyde!" Jay yelled. "You best wake up. Get in here and grab a cart!"

Jay found the fertilizer and Clyde hurried over pushing a big flat cart. Those bags were fifty pounds each, but they loaded twenty in no time. Clyde ran it to the loading dock and Jay went off shouting about where the carts at? Clyde met him there, a big poster of Miss Missouri hanging on the wall. "She's pretty, I give you that," Jay said, "but the best piece of ass in the whole goddamn state?"

They filled more carts, Jay messed with the controls for the loading dock until the door groaned to life. Clyde jumped down into the truck and Jay threw bags. Teamwork. They got over a hundred and twenty, more than they needed. Down on the ground by the truck they fogged the air with hard breaths.

"What time is it?" Clyde said.

Jay checked his watch. He spat, squinting at the light streaming out of the dock. "Been about twenty."

"We should probably check."

Jay gave Clyde a fierce look. "Still gotta light the fire." He opened the driver's door and put a cigarette in his mouth. His head shook, slowly. He pushed the truck lighter and waited for it.

"What are we doing?" Clyde said.

The lighter popped, Jay lit up. "All right, goddamn it, go check."

"Take the bags off?" Clyde said.

"No. No. Do not take the bags off their heads. Just come back with a status report."

Clyde ran. In the trailer no one was moving or making a sound. They were all dead, all of them dead. Then a bag snapped. The man, Calvin, his round back rose and fell. Clyde heard a whimper, saw a hole in the bag. Clyde stuck his finger in, tore it bigger. The man had chewed one through his granddaughter's bag too. She started to cry now and Calvin said, "It's okay," so softly that Clyde, only two feet away, barely heard it. Feeling a rush of relief, he hurried out. Jay was in the store making a racket. No reason to hide our presence or intent now. Clyde followed the noise until he found Jay dousing the remaining bags of ammonium nitrate with gas. "Well?" he said.

"They're okay."

Jay said nothing. He threw the plastic fuel can, it bounced. He crossed the floor and handed Clyde a pack of matches. "Light it."

Clyde got one lit, tossed it. It went out with a hiss. He tried two more before the fire caught, but when it did, it spread so fast it was scary.

They ran back to the loading dock, shoes slipping on the slick floor like a cartoon. Before jumping down Jay ripped Miss Missouri off the wall. He started the truck but didn't put it in gear. What the hell was he waiting for!? Clyde didn't understand this at all. Maybe Jay wanted to be sure the fire caught, the evidence consumed. A large quantity of ammonium nitrate going missing alerted the feds. Jay lit another cigarette and there they sat, the blaze lighting up Clyde's side mirror. They had been there an hour now, maybe more. They were well past recklessness. "Your gun fully loaded?" Jay asked.

Clyde knew it was. What use was it carrying an empty weapon?

Jay took his Hi-Point out and checked the chamber with a loud noise. He dropped it on Miss Missouri and flicked his eyes about the blank darkness spreading into the distance from the front of the truck. He pounded the wheel with a hammer fist. "Goddamn Dale."

"Probably didn't even check," Clyde said. "Probably didn't even come here. Wouldn't put it past him."

Jay blew smoke out his nostrils, looking like a bull. "We been very careful with every piece of the puzzle. When I bought the cargo truck off that Mexican you know I wore a fuckin disguise?"

"No."

"I did. That's what got McVeigh. FBI sketch artist." Jay opened the door to blow a snot rocket, slammed it shut with a long rattle, checked his watch. Clyde saw the worry. "We been here an hour fifteen. Fuck *me*. McVeigh's dead, in case you ain't noticed." He laid a hand on his gun but didn't pick it up. The poster made noise. *Make us proud, Miss MO.* "They seen us," Jay said. "Seen our faces."

"The woman's blind."

Jay sighed. "She's one of three."

But that granddaughter, she wouldn't be able to identify anybody, she was nothing but a child. "The girl," Clyde said.

Jay jumped on his seat. "In eight weeks we gonna kill fifty just like her! A warrior don't go around mopin about how many heads he cut off. One, a hundred, a thousand? Revolutions are bloody." Jay mumbled something to himself, made a sour face, snatched up his Hi-Point. Without saying another word he got out, marched around the front of the truck. In a minute he disappeared into the darkness. Clyde rolled his window to the cold. The fire in the store was spreading, Clyde could hear it, there were containers in there, metal or plastic, starting to pop. When the trailer door opened, light ran across the ground. Jay was in that light, stepping up, reaching back, pulling the door behind him. Watching the black ground Clyde braced himself, but heard nothing. The fire fizzed like soda in a glass.

Light fanned out again and folded away. Clyde heard Jay's feet on gravel, then flinched when he seemed to materialize out of the night only a few feet from the truck. His eyes were wild. What had happened in there? The image of a butcher knife stabbing, stabbing. Jay yanked the passenger door open and dragged Clyde off the seat, shoved the gun into him. "Didn't tell me they'd chewed through the fuckin bags," he said. Clyde felt the gun against his solar plexus, coughed. "Go fucking take care of it."

"Me."

"Only a matter of minutes 'fore the fuckin fire brigade gets here."

"Why can't we just—" Jay slapped Clyde across the face. It brought all of Clyde's senses alive. He stepped back with his hands up, too late. What a shit warrior he was, hadn't even seen it coming, couldn't even block an open-hand bitch slap.

"You know better than to question me!"

"Osu," Clyde said, out of habit.

"You're a soldier. I'm your commanding officer. And I'm giving you an order. Go in there and eliminate a serious fuckin threat to our mission. You get it? To our mission. To my family and yours too, Clyde. Your mom and uncle ain't a couple innocents no more. You fuck up you don't just fail me and my family you fail your own too and it's about time you got that through your fuckin head." Clyde felt the gun again, it hurt. He couldn't look at Jay right now, this was not the plan at all. "Goddamn you, Clyde, this is for keeps!" Jay's voice was strained, close to blowing out. "No difference between the three people in that fucking trailer and all the goddamn politicians in that building in Jefferson City."

"Yeah, there is," Clyde said.

Jay punched Clyde in the side of the head. Clyde winced and blinked. "Get a hold of yourself!"

"Osu," Clyde said, the gun now in his hand, somehow, heavy and hard. Jay shoved him. Clyde walked around the building and climbed the hollow trailer steps.

The girl was sitting up, crying silently through the jagged plastic hole. The man and the woman were still on the carpet, face up now, talking softly, planning something, planning a getaway. When the trailer pitched under Clyde's weight they went rigid so fast it was like they were playing a game for the girl's sake. Clyde shoved a forearm into his mouth, stepped over the man. "Don't," the man said. The girl scrambled under the dining table, the space in there was so small. "Don't," the man, Calvin, said again. He fought the rope on his wrists but Clyde had tied a damn good knot. Once upon a time, he'd been a Boy Scout.

The man's wife slumped against the wall. Her head was set like she was watching, but the bag hid her eyes, which were useless anyway. The end of a gray tongue poked into the hole she'd chewed. The man yelled, "Don't!" It was a command now; before it had been a plea.

Footsteps approached outside and Jay said, "I ain't heard nothing yet."

The man went rigid. He shook his head at Clyde and whispered, "Don't."

"I'm doing it," Clyde said at the door.

"We's pushing our luck, Clyde-san!"

"Just a second," Clyde said.

He shoved an arm into his mouth. Nausea rose. He had to wipe his eyes to see. He shook his head and took a step, feeling the trailer rock. The gun would not stay steady in his hand. Some warrior.

"Don't!" the man said, and Clyde waited for him to make eye contact through the hole in his bag.

These people, Clyde thought, trying to breathe, these people got nothing to do with us. Even McVeigh weighed every life he had to take against the greater good, he had the chance to kill innocent bystanders at every turn; a nosy fisherman when he was mixing explosives lakeside, a motel clerk who asked too many questions. Every time he chose not to.

Clyde shot a hole in the sofa. Stuffing burst. The man jerked against the rope, his wife screamed and kicked against the carpet like she was doing exercises. Clyde put his foot against her, shoving her into the cabinet. She split it with a loud *crack* and he fired two shots where her head had just been. Jagged holes popped into the wood, coughing sawdust.

"There you go," Jay said. He was right outside, his voice nearly blown.

Clyde looked from the door to the man and held a finger to his lips. The man nodded. Clyde smelled piss, he got down and peered under the table. It was hard to see, his eyes were flushed, the back corner, where the girl had curled into a little ball, was dark. In Clyde's vision she wavered, though she kept perfectly still. He took a breath, his first since firing the gun, shot a hole into the floor. With his mouth on Calvin's ear he whispered, "You know how to play dead?" Calvin was shivering. "Better goddamn do it, then, I fuckin mean it." He jerked a nod and collapsed.

Clyde kicked the trailer door open and Jay jumped back. "Get all of 'em?" He'd been right outside. Clyde threw the door shut. "Did you?" Jay said.

"Yes, goddamn it!" Clyde yelled. "Wanna fuckin check!?" He had half a mind to fire off one more round.

Jay let the outburst go and they ran behind the building. It was hot and bright. Embers floated out of the loading dock and rushed into the black sky. They got into the idling truck and Jay slapped Clyde's thigh. "Good," he said. All he had to do was look inside that trailer. "Good." That was all he had to do. They left the lot, drove calmly down a dark, gently winding road, and took a ramp to the highway.

Jay lit cigarettes. Miss Missouri watched from the seat, torn across her chest from the gun. "Whiskey," Jay said, pointing, and Clyde popped the glove box. The dull yellow lamp lit a fifth. He uncapped it and drank. "You a goddamn warrior!" Jay said. There were very few people on the road at this hour and Jay's headlights lit a black, empty road. "Osu!" Jay shouted, his body tensing with the word, his right arm tight. He pounded the wheel and yelled it again.

"Osu," Clyde said, realizing that he still had the gun in his hand. He wondered, had he actually done it, if he'd feel worse right now, or better.

The drive home passed in silence. Jay's spirits had lifted considerably, and he brought Clyde to Dale's car in Liberty Ridge and told him to be strong, to dig deep, to remember the koan. "Firm unshaking spirit," he said.

Clyde drove straight from Liberty Ridge to the liquor store. On Boonville's Darktown side, the clerk sold him a bottle without asking for ID and Clyde sucked on it all the way back to Jefferson City, thinking of all the times Troy had bought them beer with his older brother's ID. One guy had tricked Troy with a question, said, "I got something for you here," bending down, and come up with a shotgun from behind the counter. They ran out of that Gunn City liquor store like their asses were on fire. More thoughts came to Clyde for his letter to his old friend. He ran them around his tongue and knew he was getting drunk behind the wheel. He would either make it back home or he wouldn't. He'd already died once, he knew what it was like. What bothered him the most was betraying Jay. A part of him knew that not killing those people had been his biggest failure yet. Then an image of his Uncle Willie sitting in a courtroom as Clyde was tried for murdering a helpless family came to him, making his guts clench up. He didn't know what to do. No matter what, somebody would be disappointed in him. The simple fact of that made him sick. Someone he loved would be hurt—and hurt bad.

When he got in it was after midnight. Tina was asleep. He nearly fell climbing the trailer steps, and curled onto the sofa like a dog, pulling the afghan over him and holding the bottle close to his chest. He was too hopped up to sleep, so he just drank until he passed out.

He woke feeling something heavy. When he opened his eyes, a big bottle of sweet tea slid off his chest. It was capped, so it didn't spill, and Tina, standing over him, caught it. "Late night?"

Clyde's body hurt but his head was worse. Slowly he sat up and uncapped the bottle and asked Tina for his sunglasses. "How much sugar you put in?"

"I know how to make rocket fuel," Tina said. Clyde took a gulp. She was right, she did. "Dang, niggah," she said. "You be illin.'"

Clyde laughed and coughed, Tina could be so funny sometimes. He tried not to focus on any one thing as Tina chattered away. She'd been fooling with the Big Flavor recipe, the marketplace demanded perfection, she wasn't about to work hard to get her product into stores just to have the fickle consumer pick a competing brand. What she'd peddled at the WAC might have been good enough for crazy white supremacists, no offense, but it wouldn't cut it in the real world. In the short time they'd been in Jeff City, she'd registered the business with "D and B," a first step toward legitimacy. She went through some papers and passed Clyde the official DBA certificate they'd sent to a P.O. Box she'd rented. *Smalls Flavor Enterprises LLC*, it read. "I figure if the barbeque sauce takes off, I can put other stuff out, like hot sauce. Smalls Scorcher. With Smalls as our core brand, we can do pretty much anything once we've established a market presence. It ain't about our product, it's about our values." Clyde didn't know who this "we" was that Tina kept mentioning, and he figured she didn't either.

Had things been different, had he been able to control Tina the way Jay controlled Jan, he would have already put an end to all this. Now the forms had been sent, the damage had been done. He just didn't have it in him this morning; he gulped rocket fuel and forced a smile.

"They make it so hard you almost need a stupid lawyer just to get the ball rolling, ya know? A hundred and fifty bucks an hour? I don't think so. And half the Web sites give you the wrong instructions for how to fill out their stupid forms and then you gotta do the whole thing over again. And holy crap, insurance? Jeez Louise. Don't even get me started. If you saw how much *that* shit cost it'd make your weenie shrink, but I guess you already saw it." She laughed and slapped her hip. "Oh, and guess what? Walmart's got this Supplier Diversity Program I can get into if I register as a woman-owned or minority business."

Clyde nearly spat. "You gotta be shitting me."

"Hey, according to Walmart I'm a minority. I guess on account of my pussy. Why should I let some jigaboo or illegal mamacita take all the cake for her and her twenty-five bastardos? I don't got any more of a leg up than they do just 'cause I'm pasty. I mean, look at me," she said, spreading her arms. "I live in a *tray*-ler."

"You better hope Jay don't find out what you're doing."

Tina just waved her hand at that. Maybe she really was done with this family. "Speaking of Walmart," she said, pausing long enough for Clyde to raise his bloodshot eyes. "We got an appointment today."

"Uh . . . "

"Well, *I* got an appointment. In Boonville with, um, well, you know him, Mr. Wilson." Tina cringed, waiting for Clyde's reaction. "I need your help."

"Son of a bitch," was Clyde's reaction. On a long list of things Clyde had no interest in doing, this would have been at the top.

"He wants to taste Big Flavor! If he likes it, he'll give it a trial run in the store, can you believe it!?"

Clyde's head hurt. "When did this all happen?"

"I did some market research one day in there and we got to talking."

"Market research."

"Turns out, Jerry *loves* barbeque sauce."

"Jerry."

"Mr. Wilson, dummy. Jeez Louise, if you're gonna be any help today you best start working your head out of your bung hole." Tina got up and poured herself some coffee. "Finish your tea while I get ready, clear out the cobwebs. I got charcoal and a little grill in the trunk. I'll drive so you can recover. When we get there, I need you to do the cookin while I deal with front-office matters."

Clyde leaned back with his eyes closed and the cold rocket fuel resting on his crotch. Everything hurt and his mind was a jumble. He didn't want to participate in Tina's craziness, but neither did he want to spend the day in the trailer alone replaying Jay's threats. Surely that man Calvin had made the news. "My terrible ordeal." With no Internet or television in Lick Skillet, Jay's only chance of hearing it would be radio out of K.C. Clyde hoped that Mexico, MO, was small enough and far enough away to not be of any interest to big-city folks. If Jay found out they were alive and well, there'd be no night in the pit; there'd be an eternity in the pit. He wished he'd got some of that crystal off Chetto. A bump right about now would help. He wanted to feel strong again, he needed that aggression.

"I ain't asked you for anything in a long time, buddy. Can you do this one thing for me? I'll take you to lunch at Pancho Villa's when we're done. How 'bout that? Just like old times."

When he looked up Tina's face was such a mixture of sadness and hope that he said, "All right."

A station out of Columbia was playing Mötley Crüe and Tina turned it up. "Vince Neil is so fucking hot," she said, drumming the wheel and singing along with words that were mostly wrong and out of tune. Clyde took out his cigarettes, cracking the window. Tina surprised him by taking the pack and lighting one for herself. "There a lot of things you don't know about me," she said. They smoked. Clyde watched the gray-green country pass. "You feeling any better?" Tina said.

"Not really."

She was quiet for a time. They listened to K-Rock. Then Tina turned it down. "I know living in a trailer on the side of the road ain't, like, the life or nothing, but being down here on our own is kinda . . . fun." She smiled with her little teeth. "You like it?" she said.

Clyde nodded.

"Do you?"

"I do," he said. "Yep."

"Be better if we had an actual apartment to live in, you know, with a real bedroom, an actual kitchen, maybe a toilet you didn't have to empty yourself in a ditch. Call me crazy."

"Crazy," Clyde said, staring out the window on his side.

"I wonder how much a little apartment down here costs?"

"Probably more than we can afford."

"Oh, I don't know, you got a real job now, Clyde. I know it doesn't pay, like, great or nothing but it's a start." Clyde wondered where he'd been during Tina's shift into embracing this domestic fairy tale. She grinned and looked girlish when she said, "If we could afford two bedrooms we could have babies."

"Ain't a job, Tina, it's intelligence work," Clyde said. A part of him didn't want to knock the wind out of Tina's sails right before her big pitch to Wilson. But another part didn't want to encourage her to grab on to the dream that Clyde, thanks to Jay, was determined to expose as a fuckin lie.

Tina looked wounded. After driving several miles in silence, she said, "What you all are planning to do . . . " She shook her head.

"We ain't planning nothing," Clyde said. Tina—and everybody else—was better off kept in the dark.

"I hope you'll be able to live with yourself is all I'm saying."

Clyde didn't want to hear this crap from her right now. He didn't want to think about what his actions might mean to people outside the movement. "Probably gonna end up dead anyway," he said.

"You and how many babies?"

"Ain't gonna be any babies."

"That's what McVeigh thought before he blew the day care to smithereens."

"Well, we been studying every mistake he made so why don't you let us worry about the collateral damage."

"You know what's funny?"

"No, but I got a feeling you're gonna tell me."

"There ain't a single thing that's come out of your mouth since you started training with my dad that I ain't already heard him say."

Clyde slammed his hand into the armrest with so much force it broke off the door. "You're the one got me into this!" he shouted, scaring Tina with his anger. She stared for so long that Clyde worried they'd run off the road. He tried to fasten the armrest back to the door but couldn't. "Before I met your family I was just a normal guy," he said, and Tina finally turned her eyes back to the road. "Head in the sand, ignorant to pretty much everything. Now I ain't. I'm awake. I'm part of the warrior class now."

Tina swerved. Clyde's head banged off the window. "Sorry," she said. "But wow." She shook her head with her mouth open like he'd just said something crazy.

Right then and there he decided to tell Jay about Tina. It was the only way. If she was this worried about it there was no telling what she might do to sabotage their plans, intentionally or otherwise. Telling Jay now, after the talk they'd already had in the bar, would piss him off something fierce, but it was better than the alternative.

The rest of the drive Tina didn't say a word, giving Clyde time to get his head on straight. Lately he'd been feeling something new, and it took him several miles of countryside to realize that it was anger, at Jay, who had been the first person in Clyde's life to see just how angry he was. As Tina drove, bobbing her head to the heavy metal that Clyde had tuned out, he weighed his thoughts. He didn't want to feel this way. He loved Jay. He'd learned more from him than he had from anybody. Jay was a wise and powerful man, and he'd never given up on Clyde, even when it seemed like he had. Clyde tried to remember everything leading up to his going into the trailer at the farm store. He had to get this straight. Maybe there was something he'd missed. From the moment Jay had told him to tape the bags over their heads, Clyde had been focused on only one thing: saving those people's lives. Whereas Jay's focus had remained on their goal. Clyde hadn't thought that last night could have been another test, one to determine if he was ready to kill for the cause. If that was the case, the answer was clear, at least to Clyde. What defined a warrior more accurately than a man prepared to kill in the line of duty? Jay would say that this was the burden of the warrior class, to do the dirty work that others could not, or did not, want to do. The soldier was an instrument, a well-trained weapon. Part of training the heart, Clyde thought, might be in teaching it how *not* to feel. If it was a simple muscle, like the bicep, as Jay had said, then it too had a memory. The warrior understood how to live apart from normal human emotions and become a ghost.

Tina pulled into the Walmart. Two hours had gone by in a flash. She parked near the store and put a little sign she'd made on her window. It said *Smalls Big Flavor Sauce* and *It Packs a Hell of a Kick!* She thought that Jay's line sent the right brand message. She went in and Clyde set the grill up at the front of the car and looked for Esther. He kept half an eye on the entrance in case she came out for a smoke.

When the coals were hot he put the chicken on and it started dripping, which rose a sweet smell that attracted curious shoppers. Clyde ignored them all. He didn't work here no more, the hell with them. The automatic doors jerked and Tina marched out in front of Wilson and the assistant manager. And Esther.

"It packs a helluva kick," Mr. Wilson said when he saw the sign. "We'd have to lose the 'Hell' but 'Packs a Kick' is still pretty good."

Clyde could see Tina's jaw clench but she said, "That's no problem." After a minute she said, "I actually like that better," and Mr. Wilson grinned and nodded. "I mean, 'hell' adds the idea of heat to the customer's expectation of the flavor character, but, um, I'm not sure we need it."

"I like it as it is," Esther said, slipping a cigarette from her pack, not looking at Clyde. Today her hair was chestnut brown, a single pigtail sticking out. "And I'm the only one here who knows anything about damnation."

"I think you can see just by looking at it that it packs a kick."

"Mr. Wilson's remarkable taste-o-vision!" Esther said, raising an arm, and Wilson blinked at her.

"Not too much of a kick," Tina said, giggling. "We tailored the spice so it can be enjoyed by the whole family." Besides Clyde, she was the only one wearing a coat. Wilson and his assistant rubbed their hands together and shivered.

"Let's see what kinda kick it packs," Mr. Wilson said, all exaggerated enthusiasm.

Clyde put the chicken on paper plates. It was obvious that Wilson liked it. Esther took a few bites and made a big show of how spicy it was. "Too hot for this white girl," she said. "Ouch, somebody spray me down." She retrieved her smoldering cigarette from Tina's bumper and took her first look at Clyde.

"It's not that hot," Tina said. "She's a kidder." With that, Wilson and the assistant manager put their plates of half-eaten chicken on the top of Tina's car and followed her inside to "talk business."

lyde doused the coals and watched Esther through the gray smoke. She hung back, looking at the ground. He opened Tina's doors and waited. Esther got in and sat looking out the passenger window as if Clyde didn't even exist.

"I know," Clyde said. "I did it again."

"Yeah asshole," she said, slapping his arm and saying "Sorry" to the ceiling. "Last time I saw you, your cock was in my mouth." She shoved a hand into his chest. "I mean, I didn't think that meant we were suddenly man and wife. I was just worried about you. Sweet moustache, by the way. And by sweet I mean scary."

She rested her cigarette softly in Clyde's lips, took it back, and closed her eyes to drag deeply. She shook her head and her hair tumbled. Clyde had half a mind to take her behind the Tire & Lube Express. The other half knew he shouldn't be sitting here.

"What you been up to?" she said.

"Not much," he said. "I died."

She laughed.

"I'm serious, I got shot, then I tried to find a hospital and passed out at the wheel, rolled my truck, totaled it. I was in a coma for like two weeks."

Esther dropped her cigarette into her lap and then batted it to the floorboard. When she looked up her eyes had welled with tears. She covered her face with both hands. "Oh my gosh, Clyde," she said. "Where!?"

"Down on Troost."

"No, dummy, *where*?" She pushed her hands at him.

Clyde unzipped his coat and pulled his sweatshirt up, revealing his mangled stomach. Esther laid her insect-thin fingers on it. They were freezing but Clyde didn't mind. He took the discomfort and tried not to show it. "You poor puppy!" She leaned over and kissed his wounds. Clyde closed his eyes, not sure if she would stop there. He imagined Tina opening the door to a little surprise. Maybe she'd learn a thing or two.

Esther sat back and ran a pinky up and down his zipper absentmindedly. He made her stop after a while and she bounced on the seat, her hair jumping. "You ever do crystal meth?" he asked.

"Crank? Me and crank go *way* back."

Clyde laughed. He shoulda known.

"You ain't fucked till you fucked on meth." She let her head fall back and said, "Sorry, hun."

"I did it, other day."

"Clyde!" She shoved a hand into his chest. "Naughty naughty!"

Esther leaned over and wrapped her arms around Clyde's neck, kissing the skin behind his ear with a wet, smoky mouth. Then she moved to his mouth and sucked the tip of his tongue. "Num-num-nummy!"

Sometimes Clyde wished he'd made different choices in life. He said, "Did you know Tina's family were like, white supremacists?"

Esther raised an eyebrow. "Tina's family? And you?"

Clyde didn't really know what he was anymore. He knew he wasn't normal, that much was clear enough. He recalled the language that J.D. had used in court. "I'm a non-resident, non-foreigner stranger to the current state of the forum."

"Say what?"

"Nah, that's just . . . I'm just . . . " He shrugged. Esther waited. "I'm a good soldier, that's what I am." He made a fist, his forearm bulged. "Jay's the only person who ever saw it in me, the only one to put me to some kind of use."

Esther took a drag. Holding her breath she said, "Doing what?"

Clyde thought about telling her doing what, exactly what, maybe she could handle it, if anyone could it might be her. But instead he just smiled like he was talking crazy.

"Well, I'm a quarter Navaho," she said. "That mean they wanna kill me?"

"Why would they wanna kill you? We're friends."

"Are we?"

"Course."

"What if I was black?" she said.

"Well. Let me put it this way. We probably wouldn't be sittin here."

"They hate black people?"

"They don't like 'em much, no," Clyde said. "But Jews are the real problem. They're the ones running things. Israel. And nobody even knows it."

Esther studied Clyde, leaning against the door. "You sure they're white supremacists? White supremacists believe in the total annihilation of non-white races." Clyde took Esther's pack and lit a new cigarette. "White *separatists* on the other hand," Esther said, "don't necessarily wanna kill nobody. Like that Ruby Ridge guy. They just don't think the races should, like, mingle, and just wanna be left alone. I guess you don't watch the History Channel," Esther said, holding her hand out, fingers spread, for his cigarette. "Seems to me you're confusing your white factions."

"When'd you git so smart?"

"When I met my boyfriend."

Clyde knew who she meant and it wasn't him.

"What about you? You ain't answered my question yet." Her voice was low with smoke and trembling. "I know who they don't like and what they believe in."

"Ah, fuck," Clyde said, and this made Esther laugh. He was more confused than ever. Damn it if Jay hadn't been right about spending time with people outside the movement. They fill your head with questions and before you know it you're doubting your own beliefs. Instead of trying to come up with an answer to Esther's question, Clyde shot back. "You know what I don't get?" he said. "How you deal with these two things that are basically complete opposites."

"What do you mean?"

"You smoke, drink, do what you did to me . . . and call yourself a Christian."

For a long time Esther only leaned against the door, looking past Clyde, holding her cigarette in front of her face. He was worried he'd pissed her off, even though that had been at least part of his intent. Then she blinked and took a drag, closing her eyes. She expelled the smoke out her nostrils this time and said, "Thing about me, Clyde, I don't work so well going just one way. I tried, I really did. Before I got born again I was out of control." She smiled and so did Clyde. He could imagine. "I was probably headed for an early grave, to be honest. Then I gave that all up," she snapped her fingers and they hardly made a sound. "Started going to church, reading the Bible. I went to all the church functions, formed a Christian book club. But," she shook her head. Her hair stuck to the window. "Didn't work either after a while." She took a drag and said, "I need both. Having both keeps me balanced. But the main thing is, Jesus doesn't judge me, he forgives all my sins, and he makes me feel safe."

Safe, Clyde thought. It's been a while since I've felt that.

"You oughta come with me to church group, Clyde. You might like it."

Clyde doubted that he would, he'd been to church only twice his whole life, but he said, "Maybe I would." In the distance he saw the doors at the entrance jerk open, and Tina and Wilson step into the light. "Shit."

Esther turned, sighed, and bunched her coat around her. "Why don't you leave her fat ass and be with me!?" She grinned, ear to ear. "We'd have so much fun, can you imagine!? I honestly don't get what you see in her. What is she, anyway, fifteen?"

"Sixteen," Clyde said. He shrugged.

Tina's tiny feet slapped the pavement crossing the lot. Esther threw the passenger door open and spilled out. She ran past Tina in a flurry of jacket and hair and Tina's face turned almost red. When she got to the open door she leaned in and looked at Clyde. "Uh, was that freak sitting in *my* car?"

He took a drag, nodding.

Tina pinched her mouth tight and sank into the driver's seat, waving her arms. "Smoke 'em if you got 'em, Jesus." She rolled both windows down even though it was freezing out and kept up a constant shake of her head, watching the entrance of the store. "That chick is one heaping helping of freaky deaky." Tina shut her door and backed out. Clyde saw the little grill on the ground and didn't say anything. "But you know what?" Tina said, shifting into drive. "I'm gonna let it go." She grinned. "I don't wanna be mad right now. Thank you for helping me today, Clyde."

At Pancho Villa's, Tina studied the four-page menu and Clyde ignored it. When the waitress came over he asked if she had barbacoa tacos.

"Oh," she said. "No, sorry."

"Conchinita pebil?"

"Pebil?" the waitress said. "Si."

"Three conchinita pebil tacos, then."

"Si, señor."

Clyde grinned. Chetto had said barbacoa was the best, but pebil was good too. When he looked at Tina, her mouth was hanging open. "Hola. A-mi-go?" she said.

"Qué pasa?" Clyde said, contorting his hands into something like a gang sign.

"You talk like that around my dad?"

"If I can talk like a Mexican maybe I can *think* like one." He touched his smooth temple. Their drinks came and he said, "We got something to celebrate or what?" Now that he'd decided to spill Tina's beans, he figured the least he could do was play along for the time being and let her enjoy the success she thought she'd achieved.

She raised her Diet Coke. It took both hands. "I don't know," she said. "Mr. Wilson's interested. He's gonna take it to the regional manager. That's the next step. Well, one of 'em anyway. Boy, I got my work cut out for me. I might have to get an intern or something."

Clyde wanted to laugh but instead he said, "Sounds good," and they drank. Intern my ass.

"But, I mean, what I'm worried about is for them to actually place an order they said I gotta show I actually got the ability to, you know, fill it."

"Right."

"Like, maybe a few thousand bottles."

Clyde choked on his soda. Tina giggled. "That's what I said! But Jerry thinks I can get affiliated with a supplier pretty easy." She dug in her purse for some papers. "He even gave me a list. He even said I could use his name if I wanted to get in touch with this minority-owned business association he knows."

Clyde forced himself to hold a straight face and it was about the hardest thing he'd ever done. "Good luck," he said, raising his beer.

"Thank you, buddy," Tina said. "That means a lot." When their food came, he ate half a taco in one bite and sat back chewing, smiling. Tina said, "Like your crazy wetback food?"

During his first week as an employee of the Missouri State Capitol janitorial crew, Clyde couldn't adjust to sleeping in the daytime. The shift to night work and, he guessed, the crank, kept him exhausted and bleary-eyed but not able to catch more than a few minutes of shut-eye. Those days when he got in he sat at the table, cluttered by Tina's business research, going through the notes he'd made on his shift and sucking rocket fuel through a straw in an effort to focus his mind. When you were on it, crank was great at dialing in your intent, but when it faded, it took all those benefits with it and left you raw and mean.

It felt like days passed at that table. He would jerk awake, sweating and confused, and wonder what the hell time it was. More often than not he'd slept twenty minutes. During one of his waking spells he started the letter to Troy. After getting down some of what he'd thought about in the last few weeks, he didn't know what else he would say until the words came out, and he kept surprising himself with his grasp of the knowledge. He felt it was important to educate Troy, about not just the ways in which they had both changed, but about the movement, its purpose and politics, and the imminent threat of the Zionist Occupational Government. He got up to look through the books Jay and J.D. had given him and quote passages from them at length. By the start of Clyde's second week in Jefferson City, the letter had reached twenty handwritten pages.

Most nights, after supper downtown with Tina, Clyde would meet Chetto in the lot for some crank, weed, and margaritas before going in. On the two breaks they got each night, one and four a.m., they'd run through it again. Clyde knew that as a Mexican Chetto was not to be trusted; he just couldn't help but like the guy.

One night when they finished the thermos of margaritas, Chetto said,

"Cabron, tu gusta come to mi casa por desayuno?" Clyde had been around Chetto enough by now to understand about half of what he said.

"I wanna do what?" Clyde said.

"Breakfast, man. Special New Year shit. My wife, she make tortillas from scratch. Que bueno."

Clyde couldn't say he was hungry. He had little appetite lately. "Ever been to Pancho Villa's?" he said.

"Pancho Villa's? Cabron, that shit American Mexican. Fucking Taco Bell. No such thing as burrito in México, man. No pinche 'gordita.' My wife she make the comida Méxicana tradicional, what we eat in Algodones. What I grow up with."

Since Chetto was only about five feet tall, he wasn't much of an advertisement for the food he grew up eating, but Clyde was game. Inside he was trying to fight feelings of friendship, but he also knew that the closer he got to him, the more likely it was that this Mexican would reveal something important. "All right," Clyde said.

With the sun rising in his eyes, Clyde followed Chetto across town. The ground was flat and yellow. It hadn't snowed once and people were saying that maybe this year they'd get off easy. Chetto pulled to the curb in front of an apartment building with cars parked helter-skelter in the yard. When they went in Chetto said something in Mexican. Clyde thought he heard the word "amigo" and wondered if Chetto was saying that he'd brought a friend from work.

Two tiny black-haired girls were on the floor a foot from a large TV. Chetto kissed them and made them laugh. He said, "Rosa y Pitina." A woman's voice came from the kitchen and Chetto answered. Clyde could smell something and Chetto said, "What I tell you, mafufo?"

"Smells good," Clyde said, passing posters of fat Mexicans in funny masks in the hall.

"Los luchadores. Wrestlers."

Chetto slapped a little shelf near the ceiling cluttered with small painted figures: Animals, dead families playing instruments, and other odd stuff. "Dia de los muertos. From Oaxaca, man."

"Oh-ha-ka."

"A state in Mexico. Is where Anna grow up." Chetto nodded at the kitchen.

Clyde hadn't known that Mexico had states. It was interesting to think that Oaxaca could be for Mexicans what, say, Missouri was for Americans. He wondered how many states Mexico had and if anybody down there had ever tried to wipe out their government. Probably not. Mexicans were too lazy for that sort of thing. In the small warm kitchen in the back, Chetto's U.S. wife was at the stove. She was small and dark and about the most beautiful woman Clyde had ever seen. He'd never really followed ethnic women, but had to try real hard to keep himself from staring at this one.

Chetto kissed her and slapped her ass. "This is Anna." Anna smiled and Clyde had to look away. Chetto said, "Clyde."

"Hola, Clyde," Anna said.

"Hola," Clyde said. She spoke to Chetto in Mexican and he told Clyde to sit down at a table in the corner. Anna smiled, Clyde smiled back, that was pretty much all that could pass between them. But it seemed all right to just sit and watch her and listen to Chetto in the other room with his girls and the television. She didn't seem to mind him being there. Maybe he'd try to learn how to speak better Mexican.

"How are you?" she said, dragging the first *H* out in a way that Clyde found funny and sexy at the same time. "You like Mexican food I hope." She did it again.

"I do," Clyde said. "Si."

She smiled. "Habla Español muy bien." She laughed.

Chetto came back in and said something and filled two cups with coffee and milk from the stove. No sugar. He sat and put a cup in front of Clyde. "Café con leche," Chetto said.

"Café con . . . " Clyde said.

"Leche. Is just . . . coffee and milk."

"Huh." Clyde took a sip. Chetto grinned at him. It wasn't bad but he liked his rocket fuel better. He'd need to drink ten of these to get the same kick. "So how do you, uh," Clyde began. Chetto watched him, waiting, sipping his café con leche. "You're both Mexican."

"Si, mafufo. Méxicanos."

"I heard the capitol got in trouble a while back for hiring illegals."

Anna turned from the stove. Chetto shook his head. "No hay que preocuparse," he said to her. "I no illegal." He took out his wallet and slipped a card from it. He slapped it on the oilcloth. "Permanent resident, cabron."

Clyde bent over to read the card. The name was Ramon Garcia.

"Your name's Raymond?"

"Ramon," Chetto said, rolling the *R*. "Is not my name, mafufo. My name Chetto. Pues," he said, and Anna looked his way again. She said something. "Is no technically legal, okay, but is, como se dice . . . " He shrugged. "Is real?" He pulled other cards from his wallet. "Social Security, man, driver license, I buy all this shit for, like, two hundred dolares. Ramon Garcia? Who the fuck be he? I no know. I think . . . probably . . . muerte. Dead."

"Shit. Like those toys in the hall."

Chetto laughed. "Everybody think Chetto my, uh, nickname. If no for this shit, man, we be in México." He made a face. "Is nice, pues no like Missouri."

Clyde peeled his forearms off the oilcloth. Chetto tapped the table. "Is funny . . . you say Pancho Villa before. Pancho Villa, he write this."

Under the oilcloth was a flag or something covered with Mexican writing. "Who, the guy that owns the restaurant?"

Chetto said something to Anna and she laughed and turned smiling at Clyde and Clyde had to look away again. He finished the coffee and Anna immediately refilled his cup and said, "Sugar?"

Thank God. "That'd be great," Clyde said, and Anna just looked at him.

"Si," Chetto said, and she handed Clyde a dish and a spoon. A part of him hoped that breakfast at Chetto's would become a routine. "Pancho Villa is, uh, the hero for Mexicans," Chetto said. "He was this revolutionary, mafufo. He come from the state of Chihuahua."

Clyde spat out some of his café con leche.

"Qué?" Chetto said.

"The dog?" Clyde said.

"Si," Chetto said, and Anna laughed so much that she had to cover her face. Chetto slapped the table. "Is where the dogs they come from, mafufo."

"You're shittin me."

"No, man, is true."

Anna turned from the stove and said, "Is true."

Jesus, Clyde thought, Mexico's got some funny states. You'd never see a state in America named after a little hairless dog. But on the other hand, Mexico seemed to have its share of revolutionaries too.

After breakfast, Chetto and Clyde went in the front room and watched cartoons with Chetto's thin little daughters. Clyde had a hard time focusing on the TV and he kept getting up to look at the dead figures along the wall and then sitting back down. He looked only at one at a time and there were dozens. "You like, mafufo?" Chetto said, and Clyde nodded.

"Hey," he said, leaning toward Chetto. "You think I could buy some," he looked at Chetto's girls on the floor and said, "you know, off you? Wouldn't mind having my own stash."

"For emergency?"

"Si," Clyde said, grinning.

Chetto nodded. "When Anna leave, we go to my dealer, man. She hook you up."

"Cool." One of Chetto's girls crawled into Clyde's lap to watch cartoons. Clyde rested his hands on her bony back. He didn't feel sleepy; his body was healing fast thanks to the crank. Combat soldiers had to be able to function at a high level in stressful situations on little to no sleep. Clyde thought he could hear Anna in the shower and he imagined it, his eyes full of colorful leaping characters, his mind full of something else. He couldn't remember the last time he'd watched cartoons.

When Anna left and the show ended, they got the girls dressed and went out to Chetto's car. They passed a roach and drank Corona. It was nine fifteen. Clyde liked Mexican beer when Chetto put lime in the neck. It was freezing out and Chetto's heater hardly worked. Chetto's sunglasses had lost one of their arms and rested at a canted angle across his nose. It made Clyde laugh. One of Chetto's girls said something in Mexican and Chetto rolled his window down a few inches. In came the frostbite. "They no like the smoke," he said. Clyde didn't feel the cold.

They drove along the bleak river. Few buildings, garbage, abandoned cars, first blacks then Mexicans sitting on steps and the hoods of dead cars in sweatshirts big enough to hide shotguns. The river was dark, dirty. A small boat with a man in it drifted slowly out in the brown middle. He was fishing. Clyde wondered about using the river as a getaway after the bombing, just let the ol' Missouri take them to safety, all they'd need was a boat, even a couple canoes would do, and no one would expect it, the helicopters would be watching the city, the roadblocks blocking the highways. He pulled the pad from his pocket and wrote, "River getaway? Need boat."

The first time Chetto had seen him write in the pad he'd asked what he was doing. Clyde had said he was making notes for a book.

Chetto had whistled. "Gonna be famous, mafufuo?" Clyde thought, Yeah, but not because of this book.

A pack of Mexican children ran out from between trailers and Chetto beeped his sick-sounding horn. Clyde was pretty sure the kids were laughing at it. Outside was cold and the kids weren't wearing enough clothes.

Chetto let his daughters out his side of the car. "Grandma a casa?" he said and someone said, "Si," and pointed at the trailer that rested on cinderblocks and was in a hell of a lot better shape than *American Dreamin'*. This park was orderly and clean. The trailers were lined up in neat rows separated by shrubs and trees. There were kids playing and people were hanging around. Down the road a guy was working in his car, a couple people standing around watching. A little brown boy was riding a bike with a smaller brown boy sitting on the handlebars. "Hola, Juanita," Chetto said, knocking on the trailer door.

"Chetto, ven aquí," a woman said, and Chetto opened the door and went in. Clyde followed. "Mi amigo."

They went in. The floor was covered with toys. Chetto sat down across from a tiny Mexican woman who had to be eighty. Her kitchen table was stacked with bags of weed and crank. She was eating soup that reeked of onions. Clyde said, "Hi," taking the chair by a TV that was on top of a fake fireplace. He held his hands to the warmth. Chetto and the old woman talked for a while, Clyde picked up a word here and there. "How much crystal you want, mafufo?"

Clyde took out his wallet. "I got fifty bucks."

"Cincuenta," Chetto said, and the woman nodded and dug around in the bags. "Give to me," Chetto said, and Clyde handed him the money. She weighed bags with her hands and put a small one in front of Chetto.

"Si?" she said.

"Si," he said.

It didn't look like much. But then again, a bump didn't hold much crank. Clyde hoped it would last at least a few days.

Chetto tossed him the bag. Clyde snatched it out of the air. Despite everything, he still had a training edge. He and Chetto took a couple bumps right there in front of the old woman.

In the car, Chetto's girls started whining about being hungry. He heard them say the word "churro" a bunch of times and thought it was funny. Mexicans used a lot of funny words. He had no idea what churro was, but when Chetto said, "Want to get a taco?" he figured "churro" was Mexican for "taco." Clyde had no appetitie for food, but Chetto made a turn and they drove along the river, farther from the city, to a scrubby field where a bunch of Mexicans were standing around in blue shirts. A food truck was parked in the road. Clyde was the only white person there. Chetto ordered barbacoa tacos.

Clyde watched the soccer. Chetto explained the game to Clyde. He'd never seen it in person. America's pastime, not Mexico's, had been his thing. Chetto handed Clyde one of the tacos and Clyde looked at it in his hand. Brown meat leaking red oil onto a beige tortilla. "Churro," he said.

"Pues," Chetto said, nodding to a little cart across the street his daughters had surrouded. "Luego. Tacos first."

"I thought this was a churro."

Chetto pointed to his girls, chewing on long brown sticks. "Churro," he said. He took a bite. "You funny gringo, mafufo."

"You're a funny wetback," Clyde said, and Chetto drove an open palm into his chest, making Clyde drop the uneaten taco. "What the fuck?" he said, looking at the mess at his feet. The urge to kick the shit out of Chetto flared up.

"Qué pasa with that fucking wetback shit, maricón?"

"What do you mean?"

"You call me wetback."

Clyde blinked. "You called me a fucking gringo."

Chetto put his palm in Clyde's chest again, but not as hard this time. He shook his head. Clyde was still pissed but tried to control his heart. "You think todos nosotros la Méxicanos, we just los pinche wetback?"

"No."

"I thought you were like, cooler than this pinche wetback shit. Pues . . . "

They stood around in the dirt and Clyde said, "I didn't think 'wetback' was a big deal." He shrugged, and Chetto looked at him sideways.

"You walk up to black guy and say, like, 'What up, nigger?'"

Clyde laughed.

"No, right?"

Depends on who you are, Clyde thought. He said, "Didn't mean nothin."

"You no mean nada?" Chetto shook his head. He paced in the dirt, kicking the meat, and jerked his head at the truck. "Get your own pinche tacos."

Growing up, Clyde had heard words like "wetback" and "nigger" all the time, practically on every street corner. Nobody'd ever taken offense. Just to get away from Chetto Clyde went back to the truck. In his pocket he had a dollar, enough for one taco. He didn't even want the fucking thing but he said, "Uno barbacoa," almost getting it right.

W hen he got home Clyde lay on the bed with his heart fluttering and his mind filled with violence. He went to the table and added a few pages to Troy's letter.

You were always my best friend but when I consider what bonds us today, it's nothing but nostalgia for the past. And nostalgia is cheap. Our friendship was once strong but it was also built on pure chance— a sweatshirt—and maybe it wasn't any stronger, in the end, than the fabric it was made from. What shape would that sweatshirt be in today? It would be threadbare and tattered. You may not know that the last few years, before I met Jay, were the worst of my life. I wallowed in self-pity and accepted my sad fate as if I had no choice in it at all—I played the part of the VICTIM so well I could have won the Oscar for it and I know now that I'm not alone in this regard. Look up the word "Victim" in the dictionary and you will see a picture of the neutered white American male. All Jay has done is to show me that we DO have a choice—sometimes it's just hard to see. It's even harder to MAKE. Believe me, I know. But what's important is that I've MADE my CHOICE, Troy, and I guess you've made yours. I'm on a path toward wisdom and strength, not seeking other selfish desires such as money or fame, whereas that perfectly describes the path that you have chosen to take. I'm sure now that you can see that these paths lie at opposite ends of the spectrum when it comes to eradicating the virus that has taken root in a country I no longer recognize as America.

Clyde went on and on, pouring his heart out to his oldest friend and sadly realizing that he was lost to him forever. When he finished, signing his name, he felt as elated as if he'd just had a bump. But the feeling quickly passed, leaving him worn out and empty. He nodded off, woke half an hour later, grabbed the rocket fuel from the mini fridge, and got on the highway. After a few miles he realized where he was headed: Strasburg, the little post office, the one he'd grown up with and the only one he knew. He took a bump along the way, fighting the dry mouth with sweet tea and blinking at the shaking road.

He only wanted to see the house, to drive past it. Stopping for some heart-to-heart was not on the menu. His mom would be upset by the way he looked, and upset by the silence of the last few weeks. Clyde didn't know if his uncle had told her anything. She'd called, a number of times, but Clyde had erased all her messages without listening to a single one.

Strasburg looked even worse than it had when he'd lived there, maybe Troy had been right. Neither the town nor its outskirts had ever been what you'd call picturesque, and the winter months made all that was lost stand out that much more. Rusted rail cars sat forever on the broken tracks by the roadside. Bare gray trees against an oppressive low sky revealed dirty trailers and homes with peeling paint on small flat lots with trash frozen into the mud. Homes were surrounded by old dead cars, busted toys, thrown-out sinks, toilets, and ovens, and piles of discarded materials from never-finished construction projects slowly dissolving into the ground. Steering with his knee, Clyde took another bump. His body responded immediately, feeling strong again, fearless. If only Esther were here, he'd fuck her good. Or Tina. He wiped his nose as he passed one of the signs he'd put up for his mom.

The house was just ahead, he could see it from a distance through the trees. It looked small and neglected. Without Clyde around to manage the upkeep, it had fallen to pieces in no time. As usual, there was no one on the road so Clyde let his foot slip off the accelerator. If his mom was watching, she wouldn't know the vehicle. She probably wouldn't recognize Clyde—or want to. People had a way of not seeing what they didn't want to see. Clyde stopped in the middle of the road, stalling out. A foreclosure sign sat in the yard: *For Sale, Home & Business.* Clyde started the car and made a U-turn in the intersection. He pulled to the slippery shoulder and went through the yard, yanking the sign and throwing it into the fucking trees at the edge of their property. The house's windows were grimy, dirtier than they'd ever been when he'd lived there, but he could see through the muck that the place had been emptied. He didn't have his old key so he kicked the cheap door a few times until he'd made a big enough hole.

It was as cold inside the house as out, and his steps echoed. Except for the drying chairs in his mom's salon, the furniture was gone. Stains on the bare carpet stood out. Clyde tried a light but the electricity was off. The door to his room was closed and he cursed himself when he opened it for thinking that somehow this room, unlike all the other rooms, would have been spared. Gone was his big TV, the DVR and PlayStation, the stereo, the bed, all the clothes he'd left behind. What remained was a single five-pound weight on the floor of the carpeted closet, an old school desk he'd taken from Grain Valley High that someone—not him—had carved his name into: *Clyde Eugene Twity*, only the one *t*. A cordless phone with the battery hatch gone and a pair of shoes that weren't his were on the floor. Extension cords and the cable TV line were coiled by the door next to an ashtray with a single cigarette butt. Clyde felt so strange that he all but ran out of the house. He wished he'd never come back.

He shoved his letter into a box in front of the post office and left Strasburg, passing his uncle's house and stopping in the middle of the road. He sat there watching the rearview mirror and then backed up, passing the drive in reverse and parking in the weeds on the shoulder. He left the car door open and cut through the yard to the side of the house, pulling himself up on the deck and peeking in a window. Willie was sleeping in a chair by the wood stove, his dog at his feet. Clyde let himself down to the yard and saw the state of the woodpile. It had collapsed, spread out across the grass. All those logs had gone damp and wouldn't want to burn and Willie would have a hard time keeping warm. Clyde hated knowing that he could bring this sort of suffering to someone he loved. There didn't seem to be any way that Clyde could win. What he did, what he didn't do, who he was, and who he wasn't would all be responsible for hurting people. He shook those thoughts off with Jay's words— "Pain's just information"—and stacked the wood back into a high straight row like he usually did, careful to keep quiet. Then he pulled the blue tarp over the top of it and stood looking at the work he'd done. The last thing he did at his uncle's was slip what money he had in his wallet, a couple hundred bucks, into the mailbox. He hoped Willie would know who had done it.

He was close enough so he stopped at Lick Skillet to check on the truck. They were all around it when he pulled in. Jay walked down the street to meet him. When he got close, Clyde saw the concern in his eyes. "You no rook so good, Cryde-san."

Clyde grinned and waved it off. "Think I'm comin down with something, don't get too close."

Jay laid a palm on Clyde's forehead and said, "You're sweating. It's fifteen degrees out."

Clyde could feel it in his clothes, they clung to his skin like towels. "Yeah, maybe I got a fever."

"Think you oughta quit and hole up here and recover."

Clyde got a cigarette lit and drew on it hungrily. He squinted against the day. "Gettin good shit down there, though." He whipped the pad out of his back pocket and showed Jay how many pages he'd filled.

Jay took it and read through quickly, making noise, grinning, nodding, saying, "Fuck me." Then he handed it back and said, "That you are," clapping Clyde on the shoulder and leading him toward the truck beside the milking parlor. Jay explained that J.D. had reinforced the springs on the truck so it wouldn't sit too low to the road and give away their secrets. They'd run fuses from the back to the driver's seat through tubes mounted to the undercarriage and painted to blend in. They weren't taking any chances. They'd removed the passenger seat to accommodate a smaller barrel of explosive that would now ride shotgun and could be manually executed by gunshot at close range if the other systems failed. Suicide mission. Clyde hadn't committed to a one-way trip, but when the time came, Jay would remind him of what they'd all heard at the WAC: to be in the movement was to accept death, to accept death was to truly enter the *mai*. It was the only way to win a fight. They'd decided to hold off until the last minute to mix the ammonium nitrate and racing fuel because you didn't want two dozen barrels of volatile explosives sitting around any longer than necessary.

TWELVE HOURS LATER, IN CHETTO'S CAR, CLYDE WAS HAVING A HARD TIME with the bong. Chetto didn't seem pissed anymore about the wetback comment, they were amigos again. Clyde had never smoked from a bong before. His hands were shaking and today they'd started itching, from knuckle to wrist. He couldn't stop scratching no matter how red or raw they looked. "Got to hold your finger on the hole, man," Chetto said. Clyde could not make the bubbles. It had taken him five minutes just to warm up to the idea of putting his lips on the slobbery head of Chetto's ceramic cactus in the first place. Drugs, just like training, brought people together more intimately than most things.

Clyde kept wasting smoke, so Chetto plugged the hole and held the bong to Clyde's mouth, saying, "Suck." Clyde kept laughing and stopped only when Chetto said, "Come on, mafufo, we got like two minute." Clyde finally made bubbles. Chetto took the bong and sucked up what smoke Clyde hadn't.

After letting out the smoke, Clyde said, "What do you pay in rent?" He hated himself lately for how little control he seemed to have over his mind, his heart, his hands. More and more he was questioning his path. Where had the fierceness and commitment he'd felt after getting killed gone?

Chetto's eyes were closed. He said, "About five hundred a month, mafufo. Qué?"

Clyde shrugged, his jacket making noise. He sat breathing with his eyes jumping behind the lids. "Can't live in a trailer forever."

"There always shit available in my building, man."

"We could be neighbors."

"Desayuno every day."

Clyde laughed. He took the notepad from his back pocket and flipped it open, leafing through the many notes and drawings. He got to a page where he'd drawn Chetto's car one day while they were sitting outside.

Chetto squinted at it and then took the pad and held it up close to his face. He laughed and said, "This mi coche, mafufo?"

"Yeah."

"No esta mal, amigo." Chetto leafed through the pad, looking for more. That pad held all of Clyde's secrets. He could have stopped Chetto, but he didn't. There were sketches and doodles on almost every page, and loads of notes.

Clyde flipped the pad to a page where he'd drawn some of the cartoon characters that Chetto's daughters liked.

Chetto laughed and slapped the seat with the pad. "Excelente. You one talented hijo de puta." He handed the pad back and Clyde closed it and slid it into his pocket and took a long gulp of the margaritas.

A knock on the window made Clyde jump and spill his drink all over his legs. Chetto laughed and cursed.

"Evening, gentlemen." One of the capitol cops turned his flashlight into the car, lighting up the layers of smoke hovering in the air. A bicycle stood behind him and the radio on his hip squawked.

Chetto didn't lift his head from the seat. "Buenos tarde," he said lazily. Clyde guessed he'd mistaken the cop for capitol security, a rent-a-cop.

"Wanna step out of the vehicle for me?" the cop said. He radioed something in and drew his sidearm, which brought Clyde bolt upright in the passenger seat.

"Qué pasa?" Chetto said to Clyde.

"Get out slowly," Clyde said. "Don't say anything."

Outside, the cop had them put their hands on their heads and face the car. Clyde considered running, but he couldn't run fast anymore. If he couldn't run away, he had to stay and fight. He wanted to fight, wanted to enter the cop's *mai* and fuck him up. Most people saw a weapon and wanted to stay back, but that was wrong. You wanted to get in close, you wanted to hug your attacker. Clyde stood in front of Chetto's car, hands on his head, watching the cop pat Chetto down. When the cop saw Clyde just standing there, he turned his firearm on him. Clyde didn't like having weapons pointed at him by the state. He wanted to say, "Get your damn Roscoe out of my face, pig," but didn't. Then he did, he actually said it, and Chetto cracked up. The cop only tilted his head and said, "Get over here now." Clyde ran one option after another through his muddled mind. Dale's car was in the very next spot over. Dale had a record, and so would his car. Clyde knew how lucky he'd been to be arrested in Chetto's car. He remembered a backward sweeping move they'd done in class. Someone gets behind you and you spin with your arms up. With your lead arm you trap the weapon. With the other hand you strike the throat or eyes. It was a good technique. Clyde felt like he could make it work. Jay would be proud if he used that technique to avoid arrest. Clyde took his time coming around the car.

"If you want to turn a possession misdemeanor into a resisting felony, be my guest."

"Man, like, we work right here," Chetto said. "No big deal, cabron."

The cop got a pair of plastic cuffs out and secured Chetto's wrists. Chetto cursed and Clyde tried to get his attention. He was going to try the move and he didn't want Chetto to freak out. The gun would probably discharge and it would be close and loud. But Clyde didn't think it would be pointed in Chetto's direction. He whispered, "Hey."

"Oh, come on, don't, don't do that," the cop said, sounding disappointed and kicking Clyde's legs apart so hard that he almost fell over. "This isn't a coffee break, fellas. Keep your mouths shut." Why did pigs have to be so rough? They were all the same. High on power. Give a monkey a hammer and he'll use it to bash in your brains.

"It's a free country, man, and we didn't do nothing," Chetto said. The cop lowered him to the ground with one hand holding the cuffs. Clyde could see that it hurt. "Pinche maricón, chupa mi verga."

"I had a year of Spanish in high school," the cop said.

"Good," Chetto said.

He took one of Clyde's hands. This is it, Clyde thought. The technique could be executed from either side. Sweep left, or right. The cop brought Clyde's left hand down behind his back. He'd have to sweep to the left, freeing the arm in the process. Clyde felt the cuff and the cop grabbed his right wrist before he was ready and pulled it down and cuffed it to the other. Goddamn it. "Fight it," the cop said, "and you'll just hurt yourself." He lowered Clyde to the ground next to Chetto, and Clyde felt stupid. His mind had been too clouded by drugs and alcohol to send the signal to his body. *So that in time, our senses may be alert.* He had to go clean, get off everything, same as McVeigh had done.

A patrol car arrived and one of the new cops checked Chetto's VIN while the other got them into the patrol car. Clyde saw the capitol door guard watching from the top of the steps. In the patrol car, Chetto said, "What about our jobs, man?"

The cop at the wheel said, "What job is that?"

"We work right there, man. That's what I saying. Go ask Mr. Featherstone."

The cop who was writing in a pad looked out the passenger window. The guard was still standing there. "I think what you mean is 'worked,' " the cop said. Chetto didn't get it, but Clyde did, and it just made him feel worse.

"Qué?" Chetto said.

"We're probably fired," Clyde said.

The car pulled out. "What about my car, man?" Chetto said.

"You want us to bring it to the station for ya?" the cop said. "No problemo."

"No," Clyde said.

"I wasn't talking to you," the cop said. "I was talking to your amigo." He looked through the mesh. "We can do that if you want. I can't guarantee it'll still be there when you get back, since you'll no longer have employee parking privileges."

Clyde looked hard at Chetto. Chetto said, "Is okay, man." He didn't say another word the rest of the way to the station. He was a fast learner.

The admitting pig at the precinct asked Clyde if the address on his ID was current and Clyde said it was. It was his mom's house in Strasburg, which was no longer his mom's house in Strasburg. The *American Dreamin'* trailer was parked illegally up the hill and he didn't think, despite the tickets, that anybody knew anything about it, and no one would connect him to Dale's car in the lot. Realizing that there was nothing to tie him to the Smalls made him feel a little better. What two know one can tell. His arrest didn't have to derail anybody's plans.

He was fingerprinted, which was disappointing, but he remembered that J.D. had done time in Leavenworth, Dale had been arrested more than once, and Jay was a wanted man. The booking pig made Clyde put all his belongings in a box and he felt suddenly sick with worry seeing his notepad lying there on top. He tried to remember if he'd ever used the word "bomb." He probably had. He felt like throwing up and thought for a few minutes that he would. Maybe no one would read it. A tattered little pad, why would they read something like that? Even if they did, it had *Notes for a novel* on the first page. Clyde wasn't sure what the law said about privacy of your personal property. He tried to remember what Buggy had said about it at the WAC. When arrested, you lost what few rights you actually had.

Clyde and Chetto were put in a big cell with a drunk whose long yellow beard was matted with barf, two thin black boys who didn't look older than fifteen, and another Mexican who Chetto talked to a while, even though one of the blacks kept saying, "Speak English, motherfucker." Clyde wanted to go over there and shut him up. "America, man," Chetto said to Clyde. "It muy bueno at one chingadera, mafufo." Clyde knew that "chingadera" meant "fucking thing." We were good at one fucking thing. "That why all the Mexicans they come here. Pues, no se, amigo. Sueño Americanos only for Americans. Es un hecho. Everybody else, man, we can stay here a while if we want, cook your food, cut your grass, pick your beans, clean the kaka out your pinche toilets. Pues. If me gustaria algo mas?" He made a dismissive gesture. He was mad, and not just about losing his trabajo. "The Mexicanos, man, the fucking nigger, the Chinese, whatever you be, adios muchacho. Good fucking riddance."

That got the attention of the black boys. "What the fuck you say, Speedy?" one of them said. They came over.

"Chinga tu madre," Chetto said.

"Fuckin spic, stand up," one of them said.

Clyde jumped into fighting stance. He was both taller and thicker than the black kids, even though he hadn't trained in weeks. He thought that this wouldn't be much of a fight and he was right. He threw one punch, hitting the kid on the right in the mouth. That kid dropped to the floor in a blink, out fucking cold, and his friend jumped and ran back to where they'd been before. "Fuck you," he said when he got there. Clyde resisted the urge to stomp over there and kick the shit out of him too.

"No mess with mafufo," Chetto said.

The old drunk barfed down his beard again and went back to sleep. Must be nice to be able to sleep through that. The kid Clyde had dropped came to after a few minutes and crawled back to his friend. Clyde squeezed into a space between cold metal benches bolted to the cement that was barely big enough to fit him. Everybody in there but him and the black boys went to sleep. He wasn't tired. His mind was beyond control. He scratched at his itchy hands and forearms, they itched now too, and peeled the calluses off a couple knuckles. The dead skin he flicked in the direction of the black boys. God, he wanted a cigarette, something to drink, his mouth was so dry. The cell stank of puke, piss, cigarettes, bad breath, and alcohol farts.

He went to the bars and yelled out, "Can I get a drink of water?" Nobody answered or moved on that side of the bars. He yelled it again and a cop somewhere said, "No." Clyde looked for ways out of this situation. He couldn't call Tina. He didn't want her to be able to hang this over him, not when he was about to out her to Jay. Uncle Willie didn't drive. Then there was his mom, wherever she was. He could call Jay, but he didn't think he could face that level of disappointment right now. It was official, there was no one he could call on to get him out of this. He was trying to decide who was in the one framed picture hanging on the wall the other side of the bars when a cop yelled, "Garcia."

He said it a couple more times with increasing impatience and Clyde said, "Hey, amigo," to the Mexican lying there asleep.

He woke up grabbing at air. "Qué!?" he shouted.

"Garcia," Clyde said, nodding at the hall.

"No soy Garcia," the Mexican said, and then Chetto got up and went to the door and said, "I'm Garcia," and Clyde remembered that he was. "Soy Garcia, mafufo," Chetto said to him.

"I forgot."

A new cop came and unlocked the door and said, "Adios, muchacho."

Going out Chetto said, "Qué paso with you, mafufo?"

Clyde shrugged. "Adios, muchacho."

"Pues, mafufo, give, like, five minutes."

It took a lot more than five minutes. It took so long that Clyde figured Chetto had given up and gone home. Crawled into a warm bed with his U.S. wife and probably fucked her silly. But a cop finally called Clyde's name and led him out to Chetto and a sleepy Mexican, sitting in two bright yellow plastic chairs bolted near a window. "Gracias," Clyde said to Chetto.

"Thank Pedro," Chetto said, and Clyde nodded and shook Pedro's hand. Pedro wasn't friendly like Chetto; maybe he wasn't one of the good ones. Clyde went to the counter to get the paperwork about a court date he'd never show up for and his personal items, which brought the worry back like a flash flood. His pad was gone. Clyde tried not to show his panic as he dug through his stuff. The pad was on the bottom. He sighed and flipped it open. None of the pages had been torn out or anything. Chetto said, "Let's go, mafufo," but Clyde ignored him going through the pad. He was feeling better until he got to the last page. Something had been written at the bottom, one word. *Idiot.*

P edro drove Clyde and Chetto back to the capitol. Their cars were still in the lot. They headed up the wide steps, but halfway to the top the guard, the same unhelpful bastard Clyde had met his first day here, came out. "Mr. Featherstone told me to tell you boys you been released from your duties." He seemed pretty happy about it too.

Clyde yelled, "I hope you're working March twenty-first, nigger."

"What did you just say to me?"

"Come down here, I'll show you what I said."

"I knew you were a piece of shit from day one." The guard went back inside.

Chetto dropped his head and started picking at his acne, looking sideways at Clyde with some surprise in his eyes. "Chingado," he said, and Clyde patted him on the shoulder. Chetto exhaled and said, "Mafufo, I can no go home now. Vamos." In the east the sky was just taking on light. Clyde followed Chetto to a strip mall on the other side of town and parked in front of a storefront with a dimly lit black and gold sign above a recessed door. Nothing else in sight was open. Sitting in Chetto's car in the lot they took some crank and felt better.

Cheetahs! was a big room with a small round stage. Bare chairs and tables clogged the sticky floor, steps ran to other levels where empty leopard-spotted vinyl booths sat in the dark before a wall of mirrors that turned the club into a funhouse. A naked woman on the stage was pulling at her butt cheeks and looking out between her slippery legs at all the upside-down men. Her hair brushed the floor. She slapped her ass and someone yelled, "Puta!" like they were in pain. Clyde and Chetto sat down at a table near the stage off to one side. Everyone but Clyde was Mexican in there. A wait-ress with small breasts and dark half-dollar nipples appeared. Chetto yelled, "Margarita!" above the song.

Clyde held up four fingers and yelled, "Margaritas!" The waitress looked like Anna, Chetto's U.S. wife.

"Quatro?" she said.

"Si," Clyde said, four fingers still in the air.

He lit a cigarette and watched the stage. This seemed to be the only logical way to follow what had just happened. The stripper on the stage whipped her long hair around her small head, pretending to shoot into the audience with her finger. She raised it, blew across it, then slid it in and out of her mouth. Men howled. The song stopped and she walked off plucking bills from the floor. Clyde thought about sliding a real gun in and out of someone's mouth, what that would be like. The waitress who brought a tray holding four margaritas was the stripper who'd just left the stage. Clyde could feel the heat coming off of her. Her long brown hair stuck to her cheeks and breasts. A new song started and a new stripper hung upside down from the pole by her legs. Clyde scratched at his hands and lit a new cigarette. He whistled and Chetto said, "Te gusta, mafufo." There was no pain in Clyde now, no more peligroso. Every blink shifted his plane of vision and pulled a new thought into his head, like some kind of slide show. He didn't want to think right now about anything but drinking and smoking and fucking dark-skinned strippers. Maybe he'd been lucky, maybe that one word—*idiot*—was the extent of it, and whoever wrote it obviously had no idea what Clyde was capable of. Like he gave a shit what some ZOG pig thought about his stupid fake novel. On 3/21 we'll see who the idiot is. Drinking margaritas with Chetto, Clyde let himself feel good—that was it, just good. He deserved to feel good. He hadn't felt good for far too long. As soon as he got home, and handed Tina some story about why he'd had to quit, he'd have to convince her to abandon her plans and she'd see that all the support she'd thought he'd given her had been bullshit. Clyde watched the stripper on the pole and decided that he needed to feel good a little longer. He wasn't ready to go home, to face Tina, to face anybody. There was no rush. 3/21 was still almost two weeks away. He didn't have to go home today, he didn't even have to go home tomorrow, he didn't have to go home until the crank ran out. This would be one last run, purifying, like when Sosei went into the mountains.

Clyde raised his glass to Chetto's. He suddenly realized he'd probably never see him again. "Cheers," he said.

"Salud."

"Thanks, man," Clyde said.

"For what?"

Clyde shrugged.

"De nada, mafufo."

He took a drink watching Chetto. He knew he'd miss him. In some ways this crazy wetback had become his best friend.

After another dance, Chetto clapped Clyde on the back and said, "Time to go, mafufo. Time to face mi esposa."

"Si," Clyde said. "Mucho peligroso." Chetto grinned.

Clyde followed Chetto to his house for breakfast, the last desayuno. Qué lástima. Without the distraction of margaritas and beautiful naked Mexicans his thoughts clouded again. The Jefferson City Police had spent three hours pouring over his notes. Either they'd believed the bullshit about it being a novel and he'd dodged a very big bullet or they'd copied the whole thing and were talking to the FBI. Goddamn it, he bet they were. Fucking pigs. He wondered if he could get away with a full-borne assault on the precinct. He could visit Lick Skillet and steal some of Jay's weaponry. Pretty risky, he thought, too risky so close to 3/21. After breakfast, out in the street, Clyde said adios to his amigo. He tried to stop himself, but he also said, "Stay away from the capitol on the twenty-first of March, all right?"

"I no work there anymore, mafufo, in case you forget."

"I know," Clyde said. "Just, don't go anywhere near it that day. Stay home."

"Why? You come back to shoot the guard?" Chetto made a gun with his hand. "Bang bang?"

Clyde shook his head. "Just trust me."

"What the fuck?"

"Just trust me."

Chetto grinned and shook his head. Crazy Americans. "You got mi digits, mafufo. We go back to Cheetahs! anytime you want."

Clyde grabbed his Oakleys from the car and put them on Chetto. They looked good.

"Qué esta?" Chetto said.

"Gift," Clyde said. A last will and testament. "I don't need 'em."

"Que bueno, amigo. Gracias." They shook hands and hugged. Chetto clapped Clyde on the back. How you gonna manage without me?" Chetto said, faking a bump for emphasis.

"Not too fuckin good," Clyde said.

"Ah, no cry, mafufo. We okay," Chetto said. "This be America, man."

CLYDE BOUGHT FOUR PACKS OF WINSTONS AND A FEW BOTTLES OF SNAPPLE and filled his tank so he could drive as much as he wanted. After that he only had about twenty bucks. He'd never been comfortable in Dale's car, so low to the ground that he felt exposed, but he wanted to drive. That first morning he drove without a plan, moving from downtown Jeff City, where he must have circled the capitol a dozen times, to the nicer neighborhoods up the hill and the suburbs beyond, moving slowly along perfect roads past huge locked houses with their alarm systems and clogged driveways and manicured lawns. The American Dream was alive and well in Jefferson City, it seemed. How many of these homes belonged to state senators and congressmen? Clyde wondered.

Around midday he drove past the trailer. Tina's Firebird was gone so he went in, had a bump, sat with his rocket fuel. He got back in the car and drove around looking for a hardware store where he could buy some white paint and a brush. At home he went around to the side of the trailer facing the curb and painted over the letters that remained after those Molasses Gap boys had had their fun. Now on that side it was just blank, white paint ran in long lines down the trailer, dripping on the pavement. Clyde went out again and drove until dark. Tina called around seven, hungry and curious; Clyde told her to eat without him, he had some things to do for Jay.

"Okay, weirdo."

If Dale's dashboard clock was to be trusted, it was midnight on the nose when he passed the police station where he'd been incarcerated. He parked across the street, just out of the light, and watched pigs come and go, come and go. A black man was hauled in roughly by two pigs at one point. Later, a single pig led two black women in tight shorts and shirts that hardly covered their breasts. It was freezing out, and Clyde wondered where they'd come from. He left and drove again, the little bag of crank in his lap and the bullet in his hand on the wheel, a bump every few hours fighting the fatigue and worry. When he was stopped at lights he went through the contacts in his phone: Mom, Mr. Longarm, J.D., Jan, Jay, Tina, Troy, Walmart, Willie. Mom, Mr. Longarm, J.D., Jan, Jay, Tina, Troy, Walmart, Willie.

In the morning Tina called but Clyde didn't answer. He drove some more and finally went home, sat at the table, and read all his notes again, adding new insights in the margins. Then he went outside and did *kihon* in the road, a hundred reps of everything, then push-ups, crunches, and squats. He shadowboxed and ran wind sprints until his lungs burned. He kept himself up the rest of that day with cigarettes and crank and training, and was still at the table when Tina came in. "Pee-yew, buddy, open a window or something, why don't ya?" He smashed out his cigarette and turned the nearest window. Leaving the door open to the cold Tina went around turning all the windows and the intake fan in the roof. It spun squeaking. She dragged a sweater over her head and dropped to the couch, sighing. "What a day!"

Clyde grunted. "Sauce in the stores yet?"

She laughed. "At this point, I don't even know when that's gonna happen. I jump through one hoop they put up another."

Music to Clyde's ears. Maybe he wouldn't have to tell on her after all. "I knew they'd find some way to fuck you, just a matter of when and how hard."

"Whoa," Tina said, looking at him with exaggerated shock.

Now all he could think about was fucking. His dick was hard. He got up and stood over Tina.

"Uh, hello."

"Hi," Clyde said, unbuttoning the jeans. He tried to grin.

"What are you doing?"

"Screwing you."

Tina moved a hand to her face, giggled, and said, "You sure you're up to it? You look half dead, and, uh, I'm being *gen*erous. I've never seen you get a zit before and now you got, like, a bazillion." She ran her hand in a circle around her own face. He stripped out of his shirt and knew he stank, he could smell it but didn't give two shits. The armpits itched, one of them ached, something in there. He scratched it, gummy flakes sticking under his nails. Wiping his fingers on his jeans he shut the door. Standing over Tina, he got out of his jeans. "Dang, nigga," she said. He moved her from the couch to the floor.

"Uh, okay." She looked up at him from the carpet and Clyde got a flash of another trailer, another night, someone else down on carpet, heads lost in bags. He shook it off. "Get out of your clothes."

"Jeez," Tina said, unzipping her jeans. "Who are you? Hardly look at me for weeks and now you're like some crazy rapist."

She was going too slowly so he yanked her jeans over her shoes and threw them. They slapped the wall. He felt strong and fierce. On top of her he moved hard and breathed hard and she turned away. If you're gonna fuck, fuck hard. Her eyes were shut and she flattened her mouth into a thin line as he went at her with all he had. When he was finally done he jumped up, dripping sweat, and lit a fresh post-screw cigarette, pacing the floor, which made Tina's breasts rock back and forth. She said, "Jesus," and dragged the afghan off the couch to cover herself. With that around her body she moved into a sitting position and held her arms around her knees, staring at the door. She left at some point, then Clyde got dressed and left too.

That night he had to dump the rest of his money down Dale's tank. He drove, stretching what crank was left by taking half bumps. He smoked cigarettes with his arm out the window and his raw red hand going numb in the cold. For a while he sat in the Cheetahs! lot watching the door after trying to get in without paying. Chetto's name didn't help. One of the dancers came out when he was sitting there and he recognized her as the gun dancer. He got out and followed her to her car and when she saw him she screamed. This stopped him cold in the lot and the bouncer by the door came running. Clyde had his hands up but the guy showed no signs of slowing. "I was just gonna talk to her," he said, running around Dale's car.

"Get the fuck outta here," the bouncer said. "I kick your ass."

"You kick *my* ass?" Clyde said. "I fuckin doubt that." But instead of fighting the guy, who was about Jimmy-Don's size, he got in Dale's car and drove away, laying on the horn the whole time, his middle finger high. At a light downtown he went through the contacts in his phone again. Mom, Mr. Longarm, J.D., Jan, Jay, Tina, Troy, Walmart, Willie. At the next light he called his mom and got the message: disconnected. He guessed he wasn't surprised but hearing it made him have to pull over and open the door and think about throwing up. Once he stopped sweating he deleted her contact and got back on the road. He tried Mr. Longarm and got the loud repeating tone he knew he'd get. He deleted them, driving slowly with half his attention. Then there was Willie. He pressed "call" and listened to the phone ring against his leg over a dozen times. The clock on Dale's dash read 3:42 a.m. Willie's phone came noisily off the receiver and noisily into his bed. There was a ratty breath as his uncle dragged it to his pillow. Halfway through "hello" Clyde hung up. There was the phone number, the house address, the birthday, which Clyde saw that he'd missed this year. He pressed "delete." The Walmart contact appeared and he deleted it too. Then Troy. He was left with only four, the only contacts he needed, and every one of them had the same last name.

It was dawn. Tina was asleep in the trailer. Clyde stood across the road doing *kihon* as the sun came up over the Missouri River. He wanted to run down the bank and jump in. At a point later the door banged against the trailer and Tina said, "Really?"

Clyde was in one of the stances, throwing hard punches and, he now realized, shouting his *kiai*. He didn't break the rhythm but stopped shouting. Tina slammed the trailer door and Clyde heard its springs as she got back on the bed. When he finished his fifth set of a hundred reps he paced in the road with his hands on his head, breathing the *nogare* way and feeling the heat pushing off of his skin. Tina came out dressed and walked to her car watching Clyde with a concerned look. When he turned to her she twirled a finger beside her ear. He nodded, I am crazy, you're right. Tina drove past and Clyde went inside. On the table his phone buzzed and buzzed. It was Jay.

C lyde washed himself in the sink and made a jug of rocket fuel. He drove fast to Lick Skillet. The purifying run was over and it had worked. He felt stronger than ever. The old Clyde, uchi deshi, a damn warrior, was back.

He drove through Lick Skillet cemetery slowly, hitting only one tombstone, and parked outside the bar on the High Street. No one was around, but halfway down the hill Jay was in the road, a rifle on his back and a handgun in a thigh holster. At the bottom of the hill J.D. and Dale came out of their cabin. Jay waved and Clyde did some shadowboxing on the cobblestones waiting for him. Jay said, "Woo!" when he reached the street. He approached Clyde grinning but the closer he got, the less happy he looked, until he was standing right there with a mix of worry and suspicion in his eyes. "What the hell's happening to you, Clyde?"

"What do you mean?"

"Clyde-san, goddamn, you look like you're about ready to drop."

"I feel fine," Clyde said, throwing a couple short uppercuts. "Good, actually, really good. Started training again."

Jay watched Clyde with heavy lids. Clyde could tell that he was looking for the truth behind his bullshit, the way he always did. "What's wrong with your hands?"

Clyde looked at them. They were pretty red, pretty marked up from his fingernails. "Got some kind of rash," he said. "Probably the cheap cleaning shit they use at the capitol." Jay didn't look convinced. The dogs ran into the street and Clyde lit a cigarette, watching J.D. and Dale come over the hill. Both wore rifles. They went straight to the lean-to, pinning the netting to one side. Dale dragged the cargo door open and J.D. disappeared into the milking parlor. Dale threw a stick, the dogs scrambled.

"Come on," Jay said, putting a hand on Clyde's shoulder and walking him in the direction of the bar. They climbed in and sat on the stools. In the street one of the dogs trotted with the stick in its mouth, the others beside it. J.D. climbed into the cargo hold with a Makita. Jay put a hand on Clyde's back. "Probably my fault, Clyde-san. You're falling apart down there. I think we got enough, I think maybe the Jeff City mission's over." Clyde huffed. The mission had ended four days ago. He just didn't get what all this concern was about. Here he was feeling strong and good again and nobody could leave him be. It was like they wanted to see him helpless. The pathetic victim, the weakling they'd met last year.

Clyde was getting tired of being studied. Jay had hardly taken his eyes off him since he got there. He lit a new cigarette with his old one, shut his eyes, and nodded. The mission was over, yes it was. At least he wouldn't have to tell Jay about getting shit-canned. Behind the lids he could feel his eyeballs bursting.

"This got anything to do with, uh," Jay said, watching Clyde until he made eye contact. "Orscheln's?" Clyde realized they hadn't talked once about the murders Jay had ordered him to commit. He guessed the news hadn't made it to Lick Skillet, what a relief. He knew he had to play this answer right or he'd be a dead man.

"Maybe it does," he said. "I'm trying to control it. Can't really sleep. That's all that's wrong with me, I ain't sleepin."

Jay nodded. "We will train our hearts and bodies," he said. Behind him, J.D. heaved an empty barrel into the cargo hold and wrestled it into a space made by a grid of two-by-fours on the floor that would keep the drums in place. "I ever tell you 'bout the one I killed?"

Clyde sat up, he looked at Jay.

"Some fuckin nigger. Maybe a faggot too, different night. Not sure he's dead. Put his eye out, that much I know for a fact."

"When?"

Jay didn't seem bothered by talking about it. "Back before I had purpose. Me and J.D. and Dale used to drive to K.C. looking for a fight. Niggers, spics, chinks, faggots, whatever. Didn't matter. You know that fuckin Liberty Memorial? That big penis-shaped monument over by Signal Hill?"

"I only been downtown about two times in my life, and neither one of 'em went too good." Clyde suddenly wanted to pay a third and final visit to that liquor store on Troost. This time he'd be ready.

Jay snickered. "Well, there's a big monument over there, shaped exactly like a dick. I guess 'cause of the fact that it's a monument to the cock all the homos in the city like to hang out there, to, uh, bask in its glory." Jay blew smoke across the bar. "We used to drive through there with baseball bats swinging like we'd just been drafted to the major leagues. And you know what?"

"What?"

"Faggots fight back."

"Yeah?"

"Fuck yes. Hell yes. Holy shit. You pick a fight with a goddamn queer you best bring your A-game. We shut a few of 'em up though."

Clyde wondered where fags fit into ZOG's master plan. He'd read about how the embrace of faggotry by the media and government we were seeing today would lead to its widespread general acceptance. Soon filth, sickness, and depravity would be the norm.

"Anyway, all I'm saying, Clyde, is you ain't the only one that been there. I been there. J.D.'s been there. When he was a kid J.D. used to say, 'God put me on this earth to kill fags.' And you know what?"

"What?"

"He was right. He could just about sit in the same room with a nigger or a kike, wetback. But you toss a queer in there you better watch out."

"That why he went to prison?"

Jay shook his head. He exhaled smoke through his nose and said, "Rape."

They sat smoking and watching Dale and the dogs. Then Jay clapped Clyde on the back and slid off the stool. Even though he'd removed his hand Clyde could still feel it there. "You be all right."

Clyde didn't move just yet. His mind raced and splintered. Jay climbed back onto the stool. "What is it?"

Clyde stared at the bar top and scratched his forearms against the dry wood.

"Damn, Clyde, whatever you got eating up your insides, you better tell Papa Jay."

Before Clyde knew what he was going to say he said, "Tina."

"She okay?"

"No, she's fine." Clyde didn't know where to start. "She's been using the Internet."

Jay blinked. He looked past Clyde, then back. "For what?"

"Her, uh, sauce. She's determined to get it into Walmart."

Jay nodded slowly. He didn't seem mad. "I thought we talked about that."

"I know."

"But?"

"I told her. She didn't listen."

"She didn't listen."

"No."

"You told her."

"Yes."

"And she didn't listen."

Clyde shook his head and dragged a new smoke from his pack.

"Goddamn it, Clyde." Jay took a few steps, forward and back. The space wasn't big enough to get far. He kicked the bar so hard his foot broke through. Clyde saw Dale look over at the sound. He either had a grin on his face or Clyde was imagining it. If Jay were to drag Clyde into the street right now Dale would be beside himself. "*Clyde!?*" Jay yelled. "What the fuck did my daughter do?"

Jay was so close that Clyde could feel his breath on the side of his face. "She registered with something called Dunne and Broadstreet. She got a DBA as Smalls Flavor Enterprises or something. And, uh, I think she sent applications to the FDA and some other places."

Jay's face dropped. Clyde slipped a hand into his pocket and realized he was digging for the crank. He stopped with the slick plastic on his fingertips. Jay stepped back and kicked the bar again. He kicked it and kicked it; the boards broke and the bar leaned against Clyde, pushing him off his stool. Jay snatched that stool and swung, it shattered against the wall. He threw the one leg that remained in his hand out the nearest window, breaking off a tooth of glass. Then his hands were on his hips, his back expanding with breath as he stared into the street. Clyde got off his stool and stood. Dale was watching from the back of the truck. "Before I lose my shit altogether, Clyde, is there any goddamn other stupid fucking sabotaging shit you tried and failed to stop my daughter from pulling?"

"No."

"Is there anything else that I need to know at all?"

Clyde realized that if he was going to come clean now was the time. He shook his head. "I mean," he heard himself say, "you said the mission's over so you probably won't care too much."

"Oh, Jesus. Probably won't care too much about what!?"

"I got fired."

Jay blinked. A moment passed when Clyde wasn't sure he'd heard him. "For what?"

"Drinkin on the job," Clyde said.

Jay blew a breath. He looked at the ground and spat. "Jesus fucking Christ, Clyde. When?"

"Uh, yesterday," Clyde said.

"For drinkin?"

"Yeah."

"On the job."

"Yep."

"What'd they say?"

Clyde shrugged. "They said they could smell it."

"None of them fucking wetback beaner motherfuckers drink on the job?"

"They all do. They're fucked up all the time. It's the only way to do that work."

"Well you weren't planning on retiring from the place, were ya?"

Clyde shook his head.

"Why'd they fire you, then?" Before Clyde could say anything Jay continued. "I'll tell you why. 'Cause you're the only Caucasian. They *expect* that shit from a wetback!" Jay paced again. "Well, you're right. I *don't* give a fuck about that. You was only biding your time till the truck was good to go. Getting fired for drinking on the job is the *one* thing you actually did *not* fuck up, Clyde, congratulations." Jay stepped over broken bits of wood, breathing hard through his nose. "Is *that* it, Clyde? I mean, is there *anything* else you need to tell me?"

"No," Clyde said. "Nothing."

Jay took a deep breath. "Get your shit. We're going to Jeff City."

hey got to Jefferson City in an hour and a half, thirty minutes faster than Clyde had ever done it. Jay didn't care about getting pulled over by the highway patrol, despite the wheel guns on the dash, the breech break under the seat, a brush gun in the glove box, and a couple gallons of the nitromethane stolen from P.D. Schwab in the back of the truck. "I *hope* I get pulled over so I can shoot the pig in his face so his mama can't have an open-casket funeral. I'll git sent to prison for murder. J.D., Dale, Jan, and Missy'll all get arrested for conspiracy to use a weapon of mass destruction and they'll all go to a supermax, and you too. Maybe even Tina. Five, six lives and a revolution just . . . obliterated, because you couldn't stand up to a sixteen-year-old girl. Sosei would be ashamed of you."

After Jay's twenty-mile tirade they drove in silence. He swerved in and out of what traffic there was on 50, flexing his jaw muscles. Clyde kept his mouth busy with cigarettes, there was not a moment when he wasn't smoking. Despite Jay's reaction, Clyde was relieved he no longer had to take care of this problem by himself. Then Jay slapped Clyde's thigh. "Women," he said, snickering. Clyde grinned. "Listen, all that shit at the capitol? You did good with that."

Clyde let out a deep breath. He'd hardly moved since they got in the truck. "Hope it helps."

"Already has," Jay said. They pulled into Jefferson City just before dark. Tina's Firebird was gone and the trailer was locked. "Know where she's at?" Jay said.

Clyde opened the trailer, didn't even want to say it.

"Library?" Jay said.

Clyde nodded.

"Typing all our personal shit into every government Web site she can find. Does she know that anytime she types our fucking *name* on the Internet it alerts the NSA?"

"I told her," Clyde said.

Jay jumped into the trailer and stomped around. Clyde stood watching him go through Tina's books on the dining table. Jay flipped open one after another. Clyde couldn't even look at him right now, he felt so bad. He wondered if he could get away with sneaking a bump. There wasn't much left but there'd be enough. He told Jay he had to piss, went in the bathroom, and snorted two quick ones. Looking at the baggie with almost nothing but dust he tried to figure a way to get back to Chetto's dealer while he was still in Jefferson City. He'd have to trick Jay into it somehow. When he came out, Jay had thrown all of Tina's books on the floor. Clyde had been skeptical when he and Jay had talked about hitting a woman but he'd been right, here was the damn proof. Tina hadn't obeyed her man and now her father—the first man—was here to make it right. Clyde wondered how things might have turned out had he hit her like Jay suggested.

"Get whatever shit you want and put it in the truck," Jay said.

Clyde got his clothes and *The Turner Diaries* and the books Jay had given him. He wanted Jay to see that he'd thought to take them. As he dumped his stuff in the truck, Jay stood drinking from a bottle of tequila, his hair mashed against the ceiling, his head at an angle. Then Jay said, "Get the gas can." Clyde went out, watching for Tina's headlights. Jay flicked his cigarette away and took the can into the bedroom. Clyde could smell its stench, this was liquid nitromethane, as volatile as it gets. Jay poured it over books, papers, carpet, table, clothes. Clyde stood by the road watching him walk backward through the trailer. Outside now he said, "Give me your cigarette," puffing up a good glow. "Say bye-bye," he said, flicking it. The fire caught with a snap.

Jay crossed the road and kept to the riverside. Fire ran quickly across the floor and up the trailer walls. Drapes lifted toward the ceiling with fire, cushions popped their insides, cabinet glass split. The roof broke open and fire lapped at the trees. Winter branches smoldered. The paint on the words facing the street began to bubble. Jay's eyes were bright, he grabbed Clyde and pointed. "So much for *American Dreamin'*!" The fire burned those words right off. Clyde watched them disappear.

A car turned onto the street. "I hope to God that's Tina," Jay said.

Clyde knew it was; he could spot her headlights a half mile off.

She pulled to the side of the road and jumped out, door open. "Oh my God, Dad, what happened!?" She ran over, her eyes full of tears. "Did you save my stuff?"

"What stuff is that?" Jay said.

"All my—" Tina said. Then her mouth fell open.

Clyde kept his eyes on the trailer. The fire was awesome, talk about power. He wanted to possess power like *that*, power that was primal. One of the tires blew and the trailer lurched, tearing open at a corner and sucking half the roof in. Sparks floated above the street like fireflies, drifting to the river, hung against the gray-yellow sky. Without looking at her, Clyde knew that with this, he'd lost Tina forever. They all had.

She marched toward the trailer. Clyde took a step but Jay's hand kept him where he was. She stopped, too intense. If Tina had nothing else, she had one hell of an instinct for self-preservation. A window blew and she screamed, covering her head, beating her little feet on the pavement. She ran back to the men and stood shaking with hatred. "A fucking *month* of work!"

"Yeah, that's all over," Jay said.

"You're crazy," Tina said. "Like, in*sane*. And *you*." She flapped an arm at Clyde. "I actually feel sorry for you. You two shoulda been the ones got together. Why don't you just fuck each other and get it over with!?"

Jay took a short step and punched her in the mouth. Tina's hair burst around her head, she fell straight down like something dropped from a ladder. Jay stood over her breathing hard. Clyde felt bad for him. Tina was unconscious and very heavy, but Clyde crouched to lift her, carried her to the truck. Jay opened the passenger door and Clyde laid her across the seat. Jay stripped off his belt and used it to bind Tina's wrists. "She wakes up, she gonna kick like a goddamn mule," he said. Clyde stripped off his belt, tied it around Tina's ankles. His jeans started to fall down, he held them up. There were sirens now.

"Want me to drive the Firebird?" Clyde said.

"I'm gonna need you in the truck. Park and lock it, we'll come back."

Clyde drove the Firebird a block up the road. Jay stopped for him; they went on with Tina still unconscious, her head on her chest. In his side mirror Clyde watched the trailer, a shivering box of orange, yellow, and green.

Tina came to on the highway. As predicted, she fought. Jay put a hand on her and said, "You better calm down!"

"Jesus Chr—" she said, moaning. "I fink you fucked me up."

"You be okay." Jay looked at her sideways.

Her eyes were full of worry and her jaw was swollen and red on one side. There was already a yellow bruise. "Buddy," she said to Clyde without moving her teeth. "Does my jaw wook ah wight?"

Clyde shook his head. She closed her eyes and cried, jerked against the belt and stomped her feet.

"Take it easy," Jay said, getting a cigarette going. Clyde grabbed one himself.

"I fink you fucked me up, dad," she said, trying not to sob.

Jay studied her face, Clyde thought he saw regret. "I didn't fuck you up, Tina, you fucked yourself up. Ain't no fink to it."

"You bwoke my jaw. I need a hospital."

"Nah," Jay said, though he didn't look at her again and Clyde could see that Jay figured Tina was right. He drove, mumbling. "Don't know my own strength, I guess," he said. "You just gonna have to hold on till we get home."

"Home?" Tina said.

"You remember what that is?" Jay said. "I don't think you do, and that right there's half the goddamn problem."

Tina shut her eyes and laid her head on the seat. She lifted it after a mile and said, "Ought oh."

"What?"

She leaned over, barfing. She couldn't open her mouth more than a crack so the vomit sprayed out in a wide fan and shot like soda from her nostrils. She coughed, moaned, leaned between her legs until it was all out. Then she cried, wailing and blubbering. When she stopped she said, "Can you bwow my nose?" Jay took a handkerchief from his pocket, cranked the heater, rolled his window to the cold rushing air.

Clyde held the hanky and Tina blew, whimpering. The cab started to smell and Clyde wondered if they'd be able to make it without adding their own puke to Tina's. She leaned her head on Clyde's shoulder. It felt good having it there, and he did his best to keep his shoulder at the level she needed. Jay passed him cigarettes, nobody talked. Tina went to sleep and her heavy head kept rolling forward but Clyde held a hand against her forehead all the way home.

THE TREE OF LIBERTY

In Lick Skillet, they put Tina's face in the lamplight and Jan, J.D., and Dale took turns moving their rough fingers across her skin. Jan called Missy, she arrived and looked at Tina. The jaw was definitely broken. Jan stomped out, slamming the door. Tina refused to be in the same room or vehicle with her dad or Clyde so Jan and Missy took her to Boonville, returning the next morning with her jaw wired shut, two black eyes, and blue, yellow, and green skin. Jan got Tina settled in the cabin next door to J.D.'s and Dale's, with Dale keeping her wood stove warm. When Jay came in, Tina made a big thumbs-up and said, "Way tuh go, Dahd," her lips fishy and her face so swollen that her head looked like a block of wood.

Clyde finished the rest of the crank and then drove Dale's car to Jefferson City without telling anyone. The dealer's trailer was dark and when he knocked she threatened to call the police, first in Spanish then in English, so Clyde drove off, lights in the park coming on behind him. He got back to Lick Skillet in the middle of the night. Coming down the hill, Jay said, "Boo!" He was standing in the dark at the tree line off the road.

"Jesus!" Clyde said, his heart racing now. "What the hell?"

Jay stepped into the road, the barrel of a rifle on his back caught the moonlight. He looked at the High Street. Clyde could hear Dale's engine cooling up there. "Go for a little drive?" Jay said.

"Yeah. Yeah, couldn't sleep."

Jay nodded, looking past Clyde at the darkness. He shook a cigarette end out of his pack and offered it to Clyde. They smoked, listening to the sounds of the woods in the night. Slowly, Clyde's sight came around. All was gray and blue; even Jay's baseball hat, which Clyde knew was red, was blue. There were noises in the trees that they both shrugged off; hunting had taught Clyde how much noise even the smallest critter can make. When they finished smoking Jay said, "Try to get some sleep. Gonna need it." He told Clyde he was gonna stay out a little longer. Worried that Jay was onto him, Clyde went down the hill to his cabin. He lay on his cot but didn't sleep.

Later that day they mixed the ammonium nitrate with liquid nitromethane into twenty fifty-five-gallon drums. Each drum was big enough to hold almost four bags of fertilizer and over a hundred pounds of the racing fuel. They weighed it out in measurements of twenty pounds each using a bathroom scale; once a barrel was full it weighed probably five hundred pounds according to J.D.'s estimates. It was hard, dirty work that made Clyde's body burn and sweat his clothes damp, despite the cold, and all the men watched him in a way that made him paranoid as hell. What might have taken a few hours took all day because half the drums were sealed at the top and had to be fed through a two-inch hole using a funnel. When each drum was full Clyde went into the street to snatch a few drags off a cigarette. When they were done, the drums in the middle of each backward *J* were full of Tovex, coiled inside like snakes, and the outer drums, twenty-two in all, were surrounded by the remaining bags of ANFO. Dale connected the fuses to blasting caps fastened to lines of shock tube. Using a power drill and a two-by-four, J.D. secured the smaller "Suicide Mission" drum where the passenger seat had been, the final, fatal redundancy. He draped it with Clyde's Gadsden flag, a personal touch. Don't Tread on Me, motherfuckers. All the tools and leftover material were left in the back of the truck. The best way to dispose of evidence was to blow it up.

THE NEXT MORNING, MID-MARCH, LICK SKILLET WAS BLANKETED IN SNOW. Dawn revealed that winter had finally come, just before spring, and only Clyde, still up cleaning weapons, saw it arrive. He was sitting on a folding chair outside his cabin smoking a cigarette when Jan appeared on the hill. Slowly he followed. The blown-out sky pressed down and the horizon disappeared at the tree line barely three hundred yards distant, making Lick Skillet feel even more isolated. The day was silent and bright. Without his Oakleys, Clyde's eyes wouldn't stop watering. His boots sank into snow marked only by Jan's tracks, his own steps falling silently before the brief crunch. If someone came looking for Clyde, he would not be hard to find.

Where the street came to an end, the truck and its ten-thousand-pound bomb sat hidden in the lean-to, a few days on a calendar all that kept it from its duty. Clyde went on, past leafless trees saddled with snow and robes of ice. Under the iron Lick Skillet sign, he reached up and broke off an icicle and carried it until it slipped from his glove and stabbed the snow. Up ahead, the cemetery was foreboding and silent, its gate frozen open, the long red rungs connected by a glistening patchwork of ice.

Entering, Clyde saw that the low branches of the trees inside had been decorated with baubles of some kind, little heads, he saw now up close, with shriveled faces, glassy eyes, and mats of wiry hair. Some had little outfits hanging below.

"One of Dale's projects," Jan called, startling Clyde. He couldn't see where she was. The heads were nearly fist-sized, faces lined like hags. Tiny teeth held cigarette butts, yellow glass-bead eyes were wide open or shut in squints. Clyde twirled the nearest one on his fingertips. It was an old apple, hundreds of them hung from the cemetery trees. When had Dale done all this? "He always needs *some*thing to keep him busy," Jan said, appearing before Clyde and looking as worried as everybody. Don't worry about me, Clyde thought. I'm ready for anything. She took his arm and leaned back to catch snow on her tongue. In that instant she shed twenty years and Clyde could see Tina in her for the fist time.

At the grave where Jan and Jay had found Tina's name, she told Clyde about the Sacking of Lick Skillet. When she finished, he touched another stone; there were so many graves, densely clustered. It read *Mary*, with a date of birth and a date of death and no mystery. "Why Tina Louise?" he asked. "Why not this one? Why not Mary?"

Jan tore some grass to better read her dates. Death had come to Mary in 1854, at the age of twenty-eight, so she'd been spared the fate of her neighbors. "Probably died in childbirth," Jan said. She looked at Clyde again, her head tilted. "That's easy if you think about it. Jay Smalls? His only child? He wanted a *fighter*."

They retraced their steps in the road. It was too cold to stay put for long. Snow fell still, fat and sticky, covering their tracks. Jan squeezed Clyde's arm, then squeezed it again. Clyde looked at her and there was the worry again. "What?" he said with a chuckle. Jan kept up her stare and then stopped in the road, so they both did, standing in a swarm of snow. Jan's face was set now not only with worry but also something else, disappointment, Clyde thought. "What?" he said again, with more force, though he knew what, he knew exactly what. He started to lie to her, tried to break away but she had a tight hold, she was stronger than she looked.

"How long's it been since you slept, honey?" she said.

"Not tired."

"You think you're the only one 'round here who's ever got a hold of some meth?"

That surprised Clyde, but he said, "No. I mean, everybody here's a warrior. Makes sense."

"No, it doesn't. It really doesn't."

"Marines take it all the time, kamikaze pilots took it. McVeigh too. It's just a combat tool."

"This ain't Pearl Harbor, Clyde, and you ain't a grunt. And McVeigh's dead. You're more than a weapon of mass destruction. Jay needs you to be able to use your *brain*." She touched his forehead with a fingertip. It was warm. He lowered his eyes. "What happened to that handsome Midwestern boy who walked into my house last year? You look like you went from twenty to forty overnight. Jeans falling down, zits, you're chain smoking and twitchin and blinkin and scratchin like a dog."

Suddenly Clyde felt awful, all of the strength he'd achieved drained right out of him. He could just about handle the others but Jan was different. Squinting against the glare he said, "Fuck." After taking a few breaths to calm himself down, he said. "Jay know?"

"I don't think he's put two and two together just yet."

Jay had set his life on a good clear course and all Clyde needed to steer it off a damn cliff was a month on his own. He thought he was going to cry right there. What a pussy. Jan's boots crunched snow, she hugged him and he rested his head on her shoulder. His face was in her hair; it smelled of cigarettes and wood smoke and pot roast and pine and dogs. He breathed it in, feeling pathetic. "I'm sorry."

She ran her hands over his back and said, "I know."

When he pulled back, embarrassed, he dirtied his sleeve with snot. He avoided Jan's eyes as they walked back down the High Street without saying another word. Before they got on the road that ran down the hill, Clyde said, "I'm done with it, Jan." He almost believed it himself. "You're right. I don't need it. I thought I did but I don't, I see that now."

She squeezed his arm. "You're a good boy who just got himself mixed up with the wrong crowd for a spell."

They went carefully down, holding on to each other. "I'd hate it if Jay knew."

Jan nodded, took a few steps. "Long as you promise me."

"I promise," he said without pause or thought. They struggled the rest of the way down the road, holding on to each other. "I ran out anyway."

That day there wasn't a moment he didn't hurt. He kept to himself, didn't eat. His body ached, his mind was filled with dark thoughts. What whiskey he had he drank, what cigarettes he had he smoked in the cold of his room without a fire in the wood stove. After dark, when he thought everyone was in bed, he went up the quiet hill to the Nova on the High Street. It would not start no matter how much he cranked. He popped the hood, hooked the light on the underside and saw a big black hole where the distributor cap had been.

His head remained dark the next day, his body heavy and useless. The others passed his cabin door, sometimes opened it to look in, question him about nothing. He nodded or responded as best he could, pretending to be lost in revolutionary thought, pamphlets and books scattered all around him. By dark he was exhausted and anxious and couldn't sit still. He kept nodding off with a cigarette burning between his fingers, only to jerk awake a moment later. Eventually he slept longer than a moment, sitting in the chair in his freezing cabin, his breath visible around him. He woke once after a deep sleep, his blanket on the floor and a warm fire in the stove he hadn't built. Falling under again he dreamt vivid, feverish dreams, eventually folding what was happening in the cabin into it, Dale pinning him to the chair with a blanket while J.D. and Jay went through his things. When he finally dragged himself to consciousness he said, "What?" He tried to move but Dale had a tight hold on the blanket right in front of him, a sick grin on his face.

"Wake up, dopey head," Jay said behind him. Clyde tried to see him. Clothes were tossed from the shelves to the floor.

"What the hell?" Clyde said.

"We're staging a, uh," Jay said.

J.D.'s voice then: "Intervention, Uncle Jay."

"We're intervenin 'cause it turns out you got yourself a pretty serious habit."

"Junky," Dale said, inches from Clyde's nose.

Clyde's head fell forward, almost hitting Dale. Jan had promised.

"You can run but you can't hide," Jay said, coming around. He slapped Clyde's face, not hard, and the hand stayed there a moment, to one side of

Clyde's bloodshot eyes, cold and rough. "We don't hide shit in this family, Clyde. We deal with it. No matter what it is."

"I'm sorry," Clyde whispered.

"I know you are," Jay said. He sniffed and stood. "Get dressed. You and me's going camping, make sure this shit's outta your system for the big day. Hit the reset button. Make sure the old Clyde we took into this family with open arms is the one driving the truck 3/21. You're goin jive turkey."

Clyde wanted to say, "That's impossible." He couldn't imagine sleeping on the frozen ground, training hard without an edge. There had once been a time when to spend a few days in the woods with Jay would have been a dream. Now it was the last thing he wanted.

Dale and Jay got Clyde dressed. Dale gave him one of his heavy hunting coats, and Jay handed him a loaded Parker-Hale and a pack that held the Hi-Point, an axe, and a buck knife. A sub-zero sleeping bag hung from it.

"When Sosei lost the way he went into the mountains. He come down stronger than he'd gone up."

Jay packed his own things, taking a Parker-Hale and a Hi-Point, deer jerky and cigarettes, work gloves and a roll of plastic. They entered the woods on foot. Clyde was already hurting, his mind searching for a way out, a hole to step in, snap the ankle, a cliff to fall off of, break a leg. It was morning, still dark. They walked without words, Jay leading the way across the river on the footbridge, through the heavy snow, into the dense forest. They walked three hours before they stopped and Clyde had already thrown up twice, nothing but greenish bile, not unlike the first time he trained with Jay.

The sun rising behind the trees gave the clearing a gauzy glow. They dropped their packs and Jay looked at the surrounding trees. Long vines hung from the canopy. "Chop us some sticks for a lean-to," he said. Clyde stayed on the ground, his blood beating in his ears, his chest jumping up and down. "Clyde," Jay said. Still he didn't move. Jay stomped over and kicked Clyde in the rib cage. Snow jumped around him. It wasn't hard, but Clyde scrambled up, slapping Jay's hands away. Jay grabbed him and yelled, "Git with the program, dopey!" He shoved Clyde at the vines and tossed a machete at his feet. Clyde swung it halfheartedly while Jay went around the clearing kicking snow out of the way for a fire.

Jay used the vines and branches and brush that Clyde cleared to make a small sleep hut in a cluster of trees. "The ground on the other side of those trees looks flatter," Clyde said.

"You think it's a good idea to sleep out in the open?"

It had been a while since Clyde had been in the student role with Jay. "I don't know."

"Best forts are hidden. Somebody could come through here while we's sawing logs and cut our throats 'fore we know what hit us. Eric Rudolph evaded capture for years by sleeping in caves, not out in the open."

A creek ran on one side of the clearing, across it sloped a long snow-covered field. When the fort was finished Clyde sat down to rest but Jay said, "Git your rifle," and they jumped the creek and hiked to the ridge of the hill. Near the bottom stood a dozen albino deer. Jay and Clyde sighted them in their scopes; they were just darker than the snow and hard to spot. "I think I got a good shot," Clyde said looking at it in his shaking crosshairs. There was nothing he could do to steady himself.

"You wanna hump all the way down that hill and all the way back up it, dragging a five-hundred-pound slab of meat, be my guest. I don't know 'bout you but I ain't that hungry yet."

"I am."

"Good. That's a sign. When's the last time you had an appetite?" Clyde couldn't remember. Jay pulled a chunk of jerky from his pocket. "Chew on this."

They sat for an hour unloading, cleaning, and reloading their Parker-Hales. Clyde had fired only rifles with Mauser mechanisms, not these Lee-Enfields. They were more complicated, but fast and durable. You could drop it in the mud and not worry too much. It was a good gun to have if you found yourself in a protracted firefight.

They watched the deer in the field for two annoying hours. Finally some of them started slowly up the hill. Clyde dozed. Every time he fell asleep Jay slapped his leg and Clyde cursed him. He didn't know how he was going to get through two, three days of this shit, his body ached, his thoughts were molasses. When the deer were halfway up the hill Jay and Clyde sighted them and Jay counted down. The rifle bucked harder than Clyde had expected and he lost his animal. A cluster of them hopped into the trees and Jay said, "Bye-bye."

One lay still in the snow, bleeding out its neck and nose. Up close it was enormous, a ten-point buck, its skin pink and white and gray. Clyde got the nylon rope and Jay said, "Best tie it 'round your chest." Clyde dragged the animal up the hill by himself, in a foot of snow, with Jay, at his back, saying, "In Japan they pull cars, truck tires. Everything's training." Clyde's thighs burned but he didn't stop for longer than a breath. If he'd stopped for any longer Jay would have beat him and Clyde knew that he would have deserved it.

They hung the deer from a tree at the creek near the clearing. "It's cold enough we don't have to skin it," Jay said.

"I know," Clyde said. He'd hunted enough with his uncle that he didn't need any pointers. He had been with Willie the day he fell. He was thirteen then, so he'd laughed when Willie slipped climbing out of the deer stand, dropping his rifle and scrambling cartoon-like for purchase among the tree limbs. Then he'd kicked off and dropped, his body tumbling slowly backward on the way to the earth. If he hadn't kicked off, he might have landed on his feet. The legs would have snapped, and the pelvis too, probably. Instead he landed on his head, the rest of his body piling down on top of itself, and Clyde, even from thirty yards away, heard the dry *crack* of his uncle's neck. Clyde had been small then, under five feet and not even a hundred pounds. Willie's body had settled into an impossibly broken clump, his face packed with snow, dirt, blood. Clyde knelt to brush it off as Willie issued, from somewhere very deep within, a long, low moan. To this day it was the worst sound Clyde had ever heard.

With Jay watching, Clyde gutted the deer with the buck knife and removed the sex organs, resisting the urge to use them as a joke. They hadn't brought a kill bag but Jay had a jar of rub. Clyde smeared it in the cavity, his eyes watering. He stuffed globs of it into the ears, nose, and mouth. Then he washed his hands good in the creek and went back to the clearing to lie in the sun. His eyes and fingers burned and his mind filled with images of his uncle that he worked to shake off.

Jay went around picking up strips of vine and bark and sat down making something with it. When he finished he smacked it against his thigh. It was a *bo*, like what he used in class to hit students. "Let's do some *kihon* to get our energy back."

The ground was frozen hard and it felt good lying on it.

"Come on." Jay was standing over him now. He swung the *bo* into Clyde's thigh. *Whap!* It stung, and Clyde jumped up.

By the time they were done he couldn't hold his arms up. Jay said, "*Kumite* time," and came at Clyde throwing punches and kicks. They fought in a circle for twenty minutes. Light contact, Jay showed mercy but never stopped. The punches and kicks that landed on Clyde's chest, thighs, stomach, and arms actually felt good. There was something about getting hit that brought everything into focus in a way that Clyde had forgotten. It was a purity similar to the crank. To feel that shock to the body, that focus of contact. Jay finally said, "That enough," and went down to the creek. He stacked riverbed slate into two stands in the clearing, positioning a rock on top like a bridge. "Break it," he told Clyde.

"The rock?"

"Mm-hm."

Clyde got painfully down on one knee. His heart was flapping in his chest, like it wanted out. He'd only ever broken boards of three-quarter-inch pine. Breaking boards was nothing. Like Jay had said, even Tina could break a board. "Any pointers?"

"Hit it hard."

Clyde lowered his open hand slowly, touching the rock, making sure to tighten it so the muscles and not the bones would take the impact. He did not think he could hit a rock hard enough to break it. But after Jay said, "Any day now, dopey," he hit it, hard. The rock jumped, unbroken, and Clyde got up cradling his hand. It was punishment, "Just more fucking punishment!" Clyde yelled. If I'd had a bump I coulda broke it, he thought. No problem.

Jay huffed and grabbed the rock Clyde had failed to break. "Look," he said. He rested the rock back on the slate stands. "Get down here," he said. With thumb and forefinger, Jay lifted the rock slightly on one side. "See what I'm doing?"

"It ain't touching," Clyde said.

Jay brought his hand down with less force than Clyde had. The rock snapped in two.

Clyde held his swollen hand out. "Coulda showed me that trick a minute ago. I think it's broken."

"It ain't broken and it's not a trick."

"If that ain't a trick I don't know what is."

"Then you don't know jack shit." Jay put a finger to his temple. "Fighting here, Cryde-san, no here," he said, making fists. "I broke that rock because I know that rock. That's the only difference between how you hit it and how I hit it. I knew what I was hittin. I knew the rock's *character.* So I knew what would break it. Half of fighting's knowing what you're up against. Know thy opponent and you defeat thy opponent, no matter who, or what, it is. It's called wisdom, dopey, not cheatin.'"

At dusk Clyde and Jay spent half an hour in the trees gathering wood. Jay made a pile in their camp and Clyde knelt with two bits of slate in his cold, numb hands. He aimed the sparks he made at a little pile of paper-thin strips that Jay had shaved off a branch. Every smack of the slate made Clyde's injured hand throb more. If it wasn't broken, it was fractured, that much he knew. Clyde kept at it until dark. A spark would flint off, he'd blow on it, but the fucking fire never caught. All the while Jay stood over Clyde, watching him try. He smoked, he stared at stars, he paced kicking snow. When one of the pieces of slate disintegrated in Clyde's hand he cursed. His fingers were bleeding now. "The hell you doin?" Jay said.

"It's not working." Clyde was up on his feet.

"What's not working?"

"I can't do it."

"Won't do it, you mean."

"You been sitting here. I gave it a pretty damn good try."

"But we ain't got no fire."

"No. We don't."

"Know how cold it is right now?"

"Freezing."

"Know how cold it gonna git around three in the morning?"

"I fuckin tried. You watched me."

"We don't make a fire we're liable to die tonight, Clyde."

"I'll take my chances."

"You'll take your chances," Jay mumbled, shuffling around in the darkness. "You may not give two fuckin shits about yourself no more, but you ain't the only one out here tonight. You got a responsibility."

"I bet you could make a fire in five minutes."

"What if I was sick, goddamn it? Wounded?"

"But you ain't. I'm the one fuckin sick."

Jay whined, "I'm nuh one fuckin sick, waaaaah." He scrambled up and Clyde braced himself. But he stomped over to the pile of slate. He dug around and returned with a few pieces. Kneeling, he smacked them together right against the shavings. After a few minutes an orange spark settled there, Jay blew it softly into fire. Clyde thought, See!? What I fuckin tell you!? Jay carefully pushed the fireball through a hole in the wood and blew some more, adding twigs one at a time like he was building a fort. When the larger wood finally took, Jay held a cigarette to it and sat back smoking. Clyde watched and fell asleep and woke when Jay said, "You ain't sick, boy, you're just weak. Big difference."

"Whatever," Clyde said, irritated by all the punishment, the lessons; he'd learned enough, he was tired of playing the student role.

Until they made their way to the sleep fort, Jay knelt in front of the fire so that only his shins and knees were wet. Clyde spent the evening on his side on the ground and felt damp to his bones. They both smoked and kept quiet. In that dark silence Clyde's spirits plummeted, all he felt was hunger, sadness, worry—about what he didn't even know. His future, he supposed, but also his past. Where was his mother? He recalled Willie's disappointment the last time he saw him. Was he really prepared to destroy the man entirely? He nodded off but always woke with a start to find Jay watching, shaking his head. "Fuck off," Clyde mumbled and Jay said, "That's the crank talking." Clyde didn't think it was because he didn't think he had any in him anymore. How he wished he had, how he wished he was sitting at Cheetahs! right now, with Chetto, or out in the lot in Dale's car fucking a stripper. Or fucking Esther, who understood him, in the Walmart parking lot. He fell asleep again and again. All he wanted was a warm bed. Jay was gone. Then he was back with a fifth of Rebel Yell. Clyde didn't say anything but seeing that bottle filled his mind with murderous thoughts, he wanted it so bad. Jay took a few long pulls, smacking his lips and making exaggerated noises of appreciation. Look what I got, look what you don't deserve no more. Then he turned his snaggletooth grin on Clyde and tossed him the bottle.

"*Arigato*," Clyde said.

"*Do itashimashite*," Jay said. "Cryde-san. Don't be uh-mad-oo wiz papa-san."

When they crawled into the fort Jay fell asleep immediately, snoring at Clyde's side. Some good it would do them to be hidden from view; anyone passing by could just follow the noise. Bugs kept crawling into Clyde's hair. When he brushed them away his hand ached. He felt the stock of the rifle, the Hi-Point, the machete beside it. With his hands upon his weapons he rushed into sleep.

L ight streamed through the trees, blue sneaking through the canopy. It was past dawn; Jay had let him sleep in. Clyde hadn't slept through the night in how long? He had not stirred once and he had to piss so bad his back ached. He crawled out and unzipped, making a froth in the dead leaves. Jay laughed from somewhere in the trees.

"Morning, sunshine," he said. "Want some coffee? Was hot a few hours ago."

"What time is it?"

"Three o'clock."

"Three!?"

"Yep," Jay snickered.

"You're shitting me."

"Nope."

"I never slept that late in my life."

Jay handed Clyde a tin cup of cold coffee and lit a cigarette. "Looks like you needed it more than push-ups right now."

Clyde cleared his throat, spat into the ashes of their fire. He actually felt all right, maybe even, hell, maybe even good.

"How's the hand?" Jay said. The hand had turned so many colors it looked almost rotten. "Think you be able to shoot?"

Clyde went for his rifle, cocked it, aimed. It hurt, no doubt about it, but not so much that he couldn't pull the trigger if it came to that.

"When I used to train with Sensei Sazuki, one day he told all the shodans to go outside and find a rock. I musta looked at fifteen different fuckin ones. I finally brought one in. He had us lay 'em up on the counter by the front. Six different rocks sat up there for weeks, then months. Every day we'd come in and there they were, those fuckin rocks. We'd hold class and sensei never said nothin. Then one day, out of the blue, at the beginning of class: 'Jay, git your rock.' Shit!" Jay snickered. "He had me lay it on some bricks and then we held goddamn class like it wasn't there. I started thinkin he was just fuckin with me. But around the end of class he goes, 'All right.' Nobody else. Just me. I got down on one knee and I musta hit that motherfuckin rock twenty times." Jay smiled, a little sadly, and smoked.

"It didn't break?"

He shook his head. "My hand's gettin fuckin bigger an bigger. Goes numb. I figure it's busted. I didn't give a fuck. Sensei's watchin. 'Jay-oo,' he says. 'Some-sing today wir bleak-oo. The lock, your hand, o your spilit.' " Jay snickered. "Wasn't the rock, and it wasn't my hand."

Clyde finished the cold coffee. A whippoorwill was in the trees, Clyde couldn't spot it. Jay said, "All right." They went back to yesterday's ridge, ran down and up the hill with their rifles bouncing on their backs. Clyde's stomach made noise the whole time, his lungs burned against his ribs. He had to bend over to breathe, and when he did he dry heaved. Nothing came up. "Body's just a machine, Clyde," Jay said. "What's it say in the Bible? A vessel? You can control your body, Clyde, breathing, heart rate, pulse. Or you can let it control you. It's a choice, never forget that."

They took the hill again. From the top, Jay yelled encouragement. When Clyde wanted to quit, Jay's words kept him going. Left on his own, without supervision or encouragement, Clyde had let himself get distracted, had embraced the petty at the expense of the profound. But at Jay's side he remembered his purpose; Jay made everything crystal clear. Running alongside this man made Clyde believe that everything, for the second time, had been set right in his life.

They trained in the clearing until dusk. "Strength through repetition, Clyde!" Jay yelled. When they finished, he said, "You just did ten thousand reps. Sosei said train one thousand days and you've mastered your basics." Clyde was exhausted, but he felt better than he had in ages.

That night Clyde made the fire, it took an hour but he did it. He didn't have Jay's technique but he'd learned from his mistakes. They ate jerky that didn't make a dent in Clyde's hunger, but he didn't mind, he'd forgotten that pull of hunger and welcomed it. Jay dug into his pack and pulled out a book with *FM 21-76 Department of the Army Field Manual* on the cover. Clyde read "Survival" and "October 1970." "Hasn't a lot happened since nineteen seventy?" he said.

"I'm sure there been some minor revolutions in the plant world, Clyde, some upheavals, but I don't imagine any of that reached these plants out here. These are old-fashioned plants." Jay flipped to the table of contents. "Look at this shit. Chapter three, water, finding water. Chapter four, food, vegetable foods, animal foods, fried chicken. This a good book to own, Clyde, there's everything in here from cold-weather survival to jungle and desert. First aid. Government does *some* shit right. You hold on to it."

"Thanks."

"We'll use it later to find somethin we can eat."

"We going back?"

Jay nodded. "I think we accomplished what we needed to accomplish here. 'Sides, Valhalla awaits." He grinned.

That night Clyde slept like he used to. His body was sore again but not enough to keep him awake.

At dawn they knocked apart the fort and drank warm coffee kneeling in seiza by the dying fire, a few orange coals glowing under ash. Clyde got their packs together and Jay smothered the fire with dirt, took down the deer. He found a branch to support it between them and they shouldered it, stopping every so often on the way back to kick the snow from plants that looked edible. Carrying the deer was training, looking for food was training, everything was training.

"There some plants you don't wanna touch, let alone eat," Jay said. "Anything with a milky sack, I know I know," Jay snickered. "Leave it alone. And whatever you do don't use a leaf to wipe your goddamn ass." Clyde smiled. His Uncle Willie had told him the exact same thing when he was a boy.

"I ain't sure I could live off nothin but plants," Clyde said.

"Eric Rudolph did. Five years off plants and salamanders."

"Salamanders?" Clyde said.

"There's a lot you can do to a critter to make it tasty, Clyde." Jay banged his hands together. "Smash it between a couple rocks and sprinkle it over your cabbage like bacon bits." Jay found what looked like cabbage and tore a leaf, pressed it to his wrist. "Fifteen minutes or until it starts to bother you." This one irritated his skin from the get-go. "See? No good." His eyes were on the ground. He found another plant and did it again.

This time neither one of them had trouble. Clyde said, "It's good."

"Maybe," Jay said, putting it under his tongue.

"Jesus, lotta work," Clyde said.

"In my experience, when you're living off the land, most of your time is spent on the three F's: food, fire, and fuckin." He snickered.

"Fuckin what?" Clyde said.

"Whatever puts up the least fight."

"The four F's," Clyde said. "Food, fire, fighting, and then, fuckin."

Jay laughed and the leaf fell out. He put it back and they stayed still for another ten minutes.

"Starve 'fore you find something edible," Clyde said.

"But if this is edible look at how much we got." He kicked at the plant on the ground, big as a basketball. "That's two, three days' food. I either wanna eat this or get it out of my mouth." He tore a handful of leaves, shook them out, took a bite. "Still," he said, chewing. "You can never be too sure. Eat a bit, wait an hour, see what happens. You might start shitting your guts out. Living off the land, you wanna be afraid of anything you ain't already encountered."

"Sounds like good advice in general," Clyde said.

They each chewed a leaf, lifted the deer, and walked on.

"Some quote-unquote edible plants are gonna taste so shitty you'll wanna boil 'em or steam 'em or do some goddamn thing to 'em. And just cause it don't taste good raw don't mean it won't taste like a ham hock once it's cooked. About the only thing I like to eat raw is pussy."

Over their heads, the day glowed brighter. It must have been mid-morning. The weight of the deer tore into Clyde's shoulder and Jay said, "Let's shift it side to side every hundred paces." He kept count. The woods grew slowly more familiar. Clyde thought he could hear the river that cut through Lick Skillet at the county line where the Sacking of Lick Skillet had begun. The sun broke through and Jay stopped to feel it on his face. Clyde shut his eyes and heard the distant popping of gunfire.

Jay flipped his phone open. He said, "Nope," and put it away.

"Dale, I bet," Clyde said.

"For all I know those are nine-hundred-yard rounds. Which way they headed?" He held a finger to his temple. "I'd rather it wasn't right here." He got his Hi-Point out and pulled off three quick rounds into the ground. "Friendlies!" he yelled.

"Friendlies!" Clyde yelled, cupping his mouth.

They waited. No other shots were fired, they raised the deer and went on. Soon they found one of the paths that led to the village at the bottom of the hill. When they were close enough to see J.D.'s Bronco on the road that ran to the cabins, shots were fired not two hundred yards away, from the bottom of the hill. This was answered immediately from the High Street above, in a much bigger way.

"Goddamn it!" Jay said, dropping his head.

"What?"

"We're under attack!"

T hey came out of the woods behind the cabins near the ostriches. Those birds were climbing all over each other, bouncing off the cage. Jimmy-Don and Dale's corner cabin stood fifty yards distant, chimney smoking. Jay and Clyde hugged the back property, keeping a structure between them and the High Street. A rifle fired a round near enough that Clyde could smell gunpowder. Shots returned from the hill, raising dust in the road, chipping plaster off the cabins down here. Jay ran to the back of the corner cabin; Clyde followed, the only way in was from the street side. They hugged the cabin all the way to the front, four feet from the road. Jay banged on the wall. "It's Jay and Clyde!" Then they ran to the door. When they slammed through it a gun went off, filling the room with smoke. Clyde's ears rang, he hit the floor, Jay was on top of him yelling, "Friendlies, goddamn it!"

Missy threw down the wheel gun. It hit the cement floor, skidded. "Jay!" she yelled, running over with her hands out, sobbing. What about me? Clyde thought, getting up with nobody's help. Good thing Missy couldn't shoot for shit.

"Where's Jan?" Jay said.

Missy flapped an arm. "Out fuckin there!" She looked exhausted, her cigarette smoke drifting into her wiry hair, Jay told her to sit. With a deep, loosened voice, she told them about one of the alarms getting tripped around dawn. "We all figured it was just the two of you back from the woods, unable to hack it in the wild." She coughed smoke out her nostrils. "Well, Clyde any-way." Her eyes skipped to his and he tightened his face. "That was the only goddamn thing that got Tina out of the house in six days. She wanted to laugh at you. Her and J.D. go out there and after a minute, the place just fuckin lights up like goddamn Independence Day. Dale tears out the door and I ain't seen any of 'em since." Missy's head fell and she covered her face, dropping her cigarette to the floor. Jay rubbed her shoulders and she sniffed, got herself together. "After about an hour Jan says, 'I ain't sittin around like a goddamn idiot,' and goes out after 'em."

"When was that?" Jay said.

Missy rolled her arm to check her watch. "Been about five hours now."

"All right," Jay said, pointing at the door. "I don't know much, but I know there two to four army-trained federal agents, FBI, ATF, maybe both, out there with long-range weapons. Shots been fired, ROE. Rules of engagement. One or more of 'em's on the High Street. Who knows where the others are. It's a miracle nobody been killed yet."

"I didn't say that," Missy said.

"I'm going on the assumption that everybody's alive and in good positions out there."

Another close shot popped off and Jay yelled out the door, "Jan, that you!? I think she's in that goddamn copse right there. Somebody is. Thirty yards. We get to that we find out what's what."

"You oughta stay out of that doorway," Missy said, tired.

Jay stepped away. "Clyde, reload us." He handed Clyde the Parker-Hales.

Clyde went through J.D.'s ammo and loaded them up. Then he filled two brush guns with 30-30s. Redundancy. He was awake now, alert, without an ounce of the exhaustion or confusion he'd been feeling.

"Jimmy got any Uncle Mikes?" Jay said. Missy looked blank. "Bullet holders. Wraps around the stock." Missy jerked her head at the corner. Clyde dug through boxes and found them. "Fill 'em," he told Clyde.

Clyde filled the Uncle Mikes and strapped them to the rifles.

Jay said, "Scatterguns next door." He went to the window. "Ready?" he said to Clyde.

"Yep." Everything Clyde had done—all of Jay's tests—had been to prepare him for this.

"When we get to that door we gotta bust through. We stand around trying to figure out how to work the goddamn latch they'll leave our bodies on the welcome mat." When they moved, Clyde and Jay made a hell of a racket. Jay aimed the 30-30. His eye scrunched in the scope. He stepped into the open door and fired three quick rounds, jerking the bolt to spit out one shell before the last had hit the floor.

J ay and Clyde made the door of the neighboring cabin, slamming into it and spilling their weapons across the floor. Jay got an auto and a breech break loaded, extra rounds in pockets. He snapped the breech break shut. "Fine gun but a bitch to load if you're in a sticky situation."

"Good thing this ain't a sticky situation."

With their weapons strapped on and in pockets, they got winter gear from a pile on the floor, stood breathing hard, looking out. "I don't got much of a plan yet, son," Jay said. "For now just follow me." Jay counted to three—*ichi, ni, san*—and they ran, stomping the open snow to the nearest copse. Jay yelled, "It's me, mama," when they burst through and Clyde heard Jan in the sudden dark heave a great sob. Clyde's fingers stuck together with pine sap and he rubbed them against his jeans, they were still sticky, his hand throbbed.

"Goddamn it, Jay," Jan said. Clyde's eyes came around. Her arms were wrapped around Jay. She'd slid to her knees at the base of a tree, Jay's face in her hair, hands on her back. "They killed our baby," she sobbed.

"No," Jay said, holding her. "No, they didn't." He looked over at Clyde, Clyde dropped his eyes, he knew in his gut that what Jan had said was true. Tina had probably been dead since dawn. Jimmy-Don, Dale, and even Jan would think little of spending five hours in the wet snow defending their property, but Tina would grow tired of the discomfort in minutes. This wasn't even her fight. Tina had died on that hill, Clyde was sure of it.

Someone fired and a branch above Clyde's head twitched, he dropped to the damp ground. Jan let herself collapse into Jay completely, accepting grief the way only a woman can.

"I don't really think we should stay here," Clyde said.

"You all right?" Jay said. Jan held a hand toward Clyde.

"There are a lot of open spaces between these trees."

"Come here, Clyde," Jan said.

"I just don't want you to . . . " He couldn't finish the thought.

"Clyde."

He stayed where he was even though their hands reached out.

"Sons of bitches," Jay said, moving Jan to a safe spot. "Clyde's right. Can't shoot good from here neither. Pinned down, can't see shit." Jan wiped her face and took a cigarette from Jay. "Where's J.D. and Dale?" he said.

"Jimmy was in here with me half the morning," Jan said, wiping her face with her free hand. "Then he ran off to find Dale." Jan flung an arm at the woods. "They shot one of Dale's dogs. Heard him out there dying, the poor thing."

"How many are there?"

"J.D. thinks there's three."

"FBI?"

Jan nodded. "J.D. thinks so, yeah."

Jay's mouth went tight, he stared through the branches. "We got back in the woods we could make our way up to the hill that way. Level ground. Come at 'em from both sides. Maybe they's dumb enough to use the roads."

Jan's eyes, when Clyde really looked at them, were extinguished.

"You two on one side, me on the other," Clyde said.

"Long as we don't shoot each other," Jay said, handing Jan his 30-30. The rifle she'd been using was covered in mud and grass.

Jay said, "We kill these three maybe we can get out of here before anymore get here. It was a few days into Ruby Ridge 'fore anybody but two feds was there."

"Sounds good," Clyde said. Meet back at the main house later, where Missy's at?"

They stood a moment in the quiet. "Works for me," Jay said. "Work for you, mama?"

"Yep," Jan said softly.

Clyde looked from Jay's face to Jan's. He wanted to burn them into his brain. One way or another, he thought that they would all join Tina on that hill. Maybe tonight, maybe five nights from now, when they were freezing cold and starving, exhausted and sick, just didn't care no more. "See you in a bit," he said, running out with loud, uneven steps.

Tearing across the opening he saw a shape in the middle of the road. For a second he thought it was a shooter hunkered down to end his life, and he flinched. But it wasn't a shooter, it was Tina. Facedown in the snow, her posture was identical to the army men J.D. and Dale had placed around the map of the capitol. She was still as a stone, but a dark line trailing several feet through the snow behind her showed how far she'd dragged herself before giving in to her fate.

Clyde thought about stopping, risk be damned. He could drag Tina's body out of the open. He remembered Jan telling him about that slave who'd tried to move Gerhardt. A pain tore through his ankle and he went down in the snow, his rifle landing two feet away. He was wearing high boots and he'd still managed to turn an ankle. Tina lay not ten yards away. *Do you have a girlfriend?* Clyde remembered her saying that night, so shy. *Can I be your girlfriend?* That had been the moment he'd liked her best. It had never gotten any better than that; their best time together had been before he'd said yes. Lying there at Tina's level, cold and exposed, he wished he'd been a better boyfriend to this girl. He'd been her first and he'd been careless with her. Now Tina, who in the end had wanted nothing to do with her family's quarrel, was its first casualty. Clyde's chest tightened with sadness, burned into anger. The United States government, uninvited and armed, had come onto private property and assassinated Tina Louise Smalls, sixteen, a completely innocent girl. Any skepticism Clyde might have once held about the far-reaching powers of ZOG had been obliterated. Unlike her namesake's, the grave that marked the life of Tina Louise Smalls would have a date of death.

Clyde made it to the woods on the cemetery side of Lick Skillet, moving uphill and making sure to keep cover between him and the High Street. His right ankle was ripe, he'd torn something, the adrenaline was draining away, a dull sickness taking up more and more space inside him. But he kept moving and made it halfway up the hill, stopping only when someone on the other side of Lick Skillet started screaming bloody murder. It sounded like a woman and didn't last long.

Shots came from the woods. Jay probably. The dogs barked like mad, their noise echoing around the valley. The straps of the weapons dug into Clyde's shoulders, he kept climbing to where the ground leveled off. Through the trees he saw the High Street. He crawled to the ditch on the roadside, and into it, dug a small hole through the snow to see through. No one was around; it was quiet except for the dogs in the woods. Then someone moved. A figure ran across the street. Clyde was sorry he didn't have his rifle ready. He stripped it off, got to his knees. Nothing moved in the street now. He ran to the old bar, it was empty. Two shiny pickup trucks were parked on the High Street blocking the village road to traffic. The cargo truck still sat hidden behind netting. It hadn't been discovered, he didn't think. Clyde ran from the bar to the nearest pickup.

"Hey!" someone said, making Clyde flinch and almost lose his footing.

It was Jay. He ran over in a crouch, guns rattling.

"Fuck!" Clyde said softly. "Jay!"

"Shhh," Jay said.

"Where's Jan?"

Jay bobbed his head at the other side of the hill. "Got separated."

"You're bleeding."

"Where?"

"Damn," Clyde said, looking at Jay's ear. Half of it was gone and the mangled flesh that remained was white and bloody. "You get shot?"

Jay grabbed Clyde's arm and walked them to the far side of the nearest pickup. Once there, Jay's eyes never stopped; he barely looked at Clyde. His body rotated to take in everything, 360 degrees. He squinted into the trees across the road, brought the shotgun up, looked around, dropped it again. "One of 'em almost shot Jan. I shoved her out of the way. Actually, I *kicked* her out of the way and she weren't too happy about it till she saw me go face down. You never heard a woman scream the way Jan screamed, seeing me playin dead."

"You played dead?"

"Goddamn right, I did. And that fuckin Academy Award–winning performance is the only reason I'm standing here." Jay kept moving, kept looking, threw a one-two punch and a kick. "Fighting ain't just this." He blinked, touched a finger to his ear, looked at the blood. He patted his pockets, found whisky, gave it to Clyde after taking a swig. "I killed that one with my bare hands."

"Choke him?"

"Put my thumb in his eye. Snapped his neck." Out of habit Jay did the moves to show Clyde the techniques. "At least I know Jan loves me. Two more sprung up then and Jan took off. Like a goddamn rabbit, *pshew!* One of 'em went after her, the other come after my black ass." Jay looked behind Clyde. "He dead too," he said.

"Jesus, how many are there?"

"Four, I think, total. J.D. was wrong about that. Two still living." He looked straight at Clyde then, and it was the longest his eyes had settled on any one thing since he'd got there.

There was something odd about the stare, and it took Clyde a moment to realize what it was, that Jay wasn't actually looking at him, he was watching something beyond Clyde's right shoulder, and whatever it was he was watching he didn't like it. Someone back there said, "Neither of you fucking move."

"Follow my lead," Jay said without moving his lips. He kept staring at a man standing at the edge of the trees, a flat black scattergun pointed at them. Clyde turned slowly around to get a look.

"Get out of your weapons," the man said, jerking the gun. He took a walkie-talkie off his belt. "I got two adult males on the eastern trail. Think one of 'em's Jay Smalls. Other's Clyde Twitty. Over."

"How the hell you know me?" Clyde said.

The walkie crackled with words and the man said, "All right. Hurry it up." He clipped it back and jerked the gun. "I said lose the damn weapons."

Jay put his rifles down gently, one by one.

"I know everything there is to know about you, Clyde. Sidle up to men like Jay, Jimmy-Don, and Dale Smalls, you get noticed." The man stepped out onto the street. He was in regular clothes, but as he walked closer Clyde saw a badge hanging by a chain around his neck.

"You trespassing," Jay said.

The man didn't respond. He kept coming slowly, fanning out to keep his distance.

"Gonna wanna see that identification," Jay said, nodding. "You can't just come onto somebody's private property with a loaded weapon and expect a warm goddamn welcome. I'm gonna need to see your warrant."

The man wasn't much older than Clyde; he wore the moustache of a high-school coach, but his skin was dark, like Chetto's. He was beefy, with a winter hat pulled down to the top of his big brown sunglasses, Oakleys, Clyde thought, almost the same ones he used to wear.

"You're trespassing, amigo," Clyde said, thinking the guy might be Mexican.

"Your hands on your heads," the man said. He didn't speak like Chetto. Clyde put his hands in his hair. "You the one that killed Tina?" he said.

"I ain't killed nobody yet. Unlike you. Turn around."

"I never killed anybody." Clyde turned, connecting eyes with Jay when he did. There was something in Jay's eyes he couldn't place.

"I ain't turning till I see the identification and search warrant," Jay said.

"You oughta give me more credit for knowing who I'm dealing with, Jay Smalls. You know the law probably better than I do. So you know we are way beyond warrant." The man circled Clyde and Jay with his shotgun out until he was below them on the trail. He always kept a dozen feet between them. "Turn around, goddamn it."

"I just turned around," Clyde said.

"I ain't talkin to you. You don't put your back to me, Jay, I'll put one through your thigh."

"You ain't gonna shoot me with that," Jay said. "He got a scattergun, Clyde."

Clyde nodded with his back to Jay and his hands up like a dummy. He watched Jay stand in defiance. His weapons lay at his feet but he turned with the man's movements, never taking his eyes off him.

The agent jerked the gun at Jay and said, "You think this is the only weapon I got? Back up."

Jay took a few backward steps. Clyde kept pace with him, turning to face the agent like Jay was.

"I tell you to turn around?" the man said. Clyde didn't respond. The man gathered the weapons, Jay's and Clyde's, hung the rifles off his shoulder, ignored the scatterguns. He said, "Go."

"Go where?" Jay said. "Home and fuck your wife?"

"To that truck." He snatched the walkie again. "Sprull, what's your twenty?"

Clyde heard a voice this time. "Ten Mikes."

"All right," the man said, jerking his gun.

Jay took a step, Clyde took a step, the snow was loud underfoot. Deliberately, Clyde walked heel-toe heel-toe, like a retard. "Pick up the pace."

"I got a torn ankle," Clyde said. "This about as fast as I can go."

"I been in Iraq, Afghanistan, and Somalia. Think I was born yesterday, Twitty?"

Clyde kept putting one foot in front of the other with that exaggerated limp. The man went quiet and advanced, drawing closer. Clyde heard Jay whisper, "Good." The man was within a few feet of them now, they were halfway between the two trucks, Clyde still had the Hi-Point in his pocket, he figured Jay still had his. His pocket was zipped shut. He wasn't dumb enough to finger the zipper and give away his only advantage. He figured Jay had left his unzipped.

"I'm gettin tired of your shit," the man said, jabbing the angry end of the scattergun into Clyde's back ribs.

Clyde turned as fast as he could, doing now what he hadn't done at the capitol. He already had his arms up so wrapping the shotgun was easy, he squeezed hard to trap the barrel in his arm. Jay jumped in, punched the man in the face. The shotgun went off, scaring Clyde and nearly jerking free. But he held harder, even when he couldn't hear and could hardly see. Jay backed off and Clyde thought he was going for his gun, end this fight the easy way. Or maybe he was content to let Clyde fight this one on his own. He'd entered the *mai*; Jay had been here to witness. Clyde punched the man's face, knocking his Oakleys off. The nose shot blood, the eyes watered, he yanked the gun and it went off again. *Poooom!* The blast spread across the valley, burning Clyde's inner arm through the coat. He watched his feet and the man's feet disturb the snow but couldn't hear a thing beyond his own loud breath in his head. He kept his grip on the gun, *a firm, unshaking spirit.*

When the hearing returned, all at once, he heard the man's curses and the noise of their feet carving up the snow, the attempts to cock another shell into the scattergun, and a terrible howl coming from Jay. He was on the ground on his back, pressing at the snow with his heels and reaching with an arm. "Jay!" Clyde shouted, trying to see what had happened to him.

But the man didn't stop yanking the gun like this was a tug-of-war. Clyde kept punching, the man took the hits. His face was getting pulpier and pulpier, the skin of his forehead split. He tucked his chin, sacrificed his brow. Clyde pounded it, aiming for the bridge of the nose, driving his biggest swollen knuckle into the opened wound the way Jay had always hit the same rib with the same knuckle in conditioning drills. The man shook his head, snorted, growled. They struggled in a sloppy circle and Clyde stepped on something, slipping, almost going down. Jay must have been hit by one of those blasts, he must have been in bad shape to not be helping right now. A fan of blood sprayed out six feet across the snow from under him, black as asphalt.

Clyde threw a kick into the man's balls with so much force that it hurt his shin. He kicked again, just like in class when they did bag work. Two hard, fast kicks in one second: *bap-bap*. The man groaned. Clyde saw fear in his eyes; he'd never brought that look into a person before. God, it thrilled him. Coughing, groaning, the man yanked his weapon. He was losing strength.

"You ain't gettin it," Clyde said.

"Kill you," he said, turning his body to protect his balls. Clyde threw a kick at his knee. It buckled; the man went half down, shaking his head. Clyde saw what he was doing, he was fighting to stay conscious. Then, like he'd been surprised, the man yelled, "Oh!" He threw both hands up and ran around the truck, across the street, into the trees, his big pumping arms making helicopter sounds against his winter coat. Clyde let the scattergun fall, unzipped his pocket stepping around the truck, and fought the coat for the damn Hi-Point. He wasn't a great shot with a pistol but he could still maybe get him in his big wide back. But the man was gone, lost in the trees.

"Fuck it," Jay said. Beneath him the snow was melting into a red-black mud. He had rolled onto his front, holding his cheek against the ground. Blood fanned out around him in all directions.

"Jay?" Clyde said.

"You did good," he said. Clyde didn't feel like he'd done good. Maybe he'd entered the *mai*, but he'd let the man get away. Now someone else would have to deal with him. "You did," Jay said, as if he could read Clyde's thoughts. The one eye that Clyde could see turned obscenely back in its socket trying to place him. "Proud of you."

Clyde said what Jay usually said: "You gonna be all right." Jay's eyes stayed on the black snow. "Jay? Come on." Clyde circled Jay to see how he'd been hurt. "Is it bad?"

"Git down here." Jay rose his head and turned it. "Can't see you."

Clyde stayed where he was. "Why don't you roll over? Let me see."

"Gonna pick now to argue with me?"

Clyde knelt in the blood, he flushed with fear. "We should get you off the street."

"I ain't movin."

Clyde watched both ends of the street. For all he knew someone was standing behind a tree floating his head in the crosshairs. "Why don't you—" Clyde began, and Jay shook his head hard.

"Puttin pressure on the wound," he said, his face turning gray, slick with sweat. He spat.

"Shit." Clyde stood up. "I'm gonna go get Jan."

"The hell you are," Jay said, craning his neck, grimacing with pain. "Sit down . . . damn it . . . gotta tell you somethin."

Clyde got back down, it was cold and wet beneath him.

"You wearin a belt?" Jay said.

"You don't want me to get Jan?"

"No, goddamn it, take your belt off."

Jay rolled over, blood sprayed. His whole side was a dark shiny mess. The sleeve of his winter coat was torn and matted. He tugged at the zipper with one hand, wormed his right arm out. The arm ended above the elbow in a wet mangle that pumped blood into his lap. He grimaced, tried to sit, nodding at the street at what looked like a small dead animal twenty feet away. Where Clyde had stepped on it, blood had smeared the snow. "Git that," Jay said.

Clyde went. Jay's hand, wrist, forearm, and elbow lay in the street, the stump pocked with buckshot, the flesh there white as the inside of a fish. Clyde couldn't see bone and couldn't figure out what was muscle, what was tendon, what was blood, what was vein. He stared at it, not quite able to accept that this hunk of meat was Jay's arm, picked it up by the wrist, dropped it on the ground where Jay sat. "Sorry," he said, guessing he wouldn't want someone to be so careless with his own arm.

Jay held out what was left of his arm. "Tie your belt around it."

Clyde stripped it off. "Gonna hurt."

"I don't give a fuck. I'm in shock, anyway. Probably won't feel a thing."

Clyde fit the belt around the bleeding stump. There were no holes that far down so he tied it rope-like and it slipped off. Jay howled, rolled around shaking and cursing, his blood spraying snow. A stream crossed Clyde's face and he flinched, his mouth warm with Jay's blood. Clyde knelt on top of Jay then, pinned him, tied it quickly near the shoulder. Jay drank some whiskey. Clyde lit cigarettes, put one in Jay's teeth. His face more and more took on the pallor of the trees, the red-rimmed eyes set deeply with fear.

"What we gonna do?"

Jay shook his head. "I gotta think."

"This ain't good."

"No. It ain't. I gotta think."

"Get you to a hospital," Clyde said.

"Huh uh."

"How long you think you can last like this? Just a belt."

"Long as I ain't losing blood, maybe all day."

Clyde smoked and watched the street and the hill. "I get Jan, though," Clyde said.

Jay punched him in the arm. It hurt. "Only way I git to a hospital is turn myself in, and that ain't gonna happen. It's just a body, Clyde. Meat. Don't mean nothin." Jay held his left hand out. "Still got one, goddamn it. I can still fire the Hi-Point. I can still punch. Sosei said all you need is one good punch."

Violently, Jay's body jerked, started shivering, the teeth clacking. He dropped his eyes to his arm on the ground, pulled it in against his leg like a pet. The terrible misdirection of the hand on the ground, detached from the body, made Clyde sick, made him remember standing over his uncle that day in the woods. There are some traumas to the body that the mind just can't accept. "I'm sorry, I'm getting Jan."

"Goddamn it," Jay snapped. "I don't want her to see me like this, Clyde."

Clyde shoved the Hi-Point back in his pocket, careful to leave the pocket unzipped. "I'm fuckin sorry."

"For what?" Jay couldn't keep his head up.

"Everything."

"This ain't your fault, Clyde. You entered the *mai* while I was standin there tryin to figure out what to do."

"Yeah, but, that fuckin guy. Knew all this shit about me."

"He knows shit about all of us, just trying to psyche you out. Welcome to the movement."

Clyde had a hard time looking at Jay. He stood in the High Street behind him, watching his surroundings in an imitation of Jay. "Why didn't you do anything when he got close?"

Jay lay back flat. "Didn't want you to git hurt," he said. "Knew what a scattergun could do up close." His shoulders shook and he rolled onto his side. "I'm gonna die, Clyde, goddamn it. I'm gonna die right fuckin here."

"No you ain't." Clyde sucked air, his vision spiraled. He knelt, put a hand in Jay's hair, cold and damp. "Wanna sit in the bar? Might be warmer."

Jay shook his head. "Ain't fuckin movin." He lifted his arm from the snow and held its mangled end near the stump. "Maybe Missy could sew it back on." Then he reared and threw it, and it tumbled. "*Motherfuckers!* You can run but you cain't hide! Jay Smalls is comin! An he don't need two arms to kill with! One's plenty!"

The street was clear and bright and Clyde saw the smoke hanging in the trees above the cabin below. He wondered if Missy was still in there. He said, "I'm sorry, Jay," and marched back to where the guns had fallen in the street.

Jay threw a handful of snow at him. "Git back here!" he yelled, trying to trip him with a foot. Clyde jumped out of the way and tore down the road with the scattergun and the Parker-Hale and Jay yelling after him. "Don't you tell her, goddamn it!"

A few paces down Clyde stopped and turned back. Jay was up on his feet, standing in the High Street, his gun at the end of that one hand. He stood perfectly still. Clyde waited, watching, his chest aching from effort against the cold. Fifty yards spread between them, maybe more, open road with lots of tracks in the snow. Jay was a dark shape on one end, his body slumped a bit to the right, the coat hanging down, a sleeve ending almost at the knee. For a long moment they stood at opposite ends of the open street facing each other, the snow sparkling between them. They stood in that stillness, each watching the other, breath puffing around their heads in thin silver clouds.

Clyde said, "Jay?" He didn't say it loudly; Jay couldn't have heard it, or even seen the movement of the lips. But when Clyde said it, Jay nodded and walked straight into the woods above Lick Skillet.

lyde ran down the middle of the wide-open road even though it was a bad idea. He did not feel that he would be picked off right now by one of the two remaining ZOG trespassers. He hurt like hell, but he ignored it. To listen above his own strained breathing and the rattle of his gear for signs of the others was hard but he tried. Near the bottom where the road met the cabins something moved, making him slide to a stop in the dead center of the crossroad, his feet shooting out from under. He fell hard, didn't even try to break fall, and crawled quickly out of the open into the weeds, trying to get his breath back. Someone was coming. He didn't know if they'd seen him or not. Whoever it was they were coming fast, running on legs heavy enough to shake the ground. *Bam bam bam bam*. The ground shook and a raspy noise made Clyde think it was J.D., gut-shot, bleeding out, desperate to reach safety. God, they're killing all of us. Clyde fumbled for the Hi-Point in the frozen grass as an ostrich stomped past. Out of its pen the bird was enormous, its thick clumsy feet stabbing the ground. Clyde retrieved his gun, got to the edge of the road, saw somebody crawling into the trees. He ran down the road, out in the open again, Hi-Point cocked and expecting to find an agent, injured, trying to hide. Instead he found Dale on his back in the snow.

"Hey, fucker," Dale grunted.

"Jesus," Clyde said, standing over him.

"Good thing I ain't the feds." Dale made a gun with his hand.

"Good thing I ain't," Clyde said, showing Dale the Hi-Point, seeing now that Dale's hand dripped blood.

Dale's coat had turned red; blood was on his face and in his hair, staining the snow around him. The rifle's strap on his chest was covered with it. "Stomach?" Clyde said.

"Fuck yeah," Dale said, nodding. "A good one, too."

Dale wiped his bloody hands on the ground, balled a handful of snow, pressed it against his wound. "See they got Tina?" Dale said. Clyde looked away, he couldn't see her from here but she wasn't far away, less than fifty yards. "I dragged her out of the road," Dale said.

Clyde pulled Dale's rifle off of him. "Loaded?" he said.

Dale shook his head. "Not no more." Clyde could barely hold it the stock was so slick, he chucked it. "I'm just taking a break here," Dale said. "Don't you worry, white belt." Using his elbows he dragged himself another few feet, coughed blood onto his chin.

"I'm a blue belt now," Clyde said.

Dale pressed more snow to his stomach, pushed the ground with his feet so he could get his head against the base of a tree. He took a deep breath, blinked at Clyde like he couldn't place him just now. Clyde stood there without moving, then checked the Hi-Point even though he knew. Fully loaded. He hadn't fired a single shot from a single weapon since this conflict had begun.

"Gonna kill me now?" Dale said. "You know you want to. Might just about be a fair fight by now."

"Jay's hurt," Clyde said.

Dale spat. "Hurt?"

"Hurt bad."

Dale's eyes fell shut. He shook his head, the rough chin scraping the collar of his coat. "Poor Jay." Clyde stood, the Hi-Point hanging heavily at the end of his hand, not far from Dale's head. They studied each other in silence. Dale grinned up at him, the same grin his rat face had held the first time they'd fought. It was as if he'd just confirmed something he'd always suspected about Clyde, about who Clyde really was. He lay back with his head at an odd angle against the tree trunk and the snow crunching beneath his back and boot heels. "You are gonna kill me," Dale said. "Goddamn."

Clyde dug in his pocket for all the extra shells, chucked them at Dale, one at a time, like throwing peanuts to a monkey. Dale gathered them up, cupped them against his wet chest. Then Clyde let the gun drop into the snow right beside Dale's hip. Dale scrambled to hold it. When he had it he watched Clyde from the ground. "I knew that once you showed up, white belt, this is how we'd end up."

Clyde was surprised he hadn't heard the same thing from Jay. "You think this is my fault."

"I do," Dale said, nodding as vigorously as he could. "I really do. Who else? You know, who else?" He shrugged. Clyde looked off, heard Dale check the chamber, heard him say, "Sweet."

"Well, good luck," Clyde said, stepping into the road. He ran right into the woods. Within minutes he heard a voice. It was a woman. Missy? She was cursing like a sailor. A moment later, a gun went off, silencing her, and Clyde stopped where he was. His breath seemed impossibly loud, as loud as a dog's. His blood surged in his ears and he stood still until it slowed enough for him to hear her again. She was alive, still cursing. Keeping to the trees, Clyde moved uphill. Crouching, his knees cracked. His stupid body was going to betray him. Less than ten yards away ran an old stone wall, he crawled along it, moving uphill with the shotgun in one of his crawling hands, and a man's voice drawing close. He got to where he could make out what they were saying, saw two figures standing, one sitting. The one sitting had cuffed hands and a cigarette. As soon as he saw her, Clyde knew it was Jan. She was sitting on the ground, her head lowered.

A man stood over her, talking shit. It was the bastard who'd blown Jay's arm off. Jan wasn't listening to his hatred, she was giving it back. Clyde wished he could hear what she was saying. The other man said something into his walkie and looked around like Jay had on the High Street. He hadn't spotted Clyde, though, so he was no Jay Smalls. He held a flat black assault rifle and moved in small circles, watching, listening, looking, giving short commands. Clyde put the scattergun carefully down and slipped off the Parker-Hale, his most accurate weapon. Cocking it made such a racket that there was no way Clyde could have used it if he hadn't thought to always keep a round ready. Chambering a round in the Parker-Hale, Jay had always said, was enough to end most arguments.

Clyde brought his right leg up through the snow, cringing at the sound it made. Jan was in the scope when he looked. For a long moment he just watched her. The smoke of her cigarette drifted up around her lowered face. She wasn't crying, he didn't think; she was mad, but there was an awful stillness about her. Hang in there, Jan.

The men wore the same assault weapon on canvas straps drawn across their backs. They must have had an endless supply because the one with the moustache had left his in the High Street. Clyde would shoot that fucker first. Then he'd cock in another quick round and shoot the fucker standing over Jan, who would hesitate a moment before dropping the radio and taking up his weapon. With any luck, Clyde would get both, free Jan, and go to Jay.

Clyde centered the first one in the scope. He knew the military's teaching. BRASS: breathe, relax, aim, sight, squeeze. He'd always shot that way. He went through the first four steps twice without moving his finger on the trigger. The third time he squeezed and the gun bucked its scope into the orbital bone below his eye, blinding Clyde for a moment.

The men started shooting, blowing the snow, dirt, leaves, and trees around Clyde to bits. They scrambled on the hill shouting and Clyde knew one or both of those bastards would be on him in no time. Around him trees strobed with light, making running through them treacherous for a fully sighted man; Clyde ran, fell, and crawled blindly down, one hand in front of him. He hid behind a thick oak, rubbing his eyes until the sight returned to one, then the other.

The men had stopped shooting and Clyde chanced a look around the tree. The woods above him were empty, no one was where they had been, not even Jan. They'd run off and they'd dragged her with them.

When he reached the top of the hill Clyde left the woods and took the farm track to the backside of the milking parlor, the snow there undisturbed, pure. He sandwiched himself around the cargo truck inside the lean-to and watched the street. The two trucks sat at the foot of their tracks, blocking the road down the hill. All was quiet, and voices in the trees near the village below made Clyde realize that Jan had been taken down, not up. Probably they'd put her in the house and cuffed her to the pipes next to Missy, who would be more than ready to wave the white flag. At least they'd be warm for a while. Conspiracy to use a weapon of mass destruction. Clyde hoped Jan wouldn't get the death penalty, he didn't give two shits about what Missy got. He climbed out of the lean-to over the snowdrift, slid into the street. There was something lying in the open and it took him a moment to realize what it was: Jay's severed arm.

Jay himself had thrown that arm away, but here it was, back on the street. Clyde began to wonder if he was still conscious. Maybe he was knocked out from the rifle's scope, this whole thing nothing but a bad dream. Or maybe he hadn't even made it out of the fight with that agent. He'd been shot, just like Jay, but unlike Jay he hadn't survived, he'd died right here in the street and would never leave Lick Skillet, as much a ghost as Tina and her namesake. Eternity would be this siege—running, shooting, hiding, watching people die again and again. Slowly Clyde approached the arm. The swollen middle knuckle of that blue, bloated hand always dug into the same rib on Clyde left side. It was Jay's good arm, the fist that had broken boards, bricks, rocks. Clyde half expected it to dissolve like a projection. But it didn't, it was real, flesh and bone. Unlike Tina, and Dale, and probably Jimmy-Don, and maybe Jay, Clyde was still alive.

A thin line of bright-red blood led into the woods on the far side of the street. Clyde followed as if tracking a wounded deer. More than once he and Willie had trailed blood for several minutes until catching up to witness the last moments of life, always a profound experience, Willie had said, to approach with respect.

Clyde moved uphill until he saw Jay at the base of a tree. Clyde called out in a whisper, "Jay!" so that he wouldn't be taken for somebody else. Jay had found a good cradle of roots at the base of an enormous pine twenty yards up the ridge above the street. His head lolled to his chest. Clyde shook his shoulders until the eyelids dragged up, a corner of the mouth bent. Jay was trying to speak. Clyde told him, "It's Clyde, Clyde." Jay's eyes moved past him and Clyde turned, half expecting to see an agent before realizing that Jay was checking to see if he'd brought Jan with him. "Just me," Clyde said, placing a palm on Jay's forehead. There wasn't much heat.

Clyde went through the smoked cigarettes that lay scattered about and put the best one in Jay's lips. He found a lighter in Jay's pocket. "I, uh," Clyde said, looking at Jay's gray face. He coughed to cover the sound in his throat and tried to collect himself. He felt Jay's hand pat his leg. "Uh," Clyde said, wiping at his face, turning back. "Uh, yeah, I, uh, couldn't find Jan."

"Couldn't find Jan," Jay whispered.

"Huh uh," Clyde said. "I think she and J.D. are pickin the fuckers off. I, uh, I saw one they killed already. I think we're winning."

Jay grinned. Shouts spread through the woods below and Clyde recognized J.D.'s voice among them. Clyde didn't want to turn away from Jay right now. He tilted his ear toward the woods below. "Clyde!" J.D. yelled. *"Clyyyyyyde!"* J.D. was still alive, he must have known that Clyde was too, still out there somewhere, still in this fight.

"I, uh," Clyde said, looking off. "I think J.D.'s giving the all-clear." There was movement in the street below. "Just a minute," he said, sliding downhill and getting behind a tree.

"Clyyyyyyde!" J.D. screamed from far below. *"Where aaaare youuuu!?"*

The Hi-Point lay in the snow at Jay's side. Clyde checked the chamber, blew it clean, pressed it into Jay's hand. Clyde could hardly see; his eyes wouldn't cease and he had to shake his head to keep from embarrassing himself. Below, J.D. wouldn't stop screaming. "I think," Clyde said, having to breathe through the mouth. "I think we're almost done, Jay. This is just in case. You hear anybody coming that don't say 'Jay,' you shoot 'em, shoot anything that moves." Jay didn't react. Clyde yelled at him, the lids dragged up, the eyeballs swam in their sockets. Jay nodded and Clyde grabbed his hand with both of his, holding it tight like they did in training. For a moment, longer than he thought he could afford, he stayed that way, kneeling in seiza with Jay. Then he said, "All right," and got up.

Instead of running downhill to join the fight, Clyde climbed; he wanted a vantage. The rifle on his back jumped and he threw down the shotgun so he could take hold of branches. He ran, climbing quickly, his heart thumping, his lungs sore, thinking of Jay behind him, pushing. When he reached a spot of flat ground, all of Lick Skillet lay below, the High Street, the cemetery, the sloping field and its hiding spots, the unused greenhouse, the road at the bottom, and the cabins where they lived. The High Street was empty, quiet. Above a copse near the brake, and in the surrounding woods, puffs of smoke hung in the air where weapons had been fired. At the backside of the milking parlor, the unmarked farm track curved like a scythe before cutting straight through the orchard's thin gray trees.

"*Clyyyyyyde! You and meeee! It's you and me now, am I riiiiight!?*" Jimmy-Don's words carried up the hill to Clyde as clearly as the secrets that Chetto had whispered inside the capitol dome. They were the shrieks of a desperate man and they scared Clyde. Shooting erupted again. "*Many are being caaaaaaaalled, rememberrrrr!?*" J.D. shrieked. "*It's time to fiiiiight!*"

Something moved nearby and Clyde fumbled for his rifle. It was a dog, one of Dale's dogs. Clyde exhaled as the dog bounded toward him as if nothing at all was amiss. Clyde patted it and then it started down the hill, stopping to look back. Clyde watched Lick Skillet. The High Street and its buildings, all the roofs collapsed. Snow busy with blood and footprints dusted the cobblestones. Tire tracks ran from the milking parlor to the cemetery, crossing like braids. From here, the graveyard looked too small for how many it kept. The whole place looked small from here, insignificant, forgettable. Shots popped off somewhere down there, five by Clyde's count, from the same weapon. Another weapon answered with two. *Crack . . . crack . . .* What was powerful enough to deafen a man up close was hardly more than a cough from this distance. Only when the smoke rose above the canopy was the location of the fighting revealed. Clyde made the decision, started down the hill.

Dale's dog ran on ahead. When Clyde reached the street, someone was shouting on the hill. In that noise, Clyde checked the cargo door and climbed into the cab. The dog jumped in after him, claimed a spot on the floor between the driver's seat and the final redundancy, the suicide barrel. The truck held a powerful stench. Clyde grabbed at the ignition and found it empty. The keys— do not tell me it's going to come down to the keys are in Dale's fucking pocket. Clyde did not want to get out, make his way down, going from body to body in a firefight, no thank you. He looked at the visor above his eyes, thinking that was where Jay would have put them. He smacked it, keys fell. "Jesus," he said. Jay knew his mind and he knew Jay's. With the key marked *GMC* Clyde brought the truck to life.

The windshield fogged and he had to get out of the seat and dig around to find a rag. The truck was a three-speed. Clyde shoved the column shift up into first, feeling resistance. He didn't want to stall it and call attention to his location by cranking a reluctant engine. There was heavy snow in front of the truck on the track ahead. He let out the clutch a little more, easing down the sticky gas pedal. The truck lurched and pushed into the snow, the explosive mixture rocking in the drums behind him. Through the hole in the wall Clyde heard it slosh and spill. His eyes watered; he rolled the window to the freezing air. He yanked the column into second, where he would leave it until he made the road that led to the highway.

The track met a straight path that ran through the middle of the dead apple orchard. This must have been where Dale got all his shrunken heads. The snow nearly covered the track and dusted the branches and Clyde was happy that his route was determined by an even grid of dead trees. The gunshots behind him were hard to hear above the noise the fat tires made on the snow. Clyde wiped the windshield with the rag as the trees fanned past, lined into perfect gray rows no matter which way he watched, evenly changing from diagonal to horizontal to diagonal like a magic trick. Clyde took comfort in it. Someone's pickup sat dark and still far down between two rows.

He crawled steadily on, crunching snow, his speed never topping twenty. The orchard ended at a field that swept in a long unmarked slope to a small farmhouse flanked by an apple-red barn and a chicken coop the length of two train cars. Set against this dull landscape, the windows in the old house were warm and inviting. Trucks and tractors and ATVs and candy-colored dirt bikes littered the drive and the yard. A rusted swing set leaned to the side, one of its swings frozen to the ground. Cords of wood had been stacked against the barn, covered with a tarp. A sheepdog leapt to its feet and ran after Clyde, barking. The dog in the cab barked in return, scaring Clyde half to death. He put a hand on its head but it didn't stop.

Clyde slowed and the truck rocked against groaning springs, the explosives in the back lapping all the drums. Thank God J.D. had thought to build that grid of two-bys on the floor. At the base of the hill, a gate stood open to the gravel road that, Jay had said, led to 291, then Highway 50, a fine two-lane stretch that ran directly to Jefferson City and the capitol building. Four right turns, nothing more than that, and the first lay just ahead.

THE END

ACKNOWLEDGMENTS

N o one supported me through the writing of this book more than Johanna Lane. For carefully reading these pages no matter how often I asked, for enduring patience, intelligence, compassion, support, love, and fun, and I owe her everything.

I'm fortunate to have received tremendous support and encouragement over the years from great teachers, colleagues, and friends, like Binnie Kirshenbaum, Jesse Burch, Liesl Schwabe, Ryan Bartelmay, Caroline Murnane, Michael George, Nazgol Shifteh, Elisa Albert, Nina Weiner, Lisa Meads Casey, Diana Horowitz, E. Tyler Lindvall, Coates Bateman, Karen Branson, David Schoffman, Helen Schulman, Christine Schutt, Ben Marcus, and Rick Urdiales, may he rest in peace. For a decade of enthusiasm, criticism, and friendship, I can't thank Josh Weil enough. And for teaching me everything I know about karate: Osu, Raul Dueño!

Some people got behind this book early on: My badass agent, Bill Clegg. Dinaw Mengestu, Mark Binelli, Scott Wolven, and Aaron Gwyn, great writers all. Warren Frazier, who gave me Harry Crews and a few good meals. Meredith Turits, PJ Mark, Chris Clemans, and my family, especially my brother Steve, whose firearm, hunting, and survival tips were very helpful. And my *PW* friends, especially Rachel Deahl, for the smart feedback, and Jonny Segura, Parul Sehgal, Mark Rotella, Craig Teicher, Jessamine Chan, Gabe Habash, Rose Fox, Michael Coffey, Joe Murray, Ryk Hsieh, George Slowik Jr., and the generous Louisa Ermelino.

I'm deeply indebted to Liz Parker, Megan Fishmann, Rolph Blythe, Charlie Winton, Jeffrey Gleaves, Ryan Quinn, Debbie Berne, Domini Dragoone, and the rest of the gang at Counterpoint/Soft Skull Press for making this book a priority from day one.

Doing research I dog-eared two books more than any others: *Friction: How Radicalization Happens to Them and Us*, by Clark McCauley and Sophia Moskalenko, and *American Terrorist: Timothy McVeigh and the Oklahoma City Bombing*, by Lou Michel and Dan Herbeck. The Southern Poverty Law Center was also very helpful, especially their annual "Year in Hate" issue. Excerpts of *The Turner Diaries*, a 1978 novel written by William Luther Pierce, former head of the National Alliance, were included here in compliance with the doctrine of fair use.

This novel was also influenced and shaped by the publications, website content, podcasts, and recorded conversations of many of the white separatist, white supremacist, neo Nazi, and other extremist organizations currently active in every state of the union.

Printed in the United States
by Baker & Taylor Publisher Services